PERFECT

IMAGE

TRISH MORAN

Published by Accent Press Ltd 2019
Octavo House
West Bute Street
Cardiff
CF10 5LJ

www.accentpress.co.uk

ISBN 9781786150561
eISBN 9781786151100

CHAPTER ONE

'So as you can see, Abel, the figures for crimes committed by Labs have risen by twenty per cent in the last six months,' said the Prime Minister, Jason Whitehead. 'Here's a particularly bad example - a Lab in a highly trusted position at the Southern Bank charged with embezzlement.'

'He did maintain in his defence that he was merely trying to demonstrate how easy it was to bypass the bank's security system,' Abel countered. 'He swore under oath he had no intention of stealing the money.'

'What does that mean to you people anyway!' Police Commissioner Browne sneered. He was a large, red-faced man whose neck swelled over the collar of his stiff white shirt. He moved restlessly in his seat, flicking imaginary dust from his sharply pressed trousers.

'A Lab swearing under oath carries the same weight as a Non-Lab doing the same thing,' Abel replied.

'That's one thing I really resent! Being called a "Non-Lab"! I am a human being!' Browne spat.

'And we Labs are, too, just a different category of human being.' Abel's mouth tightened.

The Prime Minister sighed. 'I think we need to forget our differences and work cooperatively to decide what action needs to be taken. I have another serious case here, of a Lab being found guilty of hacking into confidential files at the Ministry of Defence...'

'Do you also have records of Non-Labs' criminal activity over the past month, Mr Whitehead?' Abel asked with a note of exasperation in his voice.

'At the moment, Abel, we are considering Lab activities. And the fact that this criminal was not a Compound Lab or a Government Authorised Lab, but claimed to be an Independent Lab. How many of these Independent Lab groups are you aware of, Abel? I thought we had already agreed that you would keep us informed of any new developments?'

'We have met a number of Labs who prefer to live independent lives,' Abel replied.

'But you didn't feel it necessary to pass on this rather important information?' Browne stabbed a finger in Abel's direction, 'You could be charged with withholding evidence...'

'Evidence of what?' Abel said.

'Please!' The Prime Minister held up his hands. 'Abel, Commissioner Browne does have a point there, you know. We had already agreed when the Government Lab Centres were established that we were to be kept informed of any suspicious Lab activity you came across.'

'I did not want to spread unnecessary alarm. It could cause even more prejudice against the Labs who are making great attempts to integrate into normal life on an equal footing with Non-Labs - sorry, the other group of human beings,' he answered.

'It would have been better if you'd passed on such important information immediately. Leave it to us to decide how to handle it,' Whitehead stated. 'We will expect this in future.'

'And I must disagree with Abel's view how *well-integrated* the Labs are in our society,' Browne reorganised the sheaf of papers in front of him. 'We are aware that many of your kind are now employed by UK companies and businesses and even in the Department of Education.'

'Yes,' Abel nodded. 'We are proud that one hundred per cent of Labs from the Compound secured employment within three years of us establishing our equality.'

'Are you also aware that as these super-intelligent beings quickly rise through the ranks, they leave a rather limited career scope for us lesser beings? Have you considered the feelings of mere mortals like us?' Browne asked.

Abel sighed. 'I am aware that the intelligence level of most Labs is higher than their Non-Lab counterparts, but if this makes them better suited to a post, surely you can't hold them responsible for that?'

'This is the result of a work study of one of your lot in the UK's most important car manufacturers,' Browne said, tossing some papers onto the table in front of Abel.

Abel scanned through them. 'Why are you using this as a point against us? This Lab was responsible for streamlining the factory production lines and improving the efficiency of the workforce. He saved the company over twenty million pounds in the first two years!'

'He was also responsible for the loss of nearly eight hundred jobs.' Browne added. '*That* didn't go down too well with the work force, I can tell you!'

'You can't blame us for progress!' Abel said. 'It's not the first time in history manufacturing has changed and the workers have tried to stand against it.'

'But this case did leave a bad taste, and quite a few ordinary people do blame Labs for the job cuts. There were a number of attacks on Labs around this time. And the numbers are growing,' Whitehead pursed his lips. 'We don't want to stand in the way of progress, certainly not, but it must be gradual, something the people can deal with. And it mustn't always be seen as the Labs who are leading these innovations. It's causing resentment.'

'There's another issue!' Browne bristled. 'What about these new youngsters? These Hybrids? They are coming of age now, aren't they. How old is the first one now, thirteen?'

'Closer to sixteen, I believe,' Whitehead suggested as Abel

nodded.

'And already at university - and then on to a highly paid job, no doubt. He'll be followed by a whole host of these superkids. Where does that leave the normal kids? People aren't going to take it lying down. There's going to be trouble!' Browne shook his head and glared at Abel. 'You and your Lab friends better start watching your backs. Things might get ugly! And how is the Police Department supposed to help you out when you've kept us in the dark about so much, hmmm? No doubt you'll come running to us when they start burning you in your beds!'

'If we felt we would get a fair hearing from you people on an equal footing we might feel it was easier to communicate with you, but as it stands…' Abel stood up.

Browne stood up to face him. He gave a short laugh, 'Ha! Equal footing? You descended on us innocent humans and straight away laid out your demands! What about our demands and our rights? Have you ever -'

Whitehead rapped his knuckles on the table, 'Can we have some order, please! Shouting at each other is not going to help anyone.' Both men fell silent.

The Prime Minister looked at Abel. 'Browne's right, you know. This situation is a time bomb waiting to explode, especially with the economic climate the way it is at the moment. We need to get a team of your people and ours together to think of a peaceful way forward - and fast.'

CHAPTER TWO

Ruby walked into the lounge that evening, slipped her arms around Abel's neck, and kissed his cheek.

'Hey, you've been sitting there for ten minutes in the dark! What's up?'

He sighed and patted her hand. 'It was a difficult meeting with the Prime Minister this morning.' He explained what the three men had discussed.

'But surely the Labs and Hybrids can offer help in a recession?'

'Many Non-Labs don't see us as a help but as just another threat to their jobs.' He stood up. 'I've asked Celia to arrange a meeting with some of the other Labs this week. We'll need to sort out some ideas. There are further talks arranged with Whitehead next week.'

'Abel, about what Whitehead said about Labs coming under attack from some of the Non-Labs... you don't think we are in any danger of attack, do you, here on the Compound?' Ruby asked in a small voice.

'Of course not!' He hugged her to him, glad she couldn't see the look of uncertainty in his eyes.

CHAPTER THREE

Abel struggled to wake up; something was wrong. Then he heard voices shouting. He leapt out of bed, calling to Ruby as a bright light lit the room.

'Get the children! They're burning the place down!'

He pulled the door open and was met with a wall of fire between himself and the children's bedrooms.

'Ness! Tilda! Get out of the window! I'll come around!' he shouted and headed out of the house.

'Daddy! Daddy!' his elder daughter screamed, her younger sister clinging to her neck. Snatching them up, he stumbled towards the next building where he met Celia. She wrapped a blanket around the girls as he placed them on the ground beside her. 'Where's Ruby?' he asked.

'She went inside to get the boys,' Celia answered.

Abel pulled a blanket around his body and headed for the second bedroom window as the glass exploded.

'You can't go in there, Abel!' Celia shouted. 'It's an inferno! The fire brigade are on their way.'

'I can't wait! I've got to save my family!' Abel coughed and struggled forwards against the heat.

'There's nothing you can do!' Celia sobbed as the roof collapsed with a crash.

'No! No!' Abel shielded his face as he pushed on forward. 'I must save them!'

'Abel, Abel!' Someone was shaking his shoulder. 'Abel! Wake up!'

He sat upright in bed, breathing rapidly. Ruby rubbed his

shoulder.

'You were having a bad dream, love.'

Without a word, Abel got up and walked across the corridor to the bedrooms where his children slept soundly. He gave a sigh of relief and leaned against the door frame as Ruby joined him.

'It seemed so real,' he pulled her close. 'I thought that you... the children... were in danger! I... I couldn't save you!'

'You are putting yourself under too much pressure,' she whispered. She ran her fingers along the hard muscles of his arms. The same strong arms that had always wrapped her up so safely. 'You can't take responsibility for all the Labs and Hybrids yourself. Things have changed so much over the past few years. There are so many Labs and Hybrids and Authorised Labs now, and we don't even know how many Independent Labs there are.'

'You are right, Ruby. Life isn't as simple as it was when we first gained equality. I can't manage things alone.'

CHAPTER FOUR

Celia exchanged a glance with Isaac as they arrived for the meeting that evening. Abel was looking pale and drawn as he began.

'As you know, I met with the Prime Minister and the Police Commissioner earlier this week.' He briefly explained their conversation. 'At the moment there is a good deal of tension between Non-Labs and us.'

'What do they expect us to do? Dumb down our intelligence levels to make them feel better about their own limited abilities?' one young woman demanded.

'Why can't they accept us for what we are? We have a lot to offer,' a boy added.

'I'm fed up of being treated as a second-class citizen!' a third interjected.

There were several more comments and an animated exchange of ideas.

'I understand how you feel, but we also have to see things from their perspective,' Abel gestured for silence. 'With the country in the economic situation it is in now, they see us as a threat. We need to consider ways that will help us all to move on together, without this dividing line cutting any deeper. It won't help anyone.'

Murmurs of complaint were rising again when Adam, a former rogue Lab but now one of the most respected members of the community, stood up. 'Might I make a suggestion?'

Slowly the room fell silent.

'I can understand the frustration we all feel at the moment, but getting angry and shouting won't help us. We must consider what Abel said. It's time to sit down, maybe in smaller groups, to give everyone a chance to air their views, and formulate some positive plans of action.' He turned to Abel. 'Perhaps some of the Labs who were first awakened could act as leaders of each group and make a note of their suggestions. Then we could come together and share our ideas.'

Ten Labs were selected as leaders and each of them was allocated a group. Soon there was the sound of animated but orderly discussion.

'Well done, Adam,' Abel nodded. 'You helped to avoid total chaos in here today.'

'They are young and enthusiastic. We need to channel their energy.' Adam smiled. 'I think if we give them half an hour then we can return to a general discussion.'

Adam walked across to the nearest group as Celia and Ruby approached Abel.

'You're working too hard, Abel. You're going to have to do more delegating,' Celia smiled.

'Think about it, Abel,' Ruby added. 'The Prime Minister doesn't hold himself personally responsible for the wellbeing and behaviour of every Non-Lab in the UK; neither could the US President operate without a team of helpers behind him.'

'You're right, Ruby. We need to organise the different departments we already have and have a head of each department who would keep you up to date, Abel,' Celia said.

'And each department could be responsible for promoting strong liaisons with the Non-Lab community,' Abel nodded. 'This is a good idea, but we're going to need a good PR team.'

'I'd be interested in organising that department,' Isaac said.

'This could be the way forward,' Abel said. 'Ruby, Celia, can you arrange a meeting with the Labs you think would be interested while I stay here with Adam? This week if possible. The sooner the better!'

CHAPTER FIVE

'First of all, thank you for coming at such short notice, but this meeting is urgent,' Abel stood up and smiled. 'We are all aware of the growing tension between the Lab and Non-Lab communities. It isn't surprising considering the growth in numbers of Labs and Hybrids over the last fifteen years. The numbers are now too big for me, as leader of the Labs, to manage alone. So Celia, Ruby, and I have come up with the idea of departmental leaders who would keep me and a selected team up to date on a daily basis. We already have some departments which are pretty well established: Compound finance, overseen by Celia, which also funds Compound Labs in the wider community, law enforcement through Reuben and his team, a strong medical team under Dr Shultz, and an education department via the school Amanda runs here. Isaac has already done a lot of PR work for us over the years and is happy to organise that department. We would like to develop a law department, and a commercial department to cover our different business interests.

'As well as being answerable to me, as head of the Labs, each department will be headed by a Lab and a Non-Lab and will be responsible for promoting links in the community with Non-Labs.'

'So we are going to ask for Non-Labs to apply for these positions here on the Compound?' One of the medical team looked alarmed. 'I know we have worked with Non-Lab medical staff, but up to now it has been us helping them in Non-Lab hospitals and research centres.'

'Yes, that's what we feel we need to change. The Compound is too isolated from the Non-Lab community. We need to think about not just us fitting into Non-Lab life but actively inviting Non-Labs into our lives. Now, I'll list the departments and suggested leaders, and see if anyone has further ideas to put forward.

'Reuben heads the law enforcement department. We spoke on the phone and he is all in favour of these ideas. He said there are a few Non-Lab police officers he would be happy to approach about working with him if we are going to go ahead with this. He already also has some of the Non-Lab Specials, Cam, Jez, and Otis, working with him.

'Dette would be the Lab choice to head the commercial department as she has been involved in several projects working alongside Non-Lab companies. This department will cover several sub-departments. One of those is horticultural research. We already have Bailey as Lab and Zig as Non-Lab to head that section.

'Dr Amanda Harrison is founder and head of our education department. We will need to find a suitable Lab to work alongside her. She liaises with several Labs working at Oxford and Cambridge universities, so it should not be too difficult to fill those positions.

'Celia will need a Non-Lab to work with her to head the finance department. Isaac, as Non-Lab, is looking for at least one Lab to join him in the PR department.' Abel looked around, 'Any comments so far?'

'This sounds like a sensible idea to me,' Adam said. 'Could I suggest that we continue with the Lab group leaders, perhaps renamed as Lab Councillors, and regular meetings to give Labs a platform to air their views? I would be willing to chair the meetings, with help from Leonard, and collect their ideas as I did on Monday. We wouldn't need Non-Lab colleagues at these meetings as their ideas will be forwarded to the relevant departments headed by Labs and Non-Labs.'

11

'Yes, Adam, 'Abel nodded. 'That would be useful.'

'I'd like to suggest that Pellier and I work with Isaac in PR, as we have experience working with Zorro and Jamie and their bands. Leon and Johnny could also do this job on the sports side,' Keith suggested.

Leon raised his eyebrows. 'What would we have to do exactly?'

'Pretty much what you're doing already. Promoting sport for everyone,' Keith replied.

'Oh, we could do that!' Johnny nodded, looking at his brother.

'We could take this further,' Celia sat forward. 'We could arrange sports workshops for Labs and Non-Labs, promoted and introduced by you and run by other Labs offering coaching and the chance for a Non-Lab to gain a scholarship for the kind of sports education you began yourselves. The finance department could cover the funding.'

'Other departments could offer similar workshops or even apprenticeships for young Labs and Non-Labs,' Ruby suggested. 'We already have the Non-Lab Specials, Brit and Shiva, working with the younger children at the Compound school. Shiva has said she would like to take a course in child care at the local college. We could help her out.'

'One of the ideas offered by the groups was supporting Non-Labs in educational subjects,' Adam said. 'A maths specialist suggested offering coaching to sixth form and university Non-Lab students in the Lab's own particular subject. Another had the idea of setting up weekends of outdoor activities open to Non-Labs to demonstrate the fitness programmes followed by Labs.'

Abel spread his hands. 'We have so much to offer! Could I ask you all to consider which department you would prefer to become involved in, and also to suggest suitable Non-Lab partners we could invite to work with us. We'll meet again in a few days.'

12

CHAPTER SIX

The young Hybrid looked around suspiciously as he entered the room. Leonard was seated at a large table with three other Hybrids.

'Please sit down, Rafael,' Leonard smiled. 'You probably remember Kasper, Laura, and Monika from the Lab Council meeting.'

The three others nodded, but Rafael merely scowled as he slid into a chair, 'I hope I'm not wasting my time on yet another meeting urging us to collaborate with Non-Labs. I'm not going to be forced to work with them!'

'Oh, I won't force you to. But I hope you will volunteer to do so…' Leonard began.

Rafael was already rising from his seat. 'You promised me this meeting would be different, not the usual Compound Lab crap!'

Two of the other young people murmured in agreement.

Leonard gestured for him to sit down again, 'Listen, if you'd all give me a few minutes you'll see I'm certainly not wasting your time.'

He opened a folder. 'As you're all aware, Abel and his select committee have drawn up plans for Labs and Hybrids to be actively engaged with Non-Labs, offering assistance and support in many fields.'

'Yes, we are being asked to help our Non-Lab *comrades*!' Rafael muttered belligerently. 'Why should we waste our time on them? We *are* the superior race, everyone knows that. We should be concentrating on our own development! We are the

13

future of this country! Of this planet!'

The other youngsters nodded enthusiastically.

'You are exactly right, Rafael,' Leonard smiled. 'That's why you four were selected. Because I believe you really understand what we should be working towards – the future for the Labs and Hybrids!'

'Abel and his committee don't agree with that!' Kasper pointed out.

'The Radicals do!' Laura countered.

'Hmm, the Radicals don't want to know Compound Labs, they don't trust us,' Monika said. 'I tried to get in touch with them through an Independent Lab I met. Once they knew I was with the Compound Labs, they weren't interested!'

'Perhaps the Radicals would be interested in Compound Labs who share the same ideals as themselves,' Leonard suggested.

'How would you know that?' Monika narrowed her eyes.

He shrugged. 'Wouldn't that make sense?'

Laura frowned, 'But you said you wanted us to volunteer for these projects set up by the Compound Labs leaders. Isn't that just wasting our time?'

Leonard smiled. 'Abel has organised the Compound Labs into departments, pretty much like the Non-Lab government and, as you know, he is promoting working relationships between Labs and Non-Labs. So far it is proving very popular, especially with the Non-Labs in the Hambleton area.' He read out the headline of the local paper. '*Labs and Non-Labs working together to promote community spirit.*' There was a large photo of a smiling Abel standing next to the local councillor. Ignoring the mutterings, he picked up a national paper. 'And, of course, our faithful Non-Lab stalwart, Isaac, has written an inspiring article on Abel's fine work. "*In Hambleton they're not just building physical bridges but they are bridging the gap between Labs and Non-Labs*."'

Rafael groaned and put his head in his hands.

14

'Exactly! So what has that got to do with us?' Monika asked.

'If we go along with it all and put our own Labs in each department, we can keep abreast of the Compound Lab developments. And also we'll have people in the right places when the Radicals make their move, which, if rumours are correct, will probably be in the next few months.'

Rafael sat up straight. 'So you're working with the Radicals?'

'I have made contact with them. As you know, the Radicals are recruiting Independent Labs daily. They've been especially active since the Government Lab Centre started creating Labs for Non-Labs unable to have children naturally.'

'Yeah, the "Legal Labs". I met some of them the other day. They seemed a bit Compound Lab-ish to me,' Kasper remarked.

'I met a really nice Legal Lab at uni last week. She's studying politics. She wasn't afraid to give her own opinions.' Monika countered. 'She wasn't at all Compound Lab-ish.'

'I suppose they'll be quite a mixture, considering their backgrounds,' Leonard continued. 'And we can assume the Radicals will have their eyes on some of them, at least. I also know for a fact that they're also very interested in recruiting Compound Labs and Hybrids who show an independent spirit and who are completely trustworthy,' the older man said.

Kasper snorted, 'The Radicals won't touch Compound Labs or Hybrids while Abel is working so hard to fit in with the Non-Lab ideals. We need to make a stand for ourselves! Protest! Make it known that we're not in agreement with him!'

'That's what this meeting should be about today.' Monika nodded vigorously.

Leonard shook his head, 'All that would do is make the Non-Labs create even tighter controls over Lab activities. That won't help us at all. No, we have to be much more subtle. We must appear to be working with the Compound Labs while

15

following our own agenda. If we have evidence of our own plan of action and develop our own research, we'll have a much better chance of joining forces with the Radicals.'

'So you think we should go along with this scheme of Abel's?' Rafael scowled.

'For the moment, yes. It will also give us the chance to recognise other likeminded Compound Labs and Hybrids.' Leonard smiled. 'And who knows what information we may pick up on the way that will prove very useful to the Radicals...'

CHAPTER SEVEN

'Good evening. It's good to see we have so many volunteers. Most of you will have studied in these very classrooms and I bet some of you will have mixed feelings about coming back to school again!' There was the sound of laughter as Amanda Harrison looked around the Compound school room. 'But this time it will be in the evenings, and this time you will be the tutors! You Labs and Hybrids have so much to offer our Non-Lab neighbours! There's been a great response for tutoring, especially in Mathematics and Science, so I thought we could start with those subjects.' She turned to the two Labs who stood next to her. 'Let me introduce Blake from the Faculty of Mathematics at Cambridge University, and Felicity, Head of Advanced Sciences at Cambridge House Sixth Form Unit. They are the Labs running the Compound Education Department with me. We have organised a timetable due to start next Monday, initially for ten weeks. Then we will review the progress made from both the students' and the tutors' perspective. We will give you details of the students allotted to you and a schedule of the classrooms and times they are available for use. There is also an overview available to download if you need to make any changes to your allocated times.'

Blake smiled as he flicked through his papers. 'Agnes, Virginia and Grace – we've a different schedule for you youngsters from the Compound School. We've decided that you would be most valuable tutoring standard level Maths for twelve of our top students.'

'I thought we were going to tutor at advanced level,' Grace said. 'We all achieved 100% in the exam last summer!'

Blake tapped his lip. 'The Heads of Maths and Science at both Cambridge and Oxford were worried that their advanced students might feel they were being patronised if their tutors were thirteen-year-olds. So we thought it would be better if you were allotted mainly sixteen-year-old students, initially at least.'

Ginny sighed as Henry moved on. 'I had hoped we were finally going to be recognised and valued for our true intelligence levels! It's *us* being patronised!'

'Mmm,' agreed Ness. 'Well, they did say it was the initial arrangement. Perhaps we'll get to the higher levels after the first ten weeks.'

'Huh,' a boy nearby leaned towards them. 'I expect they'll soon have everything organised the way *Abel's* daughter wants it!'

Ness felt her face flush. 'I didn't mean anything like that!'

'Shut up, Rafael,' said Kasper, grabbing his shoulder. 'You're supposed to be showing your nice side tonight. If you have one!'

'Yeah, but it just makes me...' the first boy began again.

'Just shut it!' his companion repeated.

'Yeah, shut it!' Ginny glared at Rafael.

He scowled at her but any reply was silenced with a warning nudge from his friend.

Two weeks later Ginny bumped into Kasper again as she said goodnight to Emma, one of her students.

'How's it going?' she asked him.

'Not as bad as I expected it to be,' he smiled. 'Some of these Cambridge students are really smart. We had quite an interesting discussion tonight.'

Rafael appeared in the doorway with a young woman. As she left, he walked towards Kasper and said, 'Remind me to keep my mind on the cause!'

Ginny was about to question him on this when Ness appeared, deep in discussion with a tall, thin, stooped teenager. She waved to her friend and finally ended the conversation.

'Phew!' she smiled. 'Ernest by name; earnest by nature! Still, he works very hard.'

The four of them set off towards the main gate, chatting about their first lesson as tutors. Ness stopped at a turning.

'Goodnight. See you tomorrow, Ginny.'

'Does her family still live on the Compound?' Rafael asked, looking surprised.

'Yes,' Ginny said. 'Why?'

'Oh, I thought… with her father being head of the Compound Labs, they'd live somewhere… Somewhere a bit more upmarket, I suppose,' he replied.

'Are you getting the bus home, Ginny?' Kasper asked.

'No, Mum will be at the office with Celia. I'll join her there. See you next week,' Ginny smiled and ran up the steps to the office buildings.

'I thought her mother was a Non-Lab?' Rafael said.

'Yes. She's Amanda Harrison,' Kasper told him.

'Oh, so not any old Non-Lab, then.' Rafael shook his head. 'Amanda Harrison seems to appreciate the value of the intellectual abilities of Labs and Hybrids more than Abel does.'

'Yes, so her daughter and her daughter's best friend could be useful allies to have! Remember that, Rafael.'

His friend scowled in reply.

A few weeks later they joined the others at a table during a break from the lessons. Ness was peering at a tablet that Emma, a Non-Lab student, was holding.

'Wow!' she exclaimed excitedly. 'Is that your friend in the canoe? That river looks wild!'

'Yes,' Emma nodded, 'Nell's done quite a bit of canoeing and sailing since she was young, but she said that was the scariest ride she's ever taken, even though it was with a qualified guide.' She flicked to another image. 'And here she is with some of the guys she met in Thailand. Look at that beach! It looks like paradise! Even if the camping facilities aren't exactly five-star,' she giggled, pointing to a small battered canvas tent in the background.

'How long will they be travelling?' Ginny asked.

'Well, she told me six months initially, but if they can get some work in North America, they might make it longer and go to a few places in South America, too. I hope they can as I want to join them in July, once I've taken my exams,' Emma said.

'I thought you planned on studying for your degree once you got your exams,' Kasper said.

'If I get a firm offer, I could defer it for a year and travel for a few months,' she replied.

'Why would you want to do that?' Rafael asked. 'Isn't the whole point of studying at university to achieve a good degree that will enable you to follow your chosen career?'

'A gap year can be a great experience; you can see what life is like in other countries much different than your own; you can put yourself in situations outside your normal comfort zone and see how you deal with them,' she told him.

Rafael raised an eyebrow. 'So putting your life in danger on a river or sunning yourself on a deserted beach can make you a better person? You don't need to waste your time going to these places to learn about other countries, you can find out all you need to know on the internet and on the news!'

'It's not the same!' Emma insisted. 'You can't replace real life experiences with second-hand knowledge. Building up your character this way means you have more to give in any job.'

'I agree with Emma!' Ness said. 'Ginny, we just *have* to have a gap year when we finish university!'

'Oh, my mother would agree entirely with Rafael -' her

friend pouted.

'She's right! We should use our talents to improve the future world, we don't have time to play around.' he said.

'...so we'll have to wait until I'm eighteen, Ness,' Ginny continued.

Other people around them started to move towards the classrooms again.

'Can you tag us so we can look at the rest of these photos, Emma?' Ginny asked. She looked at Ness, 'Then we can make a list of the places we really *have* to visit!'

Rafael sighed loudly and walked away.

CHAPTER EIGHT

'I can't believe it! You guys are off to Cambridge University and you're only thirteen!' Emma said. 'I'm looking forward to going to uni, but I don't feel ready yet, and I'm eighteen!'

'It's clear that, academically anyway, you are ready for this move,' Ernest said.

They were sitting outside the Compound School on a warm June evening.

Ginny shrugged. 'There are quite a few other Hybrids the same age as us at Cambridge. We'll be sharing a flat with two other Hybrids and two Labs.'

'It's only an hour by train, so we'll be able to come home most weekends and in the holidays,' Ness pointed out.

'If we want to,' Ginny added quickly. 'There'll be lots of activities in Cambridge that we won't want to miss out on.'

'Ginny, we might be able to keep up with the Non-Labs academically, but most of them will be at least five years older than us!' Ness said.

'Don't go sounding like my mother!' Ginny groaned. 'I'm going to enjoy life in Cambridge.'

'Hey, is this a farewell gathering?' Kasper said as he sat down beside Ness. Rafael propped himself against the back of a chair nearby.

'Yes, I suppose it is,' she replied. 'Are you two all set for Cambridge?'

'Yes, I'm really looking forward to it,' Kasper smiled. 'We were invited to an open political debate there last week. It was pretty lively!'

'In a limited way,' Rafael added. 'They're not really open to new ideas that challenge their way of thinking. We should be looking at new ways of changing our society for the better, tackling the big issues we face today and those waiting for us tomorrow.'

Kasper laughed, 'You've not even started there yet, Rafe! You're one of the new kids on the block!'

'Well, I'm not afraid to challenge the old fashioned rules set out by Non-Labs.' he looked at Ness. 'Some people might be happy to go with the easy option, but...'

Ness stood up her, eyes narrowing, 'If you're having a go at my father again -'

'I'm sure it won't be long before you've settled in and alienated most people at uni, Rafael!' Ginny butted in. 'Come on, Ness, who else wants to try out that new cafe in the square?'

23

CHAPTER NINE

Meanwhile, several thousand kilometres away in a laboratory in Romania, a group of people were looking at a screen showing five tiny flickering images.

'A complete success!' Dr Gil beamed at the others. 'Following Hugo's initial work on splicing DNA strips from two separate donors and fusing them to form a single DNA strand, we have been able to create these five perfect clones of a male Hybrid and female Lab. Three male and two female, all ready for the next stage.'

'The donors were proposed by Hugo himself, weren't they?' Sanjit commented.

'My research was done over a two-year period and was totally unbiased,' Hugo retaliated. 'I collected data across a wide spectrum and these two donors were of the highest calibre in every category. All my findings were submitted for scrutiny by the committee at every stage.'

'And the final decision to have you as the Hybrid donor was based on your findings, wasn't it?' Sanjit continued.

'I submitted the evidence and it was accepted by the committee. Are you feeling left out because I didn't include you in my suggested list of superior Labs, Sanjit?' Hugo sneered.

The older man flushed and was ready to make a reply when his brother Takir interrupted.

'Hugo's research was done in great detail. If we felt he'd been biased in his choice of either Hybrid or Lab we would have raised any concerns before this point. There is no shadow of a doubt that the donors proposed by Hugo as being the most suitable were the right ones, as we will see as these five develop.'

'And are we using the same speed development that my donor implemented in me?' Angus asked.

'Yes, with some modifications,' Gil continued. 'From American trials, the Radicals' medical team have perfected a method of slowing some of the effects of the ageing process; so these young ones will be able to avoid the usual illnesses and physical problems that beset Non-Labs as they enter old age, such as arthritis and organ deterioration.'

'Their selected programming during their development is of a much higher standard than we've seen so far,' said Hugo excitedly, scrolling down a list of attributes on a second screen. 'With the enhancements they'll be given when they are awakened, they will be truly superior beings!'

'Yes,' Gil smiled, 'they will be a force to be reckoned with!'

'And if they are placed in the right position,' Takir smiled, 'they'll be a force that will be a great asset to us!'

CHAPTER TEN

Ness sprang out of the car and ran to the front door as her
brother Zac opened it. She pulled him into a tight hug. 'Oh,
I've missed you, little bro!'

'Hey, I'm six! I'm nearly as tall as you now!' he said,
pulling himself up to his full height.

'Mum!' Ness threw her arms around her mother, then her
four-year-old sister, Tilda. 'I've missed you all so much!'

'You've only been gone three weeks, Ness!' Zac said. 'In
that time, I've managed to persuade Mum to let me have your
old room and we've put your stuff into storage…'

'What?' she swung around.

'Zac, don't tease your sister!' Abel smiled as he walked in
the door carrying his daughter's rucksack. 'Of course we
haven't, love. It's all as you left it.'

'Hmm, still the annoying little brother!' Ness ruffled his
hair as he ducked out of her way. 'Something smells good!
Have you been cooking, Mum?' she continued towards the
kitchen.

'No, we have!' Brit appeared carrying a large plate of
cupcakes, followed by Shiva. 'Welcome home cakes!'

'They look delicious!' she spun around to her mother,
'Where's Finn? I bet he's grown in these last few weeks!'

'He's helping Zig in the garden area. They'll be back
soon,' Ruby smiled. 'Wash your hands, all of you, before you
sit at the table.'

By the time they were ready to sit down, Zig and Finn had
returned.

Ness picked up her youngest brother. 'Oh, you *have* grown! It's so lovely to see you all!'

Soon they were seated, everyone wanting to talk at the same time.

'What's Cambridge like?'

'Are your roommates ok?'

'How are you finding the course so far?'

Ruby held up her hands. 'Whoa! Give Ness a chance to speak!'

Ness's eyes lit up. 'The course is amazing and so are the facilities they have there. And our roommates are really good, too.'

At that moment the doorbell rang. Abel went to open it.

'Come in, Amanda, I didn't realise you were on the Compound today.'

Amanda Harrison came in and greeted everyone as Ruby pulled up a seat for her at the table.

'Oh, don't let me disturb you. I was passing by and I thought I'd drop in to see how our Cambridge student is doing,' she said as Abel passed her a cup of tea.

'It's really good, Amanda. I was just telling everyone about the facilities there,' Ness told her.

'Ginny is so involved in her course already, she told me she won't be home for a few more weeks,' Amanda smiled at Ness. 'Sometimes it isn't too good to let home life distract you. Ginny is attending a conference on Early Development this weekend, isn't she?'

'Erm, yes, I believe she is,' Ness looked down, trying to ignore the smile spreading across Zig's face.

'You should see if you can get yourself involved in some of these weekend study groups yourself, Ness. Make the most of what Cambridge has to offer. I can get in touch with a few of my colleagues there who'll point you in the right direction.'

'That's OK, Amanda. I've a few things already lined up, and once we complete our first module we're going to be

27

setting up our own research projects, so we'll be quite busy.'

'Oh, well, I have plenty of contacts in the Psychology department who would be more than willing to help you out there…'

'No!' Ness cried out. 'Sorry, no thank you, Amanda. I really can manage to do this myself. In fact I've already made a start on it. But thank you.'

Amanda raised her eyebrows and was about to say something else when Zig turned to her.

'All the students from the Compound School have done very well so far, haven't they? Mariella and Ethan are Cambridge graduates, Frankie is doing well in his Media Studies. Keith and Pellier say he's a natural.'

Her mouth tightened. 'Hmm, yes! Well I had hoped our Hybrid pupils would go on to follow a career in something a little more worthwhile than Media Studies! Perhaps he'll come to his senses soon.'

'Oh, I think -' Zig began.

'I must be off,' Amanda interrupted her. 'I have to arrange a meeting with the builders about the extension to the Compound School. You said you wanted the Compound Planning Department in on it, didn't you, Abel? Ask Celia to call me tomorrow morning, would you?'

'Yes. And we need to publicise the extension of Hambleton Primary as well as the Compound School extension. Councillor Darling has agreed to officiate the openings of both schools once the work is complete,' Abel told her as he followed her to the door.

'Oh, yes. We have to play happy families with Non-Labs, don't we?' Amanda said dryly. 'I'll leave that to you. My priority is for our own students.'

There was silence as they listened to her chatter continue until the front door closed again.

Zig gave an exaggerated sigh of relief, then stifled a snigger as Abel caught her eye.

28

'She can be a bit intense, but her heart is in the right place,' he admonished. 'She has always been a great supporter of the Compound Labs.'

'Yeah, I can see why Ginny does so much extra studying,' Zig gave a mock serious face.

'Why?' asked Zac.

'So she can do really well at university, of course,' Ness answered quickly.

'You can do well and still come and see us sometimes, can't you?' he asked Ness.

'I can cram in my studies and still have time to come and see my baby brother!' Ness pulled him to her and gave him a sloppy kiss.

'Get off!' he rubbed furiously at his face. 'That's gross!'

CHAPTER ELEVEN

'So how was your weekend course, Ginny?' Ness asked her the following Monday morning.

'It was totally amazing!' she replied. 'I've never tried indoor climbing before! We'd booked for a taster lesson on the Saturday but we ended up signing up for a second session on the Sunday, too.'

Ness raised an eyebrow. 'Not Early Development, then?'

Ginny grinned. 'That was just to keep Mum happy.'

'She called around when I first got home,' Ness told her. 'She wondered why I wasn't taking lots of extra courses like you! Zig wasn't fooled, though.'

'It's just so good to have this freedom to do what I want. I can choose what activities I do - or don't do.' She sighed, 'I will go home for a weekend soon. Maybe next time you go, Ness.'

Ness looked uncomfortable. 'Ginny, I was a bit, well, sharp with your mother. She was all for getting people she knows to help me. Being a former student of Psychology here herself, she has plenty of contacts. But I *really* don't want help. I don't want to sound ungrateful, I know she means well, but I want to do this on my *own*!'

Her friend patted her arm. 'I know exactly how you feel. She can get a bit carried away. Just do things your own way, Ness. That's what I always do!'

A few days later Ness was taking some books from her locker when Rafael walked past.

'How are you getting on?' she asked.

'OK,' he nodded. 'It's better than I expected it to be, I must admit.'

'What were you expecting?' she looked surprised.

He shrugged, 'Well, considering they employ so few Lab lecturers, I'm surprised at the standards they manage to achieve. Just think what it'll be like when we get a majority of Lab staff in.'

'You need more than a high IQ to teach a subject, to bring it to life and get it across to your students,' Ness told him.

He gave a short laugh. 'I have my goals and I'm heading for them. I don't need to be inspired by some dusty old Non-Labs.'

'Oh, come on, Rafael, you've got to accept that there are Non-Labs here who have as much to offer as any Hybrid or Lab,' she countered, giving a sigh of relief as Ginny appeared. Her friend was accompanied by a young man wearing an ill-fitting checked jacket. They were talking animatedly.

'I can tell you now that Ness is not going to be interested in your very kind offer, Terence,' Ginny said, shaking her head.

'Well, I promised your mother I would pass on her message, Ginny,' he replied looking uncomfortable, 'so I will.'

'I'm sorry,' Ginny mouthed at her friend as he cleared his throat.

'Ginny's mother, hmmm... Dr Harrison... suggested you would be... interested... in some guidance and well... help or something... with your first assignment this term. I'm not a lecturer... I'm more behind scenes.' He thrust out a hand, 'Terence Atkins, research psychologist. I've worked with Dr Harrison on several occasions.'

Ness took his hand and smiled. 'Thank you so much; but I did tell Dr Harrison that I'm fine. In fact I have already sorted out my first assignment. I'll be speaking to Dr Harrison myself later this week. I'll mention how helpful you were, Terence.'

He visibly relaxed as he let her hand go. 'So glad to hear that, Agnes. So glad.' He raised his hand in a brief wave and hurried back along the corridor.

Ginny grimaced. 'I'm *so* sorry, Ness...'

'No, don't be,' she replied, looking thoughtful.

'It's great to have friends in high places, isn't it?' Rafael quipped.

'Well, if I'm going to arrange to study a select group of Hybrids from the Compound School, I'll have to speak to Dr Harrison, just as anybody else would, surely,' Ness said brightly.

'You mean you really *have* sorted out your first assignment?' Ginny asked.

'Mmm, I've been thinking about it these last few days, actually. I'm going to make a study of Nature versus Nurture in Hybrid development. I'll need to speak to your mother or someone in the school office to get the go ahead,' Ness looked thoughtful. 'I'll speak to my dad, too. It might have some bearing on the type of Hybrid that may be easily swayed by the Radicals. I know he has been worried about that lately...' She pulled out a notepad and started walking along the corridor. 'I'd better jot some ideas down while it's all fresh in my mind.'

Ginny walked next to her. 'You're a genius! I might use your subjects for some connected research of my own. You're giving me ideas. I could plot the brain patterns that show the rate of development in different areas in the groups you, or even, we, select. We could pool resources and data!'

At the mention of Hybrids who could be easily swayed by the Radicals, Rafael's eyes had lit up. He pushed himself off the wall and hurried after them. 'Hey, I might be able to work alongside you two. Not on the Hybrid development side, but on any new ideas or inventions they may have come up with and where they get these ideas from. I could look at things from a learning point of view. The best way youngsters absorb knowledge and develop their creativity.'

'So you're not too much against using friends in high places, hmm?' Ginny raised an eyebrow.

'Come on, I was only joking!' He nudged her arm.

CHAPTER TWELVE

'I had no idea he was up to such dangerous stuff in the shed. He never lets me in there.' The man seemed bemused as he followed the policeman and the ambulance crew into the hospital.

'Dad, I'm going to be fine. Don't worry,' said his son from a wheelchair. 'It's a slight burn, nothing serious. Anyway, we know I'm quick-healing. You didn't need to bring me here.'

'The policeman insisted on it after the explosion was reported by Mrs Smith next door. There was nothing I could do about it, Henry,' his father continued.

'Yes, and I'd like you both to answer a few questions,' the policeman said. 'Perhaps you first, Mr Risely, while we wait for your son to have his burns seen to.'

The policeman waited until Henry had been wheeled away then he turned to his father. 'Have you notified the boy's mother, Mr Risely? Would she be able to take him into her care tonight? If not, he will have to be taken to a temporary foster home until a suitable place can be found for him.'

'But... Henry lives with me!' the father sounded quite puzzled. 'There's no need for him to go into some foster home!'

'I'm sorry Mr Risely, in the light of tonight's events, we could not release your eight-year-old son into your custody at the moment,' the policeman continued. 'According to your neighbour, it is not the first time that such an incident has occurred, though not to such a serious level. Once you have phoned Henry's mother, perhaps you could make a statement about tonight's events.'

The man grimaced, 'Well, I'll try to speak to her, though I doubt if she will agree to drop everything and come back at such short notice. She's on an expedition in the Amazon rainforest.' He put his mobile to his ear and walked further along the corridor.

The policeman shook his head in disbelief and turned towards the side wards to find the boy.

Half an hour later the three of them sat together in the waiting room, one of Henry's hands heavily bandaged. He looked up as Abel and Ruby appeared in the doorway.

'There! I knew there would be a solution to suit everyone! I knew once you phoned the Compound Labs they'd know what to do!' The boy smiled.

The policeman stood and held out his hand, 'Thank you so much for coming, Mr...'

'Abel,' he replied. 'The young boy is a Hybrid, you say, and cannot remain with his father at the present time?'

'What happened to your hand?' Ruby looked with concern at the large bandage.

'A small accident. I was playing around with some stuff...'Henry looked up at her through long lashes.

'I thought you told me that...' Mr Risely began.

'Oh, Dad, I was just messing about... I'm so sorry for all the trouble I've caused...' tears welled behind his eyes, threatening to spill onto his cheeks.

Ruby rubbed his shoulders. 'Now don't you worry. Everything will be fine.' She looked at his father. 'His mother can't come?'

'No, she's in South America at the moment, on a search for some rare plant or other. It will be a few days before she even gets my message, according to the woman I spoke to at the base camp. And I doubt she'll come hurrying back just for this,' he sighed.

'So, as it isn't in the boy's best interest to return home at the moment,' the policeman told them, 'we were planning on accommodating him in a foster home, for the time being, anyway.'

Ruby looked at Abel. 'We can take him in, can't we?' To the others she said, 'There's a residential wing for children who study at the Compound School. There would be a room for him there. The Medical centre is on the grounds so he would have any treatment he needs.'

Henry looked up at Abel with a pleading expression. Abel gave him a shrewd look and nodded his head. 'We would be most happy to accept responsibility for Henry until his hand heals and suitable arrangements can be made for him.'

The policeman looked relieved. 'Well, if we can complete any necessary paperwork, we could have him stay there for at least a few days until he is better. What do you think, Mr Risely?'

'It's a perfect solution, isn't it, Dad?' Henry interposed.

'Well, it does seem to be the best arrangement until we get you home again, son,' he agreed.

'That actually might not be for some time, Mr Risely,' the policeman said. 'From what we gathered here this evening we are looking at a case of child neglect.'

Henry and his father both looked at him with outraged expressions.

'Neglect?'

'That's preposterous!'

'My dad would never neglect me!'

The policeman let out a slow breath.

Later that night, Henry sat up in his new bedroom in the Compound with Ruby and Abel beside him.

'Thanks so much, Abel! I knew a Lab would understand much better than a Non-Lab. No offence meant to any Non-Labs here, of course. But I haven't just been playing around with matches in the shed; I've been developing a new material that could be a major break-through for protection in fire-

36

fighting!'

'And that's how you got burnt, is it?' Ruby raised her eyebrows.

Missing her sarcastic tone, Henry nodded his head eagerly, 'Exactly! The outer skin is absolutely fireproof, but the protective inner layer is, at the moment, not sufficient to repel the heat of the fire. Hence the burns. But I have an idea on how I can alter that. And I knew they would never let me carry on with my research in some Non-Lab foster home!'

He looked up as the bedroom door opened and his father appeared.

'I've brought you pyjamas and a change of clothes for tomorrow...'

'And my notebook?' Henry grabbed it from his hands and flicked through several pages until he found a thin sheet of material, silver on one side with a foam backing. 'Here it is!' He held it out to Abel who felt the soft material with his fingers.

Henry pored over a page in his notebook. 'I think I have it! The chemical balance of the inner lining needs adjusting slightly. And... I have an idea if I could reverse the coating, it should repel, not absorb the heat...' He looked up at Abel. 'I have a list of the chemicals and equipment needed here. They will be available here on the Compound, won't they? And I bet you have decent laboratories here!'

'How about we talk about this in the morning, Henry?' Ruby said as she pulled the blankets up around his shoulders.

He pushed the notebook under his pillow. 'Yes, I am a bit tired,' he admitted. 'Goodnight. Night, Dad. See you tomorrow.'

'Did Henry's father return our call?' Amanda asked the young Non-Lab secretary a week later.

'No,' she replied. 'And I've left a message for him five times now.'

'He needs to let us have the boy's birth certificate and to set up an arrangement with his bank to make monthly payments,' Amanda sighed. 'Well, he does call in to see him most evenings, Matron says. I think I'll try and catch up with him there. Can you phone the hall and ask them to give me a call if he turns up today?'

Later that evening, she walked towards the residential building after she had been informed Henry's father had arrived.

'Non-Lab parent,' she muttered to herself. 'Probably feeling out of his depth and overwhelmed with coping with a Hybrid boy of such talents.'

She entered the building and pushed open the door of the visitor's lounge. A shabbily dressed man with a halo of grey curls sat with his back to her. Henry sat opposite him, his face lit up with enthusiasm as he described the complicated formula he had developed to modify his latest materials.

Amanda put on a smile as she neared the pair. 'Ah, you must be Mr Risely...' she began. The smile froze on her face. 'Dylan?... Dylan Risely? It can't be!'

The man slowly stood up, a look of recognition spreading over his own face, 'Amanda Harrison! Well I never! What are you doing here?' He stepped forward and shook her hand enthusiastically. 'Amanda Harrison! And you haven't changed a bit since Cambridge!'

'Oh, Dylan, it's been what? Twenty-five years?' she blushed and giggled.

'So; fancy meeting you here!' he continued.

'I'm the Education Director of the Compound School,' she explained. 'And what are you up to these days, Dylan?'

'Head of Ancient Eastern Studies at Oxford,' he said. 'Ever since I returned from the Middle East. Thought I'd better get settled for Henry's sake. His mother hasn't shown any signs of settling down herself. Have to give the boy some kind of stability.'

Amanda's eyes fell on the folder she was holding. 'Well, if you're planning on keeping Henry here at the school, we really need to formalise things. We need to see his birth certificate and arrange bank payments etc. Could you call by the office one evening?'

Henry groaned, 'I doubt if Dad will ever remember to do that. I don't want to be thrown out so I don't suppose you could get someone to call by the house, could you?'

Amanda smiled. 'You haven't changed a bit, have you, Dylan? Yes, I'll see what we can arrange.'

CHAPTER THIRTEEN

'So what's our final decision then?' Ginny asked Ness as she pushed several cards with names on them around the table.

'Definitely Cilla and Henry for the C group – the neglected ones,' she replied placing those cards on one side.

'Even though Henry and his dad deny he is neglected!' Ginny shook her head. 'But I'm glad your parents persuaded the police to keep the case out of the courts by agreeing to let Henry become a full-time boarder at the Compound School and to make sure all home visits are supervised.'

'Yes, Henry's really happy to have a place to continue his research. He's hoping to have his fireproof suit ready for testing next month. He was quite relieved to be able to trial test using a synthetic model of an arm rather than himself!' Ness said.

'Cilla has been eager to help him recording data, hasn't she? I'm glad they have each other as they don't get much family backup,' Ginny said. 'What about the A group? The overzealous parents?'

'I thought Dorian and Storm,' Ness looked at Ginny who nodded in agreement. 'And the B group, the ones from balanced family backgrounds - I thought Beth and Frank's youngest, Paul, and his friend Kirsty.'

'Great, that's our study group sorted!' Ginny smiled.

'Now we need to draft a letter to go to their parents or guardians,' Ness said. 'We need to do it tactfully.'

'Oh, that'll be easy,' Ginny pulled her laptop towards her. 'Make them feel honoured to have been selected to take part in our investigation!' As she typed, she read aloud,

'*Dear Parent / Guardian,*

I am writing to let you know that your child ...... has been selected to take part in an exciting investigation into the mental and physical development of Hybrid children, linked with Cambridge University.

The data we collect will be used to identify the particular needs of children attending the Compound School.

All data collected relevant to your child will be available for your perusal at all times.

To enable us to secure a place for your child in this selection, please sign the consent form below and return it to the school as soon as possible.

Many thanks, our names and signatures.

'There. That should do it!'

'We'd better run it past your mum,' Ness suggested. 'But it sounds OK to me. Now where should we start?'

'A base line assessment of each child, and we can add any notes about home background that we feel are relevant to a separate file, just for our own interest.'

The following week the two girls sat in Ness's room at the university and looked at the list of children on the laptop screen.

'I've put in the baseline tests results we've collected so far,' Ness said. 'Henry has the highest IQ, followed by Dorian, then Cilla. The rest come just below that.'

'On brain scans, Henry and Cilla show the most advanced creative areas,' Ginny added.

'Cilla told me she is working on developing a special kind of footwear to go with Henry's fireproof suit,' Ness told her.

There was a knock on the door and they both looked up as and Kasper and Rafael appeared. Rafael walked up behind Ness and looked at the screen.

'You've made a start already, have you?' he asked. 'I'm going to the Compound School tomorrow to give a science lesson as a start on my own project. Creativity, mmm, interesting, that's what I'll be dealing with. Seeing which kids can come up with the best ideas using given equipment. I'll share my results with you, if you think it would be useful.'

'Yes, that would be good. Make sure you include Henry and Cilla!' Ness told him. She explained how Henry had arrived at the Compound School.

'Wow! What a kid! I can't wait to meet him!' Rafael exclaimed.

'You'd have thought his parents would have had enrolled him in the Compound School already,' Kasper commented.

'His Lab mother isn't around much. She's involved in research mainly in remote places. His Non-Lab father is exactly what you'd expect when you think "absent-minded professor!"' Ness said.

The next morning, the two girls and Rafael headed for the Compound.

Rafael stopped and looked around him with surprise. 'It's changed so much lately!'

Ness nodded. 'Yes, the Planning and Construction Department have started knocking down the boundary walls and are building a new estate in the Compound, for both Labs and Non-Labs. Hopefully, it will break down the barriers between us. Eventually all the prefabricated houses, like ours, will be replaced by permanent ones. The whole village will double in size. Oh, look, there's Dad.' She pointed to where Abel was speaking to a group of teenagers, all fitted with hard hats and holding a variety of tools and wheelbarrows. 'He's organised some of the young offenders to pay off their community service hours by working with the builders.'

'Yes,' Ginny nodded. 'I read Isaac's article in the paper about it last week. Even Mum thinks it's a good idea.'

Rafael scowled as a couple of Non-Lab girls walked past them. 'I'd forgotten about Abel's new policies including *those* people in our work spaces! And now he's drafting in their low-lifes too, great!'

'You change your attitude or I'll make sure you're out of here!' Ginny jabbed a finger in his chest. 'I'll pull some strings with my *Non-Lab* mother!'

He closed his eyes. 'OK, OK,' he muttered. 'I'll put up with them!'

'You'll do more than that!' Ginny retorted. 'What makes you think you're so superior anyway? Your father's Non-Lab, isn't he?'

'And don't I know it! Come on, Ginny. Don't tell me you really believe that crap about everyone being equal, do you?' He gave a short laugh as he walked towards the School. 'But don't worry, I can pretend!'

'God, he's so arrogant!' Ginny hissed.

'Come on,' Ness pulled her sleeve. 'He won't last long here!'

Later that morning, the two girls stopped by the classroom where Rafael was working. Twelve children were engrossed in fixing wires, bulbs, and buzzers in elaborate designs around a board.

'Hi!' He smiled brightly as they came in.

'It looks busy here!' Ness commented.

'Yes. The children are demonstrating their knowledge of electrical circuits and their own creativity by designing a security system to protect a treasure chest.' He held up a small plastic box.

'Very creative!' Ginny nodded.

'I'm a bit disappointed that Henry isn't here,' Rafael continued.

'He and Cilla have hardly left Number Three laboratory for the past two weeks.' Abbi, a young Non-Lab helper, joined them. 'They're adding the finishing touches to their fireproof outfit. Here's the class list you wanted me to get for you, Rafael.'

'Thank you, Abbi, you've been such a great help this

morning!' he said, then glanced at Ginny.

She refused to meet his eye and turned to Abbi. 'Are you here on work experience?'

She nodded. 'I was one of the first to apply when the Compound School gave us the opportunity. I'm constantly amazed at what Hybrids can do at such a young age!'

'But they're still kids, aren't they?' Rafael nodded towards a group of children who were disagreeing over where to place their stronghold box and walked towards them. 'Now stop there. Everyone has the right to give their opinion, then you decide as a group.'

Abbi leaned towards the girls. 'Rafael is so clever, but he doesn't put on airs! I've so enjoyed working with him. So have the children.'

Ginny turned her garbled remark into a cough as Ness grabbed her arm. 'Well, we'd better let you get on.'

At the end of the morning Rafael typed up his observations as Abbi tidied up the equipment.

'Thank you so much for your help,' he smiled. 'I'd like to get the chance to speak to Henry. Is he working nearby? Perhaps I could drop by before I leave.'

'Oh, that area is out of bounds, I'm afraid,' she gestured towards the research wing. 'Only official personnel are allowed in there. I don't suppose they want any new ideas falling into the wrong hands, do they?'

Rafael shrugged. 'Oh well, maybe I'll get to talk to him another time.'

He picked up his laptop and headed for the door. Outside he sat on a low wall, keeping an eye on the research wing. Several people entered the wing and finally a young boy and girl came out. He stood up and followed them along the path.

'So, if we can find a way to attach the new soles to the boots using a material that doesn't melt in the heat, we will be able to get a working model ready for a trial by next week,' the boy was saying.

44

'Hey, you must be Henry and Cilla,' Rafael said as he fell into step beside them. 'I'm Rafael, from Cambridge University. I'm doing some research into Hybrid development.'

'We spoke to two Cambridge students earlier this week,' Cilla said.

'We're all working together,' Rafael smiled. 'My part of the investigation is looking into new inventions and ideas you young Hybrids have. I've heard a lot about your new fireproof material.'

'It's not just an idea. Henry is ready to try it out next week, once we've sorted out the footwear,' Cilla said.

'Wow. I don't suppose I could get a look at it, could I?' Rafael asked.

Henry shook his head. 'No one is allowed in the laboratory wing unless they get special clearance.'

Rafael looked a little crestfallen. 'Oh well, perhaps you could tell me about it. What is it made of? How does it work?'

He listened attentively, nodding and asking occasional questions as Henry described his material in detail.

'It sounds amazing!' Rafael shook his head. 'I wish I could see it.'

'Hey, I've a piece here,' Cilla pulled a strip of fabric from her pocket.

Rafael turned it over in his hand. It was a thin, silver material lined with a flexible plastic substance. He wrapped it around his hand and watched as the fabric moulded itself to its shape.

'It's almost like a second skin,' he said.

Henry nodded proudly. 'Yes, the entire suit will be totally flexible apart from the shoes. Cilla has been working with me on that.'

By this time they had reached the canteen.

'Well, I'm looking forward to seeing your invention in action! And I'll be very interested in any new ideas you come up with,' Rafael told them as he turned to leave. He nodded as Henry outlined a plan he had in mind for a lightweight, shark-proof diving suit.

Smiling to himself, he finally turned away, fingering the strip of material in his pocket. This could be a bargaining tool to get in to the Radicals. He wondered if Henry could be persuaded to join them, too.

CHAPTER FOURTEEN

Celia carefully laid her son down in his cot, 'Phew! Asleep at last! I thought Seth'd never settle tonight!' She leaned back against Isaac. 'I'm exhausted!'

He chuckled. 'Don't worry, love. You get some sleep. I'll do the night shift.' He kissed her hair and pulled her closer to him, looking down at his sleeping son. 'Does life get any better than this?'

He winced as he felt her body stiffen. 'Celia, I'm so sorry! I didn't mean...'

She turned to face him, 'No, Isaac, please don't apologise. I know we have to move forward, to appreciate what we have. Sometimes it's just hard... it's been years and we still have no idea about why someone, most likely the Radicals, wanted that blood sample from me. I still have nightmares about there being a clone of me out there somewhere!'

Isaac rubbed her shoulders as she leant her face against his chest. Both of them thought back to the time when Celia and a young Hybrid, Hugo, had been mugged and her car had been stolen. It would have been accepted as a straightforward case until Zig, with her extraordinary vision, had spotted a puncture mark in a wound on Celia's arm. The Compound Labs strongly believed it was the Radicals who had planned and carried out the attack - especially as an Independent Lab, Angus, who had joined them on the Compound, left soon afterwards to join the extreme group. A short while later, Hugo disappeared after it was discovered he too was involved with the Radicals.

'We'll never give up until we find out the truth. Vince emailed me another lead on Hungary this week. And we've one in Croatia and one in Latvia. I'm waiting further news from Iqra in Hungary, then we can organise a trip out there,' Isaac said.

'Zig and Keith said they would keep a lookout when they go with Zorro to join Jamie at the last concert on Mirrors's Eastern European tour. They could liaise with your contacts out there already,' Celia added.

'Yes. That's in Romania, isn't it? I still think the Romanian orphanage was the most promising site, and that the fire that destroyed the building was also used to destroy any evidence,' Isaac said.

'Reuben's men combed the area and found nothing. The place has been sealed off since then and that was two years ago,' she replied. 'Maybe it's time I face up to the fact that we may never know the truth and just appreciate the life we have now.'

Isaac hugged her again. 'We won't let it rule our lives, but we'll keep going until we find out what happened.'

CHAPTER FIFTEEN

Zig smoothed the leather jumpsuit over her hips and posed in front of the large mirror in the changing room. Keith gave a low whistle and pulled her close to him.

'Mmm, She-Devil! I haven't seen you dressed up like that since Zorro's farewell concert.'

'That's a few years ago. I was worried it wouldn't fit me! It won't do for much longer!' she said, patting her slightly rounded stomach. She looked at him, her modified pupils narrowing to slits in the light. 'Do you miss touring at all, Keith?'

He shook his head. 'No. I'm happy working with Pellier at SpecialEFX and I feel ready to settle down now, Zig. I can't wait to have our own little one! But I must admit I enjoy doing the odd show, especially when Zorro is making a guest appearance. He still pulls the crowds! Jamie's doing really well on his own with the Mirrors - this tour has been a sell-out in every country - but it's great to see him performing with Zorro again; they are such an amazing double act! Jamie is a perfect clone of Zorro.'

Two hours later, Zig moved to the music and smiled at Keith as he adjusted some of the buttons on the sound equipment beside the stage. He shook his head and gestured to where Zorro and Jamie were performing. Zig noticed how Zorro and his younger Lab seemed to communicate without even speaking. Jamie moved towards Keith and handed him a small microphone. Keith made an adjustment to it, listened, frowned and made a further adjustment before handing it back to him. Zig was so engrossed in watching them that it was a few moments before she realised someone was talking to her. She looked around to see a young teenage girl standing there. She was dressed in a pair of jeans and a T-shirt. Even in the dim lighting she appeared dirty and dishevelled.

'Zig, isn't it?' the girl said. 'Love your eyes. I've got them, too!' She pointed to her own cat-like eyes.

Zig smiled. 'These contact lenses are great, aren't they?' She looked carefully at the girl's eyes and felt her smile freeze. 'Yours are very realistic...'

The girl grabbed Zig's hand and squeezed it tightly, 'Zig, I need help! To get away from the Radicals!'

'The Radicals? Hey, what is it?' Zig asked as a look of fear filled the girl's eyes. She turned to see what had alarmed her. When she turned back again the girl was hurrying through the crowd with a determined looking man pushing his way after her. His dark clothes and muscular build made Zig think he was some kind of security guard. He nodded to two other men also heading for the exit as the girl disappeared.

She slid off her seat and followed them. Standing in the doorway outside, she peered into the darkness. A slight figure was moving silently up a narrow alley down the side of the concert hall. The three men were talking in low voices, then two left and hurried along the street. The third man, the one Zig had spotted first, was making his way slowly down the alleyway. Zig caught a glimpse of a gun in his hand. She slipped her high heels off and padded forwards in her bare feet. Picking up a can lying in the gutter, she flung it across the alleyway and as the man swung around she disappeared in the direction the figure had taken.

'Wait!' she hissed as the shadowy figure looked set to run. Zig grabbed her arm and pushed her back against the wall. 'Two of them are coming from the other end of the alley!'

'Follow me!' the girl whispered. They inched their way along the wall until they reached a small window. The girl pushed Zig through and followed her, pulling a dusty curtain across the opening and upturning several chairs on the floor nearby. She signalled silence as Zig began to speak and pulled her through a cluttered basement. They could hear voices as someone tried to push open the small window and curses as they stumbled into the chairs.

'It'll only give us a few minutes. Quick!' she whispered, pulling Zig behind her. They slipped through a door and closed it behind them as the voices got louder. 'Up here!' They emerged into a car park. Zig looked around her then pulled a car fob from her pocket and started running towards a small white van nearby.

'Quick! Get into the back and cover yourself up, there's a blanket in there!' she whispered as she pushed the girl into the back.

Zig was still breathing heavily as a figure appeared and yanked at the locked door.

'What do you want?' she asked.

'Open the door!' he said menacingly. 'I need a word with you. Where is she?'

'Who?' Zig gave a sigh of relief as she recognised a short, thick-set figure hurrying towards them. It was Bill, one of Zorro's older security guards.

'Just what do you think you're doing?' he asked Zig's assailant.

'I was just asking the young lady here if she knew where my friend had disappeared to. They were talking together by the stage a moment ago,' he replied.

'I've been talking to quite a few of Zorro and Jamie's fans tonight! I wouldn't know which one was your friend,' she replied.

'She doesn't know, mister. I think you'd better leave. This is a private car park for the band and their crew.' Bill sounded menacing.

The second man gave an impatient click of his tongue, 'I

just thought if...'

'Sorry, mister, don't think, just leave,' Bill stood nearer to him. With a final glare at Zig, the man turned and left.

'Zig, what are you doing out here alone in the dark?' Bill chided her. 'Especially in your condition.'

'I just came to get a breath of air, it's so stuffy in there,' she replied. 'The performance is just about over now, look, the costume guys are already bringing out some of their stuff, so I should be OK to hang on here now. Thanks for your help, Bill.'

He shook his head as he walked away. 'I'll let Keith know you're here.'

Zig let out a long breath. 'Are you OK?'

A pale face appeared as the girl pulled the blanket down from her face. 'Yes... thank you so much.'

'What do you know about the Radicals? What are you doing here?' Zig asked her.

'It's a long story.' She gave a sigh. 'I'm Annette, by the way. Me and Robert, my brother, we're Labs. We were homeless when we met Lisa at a soup kitchen in London. She told us about the commune here where Labs lived free and happy lives. After our experiences living on the streets, we were easily convinced. We'd never even heard of the Radicals.' She began to cry and put her hand to her mouth. 'I still can't believe it! That Robert's dead!'

Handing her a tissue, Zig frowned. 'I hope I can trust you! I hope I haven't put us all in danger...'

Annette shook her head vehemently. 'No, I swear! You must believe me! I would do nothing for those awful people! We had no idea! Or we never would've gone with them in the first place. And now Robert...' She lay down, sobbing into the blanket.

Zig watched her for a while then sighed and patted her shoulder. 'I think I do believe you, Annette. Your eyes look like you're one of the inmates from the Zoo.'

'The Zoo!' Annette looked up. 'The Non-Labs told me about the Zoo. You were…?'

'That's right! I was one of the early Zoo experiments!' Zig gave a tight smile. 'I managed to escape with another guy, Cam. He had a faulty nose enhancement and was due to… disappear! With help from Abel and the Compound Labs, we managed to go back and get the others held by the Radicals out safely. We call ourselves "Specials" now – it has a nicer sound than "Zoo", don't you think?'

Suddenly Annette froze as the sound of voices neared.

'It's OK,' Zig murmured, climbing into the back of the van. 'It's just Keith and Pellier. They're with me. This van's for the sound equipment. They've a few techs with them so keep out of sight for the moment. We can explain things later.'

She leaned forward and opened the back door as the men appeared.

'Bill said you were out here, Zig. Are you OK?' Keith said putting a box containing electrical equipment into the van.

'Yeah, just got too stuffy in there,' she replied, pulling the box further inside.

Pellier and another man appeared carrying a larger box between them.

'Grab that blanket, Zig,' he said, 'I'll put it under this to stabilise it. The roads aren't too smooth around here!'

'I've got it. Is that it?' Zig pulled the box inside towards her. 'You go in the front with Keith, Pell, I need to stretch my legs out. Got a bit of a cramp!'

Keith gave her a look over his shoulder but said nothing as they drove out of the car park.

'What is happening, Zig?' he asked quietly as they drove along the main road into the town centre towards their hotel.

'She's a Lab!' Pellier stuttered as Annette's face appeared above the blanket. 'And with your eyes!' Annette trembled as Zig began to recount the evening's events.

'So the Radicals are still here in Romania! Isaac always

53

said he wasn't convinced by the fire at the Children's Hospice,' Pellier gave a low whistle. 'We'd better let Abel know about this as soon as possible, before they move on again!'

'And they're probably watching us right now,' Keith frowned. 'We don't even know if we can trust this girl!'

'I don't think she's pretending to be scared, Keith! Those guys really wanted to kill her! At least one of them had a gun,' Zig said.

'I think we need to find out more about her anyway. Do they know the girl is in the van?' he looked at Zig who shook her head. 'If we can get her into the hotel without anyone noticing…'

Pellier nodded. 'Annette can wear Zig's coat and you can take her through the front entrance. Then I'll take the van to the store room and Zig can sneak into the hotel through the staff entrance.'

'They'll be watching both entrances, I'm sure…' Keith began. 'It might be dangerous for Zig.'

'Hey, I'll be OK. Pellier can make a diversion,' she said.

'I don't want to put anyone in danger…' Annette whispered.

Zig squeezed her hand. 'We'll all be fine. Just follow Keith. Here put my coat on, pull the collar up. That's it, no-one will know it's not me. Especially in the dark.'

Pellier slid into the driver's seat as Keith stepped out helping Annette onto the pavement and pulling her in close to him. He gave a brief wave to the doorman before they disappeared inside.

'Most of the equipment is to go in the large container to be taken to the airport for tomorrow's flight,' Pellier said as he drove into the storage area behind the hotel. 'I'll keep the guys talking and you head to the metal door on the left over there.' He walked towards a group of young men and women leaning against an open container.

'Hey, some of the sound equipment needs to be packed for transport tomorrow. Have you space there? Some of it is fragile.'

Zig waited until Pellier had all their attention then she slipped out of the van and headed for the door. A voice called her name as she put her hand on the doorknob.

'Zig! What are you doing down here?' Bill, the security man, looked concerned as she turned to face him.

'I forgot this,' she held up a small handbag. 'I'd forget my head, these days!'

'You're looking a bit pale. You're probably just worn out. I must admit I'll be glad to get back to London tomorrow. Are you going to the party tonight? Zorro's wife flew in earlier with a planeload of friends!' Bill grinned.

'I might just give it a miss this time. I'm feeling a bit tired. Is there a quick way to our suites through this door?' she smiled.

'Well, we're not really supposed to go this way, but as it's you, I'll show you! There's quite a crowd at the front, so I'll take you via the staff elevator. Come on,' he held the door open.

'I hope we don't meet anyone. I don't want you to get in trouble,' she said.

'Don't worry about me, but you might end up fending off a few reporters, Zig. You're well known as the She-Devil and I see you're still wearing the costume.' He noticed the look of dismay that crossed her face. 'Here, put this overall on and tuck your hair into the cap. Now you're just one of the staff!'

Zig breathed a sigh of relief as she finally knocked on their suite door. Keith let her in. 'Annette is in the shower,' he said as she closed the door behind her.

'Has she told you anything?' she asked.

He shook his head. 'I told her to wait until we're all here. I've called Abel. He's flying out here tomorrow morning. I hope we can trust her, Zig. What do we really know about

55

her?'

'She escaped from the Zoo,' Zig said quietly. 'And those men were ready to kill her!'

Annette walked into the room with a towelling robe wrapped around her. The dark smudges under her eyes heightened the pallor of her face. She took a deep breath, 'You have been so good to me... without even knowing me...'

Pellier had slipped into the room as Annette sank down onto the sofa.

'So, you escaped from the Radicals?' he asked as he sat down opposite her.

She nodded, 'Just over two weeks ago. I saw the posters in town about the Mirrors concert and I hoped someone could help me as it said Jamie is a Lab. I managed to get into the basement of the concert hall and wait for you. I was so relieved to see you, Zig. You have eyes like mine!'

'So they've started experimenting on Labs now, have they?' Pellier said.

'What experiments did they carry out?' Keith asked.

'Enhancements?' Zig suggested.

Nodding, Annette pushed back her hair. 'Eyes, as you can see, and ears.'

'You can spot the eyes straight away but the ears aren't as noticeable as Jez's,' Zig commented.

'These are the latest ones. Takir and the others were very pleased with them. A great improvement on the Non-Lab enhancements, they said.' Annette gave a short laugh. 'Much better eyes, ears, nose, but not the muscle enhancement. Robert had that. Something about the Lab heart muscle... it couldn't take it... he had a heart attack...'

Zig sat beside her and put her arms around the sobbing girl's shoulders.

'Hey, you need some sleep, you must be exhausted. You can tell us the rest of the story tomorrow.'

The two men watched as she led the young girl to the

56

bedroom. After ten minutes she reappeared.

'She fell asleep nearly straight away,' Zig told them.

'So, the Radicals have started experimenting on Labs. They don't follow the fundamental rule that a Lab does not harm another Lab. That is worrying.' Pellier rubbed his chin.

Keith looked at him, 'Don't forget that Adam – Url – was capable of that, too, at one time.'

'Where do they get the Labs? Or do they create their own subjects?' Pellier mused.

'We'll find out more details tomorrow when Annette is able to talk to us a bit more,' Zig said.

Pellier stood up. 'I think it would be a good idea if we show our faces at Zorro's end of tour party as usual, in case any of Takir's men are hanging around. We don't want to arouse suspicion.'

Zig agreed. 'But you can make excuses for me. I don't want to leave Annette alone.'

Keith kissed her. 'Don't open the door to anyone, OK?'

She smiled. 'Don't worry! I'm not in a hurry to see Takir or any of that lot again!'

CHAPTER SIXTEEN

The following morning Pellier was sitting at the table pouring coffee for himself and Keith when Zig and Annette appeared.

Zig accepted a cup as they sat down. 'I'm glad you ordered room service this morning.'

'Our breakfast should be arriving any minute now,' Keith told them.

The knock on the door startled Annette and she quickly left the room before a young man pushed the breakfast trolley into their suite.

Keith was just about to speak when she re-entered the room, wide-eyed. With a finger to her lips she pointed to the base of the trolley. Pellier bent down and reached out to remove a small black button, but Zig stopped his hand.

'Here you are, Keith, croissants just as you like them! And there's ham and cheese and even cereal. Where to start? I just love hotel breakfasts, don't you?' she laughed. 'And now I'm eating for two!'

'You're eating for about ten these days, Zig,' quipped Keith as he realised she was talking for the benefit of the listening device.

'So what time are we leaving today?' she continued. 'I can't wait to get back to England now. I need to get back to the Compound Garden. We'll have a good harvest this year. Quite a few of the children from the school have been working in it, too. And some Non-Labs, too.

They continued the conversation for another fifteen minutes until Zig begged someone to move the trolley into the corridor to stop her eating any more food.

'No, push it right away from the door!' she moaned. 'Right down the corridor!'

She gave a sigh of relief as they sat down again in the suite. 'They don't give up easily, do they? I hope that fooled them.'

Annette took a sip of her coffee and smiled tentatively. 'You have all been very patient. I'm sure you have lots of questions to ask me.'

'Well, you told us a bit about how you ended up here. How about you tell us all about yourself, right from the beginning?' Keith suggested. 'Where were you created? Who were your creators?'

Annette's took a deep breath and started to speak.

'I lived with my mother and father, and Robert, in a house in a suburb of London,' she began. 'We weren't allowed to go outside. I remember Robert arguing with Mum.

Her eyes seemed to be focused on a scene far from the hotel room.

'Just let us go for a short drive in the car with you, Mum. We won't even get out.'

'I know it's hard for you having to stay here all the time, Robert, but you can't go outside just yet. I can't explain everything to you now, but I will, I promise. Once we move to our new home it will be different. Just be patient.'

I felt cross, too. 'You've been talking about the new house for ages now, Mum!'

'Well, our budget isn't quite what we expected so it does mean we have to wait a little longer until we move. And we can't let anyone else around here know about you. We're not going to take any risks of having you taken from us!'

Annette remembered how she had jumped up and hugged her mother. The thought of losing her parents was too much to even think about. *'We'll be patient, Mum!'*

Unfortunately, Robert wasn't so patient. Although their parents and Annette herself tried to keep him occupied, he

59

often got up to mischief.

'One morning, Mum was at work and Dad had gone to the supermarket nearby. Robert was being particularly annoying. He started to light matches and see how long he could hold one before he blew it out. I got angry with him, but he wouldn't listen to me, so I decided to ignore him. I went out into the garden and hoped Dad would come back and give him a good telling off. Suddenly there was a scream. I rushed back inside. Robert was trying to put out a fire on the kitchen rug with a tea towel, but it was spreading rapidly. Before we knew what was happening, the fire quickly spread through the back of the house! We were really frightened. Suddenly there were shouts and screams and people everywhere! There was no sign of Dad so Robert grabbed my hand and we ran out through the garage doors on to the street and just kept on running. No-one seemed to notice us in the chaos.

'We ended up near the river and walked along it towards the city centre. After an hour we sheltered under a railway bridge. I wanted to go home. I was sure Mum would be home by then and everyone would be looking for us.'

She remembered the excitement in Robert's eyes. 'Look, we're free for the first time ever! Let's just enjoy it for a few hours, then we can head back.' And how she had reluctantly agreed.

'We were just about to continue along by the river when two teenagers appeared. I was terrified and I could tell Robert was, too. They blocked our way and asked for our money and phones.

'We don't have anything…' Robert had stuttered.

They had sneered and one of them had grabbed Robert and ripped his pockets. He threw him on the floor and kicked him when they didn't find anything. Then he turned to me and pushed me against the wall. Annette's stomach heaved as she recalled how his breath had reeked of alcohol and how his hands had crawled all over her body. She could almost taste the blood as she bit his lip and felt the stinging slap as he knocked her to the ground. Her ears were ringing as he loomed over her and she closed her eyes. There was a sudden crack and she felt the weight of his body slump on top of her.

'You've bloody killed him!' the second youth sounded strained. He turned and ran down the riverside path.

'Robert was pulling my arm, sobbing, telling me we had to get out of there quickly. He was standing holding a heavy branch. The other boy didn't move. He flung the branch to the ground, 'Annette, come on, come on! We've got to go!'

'We ran on towards the city and didn't stop for breath until we had left the scene far behind. We came to a park and hid under a hedge, falling asleep when we couldn't keep our eyes open anymore.

'The next morning we talked. We decided we couldn't go home now. We were killers. We'd be put in prison. And maybe our parents would be, too. The next few days we wandered around the city, eating whatever we could find, sleeping in parks and old buildings. It looked like this was to be our life, until one day we met another young girl on the street. She told us about a soup kitchen where we could get food, no questions asked. We went there for several nights. Some of the workers tried to get information from us, but we never told them anything! Until the night Lisa was working. Straight away we knew there was something different about her to the other people we had met.'

Annette gave a wry smile. 'That was the night we began to understand there were different kinds of Labs.'

'Lisa asked us about our background. We were reluctant to talk at first, but she had a way of making us relax; well she was like us, a Lab. Robert told her about Mum and Dad and she promised to find out what had happened to them. She came back the next night with details of the news story of the fire. It was believed that our parents lived alone. None of the neighbours knew much about them. It was assumed either Dad or Mum had accidentally started the fire in the kitchen. She showed us a few newspaper clips of the story. There was no mention of us.

'Lisa explained that we had probably been created illegally. It seemed likely, considering how we had been hidden away.

'"And now you've killed someone, you can't go back ever, can you?"' Lisa told us. '"You'd be put straight into prison and your parents would be in trouble as well. They'd probably be put in prison, too. But I might be able to help you out of this mess! Labs stick together!"'

'She suggested we join a commune of Labs who lived abroad. She made it sound like an ideal life. It was tempting considering the alternative was to continue living on the streets of London. We were taken to her flat where we met two other Labs, and a few days later we flew over here.'

Annette sank back into her chair, closing her eyes.

'Hey, take a break for a few minutes,' Zig said, stroking her arm.

Annette shook her head. 'No, you must know about the commune, about the people there. About what happened to Robert.'

For the next few minutes she sat silently. Then she swallowed and began to speak, 'It was about three o'clock when we arrived at the commune. We were shown around and given rooms.'

'Did Lisa show you around?' Keith asked her.

'No, Lisa handed us over to another Lab called Jackie at the airport and she drove us to the commune. She showed us around and introduced us to some of the others in the canteen that evening. We met Takir, who seemed to be in charge, and an older man, Sanjit. There was also a young man with a strange accent, and a Hybrid teenager who was very confident and spoke like a much older person.'

'How many people lived there altogether? Were they all

Labs?' Keith asked.

Annette frowned, 'There were about ten or fifteen Labs and Hybrids altogether. We met different people over the next few days. There were four Non-Labs, teenagers, two girls and two boys. They all had different enhancements. One girl had eyes and ears, like me. The other girl had nose and ears. One of the boys had nose and muscle, like Robert was given. The other had eyes and nose. We didn't get to meet them until after they... they did this...' she pointed to her eyes. 'They did tests to compare the results - Lab and Non-Lab...'

'Annette, did you know what to expect when you agreed to these experiments?' Keith asked softly.

She looked up wide-eyed. 'We didn't agree to anything! They told us they would carry out a few medical checks to make sure we were OK after sleeping rough. We had no idea what they had planned!'

Zig hugged her tightly. 'I know exactly how it feels, Annette.'

The other girl put her hands to her face, 'The awful thing was what happened to Robert...' She took a deep breath again. 'The muscle enhancements on the Non-Labs just made them fidgety, restless. They always had to be on the move.'

Zig nodded.

'But with a Lab, they said that because the heart muscle was so much stronger than a Non-Lab's heart, a Lab would need a much lower dosage. That's why Robert had a heart attack,' she sobbed. 'He died the day of the operation. He said he felt ill, then suddenly he clutched his chest and he just... fell down...'

Sobs racked her body as Zig pulled her close.

She pulled herself back, determined. 'Later that day I went to find out where they had taken Robert's... body. I wanted to see him once more. To say a final goodbye.'

She shuddered as she recalled standing outside the room and hearing two people talking.

'The eyes and ears enhancements on the female Lab are in perfect working order,' a clipped voice said. *'As expected, the tests show even better results than those of the Non-Labs. We need to take another look at muscle enhancement for Labs. The implant sends out a regular pulse to the brain to increase muscle activity. But we hadn't factored in the superior strength of the Lab muscles. The Lab heart was over-activated, hence the heart attack. Looks like this one's had it. Next time we need to lower the dosage.'* It was the young Hybrid talking to Takir.

'We'd better get it right with the girl. Where will we get more Labs? It's extremely unusual to find Labs amongst the down and outs! I doubt we'll be so lucky again,' Takir had replied.

'My God! That's awful!' Zig whispered as Annette finished talking. 'I'm so glad you escaped!'

'Yes, I was terrified. I lay awake all night, thinking they would be coming for me at any minute! Early the next morning I went down to the kitchen. A delivery van arrived and I was able to sneak into the back of it when the man was taking some supplies into the building. I stayed out of sight until we reached a hotel where he made his next delivery, then I jumped out. I walked the rest of the way into town and just tried to keep out of sight as much as I could. I knew they would be looking for me. Then I spotted the poster about Jamie's concert and it said he was a Lab! There was a picture of you, Zig, with your cat's eyes, and I knew you were my only hope, so I found out where the theatre was and got into the basement. I stayed there for ten days. Until last night.'

'How did you manage to eat?' Zig asked her.

'Our time on the streets of London came in handy,' she gave a short laugh. 'I was able to steal enough food to keep me going.'

'Well, you're safe now, Annette,' Zig said, gently hugging the girl to her.

An hour later, Abel, Isaac, and Reuben arrived. They were introduced to Annette.

'Keith has told us about you. We will look after you now and make sure you're safe. Celia has already started making enquiries about your parents,' Abel told her. 'I'd like you to show us the place you stayed with the Radicals. It is imperative we move as quickly as possible.'

'We don't need to go outside. Celia has downloaded a virtual tour of Constanta and the surrounding areas onto this,' Isaac said, sitting down beside her and opening a laptop. 'We'll start with the place you climbed out of the delivery van and work back from there,' Isaac suggested. 'What was the name of the hotel?'

'OK, let me try to remember…' Annette closed her eyes. 'The hotel was called The Garden, no… The Gardenia! Yes, that's it!'

Isaac clicked on several images of the hotel.

Annette pointed. 'There! That's where I got out!'

Isaac brought up an aerial picture of the area. Annette leaned forward, 'We had driven up this road here. We were on the main road for about fifteen minutes. We turned right into it from a smaller road.'

Isaac traced back through the journey. Sometimes Annette was positive about the route, sometimes they had to retrace several times to find a familiar sight.

Suddenly Annette sat very still, her eyes fixed on the screen. 'That's the commune boundary wall. The gate is just around to the left.'

Isaac called out the coordinates as Reuben keyed them into a tablet. 'We need to go the commune straight away. The Radicals have a way of disappearing very quickly! Let's hope they haven't done so already.'

Reuben had been speaking into a mobile phone. He looked up, 'There will be Lab guards arriving here in five minutes. Two will remain in the hotel. Two senior officers will accompany us to the commune which they will shortly have under surveillance. No-one will be allowed to leave the premises.'

'Stay here until you hear from us. Keep Annette out of sight,' Abel said as they were ready to leave.

Silence fell over the room after the three men had left.

'We'd better get packed up and ready to catch our flight this evening,' Keith said. 'Celia has arranged your papers and included you on the flight list both ways so it looks as if you came from London with us.'

'Hey, Annette. Why don't you take a rest for an hour or so? As soon as we hear from Abel or Isaac we'll wake you up,' Zig suggested.

Annette looked up and shook her head, 'No. I have to do something, while I remember it clearly.' She sat down at a desk in the window and pulled a pad and pencil from the drawer. Zig shrugged as Keith gave her a questioning look. Annette remained engrossed in her work as the others packed their bags. After fifteen minutes she stood up holding out several sheets of paper. 'These are the people I saw at the commune. The Labs...'

Zig gave a gasp as she looked through the pages. 'Angus, Takir, Sanjit – he looks so much older! And who is this? He looks familiar... My God, it's Hugo! Mmm... some of the other faces look familiar, too, though I don't know any of their names.'

'And the Non-Labs...' Annette held out two more sheets.

Zig shook her head. 'I don't recognise these at all.'

Pellier gave a low whistle. 'These are very good likenesses! You certainly have a talent!'

'The last one is the boy who delivered the breakfast trolley this morning. I only caught a quick glimpse of him from behind the bedroom door, but it might be useful. He could be working for them.'

'I'm impressed. I wouldn't have been able to describe him,

but I recognise him from your picture,' Keith said. 'Your talent will come in very useful, Annette!'

'I hope so,' she replied quietly. 'I want to get these people. The ones who killed my brother.' She pulled a folded sheet of paper from her pocket. 'This is Robert.' The face of a boy around her own age looked up at them. He was wearing a wide grin with a touch of mischief gleaming in his eyes.

CHAPTER SEVENTEEN

'There was no sign of them. Again!' Isaac sat down dejectedly in an armchair in the hotel suite later that day.

'Well, I expect they packed up as soon as they realised that Annette had gone,' Pellier pointed out.

'We did discover something,' Abel was looking at a small piece of silvery material. He'd slipped it into his pocket as the rather reluctant caretaker had shown them around the building. 'I'll have to get them to examine it at the Compound, but I have a feeling that this is very similar to the fireproof material Henry, our new Hybrid student, has been developing.'

'How would they get their hands on that?' Isaac looked puzzled. 'The only ones aware of Henry's research are those on the Compound.'

'Exactly!' Abel nodded. 'They must have a contact living amongst us.'

'This could be serious.' Reuben frowned.

'Indeed it is!' Abel agreed.

'What are you planning on doing next?' Keith looked at them.

'I have arranged a meeting with the owner of the commune building tomorrow morning,' Reuben told him. 'He said he had rented out the property and grounds to an American company on a yearly contract which ends in two months' time. He was expecting them to renew the contract as they had done over the past two years. He was surprised to hear they had decided to leave this year. I hope he can give us some background details on the company tomorrow.'

'Well, we'll be leaving here in half an hour. There are taxis picking up all the crew and equipment and taking us to the airport.'

'Annette, there is a room ready for you in the Staff Medical Wing on the Compound. There are three new trainees joining Dr Shultz's team on Monday morning. Celia has added you as a fourth. She has identity papers drawn up for you and she will fill you in on your new background when you get there,' Abel told her. 'It would be a good idea if you could make some changes to your appearance, too. The Radical sympathisers at the Compound will no doubt be on the lookout for you.'

'I can help out there,' Zig said. She held out the sketches the young girl had drawn, 'Annette has a great memory for faces, look.'

Reuben looked through them. 'I recognise some of these faces. It is a real help to know what some of the others look like.'

Isaac shuffled through the pages and nodded. 'Very useful! I'll get copies of these out to a few friends this evening.'

CHAPTER EIGHTEEN

'I suppose we might as well go ahead and book our flight home tomorrow,' Isaac sighed as he and Abel walked back to the hotel the following day.

'Did you send Celia all the information we have so far?' Abel asked him.

'Yes,' he replied. 'I gave her the name of the owner of the commune, Mr Antonov, and all the details Reuben found out about Aura, the American company who rented it. Mr Antonov said he received an email from them last week telling him that they were facing financial difficulties in the States and that's why they were terminating their lease. Celia has the bank details, too.'

'Unless Celia comes up with any new leads, I think we might as well go home. We don't know where the Radicals are based now. At least Annette is safe,' Abel said. He gave a yawn as they entered the hotel and headed for the stairs.

'Mr Abel, Mr Abel!' a voice made him turn around. The receptionist was waving an envelope at him. 'This arrived just over an hour ago. The man said it was important.'

Abel slit the envelope open and pulled out a sheet of paper, 'Who delivered this? What did he look like?'

'He was a motorbike courier. His face was hidden by his visor. He didn't say much, just that it had to get to you quickly as it was urgent,' she said. 'Is everything OK?'

'Fine,' Abel gave a quick smile and hurried upstairs with Isaac close beside him. 'What time is it? Six thirty. That gives us two and a half hours! I'll get on to Reuben!'

Isaac's eyebrows rose as he read the letter:

'Abel,

We feel it is time we met to discuss the possibility of us working together, for our mutual benefit.

We will meet you and Isaac, just you two, at the south gate of the Municipal Park at 9 o'clock this evening.

Angus'

'What do you think? Is it a trap?' Abel asked him.

'Maybe, but it's also our only lead,' Isaac replied.

An hour later the two men set off for the Municipal Park. Abel pointed out the south gate as they drove past.

'It looks pretty deserted, even at this time,' he remarked.

Isaac nodded, 'And there are quite a few places to hide: that clump of trees over there, and there's a small stone building, maybe a gardener's shed, further up the path.'

'I've let Reuben know where we're meeting Angus. He'll be keeping a discreet eye on us,' Abel said. 'I'll park further up this road and we'll wait and see who turns up.' He drove to the next junction and swung the car around.

Isaac yawned and rubbed his chin as a clock chimed out nine.

'Nothing so far…' he began, but Abel tapped his arm.

'Look.' A long black limousine slowed down as it passed the gate. Several minutes later it reappeared and slowed down once more before continuing on its journey.

'Let's go,' Abel whispered as he slid out of the car.

They were level with the gate when the black car reappeared. This time it drew to a halt. A door opened, Angus stepped out, and the car silently moved off.

The three men faced each other. Angus smiled and stepped forward, holding out his hand, 'It's good to see you both again. I'm glad you are unaccompanied. And as you can see, I am also on my own!' He turned towards the park, 'Let's take a walk, shall we?'

Isaac and Abel kept to the centre of the wide road as he

headed into the park.

'So, you think we can work together?' Abel began.

Angus nodded. 'A great future lies ahead for both of our groups if we can forget our differences and build on the ideals we share. After all, we are all Labs and we know the future is in the hands of the Labs.'

'What are you proposing?' Abel asked.

'It's simple really. We pool our ideas and resources and make plans for the future of our race,' Angus replied. 'We all know that the governments of the major countries, if not all countries, should be led by Labs and Hybrids. For the benefit of Labs and Hybrids.'

'What about the Non-Labs?' Isaac asked.

Angus smiled. 'Of course, as a Non-Lab that is going to be one of your major issues, isn't it? But don't worry, there will be positions for Non-Labs, too.'

'Our goal has been to live a life on an equal footing with Non-Labs,' Abel pointed out. 'I don't see how we can be working towards the same future.'

Angus stopped and faced him, the contours of his face etched hard in the dwindling light.

'Abel, think about what the Non-Labs have done for the Labs so far! We are treated like some poor relations. They are holding us back in every way possible! Stopping us from achieving our full potential! At best they tolerate us! Is this the life you want for your Hybrid children? Don't we have the right to plan our own future, live the life we are meant to live? You said yourself, all Labs should stand together!'

'Except for the ones you experiment on!' Isaac scowled.

Angus shook his head and gave a sigh. 'We have had a few setbacks, but we now have strict checks in place to avoid any harm coming to any Lab who agrees to help us with our research.'

There was silence. Angus shifted his feet on the dusty ground.

'So what were you hoping I would agree to?' Abel said at length.

'As leader of the Compound Labs you have influence over the people you represent. You are in a position to speak for all of us, to push for changes! To put us in our rightful place in society!' Angus's eyes gleamed.

Abel folded his arms. 'We need to sit down together, all of us; the Radical leaders, myself and some of the leading Non-Lab leaders and to put forward ideas from all parties…'

'No!' Angus swung around. 'The Radicals will not agree to take into consideration the antiquated views of a dwindling race! This is about the Labs!'

Abel faced him. 'Non-Labs have as much right to have a say in the future as Labs do. The Compound Labs do not wish to enter into any agreement with the Radicals without considering Non-Lab rights, too!'

The veins in Angus's neck throbbed as he walked towards Abel. 'The Compound Labs led by *you* do not want to enter into any agreement with the Radicals! With a new leader, who knows what is possible!'

Abel stood his ground. 'I am not the only Compound Lab to think this way. You would not be able to replace *all* of us.'

'Don't underestimate us!' he spat out, turning as the black car silently drew up beside him. 'Think it over. We'll be in touch.'

'Wait!' Isaac grabbed his sleeve as he headed for the car. 'Wait! What about Celia? You took a blood sample from her. Why? You must tell us!'

A figure stepped out of the car.

'Hugo!' Abel gasped.

Hugo shot Isaac a look of pure hatred. 'What happened to Celia has *nothing* to do with you or any other *Non-Lab*!'

Isaac dropped Angus's arm and turned to the teenager. 'Why, you…' As he raised a fist a figure emerged from the shadows and knocked Isaac to the ground with a blow to the side of his face. Abel sprang forward to shield his friend from the vicious kick which followed and crumpled to the ground himself.

'Get back into the car!' Angus hissed. With a sullen face, Hugo obeyed. The second man raised an eyebrow as he caught Angus's eye. 'You, too,' he added and turned to where Abel lay clutching his stomach. 'As I said, think it over. You either join us willingly or we take over the Compound Labs. We'll be in touch.'

An hour later, Abel and Isaac sat in their hotel room. Reuben watched as Isaac held a cold compress to his blackening eye. One side of his face was purple and swollen.

'That man,' Abel shook his head, 'he was solid muscle. I have not met a Lab as strong.'

'Some kind of enhancement?' Reuben suggested.

Abel agreed. 'It must be. What kind of people are they creating? Where will it all end?'

'Hugo!' Isaac said, grimacing with the effort of speaking. 'How *dare* he tell me I have no say in Celia's wellbeing?' He groaned again and pushed the compress back in to place.

'The way he reacted, Hugo obviously knows about the research they were doing.' Abel looked thoughtful. 'He was only fourteen at the time he left, but he was always wise beyond his years.'

'If only we could have found out more.' There was a note of sadness in Isaac's voice. 'I've still no news for Celia when we get back.'

CHAPTER NINETEEN

'You will not be allowed outside of this research station here in Austria. You will not be involved in any communications with the Compound Labs or their Non-Lab friends at all!' Hugo looked up with a contrite expression as Takir faced him across a large conference table. 'We will not let you jeopardise our organisation in any way!'

Hugo shuffled uneasily in his chair. He nodded quickly. 'I know, I know! It was stupid of me, but that *Non-Lab* demanding to know about Celia...'

'He lives with her. He has a child with her. Of course he wants to know what happened to her!' Takir interrupted. He turned as there was a knock on the door. Two young women entered. 'Liz, Jackie; are the others here yet?'

'On their way down. Ali picked them up from the airport an hour ago,' Liz replied.

A few moments later there was the sound of voices in the corridor. Two people entered.

'Hey there, you guys,' the young woman said as she slipped into a seat at the large table.

'Hi, Shana. How was your flight from New York?' Liz asked.

'Not too bad. I slept for most of it, but Willis here was working away for most of the flight!' She smiled at the young man who was looking around the room.

'Where can I set this up?' he asked.

Hugo jumped up and helped him set up his equipment.

The door opened again and Dr Gil came in. 'I hope I

haven't missed anything?'

'No, just setting up now,' Willis said. 'Well, as you know, after an accelerated growth programme, our five special clones were awakened at the equivalent of fourteen Non-Lab years. Since then they have lived with their foster Lab parents in Arlington, New York and have achieved good results at the local High School over the past two years. We have kept you updated on their progress.'

'Arlington High has a good reputation and a high intake of Labs and Hybrids,' Liz commented.

Shana nodded in agreement. 'The location was carefully chosen. We have selected New York University and an annex of it, New York State Sports College, for the different courses we have planned for them when they are eighteen.'

Willis clicked a button and a page of data appeared on the screen, 'They quickly settled into school life. Pretty much as expected.' He clicked a button and pointed to the screen, 'These three are performing in the top 2% in their areas. Bruno is doing exceptionally well in Politics, as we planned, and has already been approached to work with the local council on a project for young people from dysfunctional families. Jude will also be working with him on this. The two of them have set up a political forum in the school called Green Shoots which is proving to be very popular. Celeste is once again taking the leading role in the Drama department end of term performance. She is also involved in two main charity organisations – one of them linked to the same one Bruno and Jude will be working on for the council, the other a scheme to promote green living through drama workshops in inner city schools.'

'What about Jane and Max?' Hugo asked. 'How are they performing in the Sports department?'

'They are a bit of a worry. Look at their results. They're only performing in the top 7%. It's not their fitness levels and commitment, it's just that there's tough competition from the

Labs and the new Hybrid students. We were very pleased to hear you have inserted the eyes, ears, and nose enhancements into Labs successfully. We want to arrange for the first of the operations to begin during the next school vacation. But what about the muscles? Have you corrected the dosage for Labs and Hybrids yet? We don't want any more mistakes. We need this enhancement to work.'

'We have now almost perfected the muscle enhancements. In fact our latest trials show a great improvement on our earlier ones - the muscles are not just more flexible but also harder and stronger. Our latest Lab subject is working for us as a bodyguard. Initially, there was a slight heart problem but we are confident this will be remedied in our next trial, scheduled for next week,' Takir told him.

'So you haven't actually had a successful Lab trial on muscle enhancement up to now, then?' Willis looked annoyed.

'With all respect, Willis, we have an unlimited supply of Non-Lab subjects; youngsters that we can pick up and who won't be missed. It is a different story with Lab subjects. It's not so easy; but we have now located three new Lab volunteers without any family issues,' he replied.

'Do these Labs know what it involves?' Shana asked. 'Our benefactor was concerned about any legal backlash that may arise.'

'Everything is in order,' Takir assured her. 'The operations will go ahead at the end of this week.'

'So we can start the enhancements implants during the next vacation? Good. I can report back to our benefactor that it's all in hand. It will enable us to move on to the next stage of our plan. We need these five youngsters to be ready to take up their roles once they get to university, to lay the groundwork for their future careers. With influential people in politics, the entertainment industry, and high-profile sports, we will have the means of being the biggest influence on the youth of one of the most powerful nations of the world. And whatever the

77

US does, the UK soon follows!' Willis rubbed his hands together.

Shana stood up. 'As well as bringing you the latest data and facts on our famous five, I've persuaded Willis to include a few clips so you can get an idea of what these kids are really like. You will be hearing a lot about them over the next few years! Here's a taste of what's to come - here are Bruno and Jude in action at one of the Green Shoots meetings.'

A young boy stood up and introduced himself as Bruno. He was tall and slim with light golden skin. His dark brown, tightly curled hair was cut close to his head. He smiled with a confidence beyond his years as he turned pale green eyes on his audience. Beside him sat a similar-looking young man with slightly longer hair who nodded as Bruno outlined the role of today's youth in the future of the United States, adding some of his own comments from time to time.

Hugo leaned forward, transfixed by the two men on the screen. He felt a hand on his back.

'You have a very personal interest in this particular group, DNA wise, don't you, Hugo?' Shana smiled.

He blushed. 'I am proud to have been involved...'

'Of course! I find it hard to remember that you're actually one of the donors of these youngsters! You're still a kid yourself!' Willis laughed.

Hugo was stung. 'I am a *Hybrid*! And it is a long time since I ever felt I was a *kid*! At fourteen years old I had already proved my worth in the advancement of cloning. It was my research that made it possible to merge DNA from two donors to create a clone of them both. Dr Gil himself worked on that project with me. I find your attitude towards me patronising to say the least.'

'Hey, that's OK,' Shana patted his shoulder. 'The development of these youngsters is teamwork! And we're all part of the same team, totally committed to this project.'

'Shana is right,' Takir spoke up. 'We're a team working

towards the same goal. There is no room for personal disputes.'

Willis nodded. 'My apologies if I have offended you, Hugo.'

The young man acknowledged him briefly and quickly dropped his eyes. Shana wondered what expression he was hiding as his body trembled slightly.

'Can we see the clips of the other three?' she asked Willis.

'Sure,' he said. 'This is an interview Celeste gave to the local newspaper after the success of the end of term play at their school last year. She was Maria in *West Side Story*. It went down a bomb!'

A tall, slender girl appeared on the screen and smiled with assurance into the camera. She pushed thick, wavy black hair back over one shoulder. Her narrow eyes were, like Bruno's, a pale green. As she spoke, her face lit up with an intense energy.

Takir let out a low whistle. 'I had forgotten how beautiful she is!'

Willis nodded in agreement. 'She certainly is, and it's not just that; she has a great presence, she's very persuasive in her arguments. As with Bruno and Jude, in a few years she will be somebody to be reckoned with'

The others agreed as she explained to the interviewer the reasons they had chosen *West Side Story* and the message that they hoped to put across. Shana glanced at Hugo, his eyes riveted on the screen, his mouth curved in a smile.

'We have certainly done well with these three,' Willis continued. 'And now, let's see Jane and Max in action.'

The next few clips showed each of them in several different competitions, including sprinting, swimming, and gymnastics. In some they gained first place, in others second or third places. In two they came fourth.

Willis shook his head. 'That is why the muscle enhancements are so important. Especially in the gymnastic events. We don't want fourth place. We don't even want second and third places, we want firsts every time! So does our benefactor.'

'And firsts are what we are going to get!' Takir assured him.

The conversation turned to the timetable for the enhancement operations on the try-out Labs. The results were to be sent directly to Willis at the US office. Takir reassured them that everything would be perfect when it was time for Bruno and the others to be flown out to the new Austrian research centre for their enhancements.

CHAPTER TWENTY

'My God, Isaac! What happened to you?' Celia rushed forward as he was wheeled through the arrivals gate at the airport. He attempted a painful smile and patted her hand.

Abel reassured her, 'He'll be fine, Celia. He's suffered a broken cheekbone, but they'll soon sort him out at the Compound.'

'Ruby told me some of the details before I left. She said you were in some sort of fight with members of the Radicals. What was it about?' she continued as they sat in the ambulance.

Abel explained to her what had happened. She felt Isaac's eyes on her as he spoke.

'So we know for sure they were involved,' she said softly squeezing his hand gently. She took a deep breath. 'We have to find a way to infiltrate the Radicals.'

'I agree with you there, Celia, as it looks like they have at least one spy in our camp!' Abel's face looked grim.

Celia nodded, 'Yes. Keith told me you had found a sample of material very similar to Henry's invention. So how do we go about discovering their identity?'

'I have some ideas,' he said.

Once Isaac had been attended to and was sleeping in the Medical Ward on the Compound, Abel and Celia joined Ruby, Zig, Annette – now known as Anya - Keith, and Pellier at Abel's home.

'I've made a list of all the Labs and Hybrids who have visited the Compound at least once since Henry arrived,' Ruby told them, 'But then, we also need to consider who else those Labs could have been in contact with.'

'Let's start by looking at your list and picking out those who are possibilities,' Zig suggested. 'They're the ones we can keep a careful eye on.'

'I can help you out there!' Anya sat forward eagerly. 'Not many people here are aware of my enhancements. They wouldn't know if I was watching and listening.'

'Unless they are working with the Radicals and they know all about you!' Pellier pointed out.

'If I meet anyone who seems to know my background, I will report them immediately,' she said, turning to Celia. 'If you could arrange it so it looks as if my research takes me to most areas of the Compound, I'd have a good excuse to look around.'

'I could do that easily enough,' Celia looked at Abel. 'Annette, sorry, Anya, should be safe.'

'Please let me help! I want to find these people as much as you do. I will do everything to find the people who killed my brother!' Anya pleaded. 'When I see my parents tomorrow I want to be able to tell them that I'm also doing all I can to seek justice for his death.'

Celia looked at Abel. She had told him of Annette and Robert's background. She had traced their parents, Denise and David Markham, to a small terraced house in a south London suburb.

'David wanted to move out of London, but I wanted to stay near our old home in case the children came back,' Denise had told her. 'I could never accept that we wouldn't see them again.'

Celia had been moved by the couple's story. They had spent a fortune on unsuccessful attempts to have their own child through IVF and had given up hope until the government had introduced the Authorised Labs scheme, which had soon become known as Legal Labs. Couples could apply to have a cloned child if they were unable to have one naturally. The couple had jumped at the chance and were devastated to find their application rejected due to their age and David's poor health. Through an extensive internet search, David had come across an advertisement offering the chance to attend a conference on cloning by a medical group in Switzerland and had felt there might be a chance to find out some information about creating their own offspring, even illegally. Their dreams became reality when they were given such an opportunity to do so, at a phenomenally high price. Downsizing to a much smaller house and cashing in all the assets they had, the Markhams finally had the son and daughter they wished for and welcomed Annette and Robert into their home as young teenagers. Shortly afterwards, the company vanished without trace, and without providing any of the legal documentation that had been promised for their offspring. Fearing that they may lose their children, they planned to move to a country location to start a new life once they had saved up enough money to do so.

'Anya's parents were devastated to hear the news of Robert's death, Abel. That was the first thing Denise Markham said she wanted. Justice for her son,' Celia told him.

He was silent for a few moments. 'OK, Anya, but you must stay on the Compound at all times unless you are with someone that you know you can trust.'

The girl nodded. 'I will.'

She sat down beside Celia as the others discussed the list of possible Radical sympathisers with the others.

'Thank you,' she said.

Celia squeezed her hand. 'We are all seeking justice!'

'And we won't give up until we find it,' Anya whispered.

CHAPTER TWENTY-ONE

Ness, Ginny and Rafael spread out the sheets of paper across the table top.

'We have all the data, now we need to organise it and cross reference everything,' Ginny said. 'Then we can each present our investigations from a different angle to highlight the area we are each concentrating on for our individual assignments.'

After an hour they felt they had organised everything satisfactorily. The work was scanned and each one had a copy on their tablets.

'So that's nurture and developing skills, IQ and creativity, Hybrid brain development. Oh, and didn't you say you were also going to formulate a hypothesis on which groups you feel would be more likely to be vulnerable to influence by the Radicals, Ness?' Rafael asked.

'Mmm,' she nodded, 'Dad was very interested in that idea but he wants to keep that information separate.'

'You could share it with us, though, couldn't you? We don't need to refer to it in the assignments we hand in, but it would be interesting for us to consider,' he continued. 'We might want to challenge some of your ideas.'

Ness busied herself tidying up the papers and packing up her tablet. 'I'll speak to Dad.'

Later that evening, back at the university campus, Ginny sat on Ness's bed.

'I think this assignment is bringing out the best in Rafael, don't you, Ness?'

'I suppose he is mellowing a bit, not so critical and high-handed about Non-Labs these days. Maybe it's because he is spending more time with them here and at the Compound.' She looked thoughtful. 'You know Dad discovered that there is a supporter of the Radicals on the Compound?' Ginny nodded. 'Well, they drew up a list of possible suspects. And Rafael and Kasper are on it.'

'I know Rafael can be a bit full of himself about being a Lab, but...' Ginny looked thoughtful. 'I have to admit, at times he does remind me of...'

'Hugo?' Ness inserted.

Ginny nodded again. 'But not Kasper!'

'Zig thinks we don't just need to think about the obvious suspects, but the ones who seem to be a bit too nice, too.'

Ginny sighed, 'I see what she means. And if Rafael *was* a Radical sympathiser, I suppose Kasper would probably be aware of it. What are they planning to do?'

'First of all, monitor any suspects carefully. There are about twenty. Hopefully, after a week or two they will have narrowed that number down even further,' Ness told her.

'And then?' her friend asked.

'As Zig said, "Then we move on to Plan B - as soon as we work out what Plan B is!"' She smiled.

'Well, we can help, we can be vigilant,' Ginny suggested.

'I've already told them we will keep our eyes open.'

CHAPTER TWENTY-TWO

'What do you think about these enhancements we're getting, Celeste?' Bruno asked her as they walked to school one morning.

'Absolutely amazing! We'll be able to see and hear and have a better sense of smell than everyone else! We'll be suppler and be able to move quicker than everyone! It won't just be our brains that are superior! I can't wait!' she beamed. She frowned as she heard him sigh. 'What's up? You don't seem so pleased.'

Bruno shook his head. 'I know we score highest on all the IQ tests they've done so far and I'm quite happy with that. Do we really need all this for our future roles? I find the idea of having animal implants…'

'They are not animal implants, they are modified to fit our bodies perfectly. The enhancements are handpicked to raise our own human senses to a whole new level! Above any other Lab or Hybrid. Six years of research have gone into this. What's not to like?' she said. 'I'm sure you'll feel different once we have them.'

'You're probably right,' Bruno conceded. 'Jane and Max are really excited about the muscle enhancements. Both of them just hate coming second or third!'

Celeste nodded solemnly. 'Yeah. We've no space for that. We're top scorers. That's what's going to getting us where we want to be! Anyway, we'll have all our enhancements over the next few months so we're ready for the start of uni next September.'

'Yes, and we'll have had a few months to get used to them by then,' Bruno reluctantly agreed.

'Hugo is coming to see us tomorrow. He's really keen on these enhancements and I'm sure he'd be the last person to put us in any danger,' Celeste suggested. 'Ask him about any doubts you have.'

'You're right. If Hugo is all for them, the enhancements must be OK. He's always been overprotective of us. He's had quite a few arguments with Takir over our treatment!'

'I don't think Takir is aware of how often Hugo visits us,' Celeste said.

'It's probably better that way, to avoid any more arguments,' Bruno shrugged.

CHAPTER TWENTY-THREE

'Second year seems like even more work than first year, if that's possible!' Ginny groaned as she closed her laptop and collected her papers together from the desk.

'And you're still planning on getting your MA,' Ness reminded her as they headed for the library door.

Ginny pushed her heavy rucksack higher on her back, 'I might just take a gap year before going for an MA.'

'Still talking about wasting a year of your life, Gin?' Rafael said as he and Kasper fell in step beside them. 'You're not going straight out there to save the world?'

'I thought I'd leave that for you to do!' she retorted. 'You know so much about everything, it should be easy for you to save it all by yourself!'

'Are you going to be around this weekend?' Kasper asked them.

'No. I'm going home. I'm babysitting for Celia and Isaac,' Ness replied. 'Are you going home, Ginny?'

'No. I'd have to watch Mum and ditsy Dylan play happy families! Gross! Tina and Kiri were talking about going shopping Saturday morning. They want to buy something new for a party over in the Plantagenet House Saturday night. They said I could go, too, if I wanted,' she smiled.

'Gin, you're only fourteen. Most of the students at Plantagenet are twenty, twenty-one!' Ness frowned. 'You could always join me at Celia's, we could watch a movie once the baby is asleep.'

'Hey, I'm nearly fifteen, I'd like to live a little! All I seem to do is study and watch movies! There must be more to life than this!' Ginny retorted.

On Saturday morning, Ness tapped on Ginny's door, 'I'm off now, Gin. See you on Sunday.'

'OK,' Ginny yawned. She reached for her mobile as a text came through. She smiled. Kiri and Tina would meet her at TeenChic at half past eleven.

Over the next four hours, Ginny spent more than she usually spent in a month. Like the two older girls, she was laden down with bags, hers containing two new tops, shoes, jeans and makeup as they headed for Tina's and Kiri's rooms on campus.

'I can't believe you're only fourteen,' Tina said as Ginny tried on one of her new tops and the jeans. 'You could easily pass for sixteen, maybe eighteen.'

Ginny beamed with pleasure. 'So you don't think I'd look too young if I go to this party with you, then?'

'No way,' she said. 'Let Kiri do your hair and makeup and no-one will even think you're fourteen. She's really good!'

'Cocktail time, girls!' Kiri said coming into the room with a tray of drinks. 'Go on,' she urged seeing Ginny's smile waver. 'You don't have to get drunk! It'll just make you more relaxed.'

'I'll drink to that,' Tina raised her glass. 'We work hard all week, we need a bit of relaxation time!'

'Hear, hear!' Kiri clinked glasses with the other two girls.

Ginny took a sip of her drink and pulled a face as the sharp tang hit her.

Kiri laughed. 'One of my specials! Just to get us into the party mood! Come and sit over here so I can start on your makeup.'

Ginny watched in the mirror as she was transformed from a gawky fourteen-year-old into a glamorous beauty. The cocktail had left her with a warm buzz.

'Wow,' she said finally. 'That doesn't even look like me,

anymore!'

'I told you she was good!' Tina said as she reappeared from her bedroom wearing a tight black dress and heels so high that Ginny wondered how she could walk in them.

With Kiri dressed up in a similar outfit, it was time to leave.

Before they had reached the block where the party was being held, they could hear the loud music. Ginny took a deep breath as Kiri knocked and the door was opened by a smiling blonde girl who welcomed them in. Tina introduced her to several people then was led away by a boy from her classes. She looked around for Kiri and saw her in a corner talking to the blonde girl and two boys. Kiri caught her eye and beckoned her over.

'This is my super clever Hybrid friend I was telling you about!' Kiri said.

Ginny gave a deprecating shrug as one of the boys looked at her with raised eyebrows.

'Oh, we've several Hybrids in our physics classes. So intense! I didn't think Hybrids went to parties! I thought they just studied!'

The other boy put his arm around Ginny's shoulders, 'Well, Ginny here is convincing us they're all really human – sort of!'

Ginny laughed and moved out of his reach towards a small table that held drinks. She poured what looked like water into a glass and took a sip, choking as it burnt her throat.

'You're a vodka drinker then, are you?' he held up the bottle, 'Mind you, I think this is more anti-freeze than pure vodka!'

She turned back to find the others had moved away.

'Come on, let's dance,' her partner said, pulling her into the lounge where furniture had been pushed to one side.

'I'm Thomas, by the way,' he shouted into her ear as they danced to a loud rock song.

Ginny was relieved when the song finished and was about to move away when Thomas pulled her close to him as the next slow song started.

'So, what are you studying, Thomas?' she asked, pulling back from him.

'Psychology,' he shook his head. 'It's a hard slog. You people just find it all a piece of cake, don't you?'

'No! It's pretty tough!' she shook her head.

'I bet you say that to all of us – what do you call us? – Non-Labs?'

She stopped dancing and stepped back, 'Thank you, Thomas, but I think I need a bit of fresh air! Excuse me.' She was dismayed to find him catching her hand and leading her to a small courtyard outside. Sitting down on a wooden bench, she took a deep breath.

Thomas moved closer to her, playing with her hair as he spoke, 'I heard that not only are you Hybrids gifted brain-wise, but also physically, too!' He nuzzled her neck.

Ginny pushed him off her and tried to stand up. 'I'm sorry, but I'm not interested…'

'Hey, come on, now,' Thomas's face drew close to hers. Ginny realised by the glazed look in his eyes that he'd had quite a lot to drink.

She put her hands against his chest and pushed him away again, 'No thanks!'

'Aw…' he wheedled.

'She said she's not interested!' The familiar voice made Ginny look up. Rafael was standing in front of the bench.

'Just back off!' Thomas began.

'And let you get done for sexual assault of a minor?' Rafael glared at him. 'She is only fourteen, you know.'

Thomas released Ginny straight away and stood up.

'Bloody prick teaser!' he spat at her as he turned to go back into the house. Rafael made as if to go after him, but Ginny grabbed his arm.

'Leave him, please.'

'Get your things,' he said without looking at her. 'I'll walk you home.'

A subdued Ginny fell into step beside him a few minutes later. They walked in silence to her apartment.

'Thank you, Rafael,' she said as she turned the key in her door.

He gave her a curt nod and walked away.

CHAPTER TWENTY-FOUR

Ness walked in to the kitchen early on Sunday morning to find her family clearing up the breakfast table.

'Hi,' she said, slipping into a seat at the table and pouring a cup of tea.

'Want some toast?' Ruby asked her.

'No thanks, I had breakfast with Celia and Isaac earlier,' she replied. 'They said they'd be calling by later this morning.'

'I'm going over to Mark's house,' Zac said as he put the last plate in the dishwasher.

'OK,' his mother smiled. 'And Shiva is taking you other two to the park soon, so get your coats on.'

'I could go too,' Ness suggested but her father put a hand on her arm.

'Anya is on her way,' he said. 'I'd like you to hear what she has to say.'

Half an hour later Zig and Anya appeared, closely followed by Celia and Isaac.

'You know we have become aware that there is at least one Radical informer on the Compound, don't you?' Abel looked at Ness who nodded.

'Yes. Zig told me some of the names that were suggested over the last few months. Have you any further evidence? Can you name anyone for definite now?'

Abel looked at Anya. 'Perhaps you could explain what you've noticed.'

'From what I have seen and heard, there are quite a few

Radical supporters who live here or visit the Compound,' Anya began. 'And they seem to be well organised.'

She opened a folder and pulled out a sheaf of sketches and notes.

Ness picked up one of them. It was a good likeness of Adam. He was looking to one side as if catching someone's eye and sharing a private joke. There were two similar pictures of Leonard and Rafael. In another sketch, Kasper was looking down as if hiding his expression.

'These four people have the most trouble accepting the Non-Labs that are working alongside us on the Compound. I have heard them make several disparaging comments about them on different occasions,' Anya looked thoughtful. 'From their faces I think that they share something that the rest of us don't know about. I feel they are most likely to be the Radical sympathisers.'

Abel sighed and shook his head. 'I think you are probably correct. We have grown lax with Adam over the years, but we knew what he was capable of doing in the past. Perhaps he hasn't changed as much as he'd like us to believe. We must be more vigilant.'

'So what do we do next?' Zig asked.

'If we keep an eye on them they will lead us to the Radicals, surely?' Celia ventured. She looked at Isaac.

'We must move slowly,' he said. 'The Radicals have a spy in our midst, we need to have our own spy in their camp.'

'That could put someone at great risk,' Abel said. 'We know how ruthless they can be.'

'It would have to be a Hybrid or a Lab who was aware of the dangers. And someone they would not suspect,' Isaac added.

There was silence for a few moments.

'In the meantime we must keep a careful eye on these four,' Abel said.

CHAPTER TWENTY-FIVE

Later the same evening, Ness and Ginny sat giggling over a cup of tea and a homemade cake Ness had brought back with her.

'I suppose I could have got rid of him myself, but Rafael made it easier. And he walked me home.' Ginny sighed. 'You were right, I'm certainly not ready for those kind of parties yet! In fact, after the shopping and the dressing up, the actual party was a bit of a let-down!'

'What was Rafael doing over that side of the campus? He doesn't live anywhere near there, does he?' Ness asked.

'No, though I suppose he might have friends over there,' Ginny said. 'Anyway, how was your weekend?'

'Pretty quiet. The baby went to sleep quickly and I got my essay finished on Saturday night. On Sunday Anya came round to talk to Dad,' Ness hesitated.

'And?' Ginny prompted.

Ness told her about the sketches Anya had made and the discussion that had followed.

'I'm sorry that your father is a suspect, Ginny,' she said quietly.

Ginny bit her lip. 'I'm not really surprised, actually. Since I was very young he has always had a rather dim view of Non-Labs and talked about a great future for Labs and Hybrids. It's an interesting idea, to get a spy in the Radical camp.' She stood up and stretched. 'I shouldn't have wasted this weekend. I think I'll go home next weekend.'

CHAPTER TWENTY-SIX

'So, how are your studies going, Ginny?' her father asked her the following Saturday as they sat down to lunch at his house.

'OK,' she replied. She pushed the food around on her plate. 'Actually, I know I shouldn't complain, there isn't a better course in the UK, but, sometimes...'

Adam raised a questioning eyebrow.

'Well, I feel I know more than some of the lecturers; most of them in fact,' she sighed. 'And often I feel held back by the Non-Lab students in our classes. We have to go slow to let them keep up!'

Adam nodded. 'I can understand your frustration. Are there other Labs and Hybrids who share your views?'

'There are a few, like Rafael and Kasper, but they're not on my course,' she said.

'What about Ness?' he continued.

Ginny grimaced. 'She's a great friend, my best mate - but she'd never complain about Non-Labs, she'd feel like she was betraying her mum. And Abel is always on about equality for everyone!'

Adam patted her hand. 'It's hard for you young Hybrids at the moment; but I think your time will come in the future.'

'What do you mean?' Ginny looked up at him.

He pushed away his plate and looked at his daughter. 'Well, you know I've always believed that we Labs and Hybrids can do great things in the future?'

She nodded.

'This may sound like treason when you think of Abel's

96

views, and he is head of the Compound Labs – but there are some of us who have a vision of a future where Labs and Hybrids have their say and are in a position to put their ideas into action, even if it does mean offending a few Non-Labs in the process.'

'You mean the Radicals, Dad?' Ginny looked worried. 'Abel says they are ruthless and their kind of future will mean a dictatorship!'

Adam smiled. 'That's what the Compound Labs want people to think. The Radicals have a sound philosophy on how a country should be run.' He stood up and picked up a pencil and pad from a nearby desk. Sketching a box, he divided it into three layers. 'Look, this is our society – any civilised society – here at the top, we have the rulers, then come the auxiliaries, they defend the country, and here are the producers, the workers. Each person in that society has a role they should play according to their abilities. A person who builds houses isn't always the best choice to, say, govern a country. A talented teacher would not be a good choice to construct a building. Do you understand?'

Ginny nodded. 'That does make sense. So each person chooses what skills they want to develop?'

Her father spread his hands. 'No, not exactly! How would we know that people would make the right decisions? They need evaluating and guidance to find their perfect role. That would be the job of a chosen few Labs and Hybrids. Non-Labs would not be able to make an unbiased and unemotional choice. Read the history books to see the mess they have made of the world so far! Have you heard of Plato's *Republic*? I've a copy here somewhere.' He walked to the bookshelf and scanned the titles. 'Here it is. Read it, Ginny. These aren't new ideas.'

His daughter took the book from his hands. 'A lot of what you say makes sense, Dad. What kind of role would I play in an ideal society?'

'Think about the research you are working on now. What good use can it be put to later? That's where you could make the most impact in helping Labs and Hybrids move closer to their goals.' He looked serious. 'And don't let Non-Lab fears and prejudice stand in your way.'

On Sunday morning Adam and Ginny chatted together as they drove to her mother's house.

'What do you think of Dylan?' Ginny asked her father as they neared her mother's house.

'Seems bright enough in his own sphere,' he shrugged. 'Your mother seems happy with him.'

Ginny kissed his cheek as she got out of the car, 'I'll be back up in a few weeks, Dad. I've enjoyed our discussion.'

'Me, too. But we'll keep our conversation to ourselves for the moment, OK?' he winked.

She nodded and turned to her mother's front door as the car drew away.

'Ginny! It's lovely to see you!' Amanda hugged her for a moment. 'Come in! Lunch is nearly ready.'

Ginny rubbed at a burn mark on the polished wooden table as they sat down a short while later.

Amanda smiled ruefully. 'Oh that was either Dylan or Henry! I keep telling them not to put hot plates on the table. Or dirty archaeological tools or red hot bits of Henry's experiments!'

She began to spoon vegetables on to the two plates.

'Henry's doing really well at school, Mum. You must be proud of all your achievements there,' Ginny said as she helped herself to rice.

Her mother frowned. 'There have been a few unsettling moments lately.'

'What do you mean, Mum?' her daughter asked.

Amanda sighed. 'I just don't know if we can keep our school safe from these new Labs, the Radicals. It would be an absolute disaster if they managed to infiltrate the school and influence our students. I can't help but worry about what future plans they may have in store for us. I've spoken to Abel about it and he's working with Reuben to create an undercover security team to work behind the scenes.'

Ginny patted her mother's hand. 'Don't worry, Mum, there are enough Labs and Hybrids that can see reason to stand up to those Radicals! I'm sure Abel and Reuben won't let them get very far.'

'I hope you're right,' Amanda smiled. 'Anyway, enough talk of the Radicals! Tell me what you have been up to lately. Did you get your last assignment in on time? You really mustn't leave everything until the last minute, Ginny! Your second year is flying by and your final year will be even busier.'

CHAPTER TWENTY-SEVEN

Rafael found Ginny in the library late the following evening, 'Are you still working? I thought you would have packed up for the day by now!'

'Just finishing off notes for my next assignment. I decided to follow my mother's advice for once. I really need to get my head down,' she frowned. 'I shouldn't complain, really, but I thought this year was going to be, you know, exciting, challenging. Perhaps things will step up a pace in the final year.'

'In what way? Parties and things?' Rafael sneered.

'No! I'm talking about lectures.' Rafael slipped into the seat opposite her as she packed her laptop and notes away. 'OK, in the first year, we took it a bit easy. But this year I thought we'd have exciting, eye-opening discussions. That we'd all be ready to change the world! But we just continue to plod along!' She gave a short laugh.

Rafael leaned forward. 'So you're finally admitting that we Hybrids are being held back by the Non-Lab students?'

Ginny glanced around her. 'Well, maybe a university run on similar lines to the Compound School would be a help.'

Rafael nodded. 'I think it will come to that - despite the opposition we get, even from our own kind.'

'You mean the Compound Labs?' Ginny said in a soft voice. 'Well, I can understand how they don't want to offend anyone. At the end of the day we do all have to live together, for the moment anyway...' She bit her lip, 'Hey, I better get going! Ness will wonder what's happened to me! You must tell her you found me studying here next time you see her, she'll never believe me when I say I've been here all afternoon!'

She was aware of the thoughtful look Rafael gave her as he stood up and followed her to the door.

Over the next few weeks Rafael seemed to seek her out at different times of the day. One Friday evening he sat down opposite her in the library.

'Hey, still working? I'm impressed,' he said. 'I didn't think your resolution would last!'

She raised her eyebrows. 'I told you, the new Ginny is almost all work these days!'

'How are the lectures going?'

She shrugged. 'Not much has changed. But I'm getting into my own work. Something I can really use later if I can find the right sponsors.'

'Am I allowed to know what it's about?' he asked.

'It might sound a bit far-fetched, and I'm only at the early stages yet...' She hesitated.

'Far-fetched doesn't mean impossible these days, you know. I've a few ideas myself on developing different kinds of materials that could be used for medical purposes and in industry. Like you, I'm at the early stages yet...'

Ginny took a deep breath. 'You know I've been researching the brain development in Labs and Hybrids?' He nodded. 'Well, these past few weeks I've been looking at Non-Lab brains, too. I've been considering ways to implement programming at a very early stage of development so that a person would be moulded to fit into his or her future career which would be decided upon by market demand. A bit like Plato's *Republic*. My dad told me about the book, I've been reading it.'

'Ginny, I've always known it, you're wasted with the Compound Labs!'

She shook her head. 'I never thought I'd say this, but the Compound Labs don't seem to hold all the answers to our future.'

Rafael put his hand over hers. 'I wondered how long it would take you to reach that conclusion.'

Over the next few weeks Ness noticed how Ginny and Rafael were spending more time together. Often she would come upon them huddled in the library in earnest conversation.

'Hey, you two always seem to be together these days!' she said to her friend one day as Rafael was just leaving them. 'I hope you haven't fallen for him since he came to your rescue that night at the party.' She noticed the blush quickly spread across her friend's face. 'Ginny, you must take care! Don't forget, he's high on the list of Radical supporters.'

'Oh, Ness! Of course I'm not falling for him. He just happens to be a talented and interesting person – even if he is rather arrogant! Anyway, what is the latest news on the Radicals?'

'Nothing new,' Ness told her. 'Dad has a few people keeping an eye on things.'

'Has he got a spy in the Radical camp yet?' Ginny asked, but Ness shook her head.

'Reuben has a couple of his team working on the Compound trying to get their attention. But, as you know, the Radicals are very slow to approach Compound Labs.'

Ginny nodded thoughtfully.

CHAPTER TWENTY-EIGHT

Shana watched as Celeste drizzled olive oil over the steaming bowl of pasta. She had tied her long curly hair back into a rough bun. A few wisps had already escaped and brushed across her slender neck. Even in jeans and a T-shirt she looked stunning. In fact, they all were; Bruno's strong muscles flexed as he carried two chairs through from the lounge, Jude was equally imposing as he leant back against the French windows laughing at something Willis had said. Hugo had made the right choices when it came to physical attributes.

'This smells delicious,' Shana said as Celeste opened the oven door and took out a plate of garlic bread.

'Hands off, Bruno!' Celeste slapped his hand away from the plate. 'Wait until Jane and Max arrive. They'll be here any minute.'

They were all sitting down as the door opened and the last two appeared.

'Sorry we're late!' Max apologised.

'You were just making sure you didn't have to do any of the cooking!' Jude grinned.

'Hey! We've been cooking! Look,' Jane lifted the cover off a large dish. 'Crème brulee!'

'A la Max!' Max added. 'I don't remember you doing much of the cooking, Jane!'

'I helped you clean up!' She smiled.

For the next few minutes there was silence as they all ate.

'This is superb!' Shana said. 'You've got the apartment looking really good, too. What's your accommodation like over at the Sports College, Max?'

'Good. Not quite as spacious as this place, but it's right next to the sports complex, so it suits us fine.'

'How is the course going?' Shana asked them.

'We're in demand for most ball game teams and we're both excelling at kickboxing and judo,' Jane said. 'We do meet a few challengers. We'll be glad to get the muscle enhancements.'

Max nodded eagerly. 'That'll be over the Easter break, won't it?'

'Yes,' Willis said. 'You will all be getting the first of your enhancements. You two will have the muscles, Bruno nose, Jude ears, and Celeste eyes. Over the next few months you will undergo several operations until you have all the enhancements.'

'Why can't we have more than one at a time?' Celeste asked. 'The trial Labs did, didn't they? And nothing has gone wrong since the latest adjustments, has it?'

'Nothing has gone wrong with Lab enhancements in the past year, but it's just an extra precaution we are taking. You people are too special to place in any danger whatsoever. You have an important job to do! Each enhancement will be carefully monitored before the next operation. By the end of your second year you will each have all the enhancements.' Shana said.

'I can understand the muscle operations for Max and Jane, but how will these enhancements help the rest of us?' Bruno asked. 'We are already very intelligent and physically attractive.'

Shana leaned forward, her eyes shining, 'With the talents you have, you're already influencing many others. Just think what you can do with superior senses. You'll stand out from everyone else. You will be the ultimate human beings!'

Celeste lay down her fork, a smile spreading over her face. 'Think what power we can have over people.'

104

'Exactly!' Willis nodded.

There was silence for a while. Bruno shuffled uneasily and then pushed his chair back. 'Who's for a taste of dessert a la Max?'

The tension dispersed as dessert plates were passed around the table.

'And how are you others getting on here at New York Central?' Willis turned to Jude.

'Everything is going exactly to plan. Bruno and I are on the chair of the debating society. We already have plans to start a political group similar to Green Shoots, to involve students in political discussions and volunteering at social centres. Celeste has, of course, been chosen for the lead part in the end of year drama performance,' he answered. 'We're making our mark.'

'And with enough good deeds to ensure a loyal following!' Celeste smiled.

Willis smiled and nodded. 'Good, good!'

He gave Shana a sigh of relief as they drove off later that afternoon.

'If all goes well, we'll have the perfect templates for Claude,' he said.

'And when will they get to meet him?' Shana asked.

'During their final year,' he replied. 'He'll have had all his own ops and enhancements by then. It's been arranged that he'll work as an intern in one of the senator's offices and he can get involved with the volunteer work Bruno and Jude are doing.'

Shana nodded. 'I'd like to take a close look at the background they created for Claude. It's got to be something solid that can be checked out. We don't want anything coming up later on.'

Willis gave her an appreciative glance. 'You've got a point there. I'll mention it at the next meeting.'

'The Radicals don't suspect anything, do they?' she asked.

'No. Their five will still have a very important role to

play.' He gave a chuckle. 'That young Hugo is not going to be
too pleased to have his little crew upstaged, though!'

CHAPTER TWENTY-NINE

'You mean I could actually go to one of the meetings?' Ginny's voice held a tremor of excitement as she faced her father.

'Yes. I've been thinking about this for the last three months, since we had our first talk about the Radicals. Last month I proposed that you're ready to become a team player of the Hybrid Radical group. They looked into things and found another Radical supporter willing to second my proposal and you were accepted. Rafael has been a member of our team for a while now. You can attend the next meeting with him. There will be a few other youngsters that you will be surprised to see there, I'm sure, Ginny,' her father told her. 'But remember, discretion is paramount at all times. We're building up a strong following, but we're not ready to take on the Compound Labs yet.'

'Of course, Dad. I can't believe I've been accepted! Thanks so much!' He felt her body shake as she hugged him.

'It's what we used to talk about when you were just a little girl, remember, Ginny? We used to talk about a great future for the Labs and Hybrids,' he smiled at her. 'For a while I was afraid I'd lost you to the Compound Lab way of thinking, but we're both on track now!'

Ginny was still trembling as she dressed for the meeting that evening. A pile of discarded clothes were spread on the bed as Ness came into her bedroom.

'I thought you were going to the library to study with Rafael this evening, Ginny. This looks more like getting ready for a date!'

'We might go on to see a film later,' Ginny tried to sound casual.

'So it is a date!' Ness sat down on the bed. 'Ginny, remember...'

'Yes, he's on the *most wanted list*. I know!' she snapped. 'Until he's proven guilty I am allowed to talk to him, aren't I?'

Ness took a deep breath, 'Ginny, have you thought...'

Ginny faced her friend, 'Ness, please. I'm just going to go through my assignment with Rafael and get some of his advice on a few points. Then we're probably going to relax and watch a film. That's all.'

She grabbed her jacket off the bed and headed out. 'See you later.'

Ness sighed and went back to her own room. She also had an assignment to complete. She wanted to ask Ginny for some advice herself, but her friend had seemed preoccupied these last few months. She sighed again and opened her own laptop and turned it on. Groaning, she remembered that it needed charging. And that the charger was in her locker in the college building which would be closed by now. She fished around in her laptop bag and pulled out a memory stick. Ginny wouldn't mind if she borrowed her laptop, would she?

Ness walked back into Ginny's room and saw the laptop on her desk. She picked it up and carried it through to the lounge. As she unzipped the case a notebook slid out of the pocket and landed open on the floor. She switched on the computer and reached down to pick it up. As she was about to slip it back into the pocket it fell open and she glanced at the text.

'R – about 20, all courses. H & L. Compound led by A and L. Mtgs diff loc.

Her brow crinkled as she tried to make sense of it. Ginny certainly made cryptic notes for her assignments. She pushed the notebook back into the pocket and inserted her memory stick into the laptop. As she worked on her own assignment she had a niggling feeling at the back of her mind. She pulled out the notebook again and flicked through the pages. The notes for her other assignments were much clearer, so why was this page so hard to decipher? She looked at the initials first. Ginny had been spending a lot of time with Rafael lately, so he could be R. H& L probably stood for Hybrids and Labs. What about A&L on the Compound? Abel was the Compound leader, but L? Leonard worked there, but he spent more time with Adam. They held regular meetings with the young Lab and Hybrid counsellors. And Adam was a Radical suspect. Maybe R stood for Radicals, not Rafael? She read the message again, putting in what she thought the initials stood for:

'Radicals – about 20 on all courses. Hybrids and Labs. Compound led by Adam and Leonard.'

Ness sat back in her chair, her hands trembling. So this is why Ginny had been so preoccupied these last few months, she had followed her father into the Radicals, or followed Rafael, or even both of them! It couldn't be true. There must be another explanation.

Ginny pushed open the door to the apartment later that evening to find Ness sitting motionless on the sofa in the darkness.

'Hey what is it?' she asked. 'If it was about how grumpy I was earlier, I'm sorry. There's just so much stuff to do at the moment.'

'Stuff like this?' Ness pointed to the open notebook on the table in front of her and read out, '"Radicals – about 20 on all courses. Hybrids and Labs. Compound led by Adam and Leonard."'

'Where did you find my notebook?' Ginny grabbed it from the table. 'Do you make a habit of going through my things when I go out?'

'Out to the library, you mean, like tonight, Ginny?' Ness

looked at her. 'Funny, when I called by earlier they said you hadn't been in tonight!'

Ginny sat down with the notebook clutched in her hands. 'OK, Ness. You've got entirely the wrong end of the stick here...'

'No, Ginny, it's not me going wrong here, it's you!' Ness's eyes stung with tears. 'I don't know what to do about it, but Dad will.'

As she got up, Ginny grabbed her arm. 'Ness, have you said anything to Abel about these crazy ideas of yours?'

'Not yet,' Ness's face crumpled. 'I told myself you'd come in and give me a reasonable explanation for all this. But you can't deny anything, can you, Ginny?'

'Ness, listen for a moment, please,' Ginny pleaded. 'I swear it's not how it looks!'

Ness sat down again opposite her.

'I was going to tell you, and Abel, eventually, but not yet, not until I have enough evidence,' Ginny took a deep breath. 'You know Abel's idea about getting a spy into the Radical camp? Well, I'm that spy.'

A look of alarm spread across Ness's face. 'No way, Ginny! It's far too dangerous!'

Ginny looked up, her face pale and strained, 'I have to, Ness. It's my father that is involved in all this. And Rafael. I know he's a pain sometimes, but I can't turn my back on him. If I can get enough evidence to help Abel break up this group, we can get them out!'

Her friend didn't look convinced as she continued. 'Think about it. I'm the ideal candidate. My father has always influenced the way I think. And I've built up a closer relationship with Rafael since he came to my rescue at that awful Non-Lab party! So, even if I was discovered - which I won't be, my father wouldn't let them harm me. Neither would Rafael, I'm sure.'

Ness shook her head. 'Ginny, they might not listen to your

father, and who knows how Rafael would react. It's just too dangerous. Reuben will have someone who is trained to do this kind of thing.'

Ginny looked stubborn. She held up her hand as Ness opened her mouth to speak, 'It's too late, Ness. I'm already involved. I went to my first Radical meeting tonight.'

Ness looked unhappy. 'We should ask my dad what he thinks first.'

Ginny shook her head vehemently, 'No! We are still little girls in his eyes! We always will be. He'd never even consider it! We'll let him know as soon as I've information to hand over to him. Ness, I know Adam is nothing like your dad, but would you ask me to turn my back on my own father?'

Ness sat silently, clasping and unclasping her hands.

'More Hybrids and Labs are joining the Radicals every week. We need to know what we are up against, how to counteract their plans before they go any further. We need to know what those plans are! We've seen what they are capable of doing!' Ginny pleaded. 'I'll keep my head down and just see what information I can pick up. I'm in the best position of all of us to try this. I've got Dad and Rafael on my side. No one else can say they have Radical sympathisers to look out for them. Please trust me, Ness. I'm going ahead anyway, but I would like your support.'

Her friend took a deep breath, 'I don't like it, but I know what you're like once you have an idea in your head. I won't say anything at the moment as long as you promise to pass on any information you get, don't try and act on your own.'

'Thank you so much, Ness!' Ginny hugged her. 'I promise I won't do anything stupid! My job is just to collect information. I'll leave it to your dad and the others to decide what to do with it.'

111

CHAPTER THIRTY

'Hey, can I join you here for a moment?' Celeste sat down opposite the truculent-looking character in the soup kitchen in a run-down part of New York.

He sniffed and rubbed his sleeve across his nose and answered without looking up at her. 'It's a free country, sit where you like.' He sniffed again.

Celeste watched him pick up his mug with trembling hands. 'You're not looking too good, are you? I don't think you've been taking much care of yourself. Perhaps we can help.'

The young man gulped back the rest of his coffee and gathered up his plate and cup.

'No thanks, I'm fine.'

She watched him place them in the aluminium container left at the side of the room and walk out of the door, giving a brief wave to the youth serving plates of sandwiches to a long and bedraggled queue.

Bruno slipped into the seat next to her. 'Not much here tonight.'

'That guy seemed promising. He would need some cleaning up, though,' she said. 'Even if he's not academic, with some help from us he could get a sports scholarship. I'm going to see what Thomas knows about him.'

The following night Celeste was serving the coffee as the young man arrived. He took the mug with shaking hands and gave a curt thanks without looking at her. Ten minutes later she joined him on the bench. He carried on eating and

112

drinking, ignoring her presence.

'Hi, it's Dale isn't it?' she ventured. 'Do you come from round here?'

He shook his head without looking up.

'We provide a place to stay and get cleaned up as well as food, you know,' she said. 'A hot shower can make you feel so much better! And you could sit down and chat with some friends.'

'I've got the only friend I need.' He gave her a knowing look.

'Drugs are never good friends,' she said, 'they're all take and no give.'

'My friend gives me plenty!' Dale stood up.

Celeste called after him, 'I can show you better friends who'll get you back on track.'

'Back? I've never been *on* track! I'm a lost cause, lady.' He gave a gruff laugh and walked away.

Celeste continued to chat to him each evening for the next week though each night he refused her offers of help.

The following week he looked around and felt disappointed not to see her there. She didn't turn up again until the end of the week. This time he gave her a smile.

'I thought you'd left,' he said as she slid into the seat opposite him.

'No, just busy at college, extra rehearsals for the end of term production,' she answered.

'College? I was too stupid for school, never mind college!' he shrugged.

'I don't believe that for a moment! Why don't you ditch your so-called "friend" and give school another go?'

He stopped eating and looked at her. 'Why would a good-looking college girl be interested in what I do?'

'I don't like to see you wasting your life,' she answered.

By the end of the next week Celeste found Dale waiting for her when she arrived to do her shift.

'About that school stuff. Could you help me?' he asked.

She smiled broadly and handed him a card. 'There are four other guys like yourself making a start tomorrow. Just turn up at that address at nine o'clock. I'll let them know you're coming. I'll drop by myself later in the day to see how you're getting on, ok?'

She hardly recognised the young man who stood before her the following afternoon. He had showered and shaved and had been given a haircut. Though worn, his jeans and T-shirt were clean. They showed up his thin frame.

'Hey, look at you! Had a good day?' she asked.

'Yeah, it's a neat place. Even got my own room,' he answered, running a shaky hand through his hair. 'Come and see.'

He led her to a corridor flanked by wooden doors. He pushed open one of them to reveal a small room simply furnished with a bed, chair, and desk. There was a small pile of books on the desk.

'First lesson tomorrow,' he took a deep breath. 'They even gave us some books to have a look at. We've got everything we want here.'

They walked back up the corridor to find Bruno and a group of six teenagers sitting and chatting in the lounge.

'I think I can make some good friends here,' he said.

'So you won't be needing the old ones?' Celeste raised an eyebrow.

He shook his head emphatically. 'No, no. They warned us, one slip and we're out. You've been real patient with me, I won't let you down, Celeste.'

They sat and chatted with the others for a while until Bruno and Celeste rose to leave.

'What do you think, Bruno?' she asked him as they climbed into her car. 'Producers? Auxiliaries?'

'Auxiliaries. Yes, definitely auxiliaries.'

114

CHAPTER THIRTY-ONE

'*An ideal society consists of three main classes of people:*
  guardians (rulers)
  auxiliaries (warriors)
  producers (craftsmen, farmers, artisans, etc.)
In an ideal society, these three classes must build a relationship of mutual benefits. Each group must perform its own function, and only that function, and each must be in the right position of power in relation to the others. Rulers must rule, auxiliaries must uphold rulers' convictions, and producers must limit themselves to exercising whatever skills nature granted them (farming, blacksmithing, painting, etc.) An ideal society requires that each person fulfils the role to which nature fitted him and not interfere in any other business.'

Ginny finished reading out loud. She looked at Rafael, who was leaning back against a tree chewing a blade of grass.

'What about him?' she asked as a plump, red-faced man walked past them.

'Definitely not warrior! I'd say producer,' he answered.

'And her?' Ginny pointed to a young woman dressed in an ill-fitting tweed suit.

Rafael pouted. 'Possible guardian, as she is a Lab. But she may turn out to be another producer. There's only room for so many of us at the top!' He sat up as Ness approached them. 'Now where would you put Ness?'

Ginny laid the book on the grass beside her. 'That's not fair, Ness is a friend!'

'Producer or warrior, maybe?' Rafael said.

'What are you doing?' Ness said as she sat down beside them.

'We're just playing a game,' Ginny explained. 'What role would different people play in Plato's ideal society?'

Ness picked up the book. 'Hmm, it sounds like an ideal society if you're a guardian. I'm not so sure it would be ideal for the others. Does "*not interfere in any other business*" translate as "shut up and get on with it"?'

Rafael sat up and rested his arms on his knees. 'In an ideal society, each person would make a positive contribution.'

'Even Non-Labs?' Ness asked.

He nodded. 'There is a place for everyone according to their abilities. Each Non-Lab can work in a capacity suited to individual skills.'

'So everyone can choose what they want to do?' she asked.

'According to their own skills and abilities, yes,' he replied. 'If a person is gifted intellectually, they will be given a choice of suitable positions. Those of a more practical nature would be given a choice of positions suited to their abilities.'

'What if a producer decided they wanted to become a guardian?' Ness asked.

'They wouldn't, because their whole design would make them suited and content in the role they were given,' he continued.

'So,' Ness frowned, 'the intellectually gifted people would be the ones to govern the country?'

'That would make sense, wouldn't it?' Rafael said.

'So that would mean Labs and Hybrids would rule the country?' she continued.

'Again, that would make sense, wouldn't it?' Rafael repeated.

'That does sound fair enough,' Ginny nodded in agreement. 'They are educated and intelligent. You could trust them.'

116

'They would decide who and how the country is to be ruled?' Ness asked. 'No democracy?'

Rafael gave a short laugh. 'Democracy hasn't exactly worked so far, has it? The Non-Labs haven't made the best decisions, have they? Isn't it time to give the intellectually gifted people a chance to implement some of their ideas?'

Ginny looked thoughtful. 'It does sound like a good idea.'

Ness shook her head. 'I think it would be dangerous to hand over too much power to one group.'

'At the moment, it's the group who are intellectually inferior who have too much power!' Rafael said vehemently. He stood up and glanced at his watch, 'I have to go. Perhaps see you later, Ginny?'

The girls watched as he walked away.

'He's pretty passionate about it, isn't he?' Ness said. 'And you sounded quite convinced yourself, Ginny.'

'That's what I want *him* to believe.'

Ness frowned. 'I hope you know what you're getting yourself into, Ginny. It might be harder to get out of than you think.'

Her friend smiled. 'Don't worry, I'll be fine. We're going to another meeting tomorrow evening. Are you going home this weekend? I thought I could speak to Abel, let him know what I'm doing. I already have some news to report to him.'

Ness raised her eyebrows, 'I don't think he's going to be too pleased, with either of us. It's probably better if we face him together!'

'You did *what*?' Abel stood up so suddenly that the chair he was sitting on crashed to the floor. 'And you stood by and watched, Ness? Without saying anything?'

Ginny's lip trembled but she held her head high. 'Don't blame Ness. She didn't know anything about it until too late. I know you think this could be dangerous...'

'*Could be?*' Abel ran his hands through his hair and paced

117

around the room. 'We'll have to think of a way of getting you out of this situation without raising any suspicions.'

'No, Abel!' Ginny clenched her fists. 'I've gained their trust, I'm accepted by them now. I can get inside information that could help you!'

'It's too dangerous! You're just a child!' Abel waved a hand in dismissal. 'What were you thinking of? This isn't a game, you know!'

Tears stung Ginny's eyes but she bit them back. 'No, it's not a game. My father and friends are involved. And soon there will be more! We've got to do what we can to help stop the Radicals and get them out safely!'

Abel stood looking down at the floor. Ruby and Ness sat silently at the table.

'If it was your family involved, wouldn't you want to do something?' Ginny pleaded.

The silence continued for a few moments until Abel gave a loud sigh and sat down opposite her.

'You said you needed a spy in their camp, I'm the best person to be that spy! My father wouldn't let me come to any harm if I was discovered – but I'll make sure I am not,' she added quickly.

Abel put his hands over hers. 'Ginny, your father has actually… put Labs' lives at risk carrying out his own research before now. There is no guarantee that he would protect you if you were discovered. We can't let you go ahead with this.'

'But that happened before I was born, didn't it? He'd *never* let anything happen to me! I *know* my father wouldn't!' Ginny snatched her hand back in outrage and stood up. 'Anyway, I'm in with the Radicals now! If I backed out at this point it would arouse suspicion, don't you think? Then I *would* be in danger!'

Ruby looked at the stubborn expression on the young girl's face. 'Ginny has a point there, Abel. And it looks as if she has already made up her mind. Perhaps we should accept her help

118

and offer our support to make sure no harm does come to her.'

Ginny breathed a sigh of relief. 'Oh, thank you, Ruby.'

Abel shook his head. 'How can I agree to a young girl, my daughter's best friend, risking her life like this? No, it's impossible.'

'I'm sorry, but you can't stop me, Abel,' Ginny said softly and headed for the door.

'Ginny, wait!' Ness cried. She turned to her father. 'I know you don't like this situation, Dad. I don't really agree with Ginny myself, but like you just said, she's my best friend. We can't let her do this alone.'

The discussion continued for another hour before Abel finally spread his hands. 'OK. I, *very* reluctantly, agree to your proposal Ginny, as long as you give your solemn word to agree to certain conditions. You must promise that your role is *only* to collect information and you are not under *any* circumstances to take any action yourself.'

Ginny nodded. 'Of course. That's exactly what I said to Ness, isn't it, Ness?'

Her friend agreed. 'She did, Dad. She promised me that earlier.'

'Well, let's discuss what you can do and what you are definitely not allowed to do. We need clear boundaries if we are to agree to this,' Abel said finally.

For the next half hour Ginny listened and nodded to all the suggestions put to her by Ruby and Abel.

Finally she smiled and pulled a piece of paper from her pocket. 'Look, I've been to two meetings already. Here's a list of the names of some of the people who attended. I don't know all their names, but I've written down the ones I know from university. There were five Labs who aren't at uni. One was called Denzil, I didn't get the other names. I wish I could get some photos of them.'

Abel shook his head. 'Too dangerous. You could easily be caught with equipment.'

'Could we get Anya to sketch them, if you described them to her?' Ness suggested.

'A brilliant idea,' Ruby smiled and picked up the phone.

Anya arrived a short while later and listened carefully as Ginny described the new people she had met at the two meetings, sketching and altering until Ginny nodded with satisfaction.

'That one is Denzel. And his friend was called Harry or Harvey, I didn't quite catch it at the introduction and after that everyone just called him H.'

Finally Abel sat back and gave a wry smile, 'I would never have condoned your decision to become our spy, Ginny. Never. But the information you have gathered is going to prove very useful. If at any time you feel it is getting dangerous, you must just leave. Do you understand? Your safety is paramount.'

CHAPTER THIRTY-TWO

Celeste, Bruno, and Jude were sitting on the grass bank outside the university. They smiled and greeted several of the other students as they passed by.

'You seem a bit on edge, Bruno,' Jude remarked. 'You're not worrying about the exams, are you?'

His brother shook his head. 'No, I don't see them as being too much of a challenge.'

'You're not kidding, we could do them with our eyes shut!' Celeste grinned.

'So what is bothering you?'

Bruno sighed. 'It's the enhancements. The final ones we're getting over the summer vacation.'

'I can't wait to get the eye enhancements! Just think what that will mean!' Celeste beamed. 'I love being able to hear, and smell things better than anybody else. And with our lower dosage of muscle enhancement, we're not up to Max and Jane's standard, but we can easily outrun and out-jump any Non-Lab, and most Hybrids for that matter! It's been a great help in dance. I'm easily the best! And being the best it what it's all about, isn't it?'

'Yeah,' Jude nodded. 'You said yourself, Bruno, that our energy levels and stamina have notably improved with the muscle enhancements. It certainly helped us keep up with the campaign for the New Outlook party last month. We got ourselves noticed by several of the senators, and not just the ones on our side! And we heard a lot more than they intended us to, as well!'

'Yeah,' Bruno grimaced. 'It's just sometimes I feel like a bit of a freak.'

Celeste's expression was stern, 'Don't you even think that! We're not freaks! The others just can't keep up. Don't forget what our role will be in the future.'

Jude nodded. 'She's right, Bruno. With our superior abilities we are designed to be the rulers, the leaders!'

Bruno smiled. 'Yeah, I know you're right!'

'Exactly. It's in our makeup,' Celeste said emphatically. She stood up, 'Classes start in five minutes. Are you coming down to the Rehab Centre this evening?'

Jude shook his head. 'There's a uni council meeting this evening and we want to make sure we're on next year's council, too. We need to make a big impression in our final year.'

'OK,' Celeste said. 'I'll ask Max and Jane to come with me. They were talking about arranging extra boot camp sessions. The enhancements won't be so obvious in the Non-Lab recruits then. With their muscle enhancements, they'll be guaranteed a scholarship for the Foundation Physical Diploma course at uni next term if they pass their basic academic skills lessons. Five will definitely get through with a bit of coaching.'

'Their success story will reflect well on us. That'll be great advertising. And they'll be our number one supporters next year,' Jude nodded. 'Let them know we'll be there tomorrow evening, and any evening we have free over the next month, Celeste. Let them know we're going to get them into uni!'

122

CHAPTER THIRTY-THREE

Ginny smiled as she looked around the common room at the people she had spent so much time with over the past three years. They had gathered together to celebrate, or in the case of a few Non-Labs, commiserate, over their final results. They had all joined in decorating the room and setting out food and drinks for their final party. Labs, Hybrids and Non-Labs; she had made friends in each of the groups and would miss their company. She walked to the French windows that opened onto a grass courtyard. Some students were sprawled on the grass enjoying the hot June sun. A few had set up a game of volleyball using the congratulations balloons one of the students had provided.

Hearing her name, she turned to see Rafael walking towards her.

'Hey, I didn't know you indulged in the bad habits of Non-Labs,' Ginny smiled as she clinked her glass of champagne against Rafael's.

He smiled and took a sip of his drink. 'I'm happy to celebrate our success, all Labs and Hybrids getting Firsts - as we knew we would before we even started here. I'm surprised you made such a fuss about revising; even postponing your research for the Radicals.'

Ginny looked down at her glass. 'Yes, well it's best not to get too confident... Anyway, what are your plans for next year? Did you get a firm offer from Futuretech?'

He nodded. 'I'm starting work for them next month, and they're going to sponsor me to get my MSc here. I'm planning on keeping in touch with Henry, too. See if he and Cilla come up with anything else the Radicals will find useful. In a way, I'm quite pleased that Ness is heading off to New York. I was always nervous about her getting suspicious of us spending so much time together and maybe finding out about where our loyalties lie.'

Ginny blinked hard. 'Yes, but I'll really miss her!'

He leaned in to whisper to her, 'With you continuing your MA here, we'll be able to concentrate more on our work with the Radicals. Keep our eyes on our future goal. You know that Kasper is continuing his studies in Paris? He's joining the European Radical group. We're really making a mark now!'

'Hey, what's happening here?'

Ginny took a step back as Ness appeared behind Rafael.

'Nothing, we're just getting sentimental about finishing here and moving on and you going to New York.' She hugged her friend. 'I'm going to miss you so much!'

'I'll be home every month or so and you can come and visit me there,' Ness said. 'Anyway, it's only for eight months.'

'This feels like the end of an era!' Ginny sighed. 'Who knows what will happen after that?'

'Yes, who knows?' Rafael said, catching her eye over Ness's shoulder.

CHAPTER THIRTY-FOUR

'Name... Agnes... Devon... Age... 16... Nationality... British Hybrid...' Ness looked up as Ginny sat down beside her at the table in the lounge in her Compound home.

'Am I disturbing you, Ness?' Ginny asked her.

She shook her head. 'No, I'm just filling in yet another form for university.'

Ginny squinted at the computer screen, 'Yes, there does seem to be a lot of form-filling! I've one more to do for accommodation, then I hope I'm finished!'

'Are you looking forward to doing your MA, Ginny?'

'Yes, I am. And Martin and Jodie from my degree course are staying on to do their MAs, too. And Rafael of course. All in different departments, but we'll get to see each other.' She gave a sigh. 'And much as I love my mother, it'll be great to have some space between us again! It was hard living at home again over the summer after the freedom of uni for three years.'

'I'm going to miss Mum and Dad and all the family so much,' Ness bit her lip.

'I can imagine! I still think you're very brave going all the way to New York to do your MA, Ness.' Ginny shook her head.

'Well, the university has a really good reputation. And the course sounds brilliant. But you know the main reason I'm going so far is that I'll just be another Hybrid amongst many Hybrids and Labs! No one will know about my parents and think the only reason I was accepted is because of my famous

125

father! Like quite a few did at Cambridge,' Ness said. 'And now he's decided to stand as an Independent MP for Hambleton, he's going to be in the news even more. I really feel I need to make a go of things on my own.'

'I can understand how you feel, Ness. And I can visit you there! Another bonus!' Ginny clapped her hands together.

Ness smiled. Her friend had never lost the enthusiasm and energy she had displayed since she was a toddler. 'Ginny, you will be extra careful about the Radicals, won't you? I won't be there to keep an eye on you anymore!'

Her friend's face grew serious. 'You don't have to worry at all, Ness. I promise I'll be really careful. Nothing has happened to me yet, has it? And even your dad has said the information I picked up has been very useful.'

Ness hugged her. 'I'll miss you so much! I'll be in touch every day!'

The next few weeks flew by as they prepared for the new term.

On the last morning, Ness hugged her younger brother and sister to her, 'Hey, I'll be back in a few months to see you all!' she murmured with a tremor in her voice. 'It'll be just the same as when I was at Cambridge.'

'Come here, love. Oh, what are you doing, travelling so far away from us? You're only sixteen,' Ruby said in an unsteady voice. 'Don't forget now, if you don't like it, just get on a plane and come straight home!'

'I'll be fine, Mum. Just think what you were doing at sixteen! You left everyone you knew and joined up with a band of outlaws!'

'Hey! Who are you calling outlaws, young lady?' Abel said as he came into the room followed by Zig.

'Well, Labs weren't legally recognised then, Dad,' Ness grinned. 'Honest, Mum, I'll be fine. I need to do this, to stand on my own two feet. Anyway, Cam and Otis are picking me up at the airport and they've promised to help out if I need

126

anything, so I won't be completely on my own.'

'I'm sure Cam and Otis will look after you and you're bound to make loads of new friends there, too,' Zig's eyes glistened. 'Oh, we're going to miss you, Ness! Give me a hug!'

Abel patted his daughter's shoulder, 'Have you everything, Ness? It's time to leave for the airport.'

'Yes, Dad.' Ness drew a deep breath and gave her mother a final hug before getting into the car.

A week later Ness sat in front of her laptop chatting to Ginny back in England.

'Our apartment is huge! My room is as big as our old lounge! Look,' she said, getting up and moving the screen around her.

'Don't make me jealous!' Ginny pouted. 'I'm squashed into this tiny room this year!' She moved her own laptop around.

'But you do have a great view of the river,' Ness peered into the screen.

'Yes,' Ginny conceded. 'And I have my own bathroom this year. The three girls I share the kitchen with are great, too. I can't really complain! What are your roommates like?'

'Lovely,' Ness smiled. 'There are two girls, Elise and Aisha, and one guy, Barry from California. We're all on different courses. The girls are undergrads - Elise is Physics, Aisha is European Culture, and Barry is an MSc in Biology. Doing a master's is strange, I'm mainly doing my own thing. How's it going for you?'

They chatted for a while about their work and people they had met.

'How is Rafael? Anything new on the Radical front?' Ness asked. 'You are taking care, aren't you?'

'Don't worry. There are two Labs who have joined me undercover now. Your father arranged things so it looked like

I had recruited them - that gave me extra credibility. Actually, there's nothing much happening at the moment. Same old meetings hinting that something will be happening before too long. We're told the numbers of new Radical supporters is growing every day. Anyway, what about your social life? What kind of things do you get up to? Have you met anyone interesting yet?'

Ness laughed. 'I've only been here a week, Ginny!'

They chatted for another half an hour until Ginny had to go to a lecture. Ness gave a rueful smile as she put the laptop away and got ready for bed as it was very late. She *had* met someone interesting, who had seemed friendly enough - although it had ended rather disastrously.

She recalled the details of their meeting. It was after her first lecture, which had been held in the old part of the building as the usual room was being painted. She had listened eagerly, joining in with her own comments and scribbling notes down whenever an interesting point was made. The morning session had sped by and soon it was time for lunch. The other students had already packed up and left as Ness struggled to close the zip on her bag. Finally, she grabbed it in her arms and hurried out after them, but saw no sign of anyone in the empty corridor. She gave a sigh and pushed a door leading into another corridor, but soon decided this was not the way back to the main building and the canteen. She retraced her steps and started out again through a different door. A feeling of panic came over her as she realised that this was not the way out either.

'Damn!' she had cried as her books fell from her arms and spread across the floor. Kneeling down, she was gathering them together when she heard a voice.

'Can I help you?'

Ness looked up into a pair of green eyes in a sympathetic face. She stood up, blushing as she pushed the books back into her bag.

'I dropped my books… I was trying to find the way out… back to the canteen…' she stammered.

He lifted the bag from her arms and squinted at the zip. 'Something's caught in it. There, that's better.' He slipped the books neatly into it and handed it back to her. 'I'm heading for the canteen myself, so we can walk together. You're new here, aren't you? From England?'

Ness nodded as she fell into step beside him. 'Yes, and the place seems so big!'

He smiled, a dimple appearing in his cheek. 'It does at first, doesn't it. You'll soon get used to it. I'm Bruno, by the way.'

'Ness,' she replied taking his outstretched hand. 'Did you have a lecture in this building too?'

He shook his head. 'They don't often use this annex unless they're decorating lecture halls.' He noticed her puzzled look. 'Sometimes I just enjoy the peace and quiet over here.'

'It can get a bit noisy,' she agreed.

He grimaced. 'I'm trying to get used to it.'

'Are you new here, too?'

Again he shook his head. 'No, final year. Look, we're at the canteen.'

There was a soft buzz of voices as they made their way into it.

'Oh, the pasta looks good, I think I'll have some of that. What are you going to have?' she asked as they made their way along the counter.

'I'll have the same,' he took his plate and followed Ness as she led them to an empty table at the side of the room.

'Well, it's pretty quiet in here at the moment,' she remarked as they sat down. 'What are you studying?'

'Politics,' he replied. 'We've been looking at how different countries are governed today and also the way things were run in the past. Right back to ancient times. It's fascinating.'

Ness raised her eyebrows. 'I bet it is. There have been so many different societies and governments over the centuries.'

'Yeah,' he said. 'And we still haven't put an end to war! Anyway, what made you decide on New York City to do your MA?'

'It seemed to offer the psychology course I was looking for. I really enjoyed my first lecture this morning,' she replied.

'And you don't mind living so far from home?' he asked.

She bit her lip. 'It's a bit hard. I promised myself not to Skype anyone in England for a least a week or I might end up on the next plane home!'

'There are lots of things you can do here to keep busy so you don't get homesick.'

She looked up as three loud youths sat down at the table next to them.

'There are plenty of sports clubs if you're into that. You can use your student card at the Sports Academy five blocks down from here,' he continued. 'There's a regular bus service just outside the main entrance.'

'Oh, that sounds good. My roommate picked up a few leaflets about a really great...' she stopped talking as she looked up.

Bruno had put down his fork, his forehead was covered in a sheen of sweat.

'Are you OK?' Ness looked at him anxiously.

He shook his head and stood up. 'I think I need some air. Sorry.'

Ness dropped her own fork and took his arm, helping him towards the door. He half stumbled down the grassy embankment pushing her away and grabbing a tree trunk as he lowered himself onto the ground.

'I'll get someone to help!' she cried, looking around her.

'No! No, I'll be fine,' he rasped. 'I just need a few minutes, that's all.'

He lay back down onto the grass holding his hands to his ears and taking deep breaths. She rubbed his arm gently, noticing a small flower tattoo inside his right wrist. 'Look, I really think I should get help.'

'No. Don't!' a voice ordered. A tall, slender girl and a young man were running towards them. 'It's OK. We're here now.' She turned an angry face to Bruno. 'What happened? You can't go on like this! You have to learn to be in control!'

'He's not very well,' Ness began.

The girl turned cold green eyes on her. 'We have everything under control. Don't worry, you can go now.'

Ness stood looking at her.

'He's our brother. Bruno, tell her,' she said.

The second young man was helping Bruno to his feet.

Looking at the similarities between the three of them, Ness realised they must be siblings. She looked at Bruno questioningly. He nodded.

'Yeah, I'll be fine. Thanks Ness.'

The girl looked at her pointedly until she turned to leave.

'Well, if you're sure you're OK...'

He nodded and gave a weak smile.

Ness hadn't seen any of them since that day. She sighed as she picked up a book from her bedside cabinet.

Her mind was still on the books she had been researching for 'Nature versus Nurture' and the ideas she was collecting for her assignment as she left the library the following afternoon. She was startled by a hand on her shoulder.

'Sorry, I didn't mean to make you jump.' Bruno was smiling at her. 'I tried calling your name but you didn't seem to hear me.'

Ness put a hand on her chest. 'Oh, I was miles away!'

They fell into step together, as before.

'Are you feeling OK now?'

'Fine. I really want to apologise for what happened. Your first day as well, and I bet you didn't even get to finish your own lunch, did you?' he frowned.

'That's OK,' she replied. 'Did your sister and brother look after you? She seemed, well, almost angry with you for feeling ill.'

Bruno smiled. 'Yes, she can be a bit prickly! But she means well.'

Ness looked away; she hadn't been too impressed with the girl's attitude towards her brother and to Ness herself.

'Hey, let me take you for a meal now! I bet you haven't eaten yet, have you?'

'No, but it's OK, you don't have to, really!' she said.

'Oh, have you got something else arranged?' he asked. She shook her head. 'Well, let's go then! I know a great little Italian place not too far from here.'

After a short drive they arrived at a small, rather shabby restaurant off a main road quite near the campus. The owner recognised Bruno and greeted him warmly. He told them about the day's special dish as he led them to a table near the window.

'Not much of a view!' Bruno said, looking out at the quiet side street. 'The Turkish guy that runs that corner shop opposite is a real character! He's told me that many different stories of how his family came to live in New York, I don't think he actually remembers himself! Looks like he's got the headlines in upside down again,' he chuckled.

Ness squinted but couldn't make out the sign at all. 'You must have amazing eyesight!'

He blushed. 'Oh... I noticed it on the way in! Now this place, the décor isn't up to much either, but wait until you taste the food!'

Ness had to admit the food was good a short while later as they both tucked into generous plates of spaghetti.

'This is really good, almost as good as my mother makes!' she said.

'Your mother's a good cook, is she?' Bruno asked.

'Yes, and my dad, when he gets the time to cook,' she replied.

'What does your dad do?' he asked her.

Oh, he... works in a government office. What do your parents do?' she said quickly.

'We lost our parents when we were young, a car crash. We were brought up by foster parents,' he said.

'Oh, I'm so sorry!'

He gave her a brief nod. 'Do you have brothers and sisters back in the UK?'

Ness smiled and told him about her brother Zac, and how they teased each other, and about her two younger siblings.

'I'll be so glad to get back to see them all soon,' she said. 'Are your brother and sister studying here, too?'

'Yes, Jude is taking the same course as me. We set up Conscious Decisions, a political and social awareness group for students. Celeste is taking Performing Arts,' he tilted his head to one side and turned towards the door. 'Well, speak of the devil! I'd recognise those footsteps anywhere!' He stood up and waved as the door opened and Celeste and Jude walked in.

Ness raised her eyebrows, ready to comment, but his brother and sister had arrived at the table.

'We thought we'd find you here, little brother,' Celeste smiled and kissed his cheek.

'We're the same age, Celeste!' he protested.

'You'll always be little brother to me!' she smiled and turned to Ness, holding out her hand. 'Hi, you're the girl who helped out Bruno the other day, aren't you? Sorry I was a bit sharp with you, my little brother worries me sometimes! I'm Celeste and this is Jude. And you are...?'

'Ness,' she said, shaking hands with them both. She noticed, like Bruno, they had the same small flower tattoo on the inside of their wrists.

'I'm treating Ness to make up for ruining her lunch the other day,' Bruno explained.

Soon two more plates of spaghetti and a fresh plate of garlic bread appeared on the table.

133

'I was just about to tell Ness about Conscious Decisions, see if I can get her and some of her friends interested in joining us,' Bruno said.

Jude nodded. 'We'd love to see you there. We think it's important that we get as many young people involved in politics as we can.'

'And not just in political discussions, but in community work, too,' Celeste added. 'We can always do with a helping hand with the guys we get off the streets. Most of them need some tutoring to get to a decent level of education so they don't end up back down there again.'

'I did some tutoring back in England,' Ness told her. 'With the higher achievers looking for good grades for university. I'd be happy to give a few hours a week.'

'Great!' Celeste smiled, pulling a card from her bag. 'Call by here one evening and speak to Mac. Tell him we sent you!'

Ness smiled back. Celeste seemed so different than the first time she had met her, much more relaxed and friendly. In fact, her smile seemed vaguely familiar.

They continued to chat together for another half hour, then Jude glanced at his watch. 'I hate to break things up, but we need to get going if we're to catch the game with Max and Jane.'

Bruno stood up and helped Ness get her coat on. 'I'll drop Ness off and join you guys in half an hour.'

As they drew up at her apartment block Bruno asked for her phone and synced his number into it.

'I'll be in touch, Ness.'

'Thanks for the meal, Bruno,' she smiled. 'It was lovely to meet your brother and sister, too.'

She tapped the tattoo on his wrist. 'What is that meant to represent?'

He shrugged. 'Just a family thing.'

CHAPTER THIRTY-FIVE

'Have you made any progress on your research into programming?' Adam asked his daughter one evening as they drove to a Radical meeting.

'I've a few ideas.' Ginny flicked through a notebook in her hand to hide her face. 'It's trickier than I thought to programme a Lab after their awakening, or a Hybrid.'

'There'll be a Lab there tonight that I'd like you to meet,' her father said. 'He was involved with awakening of the first Compound Labs and knows a bit about how they were making changes to the programming planned by the Non-Lab scientists. I'm sure you two could put your heads together and pool your ideas.'

'Yes!' Ginny tried to sound enthusiastic.

The meeting went much as usual for the first hour. New Hybrids and Labs converted to the Radical vision of the future were introduced. Ginny didn't recognise any of them and tried to memorise their faces and names to describe to Anya later in the week.

Adam and Leonard talked to the group about the headway the Radicals were making in several European countries and also in America.

Ginny's ears pricked up as they mentioned an important group of five youngsters who were studying at New York University, a group the Radicals were planning on using to raise their profile. Adam looked across at his daughter.

'Ginny is planning a trip to see a friend who is studying at NYU next month, so we could use this trip to our advantage,' he said. 'I will accompany Ginny and we will arrange to meet these youngsters to see how they are recruiting new Radical supporters and what their plans are for the future. We may be able to use some of their ideas here in the UK.'

The group broke up shortly after that. A few people were still chatting to each other as Ginny picked up her jacket and bag.

'Ginny, this is Carl, who worked in the Compound when the first Labs were awakened. He is very interested in working with you on the programming project you had in mind,' her father said.

Carl shook her hand firmly. 'It would be a pleasure to work with Adam's daughter! He is so proud that you joined our group. For a while he was afraid you would be swept along by the Compound Labs and their fear of taking on the Non-Labs.'

She smiled widely. 'I would love to work with you, Carl.'

'Where are you with your research so far?' he asked as Adam patted her shoulder and walked away.

'Well, I've tried a few behaviour-changing investigations on the laboratory mice, but I don't know how this could be transferred to Labs or Hybrids. My father said that one of the earliest awakened Labs did have a technique for programming Labs, but her research was destroyed by the Compound Labs when they discovered what she was doing.'

Carl's mouth thinned as he shook his head. 'I know. What a waste! I've been able to carry out a limited test on behaviour changing in Non-Labs, so at least it's a step up from mice! How about we arrange a session at my laboratory one day next week? I am available any morning that suits you. Let me give you my address and phone number and you can say what time would suit you the best.'

Rafael and Kasper joined them as they were saying their goodbyes.

'Ready to go, Ginny?' Rafael asked.

He whistled as they walked along the darkening street back

to the campus.

'I really feel like things are finally moving! You're getting your research off the ground and you're getting to meet some of the main players in the Radical movement in New York!'

'Yes, it is exciting isn't it?' she replied.

She phoned Abel as soon as she got home that evening. As she expected, he wasn't too keen on her going on the trip to America but she persuaded him she would be in no more danger in New York than she was in England. She was more worried that Ness could be in danger of being used as a tool in the Radical movement, as she was the daughter of one of their greatest opponents.

'I'm aware that my daughter, in fact any one of my children, could be used by this group. There are already security measures in place around Ness, but I'll make sure that Reuben knows this information as he may need to increase them,' Abel said. 'The information you gather is invaluable to us, Ginny, but you must always make sure you don't put yourself in any danger.'

'And I'm sure you have security measures around me, too, don't you?' she said.

'It's best if you remain unaware of who's watching over you,' he replied. 'If they do become suspicious of you the first thing they will do is look at your phone contacts. Make sure you always use the one that can't be traced for you to communicate with me or any of us here on this business.'

Ginny agreed. There was a few seconds silence before she continued. 'There's another thing, Abel. I have a really big problem.'

'Yes?' he said.

She went on to explain about her arrangement to meet Carl to further their research on programming a living brain.

'And he wants us to do trials on Non-Labs,' she added quietly. 'I've managed to put him off this week but if I continue to do so, he's sure to become suspicious.'

She heard Abel take a deep breath. Finally he spoke, 'I will need to talk to Celia about how you can deal with this, Ginny. We'll be in touch.'

A few evenings later, Ginny sat talking to Ness on Skype.

'I'm so excited that you're coming,' Ness beamed, then her smile faded, 'but you won't be putting yourself in any danger with the Radicals, will you?'

'No, I'll be meeting the five young people with my Dad. I'll let you know who they are so you will be forewarned if you do come across them,' she replied. 'Perhaps you've met them already.'

Ness shook her head. 'Not that I'm aware of! Anyway, I haven't really heard any of the students talking about the Radicals or their ideas at all here, not like we did at Cambridge.'

'Well, we only got to hear about that through your dad, and then from my dad's involvement with them,' Ginny pointed out. 'Anyway, we're also going to make time for us to have some fun and catch up on the gossip when I get there!'

'You bet!' Ness beamed again.

Ginny's mood was lifted even more when Celia called round to see her one evening.

'Abel told me about your predicament with Carl,' she said. 'I've discussed this with a few of my colleagues at our own research centre and we've come up with a plan...' She opened her laptop and put it on the table between them. 'They faced the same problem as the Radicals when trialling out new tests, but unlike them, they did not consider putting anyone's life at risk, so a group of them have created a virtual Lab for testing purposes.' She opened an app and a 3D figure appeared on the screen. 'Meet Val. He, or she, can be programmed to carry out simple tasks, such as running, walking, swimming etc.' Val demonstrated these skills as Celia instructed him. She typed in a code and the screen was filled with the close up of a brain.

'This is a 3D image of his brain, similar to the ones you made when you were five, remember?' Ginny smiled and nodded. 'But quite a bit more complicated! Here's an image of the heart, lungs, and kidneys, et cetera. You can also take readings of skin temperature and sweat levels. A member of our research team said that one of these Vals can be set up as a virtual Lab and be trained to function at the given level of a mature Lab. You can set it up with its own life and monitor the effects your research will have on it.'

Ginny looked at her in amazement. 'Wow! That certainly is something! We won't have to put any Non-Lab into a potentially harmful situation. But... no one is going to believe I came up with all this in my research!'

Celia smiled. 'I'm glad that occurred to you! No, what you can do is give him the bare bones of the idea. Tell him about the research you did on brains when you were much younger and that's how you got the idea for a virtual Lab. I've downloaded a folder with the instructions for building a basic model onto your memory stick. Point out all the advantages of using what is, in effect, a Lab rather than a Non-Lab subject for tests. There must be plenty of advantages. Let's make a note of the most persuasive ones and sort out a good argument. Hopefully, he'll be hooked and you can both build your own virtual Lab. If you come up with any improvements, we'll be happy to upgrade our own Val!'

Ginny gave her a hug. 'Oh, Celia! You've taken such a weight off my mind! And this looks really interesting. I can't wait to make a start on it!'

CHAPTER THIRTY-SIX

'So that's it then?' he looked at the older man. 'No more operations?'

'No more operations,' he replied.

'No more enhancements? No more drama, deportment and voice training?'

'No,' the raspy voice reassured him. 'You're ready now, Claude. Soon, I will arrange for you to meet the special group who will work closely with you. I have arranged paperwork to verify you have successfully completed a master's degree following an online course with West Coast Urban and Political College and now you have been enrolled to study for your doctorate in Politics, which you will start next month. The programming and education you have already received gives you knowledge far beyond what will be asked of you.'

'Then why do I need to study something beneath my intelligence?'

'To put you in a prominent position so people will notice you. Over the next few months you will be given the opportunity to gain some practical experience working as an intern with Senator Jordan in New York. You must use your intelligence and charm to win supporters. It won't be difficult, you have been created and designed to do so. Your close team is made up of people who have been endowed with similar enhancements to your own.'

'They were the templates for me, weren't they, Father?' Claude smiled.

The older man nodded. 'They were created to ensure the

enhancements were completely safe and suitable for you. Now their role is to support you fully. Each member of the group is also beautiful and intelligent, though not quite on the same level as you. But remember, although you are perfect...'

Claude raised an eyebrow. 'Yes, I've learnt in my communication lessons that I can't acknowledge this fact in public. Non-Labs like modesty – even false modesty – so when someone says I am perfect I have to smile deprecatingly. And I also have to hide my repugnance of ugliness. That could cause me to lose popularity.'

'I'm sure you hate having to look on this ugly and crippled body as much as I do!' A look of contempt passed over Arnold Warner's face as he looked down at his own gnarled hand. 'I have loathed being a prisoner inside this useless shell for more than half of my life!' He breathed hoarsely and closed his eyes. 'It's time I told you a bit more of my own background and how I came to be like this. About my miserable existence until I realised there could be a purpose to it all.'

Warner took a sip of water from a cup on the table beside him and set it down again with an unsteady hand. He took a deep breath and began in a low voice.

'Many years ago I was a young man very similar to you in appearance, though not so perfect, of course. Still, I was a pretty good baseball and football player and I was never short of girlfriends!' He gave a brief smile at the memories. 'I was having a good time until school ended and I didn't have enough credits to get me into college. So I thought about getting a job. But there weren't that many jobs that appealed to me. I drifted for a while, getting in with the wrong crowd. One day the police were involved and that's when my father got angry and gave me an ultimatum – find a job or leave home. So I did both: I joined the army. For the first year, it was OK. Long days and hard training, but I really got into it and started to enjoy myself. Our first tour of duty was in the

Middle East and that really opened my eyes. The people out there, some just tiny babies, all involved in this mess which was not of their making! When I came back home, physically I looked the same, but inside I was different. I wanted to do something about it all. I decided that when I had finished my three years in the army I was going to study politics. But it didn't quite work out as I had planned. Our second tour of duty was in the same region, but by then things were getting worse. We were there as a peace-keeping force, but most people resented our presence and we ended up having to defend ourselves against attacks from the very people we were sent to help.'

He sat quietly for so long that Claude thought he had fallen asleep.

'And then?' he whispered.

Warner slowly raised his head.

'There was a suicide bomber, young kid, no more than fifteen. Six of us caught the worst of it. All I remember was a lot of noise and shouting and the next thing I was in the base hospital. I tried to ask about the other guys, but no-one answered me. Then I was out of it again until I came around in the military hospital near Washington. I learned that of the six of us, I was the only survivor. And when I realised how badly injured I was – I'd lost a leg, part of my left arm, half of my face! – I wished I wasn't!'

His hand trembled even more as he picked up the glass on the table. He splashed some of the water on to his lap as he held it to his mouth.

'Couldn't they operate, repair the damage?' Claude asked incredulously.

Warner shook his head. 'They didn't have the technology back then. They fixed me up the best they could. Then I was put out to pasture with the other broken soldiers! For the next year I just sat around feeling sorry for myself and all that I had missed out on in life. Then one day a feisty little nurse, about

142

the same age as me, came to work on our ward. She was a redhead with a temper to match! I was giving my usual speech about wishing I had died with the others as she sorted out my tray of medication and she spun my wheelchair round so I was facing her and told me to stop feeling sorry for myself and to think about the families of those who hadn't come back. We had a long and loud argument about who was better off, then she said something which shut me up. She said maybe I had been spared for a reason. I'm not religious, but I began to think there might be something in that.

'I thought about my earlier plans about studying politics and got help to set up an online course on my laptop. After about six months I was totally disillusioned with what US politics had to offer and I began to investigate other political systems. None of them appealed to me so I began to look back through history to see if at any time there was a system that worked. And finally I looked to the philosophers.'

'Plato,' said Claude, smiling.

Warner nodded. 'He seemed to have the best ideas. A society where everyone was happy in their own role. I realised that's why I had been saved. To build the perfect war-free society!'

'Where did you start?'

'My first step was to make as much money as I could. I'd had a payoff from the US army which I had invested and it had done well. It was easy to persuade some of the other veterans to invest with me and we did OK. My big chance came when one of the doctors came to me with an idea he had for developing a new kind of artificial arm that looked and acted much more like the real thing. He said if he had a backer he was sure he could go on to develop other limbs, too. No-one else had confidence in him but I thought this was going to be the big break. My own savings weren't enough, so we spent the next year knocking on doors until we had just enough then finally we set up our own small business. We soon had interest from one of the leading hospitals in Washington and were well on our way to making our name in the medical world. After two years it was one of the most successful and profitable businesses in the US. At that point, I was ready to go it alone and so we went our own ways. I started to build up a business in my own name and after a few years Warner Enterprises were renowned worldwide.

'When news broke about the Compound and the stage of developing new human forms, I knew that the time was right for me. I had investigators find out about the inevitable splinter groups that spring up following such medical breakthroughs and soon I was in touch with what is now the most powerful Independent Lab group, the Radicals. Through their research I have been able to realise my dream and create you, a perfected version of me! You will be the leader of a better society.'

His face betrayed his exhaustion as he sat back and closed his eyes.

'I'll let you rest, Father,' Claude said, standing. 'You don't have much time left, do you?'

'No,' the old man shook his head. 'I just hope I live long enough to see you make a start.'

Claude stood up and left the bedroom, quietly closing the door behind him. He went to his own room and sat by the window looking out at the starry sky. The events of the last few years played themselves out in his head: Being awakened and meeting the man he had always called 'Father'; learning about his background – he was actually a Lab, a clone of his father. From the beginning, his father had told Claude that he was dying and they would have a limited time together. During his first year, Claude was made aware of the many talents he had been programmed with, far more than any other Lab had ever been endowed with. He learnt to use and control the enhancements that made him superior physically to any other Lab or Hybrid. Over the years they had travelled extensively to give him a taste of many different cultures. They had seen places of overwhelming natural beauty, enjoyed festivities celebrated worldwide. He had been taken to see impressive monuments created by human hands and looked around museums that demonstrated how cruel and destructive the human race could be.

On long evenings, before a fire in the colder months or enjoying a light breeze on the veranda in the warmer ones, he had listened as his father told him of the world they lived in. Warner told him how much had changed over his lifetime. Before, there had only been ordinary humans, Non-Labs like himself, but now there were Labs, cloned from humans, and the Hybrids, offspring of Labs and Non-Labs, intelligent beings who were making a mark on the modern world. A world which was headed for certain ruin in the hands of the Non-Labs and their never ending wars.

Claude remembered how his father's eyes had shone as he told him of his vision of the future, where the gifted ones would rule the world fairly and the others would be given the positions most suited to their own particular talents and abilities, which they would be happy to fill. He talked of past mighty empires that had spanned the globe and, becoming complacent, had all ended, each crumbling under a new power. Warner recognised that even in times of peace, a military force must be always at the ready with specially chosen people highly trained in defence. Nowadays that meant ready to defend or attack with technology as well as with physical power. But in this new world, under the right rulers, there would be no place for war.

Warner's dream was for Claude, his own Lab, to be the leader that brought the present structure to an end and implemented this brave new world. Claude had been created to be perfect in every way so that he would be superior to all other humans and Warner had made sure he was fully prepared for his future role. He was all that Warner had wished he could be. Claude was the perfect image of him.

Over two years, Claude had had many operations to perfect his physical appearance. His handsome face was perfectly symmetrical. He had been carefully trained to use his voice and to move and use gestures that could rival any famous actor's. Finally, he had had the enhancements trialled and perfected by the Radicals' specially selected team so that his senses and physical abilities were well beyond the ordinary levels.

Late that night, Claude awoke to banging on his door.

'Mr Claude, Mr Claude, please come quickly!' he heard Fatima's urgent plea. 'It's your father, Mr Claude!'

Claude pulled his dressing gown on as he hurried after the housekeeper along the corridor. Two other servants stood outside his father's bedroom, eyes wide with fear as they pushed open the door.

In the dimly lit room, Claude watched as a nurse adjusted the morphine drip attached to the old man's fragile arm. The doctor looked up at him and shook his head. 'There's nothing else we can do now, except ease his pain.'

Claude sat down by his father's bed and gently took his hand. The old man struggled to gather his strength to speak.

'You know what you must do, son.' Claude nodded. 'Remember all we talked about. Our brave new world!'

'Yes, Father,' Claude said gently as his father's eyelids fluttered and closed, then his body grew still.

Claude watched dispassionately as the others moved around the room. The doctor stepped forward and nodded at him as he pulled the sheet over Arnold Warner's face while Fatima stood sobbing in the middle of the room. He felt irritated when the nurse put her arm around his shoulder as if to comfort him. He didn't need comforting. A feeling of exhilaration washed over him. Finally, he was ready to step into the role his father had created him for, to become the leader who would change the course of history.

CHAPTER THIRTY-SEVEN

Death of Billionaire Philanthropist

Today the world is mourning the passing of the man who fought back from near death to go on to make an impact on so many lives.

Claude went on to read about his father's horrific injuries serving in the Middle East and how he had become one of the wealthiest men in the world, and one of the most generous sponsors of several charities. There were remembrance services being held in many capital cities in his honour. The US President was to speak at his funeral.

A voice made him look up. Hughes, Warner's PA, was standing in the doorway. 'Are you ready to leave, sir?' she asked gently.

Later that day, Claude stood silently beside the president as his father's coffin was lowered into the ground. He blinked rapidly and gave a slight cough, keeping his eyes downcast. He had practised his 'grieving pose' several times before the ceremony. Masking his surprise at the open grief of some of those around him, he found more difficult. Their housekeeper, Fatima, was sobbing and dabbing at her eyes with a tissue. Two older men stood near him. Both had served in the forces with Arnold Warner in their younger days. One held his jaw tight and blinked hard against the tears which shone in his eyes. Claude himself felt no grief as he had known his father was dying from the day he was awakened.

Later, he had to suppress a sigh as the family solicitor spoke at length about the good work his father had done to help so many people around the world. He adjusted his expression to demonstrate sadness and gratitude when he finally read out the details of Arnold Warner's will. Several charities were to benefit from his passing, but the bulk of his considerable wealth was to go to Claude himself.

And Claude knew that Warner's wealth was going to make an even greater difference to the world after his death than his generosity had ever done in his lifetime. Claude was going to use this wealth to help the Radicals establish the new, peaceful society that his father had dreamed of. The idea filled him with excitement.

Across the Atlantic, Abel read out the same headlines. 'So Warner has died. There is talk of the Lab he had created inheriting Warner Enterprises. There are strong rumours that Warner himself sponsored the Radicals. I wonder how far his Lab will be involved.'

'I'm sure we'll find out soon enough from our contacts in New York,' Isaac said. 'I don't think it's a coincidence that Adam and Ginny have been invited to New York at this time.'

Abel frowned. 'I still wish that Ginny hadn't got herself involved in all this! It's too dangerous. I'll see what Reuben can tell me about the situation.'

'Reuben said he can have her out of there straight away if things seem at all dangerous.'

'She's hardly more than a child! She should not be in that situation in the first place!' Abel frowned. 'Why did I ever listen to her?'

'She was already involved before she told you about it,' Isaac pointed out to his friend. 'If you make too much of a fuss, it will only draw attention to her. That could put her even more at risk. We're going to have to trust Reuben.'

'I suppose that's all we can do.'

'We could also counter the Radicals' views of an ideal society by getting more publicity on your views of the

Compound vision of the future. How about we jot down some ideas?' Isaac suggested. 'You could use them in your speech at the political forum next week and I can get them into some of the major news outlets online.'

Abel nodded eagerly. 'An excellent idea! The Radicals are all for slotting people into their places and taking away their freedom of choice. We need to promote our vision of everyone having an equal chance to fulfil their personal dreams, whatever their abilities and whatever their background is. There will be a fair representation of all backgrounds at the forum.'

For the next two hours, Isaac typed up ideas with suggestions and amendments from Abel.

CHAPTER THIRTY-EIGHT

Ness and Ginny stood in the airport arrivals hall hugging each other.

'It's so lovely to see you again!' Ginny cried. 'I've missed you so much!'

'I've missed you, too!' Ness replied.

'Come on, you two,' Adam smiled. 'I've a taxi to take us to the hotel. We'll have lunch there, then I've got a meeting. I'm sure you two girls can find something to do for the rest of the day.'

'If you're busy until tomorrow can I stay at Ness's place tonight, Dad?' Ginny asked. Both girls smiled as he agreed.

'How do you find New York, Ness?' Ginny asked her as they sat down to lunch an hour later.

She let out a huge breath. 'Very big and noisy at first, but I'm getting used to it! The people at the uni are friendly and my roommates are great. You'll meet them later, Ginny. They love meeting people from England! Now tell me, how is everyone at home? I miss them all so much. I can't wait until Christmas when I can go back to see them all!'

The three of them left the building together that afternoon. Ginny watched as a tall, muscularly built young man opened the door of a dark saloon car for her father then turned back to her friend as it drove off.

'Right, what are we going to do first? We'd better make the most of the time you are free!'

They headed off to a nearby shopping mall where they spent a few hours. Then Ness led them to a quiet café off one of the busy roads.

'This is so nice after the bustle and noise of the shops!' Ginny exclaimed, leaning back into her seat and looking around her. 'How did you find it?'

Ness blushed and gave a smile. 'Actually, Bruno brought me here.'

Ginny leaned forwards, 'Bruno? You never mentioned him before! Tell me more about him! Is he a Hybrid, too? Is he your boyfriend?'

'You know, I can't work out if he and his brother and sister are Hybrid or Lab. It's funny, isn't it, usually you get the feeling straight away,' Ness told her.

'And is he your boyfriend?' Ginny repeated.

She laughed. 'He's just a friend. I met him on my first day, actually. But that didn't go too well!'

She explained about their first disastrous lunch and how his sister and brother had come along.

'I found Celeste a bit intimidating at first, but she's OK once you get to know her,' she admitted. 'They seem a close family. They've all got this sort of flowery tattoo on their wrists, he said it's a family thing.'

'So you've been out with him a few times, seen his tattoo, and met his brother and sister! It sounds serious!' Ginny raised an eyebrow.

'We've only met up a few times, usually just for coffee or a meal. Just as friends, that's all.' Ness smiled. 'And what about you? Have you made any interesting friends, anyone you've your eye on?'

She noticed how Ginny stammered a little as she said there wasn't.

'Are you still seeing a lot of Rafael?' Ness looked concerned.

'I have to, to keep up with the Radicals,' Ginny said. She noticed how Ness was looking at her. 'Well, of course I do consider him a friend, but that's all.'

She told Ness about Celia's help with her research with Carl.

'It's really amazing how you can input a new programme into a mature brain, rather than during the developing years as the first Labs were programmed. I can see why the Radicals are getting excited about it. You could eventually use this to control how people behave and their expectations,' she said.

'Isn't this dangerous?' Ness frowned. 'Do you think you should be helping them with this research, Ginny?'

'They're already quite advanced in their own research. I'm in a position to pass their ideas on to the Compound Labs' research team, so at least we know what they're capable of doing.'

Ness squeezed her friend's hand, 'I wish you hadn't got involved in all this, Ginny. I worry about you!'

Ginny gave a little laugh, 'Don't worry about me! I'll be fine!'

In a private suite of the Regency Hotel on the outskirts of the city, Adam stood up as Takir, Shana, and Willis entered. They shook hands and sat around a low glass table by a long window looking out over the distant skyscrapers.

Adam sat back and looked at Willis. 'Takir told me there is to be a new Lab introduced to the group.'

'Not just a new Lab!' Willis spread his hands on the knees of his linen suit. 'Claude, the only Lab there is of Warner, who we can now officially reveal to be our benefactor. He had him created specially to fulfil the role he himself would have liked to perform if he had been physically capable of it.'

'Which is?' Adam prompted.

'Well, as you know, the Radicals' vision of the future is to create a new society based on Plato's ideas, with each person fulfilled in the role they are adapted to. Warner's dream is for his Lab, Claude, to be the leader of the Radicals, the ruling level,' he explained.

'We were led to believe that Bruno from our group of five was to be the leader, with support from the others,' Adam said.

Willis smiled. 'Warner was happy for you to assume that conclusion so that you would create the perfect templates for his own Lab.'

'But the group of five are highly valued. They will be Claude's personal advisory team. They will work closely with him,' Shana added quickly.

'And when will Claude be introduced to the team?'

'Tomorrow,' she said. 'The meeting has been arranged here at three p.m. Claude also wants to meet some of the people involved in their creation, so we would like you two to be present.'

Later Adam turned to Takir as he was being driven back to the hotel. 'I don't think Hugo is going to be pleased to hear how our five are being demoted!'

Takir gave a short laugh. 'Certainly not! Perhaps that's why he wasn't invited tomorrow. He'll have time to get used to the idea.'

Ginny listened quietly as her father told her the news on her phone the next morning. 'So you won't be able to meet our five yet, I'm afraid. Depending on what happens today, I may be able to arrange a meeting later in the week.'

'OK,' she replied. 'Ness has been in touch with Cam, Otis, and Jez, so I'll stay here for another night and catch up with you in the morning.'

She turned to her friend, giving her a thumbs up. 'Dad's at an important meeting this afternoon so I can stay another night! What time are we meeting Cam and the others?'

'Not until six. I have to go into uni for a lecture this morning, but we could meet at the canteen for lunch.'

'Great!' Ginny agreed. 'Perhaps I'll get to see your new "friend"!'

'I was hoping you would, too, but he's texted saying he's

busy himself this afternoon. Perhaps later in the week,' she said.

'So how are you finding life in New York?' Ginny asked Otis that evening.

'Out of this world, man!' He gave a huge grin. 'Everything's bigger and faster than in the UK! It's brilliant!'

'Yeah, it's awesome!' Jez nodded.

'What about your work? Are you the only Specials working for Reuben? It's not dangerous, is it?'

'We're the only Specials so far. We're never in any danger; we use our enhanced senses to do the ground work,' Otis told her. 'Cam sniffs things out, Jez listens in, and I see things no one else can spot! Then Reuben sends in a skilled team to investigate anything suspicious.'

'So you're all planning on staying here for a while, then?' Ginny said.

Cam shrugged. 'I'm not sure I want to stay here too long. I miss England, and the Compound and the people there.'

'I know what you mean, Cam,' Ness gave him a smile. 'New York's great, but home is something else!'

'Well, tonight let's enjoy ourselves in New York!' Otis said. 'They've opened a new roller-blading rink in Central Park, let's start there!'

CHAPTER THIRTY-NINE

'So we are now the *support group* for this new guy, are we?' Celeste tossed her head angrily and strode to the window.

'A very important support group,' Shana tried to pacify her. 'Claude will depend on the help of all five of you, especially at first as he settles into New York and his new role.'

'But we were led to believe that Bruno was being primed to be the leader with our support!' Jude said.

'What about all the enhancement operations we have gone through? What was all that about?' Jane asked.

'You have been designed and created to be superior to all other Labs and Hybrids in every way. Your roles are still to be part of a powerful group to lead the country to a new way of life,' Shana continued. 'Please be open-minded about Claude. Meet him and talk to him. I'm sure if you just give him a chance that you'll all get along fine and will work together to achieve what we all want in the long run.' She turned away to take a phone call.

'Don't forget, Claude holds the key to the Radicals' finances. There is no funding without his say-so,' Willis pointed out drily.

'You mean he is solely in charge of the finances?' Max asked.

'Absolutely,' Willis said. 'That was stipulated by our benefactor, Arnold Warner, in his will. All his assets are now in Claude's name and it is stipulated that Claude is to be accepted as the leader of the Radicals. He has financial advisors on stocks and shares in the companies he owns, of course, but he is in complete control of the financial backing for the Radicals.'

'He's on his way up now,' Shana said, putting her phone down.

A few minutes later the door was opened and two bodyguards stepped in followed by a young man. A silence fell over the room as Claude looked around at the faces. His lips twitched as he heard a slight intake of breath. He was relieved that his physical appearance had the same effect on these people as it had had on others on so many occasions.

Shana smiled brightly and stepped forward. 'It's really good to see you again, Claude. Let me introduce your new team who have all been impatient to make your acquaintance.'

Each person seemed mesmerised by his vivid blue eyes as he was introduced to them. Celeste was very much aware of the tang of expensive cologne and a faint musky odour of Claude's skin as he approached her. He noticed the slight tremor as he took her hand.

After the introductions Claude looked around the room with a smile that dimpled his cheeks. 'I've heard so much about you over the past few years; you don't know how much I have been looking forward to becoming involved with the work you have already started.'

'Well, to be honest,' Max began, 'this is the first time we have been made aware of your existence, let alone that you would be joining the Radicals as the leader.'

Claude gave an apologetic shrug. 'My father felt that it was best for me to be fully prepared for my role before meeting you. Perhaps if I tell you something about the conversations I had with him and his vision of a new world, the one all Radicals are striving for, you'll understand his plans. All this came to him after he faced many dilemmas in his own life.' He stood up, his eyes shining. 'If only you could have sat with me and heard what he had to say. As I listened to him I felt I was transported into his vision of the future!'

He told them about Warner's early life as a carefree teenager and then his time in the army. His own emotions shone through as he described his father's time in hospital. The faces of those listening reflected the anguish and despair Warner had lived through.

Claude paused and took a deep breath. 'But finally the day arrived when he saw his purpose in life. Despite his physical disabilities, he eagerly took up political studies and followed a line of research which led him to a firm belief in how a new society should be formed. He had finally found the reason he had been put on this earth. And though he was, as he put it, "a prisoner inside the useless shell of his own body", he realised that the Radicals could offer him a way to fulfil his dream, through me, his Lab.

'So, here I am. My father had great confidence in my ability to take up the reins and lead us all into this brave new world.' Claude gave a disarming smile. 'But I know that, despite all my programming, all my training, all my enhancements, I cannot do it alone. I need the support of this specially gifted team. Can I depend on you? Can we go forward together?'

There was silence for a few minutes as Claude looked around.

'Yes. Yes, I think we can,' Bruno said quietly.

Jane and Max exchanged glances and nodded. 'Yes, we agree.'

'You've won me over,' Jude smiled.

'You certainly are persuasive,' Celeste said with a smile. 'Let's hope your charm works as well on the Non-Labs!'

Claude spread his hands. 'Together I'm sure we can persuade them to see our point of view.'

Willis cleared his throat. 'Well now we've established we are all fighting for the same cause, perhaps we could tell Claude about the work we've been involved with over the past few months.'

'Surely Claude's already fully up to date on our work?' Celeste raised her eyebrows.

He smiled and shrugged. 'Not straight from the horse's mouth, as it were.'

Shana stood up and motioned for the others to sit around the glass table in the window alcove. Celeste was once again very aware of his special scent as Claude walked past her. The others seemed to be similarly affected, too.

'We'll start with the roles each person has been designed to fill and what they have accomplished so far. You'll find that we have each made quite an impact already, Claude.' Willis looked around the table. 'Perhaps we can begin with you, Celeste?'

'As you know, we have all been trained and programmed to fulfil certain positions. At the moment we are all studying at New York University.' She went on to describe the courses they were each enrolled on. 'Of course, the actual studying isn't really challenging for us, but it puts us in a prominent position and enables us to engage with the public in many other ways, too. We all know the importance of each member of society finding a satisfying role to play at whatever level suits them.'

Bruno took up the story. 'This is where the soup kitchen comes in. Celeste, Jude, and I set this up. It's where we select certain Non-Labs we feel could be an asset to our cause. Those selected are cleaned up, then there's a further selection to identify those with reasonable physical strengths. These are trained in boot camps, run by Jane and Max with a few Lab and Non-Lab helpers. By using modified muscle enhancements, which, of course they are unaware of, we have been able to get six of those we selected enrolled for the Sports Science Diploma here at New York University.'

'Excellent publicity as well as earning their support,' Claude nodded. 'What happens to those who can't be enrolled for a sports course?'

'We select any that show IT skills and enrol them on a suitable course. So far we have three. Another five have been enrolled on a catering and service course at a technical college and four more onto a child care diploma at the same college,' Bruno said.

'We hoped to be able to finance further courses in sanitation and recycling, and retail, to offer training for the others we rescued,' Jude added.

Claude looked impressed. 'You have been busy! I would like to get involved in this as soon as possible. It will be good publicity for me, too. I'll arrange funding to extend this programme. Draw up some outline plans and I'll get the accountants to take a look at them.' He turned to Celeste. 'Tell me about your role in the entertainment industry. How do you use your remarkable beauty and theatrical skills to influence people's behaviour?'

'The entertainment industry has been a great influence on how people behave and on their opinions over the last few centuries. Once I become a famous name, people will feel they know me and like me. They'll want to please me and be like me! The same goes for Jane and Max. They are excellent role models as well as being outstanding athletes.' She smiled as the others nodded in agreement.

'Half of the students at uni are already members of the Celeste fan club!' Jude said.

'And I'm working on the other half!' she quipped, pushing her hair back over her shoulder.

After several hours, Claude stood up and addressed the others. 'We have made a great start on our work together today. Now I'd like to invite you all for a meal at Lola's. I have a table booked for us all at eight o'clock. It will be good to be seen together in public.'

That evening Celeste noted how conversations stopped and all eyes followed Claude as he made his way to their table in the restaurant. She also noted the quick smile of satisfaction on his face.

During the meal, as the others chatted, Claude turned to Adam. 'Willis tells me you are involved in the Radical movement in the UK.'

Adam nodded. 'We are building up a sizeable following of both Labs and Hybrids who are disillusioned with the way the Compound Labs are pandering to the whims of the Non-Lab governments. We need someone who is not afraid to stand up for our rights and put us in the place we deserve to be. My own daughter is a recruit to the Radical movement.'

Claude looked interested. 'I would like to meet some of the young UK supporters. Once we have implemented changes here in the US we intend to expand into Europe.'

'My daughter is here in New York at the moment visiting a friend from the UK who is studying here,' Adam told him. 'She would be delighted to meet you.'

Flicking open a tablet, Claude scrolled down the screen, 'I have an appointment with the Senator tomorrow at eleven. Could we meet up in the morning, at nine o'clock?'

He handed his card to Adam who agreed.

Later that evening, Celeste and her siblings climbed out of the car that Claude had supplied to take them home. No-one spoke until they were seated in the lounge with a pot of coffee on the table in front of them.

'So, what do you think?' she asked.

'He is stunning,' Jane said. 'Perfect physically, and a perfect charmer.'

'I have to agree there,' Jude nodded. 'The other customers in the restaurant couldn't take their eyes off him.'

'Yeah, the staff, too,' Bruno added.

'The way he speaks, the way he talks, the way he moves, even his smell - he had everyone eating out of his hand,' Celeste agreed. 'Whoever designed and programmed him knew what they were doing.'

Max spread his hands. 'I hate to admit it - I was ready to dislike him, but he has completely won me over. He is the perfect choice to lead the Radicals, no offence meant, Bruno.'

'None taken, Max,' he replied. 'I'll be quite happy to give him all the support he needs.'

CHAPTER FORTY

Ginny wiped her hands on the sides of her trousers as the lift drew to a halt at the penthouse suite.

'Don't be nervous,' her father patted her shoulder. 'Claude's a really nice person. He just wants to meet some of the young Radicals from the UK. You are a perfect example and you happen to be in New York at the right time!'

Ginny tried to quell her nerves as the door was opened by an expressionless young man. He showed them into a large office and told them to take a seat. Almost immediately afterwards the door reopened and Claude entered smiling. Ginny took a sharp intake of breath as she looked into his blue eyes, reluctant to take her hand from his warm, firm clasp. She cleared her throat as she realised he had asked her a question.

'I'm sorry...' she muttered pulling her hand free.

A smile played around his lips as if he had read her thoughts. 'I was just asking how you find New York?'

'Oh, I love it, very much!' she replied quickly.

He nodded. 'Good. Willis told me about the research you're doing on programming Lab brains. He was very impressed with the Virtual Lab you designed. I know there were some problems with finding suitable Labs for earlier investigations. You've solved the problem! We need bright youngsters like yourself on our team!'

Adam smiled proudly at his daughter, who murmured about all the help she got from Carl. 'Don't put down your own efforts in all of this, Ginny. You have worked hard and deserve praise!'

'No, your daughter is right. I have to remember that rule myself – modesty, even false modesty, goes a long way with the Non-Labs! Even when I know I have been created and designed to be perfect!' He turned away giving her a slight wink. 'I do enjoy the effect I have on people, though.'

Ginny blushed furiously and looked down at her hands.

Claude sat down opposite them with a more serious expression. For the next hour they discussed the Radical movement in the UK and their plans for the future.

'Once we have an official Radical party set up here in the US, it will be easier to extend our ideas across to Europe,' Claude said. 'I think it would be a good idea if a male and a female Hybrid from the UK could come and work with my team as we establish ourselves here. For a month initially. They could later help in our European extension.'

Adam nodded an agreement. 'That sounds very reasonable to me. I'm sure there would be no end of Hybrid volunteers from our ranks. In fact, what about Ginny?'

'Exactly what I was thinking,' the young man smiled. 'What do you say, Ginny?'

She nodded. 'I'd love to volunteer.'

'And what about Rafael as the male? He's done a lot for the Radicals already. And you've worked together well over the last few years. He would be a good choice,' Adam said thoughtfully.

'Yes, he'd be good,' Ginny agreed.

'If Ginny and Rafael join Celeste and the others working with the underprivileged youngsters it would provide a good cover story and we could collect and implement some of the ideas you have in place here. We have Radical contacts at both universities so it will be easy to arrange some kind of student exchange,' Adam suggested. 'I'm sure the Compound Labs would be happy with this idea, too, and wouldn't suspect a thing.'

'An excellent idea,' Claude nodded. 'We'll get this

arranged as soon as possible. I'll get someone from the Radical admin office to give you a call tomorrow, Adam.'

Ginny was bubbling with excitement as she met Ness outside the university buildings that afternoon.

'I have so much to tell you! Can we go to that café again? My treat!' she urged her.

As soon as they were seated she leaned across the table, 'Guess what? I'm coming to New York for a month! We'll have a whole month together. Well, I'll be working and you'll be studying, but…'

'What work?' Ness asked her.

'With the Radicals. With Rafael, well, he has to agree, but I'm sure he will,' she continued.

They both stopped talking as the waitress came to take their order.

'What do you mean, Ginny? Explain yourself!' Ness leaned forward. Her frown deepened as Ginny finished telling her about Claude's proposal.

'Oh, Ginny! This sounds far too dangerous! You seem to be getting more and more involved. You were only going to collect information,' she cried.

'And that's what I will be doing! I will be simply collecting ideas to take back to the UK Radicals, but I'll just make sure that the Compound Labs get to hear of everything first!' she explained as she bit into her pizza. 'This is gorgeous! Oh, and talking about gorgeous; picture in your head the most amazing man you have *ever* seen, *ever*!'

Ness sighed. 'Ginny…'

'Got him? Well, multiply that by one million – no, one *billion* – and you have Claude!' Ginny groaned. 'He's the new Lab who's been created to lead the Radicals. Perfect in every way. I actually lost my breath when he shook my hand! His eyes, his hair, his smile, the scent of him… Oh, and his voice! We're going to be working with him and the famous five, whoever they are. Dad says they're an impressive bunch.'

CHAPTER FORTY-ONE

'It's only for a month, Mum,' Ginny said to her mother as she sat down with her on her first visit home on returning from New York. 'I'm going with Rafael. We'll be working together on our own projects with input from some of the US students. It's such a great opportunity!'

'It does sound interesting, Ginny,' Amanda Harrison nodded.

'Yes. And this extra work will go down great on my CV. Don't forget, there are more and more Hybrids competing for the top positions these days.'

'There is that point. What does your father think?'

'He's all for it. He's helping organise things with some Compound friends over there,' she replied. 'They know Abel and Ruby.'

'Well, if they're friends of Abel and Ruby they should be OK.' Amanda sounded convinced.

'And Ness is over there, too,' Ginny continued. 'I thought I'd call by and see Abel and Ruby over the weekend. She gave me some stuff for her brothers and sisters.'

'I'll come with you,' Amanda said. 'I've some new plans drawn up for the school extension that Celia needs to take a look at. I can leave them with Abel.'

Later that day they drove up to Ruby and Abel's new home on the outskirts of the Compound.

'Wow,' Ginny said as she looked around her. 'Everything looks so different!'

'Yes, it's much better without the Compound boundary

wall and it's freed up so much space. There are twenty more houses on this side of the main building and another ten to be built on the north side,' Amanda said.

'Who lives in these houses?' Ginny asked as they walked up to the front door.

'The correct percentage of Lab and Non-Lab families, just as the planning committee wanted,' she replied drily. 'It keeps everyone happy!'

Ruby greeted them with a smile and gave Ginny a hug. 'It's so nice to see you again, Ginny!'

'Ness sends her love to you all, and can't wait until her trip home at Christmas. She sent you these,' Ginny said, holding out the bag to Ruby.

Abel joined them in the lounge as they sat down and watched the children exclaim over the presents from their sister.

They chatted for a while about Ginny's trip to New York and she described in detail Ness's apartment and roommates.

'I can't wait to spend a whole month there,' she added. 'We're going to meet up with Otis, Cam, and Jez, too. We only managed to get to see them briefly on this trip, they were busy working.'

Abel picked up the phone as it started to ring.

'It's Celia,' he said to Amanda. 'She wondered if you'd have time to discuss the extension plans with her today.'

'Of course. Is she at the Compound office now?' Amanda said, standing up as he nodded.

Fifteen minutes later Ginny, Abel, and Ruby sat alone in the lounge.

'Zig has the children and Anya's on her way over,' Ruby said as she placed a tray of coffee on the table.

'Celia will keep your mother at the office until I call her,' Abel said to Ginny. 'Well, how did your trip go?'

She took a deep breath. 'Things are really happening fast. The Radicals have a new leader, a Lab, Claude, a clone of the

Radicals' Benefactor, Arnold Warner. He's going to be studying politics in New York and working as an intern with Senator Jordan. The Radicals want him to make as much of an impression as he can. That shouldn't be too hard. Claude is, in his own words, "designed and created to be perfect" - and he *is*, absolutely stunning and a real charmer!'

'And you'll be working with him?' Ruby said.

Ginny felt her face flush. 'With Rafael and some others. We'll get to meet the Radical five, too.'

'It's a pity you didn't get to see them on this trip,' Ruby said. 'Has Ness said anything about these people?'

Ginny shook her head. 'She's met quite a few different people, but no special group of five.'

The doorbell sounded. Ruby led Anya into the lounge. After exchanging greetings, Ginny turned to the girl. 'Just wait until I describe Claude to you!' The two girls sat for twenty minutes until Ginny was satisfied with Anya's sketch.

'That's him! Isn't he gorgeous?' she smiled.

'Yes, he certainly is!' Anya nodded, reaching into her bag to pull out another pencil.

Ginny frowned as she caught sight of a sketch of a young boy and pulled it towards her. 'I saw him, or someone very much like him, but he looked much older, and meaner too. He was the bodyguard with the driver who collected Dad.'

Anya's voice faltered. 'Tell me what this man was like, exactly!'

Her hands sketched swiftly as Ginny described the man.

'His face was quite like that boy's, but he's a few years older. He looked much harder, in fact his eyes were quite frightening. He obviously works out, from his six-pack!'

Anya placed the sketch on the table in front of them.

'That's exactly like him!' said Ginny.

Abel walked over and looked down at the sketch. He drew a sharp breath. 'He's the bodyguard who broke Isaac's cheekbone!'

'He's my brother, Robert!' Anya said softly as a tear ran down her cheek. 'I thought he was dead! I abandoned him! Oh, what have they done to him? We must get him out of there!'

Abel frowned. 'He's working for the Radicals now. We need to give this careful thought. He might not be the brother you last saw.'

'No, Robert isn't like them! They must have done something to him! If I could speak to him…' Anya cried.

Ruby stood up and put her arms around the girl. 'It might not be so easy, love.'

'I could get a message to him,' Ginny offered.

'We are not going to take any risks of you being discovered, Ginny,' Abel said. 'But don't worry, Anya, we'll find a way to get in touch with him.'

Anya was quiet for the rest of the evening and only spoke as Ginny stood up.

'I'm going to meet Mum up at the office. Bye, Anya.'

'I'd better get back home myself,' she said and joined her on the way out.

She put her hand on Ginny's arm to stop her as they neared the Compound office building where Amanda and Celia were standing talking.

'Ginny, I know it's a lot to ask you, but do you think you could somehow give Robert my mobile number? If you can do so without putting yourself in danger?'

Ginny was struck by the look of pain in the other girl's face. She took a deep breath, 'OK. I'll see if I get the chance to give it to him. I can't promise anything though.'

Anya breathed a sigh of relief. 'Thank you so much! I know he would never become like *them*. If we can just make contact, I'm sure he'll be able to explain everything!'

Ginny smiled as her mother waved to them. 'I'll do what I can.'

CHAPTER FORTY-TWO

'You've never seen a baseball game?' Bruno looked at Ness in amazement. 'We'd better remedy that as soon as possible! There's one on tomorrow night at the Uni Sports annexe at seven, Max is playing. I'm going with Celeste and Jude so why don't you join us? I've a tutorial until five thirty, but I could meet you down there if you want.'

Ness nodded. 'That would be great. My friend Ginny wants to go to one when she comes next month. At least I'll know a little bit about the game!'

The following afternoon she was making her way to the fields behind the sports building when she saw Celeste ahead talking to a tall, athletically built young man. Celeste waved as she walked towards them.

'Hi, Ness, Bruno said you were coming!' She turned to the young man next to her, smiling. 'Meet the star of the opposing team, Dale. We were a bit worried when we heard we were up against him tonight!'

'Hey, I was the one worried when I heard your brother was playing tonight!' Dale laughed.

Ness looked puzzled. 'Is Bruno playing?'

'Not that brother, Max. Their other sister, Jane, is a champion player, too,' Dale explained.

'Max said he'd leave a ticket for you at the reception. I'll go and pick it up now,' Celeste said.

Dale watched with undisguised admiration as she walked away.

'I thought Bruno just had one brother and sister,' Ness said.

'No, there's five of them. And they're all absolutely amazing people.' He turned to face her, 'I wouldn't be here now - hey, I might even be dead by now - if it hadn't been for those people, especially Celeste. She picked me up from the gutter and put me back on my feet. I was a no-good dopehead but she just wouldn't give up on me. The shelter they set up helped me get my grades and got me enrolled here. Max and Jane have been giving me and some of the others extra coaching, even though we're going to be playing against them!' He smiled as Celeste joined them, 'I was just telling Ness here how wonderful you all are!'

'Hey, you were in a bad place, we just showed you a better place to be, Dale!' She smiled and patted his arm. 'Anyway, let's see how all the training has paid off! Let's head for the gate, Ness; Bruno, Jane, and Jude will be here in a few minutes.'

As they made their way to their seats on the bench, several of the other students stopped to exchange a few pleasantries with Celeste.

'You seem very popular, Celeste,' Ness said admiringly.

'Oh, the guys at this place are a great bunch!' she said. 'They're like family to us. What about your family? You must miss them.'

Ness nodded. 'I do, but I really had my heart set on doing my masters here in New York.'

'What are your family like? Is it your Mom or your Dad who is a Lab?' Celeste continued.

'Dad. What about your parents? You know, I can't work out if you are Lab or Hybrid. Usually it's pretty obvious,' Ness told her.

Celeste seemed about to reply when there was a shout from nearby. She waved as Bruno, Jane and Jude made their way towards them. Bruno wore a pair of dark glasses, despite the overhead cloud.

Soon they were all watching the match intently. Ness

listened carefully as Bruno explained how the game was played. As he leaned towards her, she noticed he was wearing two tiny earphones and had a small device in his shirt pocket.

'It's similar to rounders, which we play in junior school in England,' she said, 'but it's not such a popular game as it is here!'

Once she had an idea of what was happening, Ness began to enjoy watching the game. Max was easily the fastest sprinter and had the quickest reactions when catching and fielding the ball, with his team soon taking a strong lead. He proved himself to be just as skilled a batter when the teams swapped.

At the end of the match the two teams shook hands and Celeste, Ness and the other two went down to speak to their siblings.

'You've got them running now!' Celeste beamed, hugging her brother.

Max nodded enthusiastically. 'You bet! No more second places!'

Other people also came to congratulate the team, including a scout from one of the higher league teams.

'I heard you were good, but I had a pleasant surprise to see just how good you are!' he said. 'We're doing some try-outs next week for new junior players. We'd be most interested in seeing you there,' he handed Max a card. 'Give my secretary a call and we'll arrange something.'

Max smiled. 'Thanks so much. I enjoy the game at uni level but I'm not really a baseball player.'

The scout held up his hands. 'Why not? With your skills we could have you playing in the main team before next season is out! We're talking really good money here, you know.'

'I'll hang on to your card, thank you.' Max shook the man's hand.

As they all walked back to Bruno's and Celeste's cars Jude

looked at Max. 'How many cards have you and Jane got now?'

'Eight,' he grinned.

Jane nodded. 'It's great, but we really need to have a serious chat and decide which Olympic sport we are going to go in for. We've a year's training to consider.'

'Did you enjoy your first baseball game?' Bruno asked Ness as he drove her home later that evening.

She nodded enthusiastically. 'Yes, I haven't seen anyone run as fast as Max in those last few minutes since…' she stopped, realising she was about to say, since Shiva. Bruno looked at her questioningly. 'Since that really fast guy, I can't remember his name, you know, the one from the Sudan.'

Bruno nodded. 'Yeah! Max thinks he will be able to beat his world record in a few months. Jane will, too.'

He pulled up at a petrol station, 'I'd better stop here and fill up.' Stepping out of the car he tossed the player and earphones on to his seat. Ness watched as he filled the tank and then walked to the kiosk to pay. She picked up the earphones and put one to her ear, pressing play on the device. Nothing happened, even when she skipped forwards and back a few tracks. Puzzled she put both earphones to her ears and tried again. Still nothing but a low hum. A hand came down over hers, taking the device from her, making her start.

'I didn't hear you come up!' she laughed.

'I asked if you wanted a hot chocolate,' he said.

'Oh… no thanks,' she said. 'I just wondered what music you were listening to.'

'Oh, it's just some calming stuff, sort of blocks out background distractions.' He gave a brief smile, pushing the device into his pocket.

Ness smiled and looked out of the window. It hadn't cut out background noise for her, it had cut out all the noise around her completely; and yet Bruno had been able to carry on a normal conversation with her and the others at the baseball game while wearing it.

She turned back to him. 'Hey, I was saying to Celeste, I can't work out whether your family are Labs or Hybrids. Usually you can tell pretty easily.'

He raised his eyebrows. 'And what did she say?'

'Well, she didn't really say -' she began.

'Man! I nearly hit that cat! Did you see it? I bet that used up some of its nine lives!' Bruno interrupted, swerving to one side. 'Are you OK?'

Ness sat up in bed late that night with her laptop open on her knees. She should have called her father or at least called Ginny, but she needed to do some research herself first. She typed in *Bruno Marcel* and came up with a list of the societies he belonged to at the university and some of his school background. He was classed as Hybrid, but there were no details about his parents. She found similar results when she typed in the names of the other four. She sighed and sat back, considering the facts she did know about them.

All were exceptionally gifted, even in comparison to other Hybrids and Labs that were students at the university. All were outstanding in their chosen subjects. Jane and Max were remarkable athletes. Bruno and Jude were top of their classes in politics. They had been accepted to begin internships with a leading senator in New York the following year. The rumours were growing that Celeste had been approached by a major film company to play one of the leading roles in what was expected to be a blockbuster film.

None of them showed any signs of being involved in anything dubious; in fact, they had all been involved in voluntary work with a well-known charity helping addicts and abused youngsters.

Jane and Max's exceptional skills were obviously down to enhancements, Ness felt. She frowned as she remembered the first time she had met Bruno. She had been terrified as she had watched him sitting clutching his head in such pain. She replayed the scene in her head:

'I'll get someone to help!' she had cried, looking around her.

'No!' he'd insisted.

He lay back down on to the grass holding his hands to his ears and taking deep breaths.

'I think I should get help.'

'No. Don't!' Celeste had ordered as she ran towards them. She had been angry with Bruno. *'What happened? You can't go on like this! You have to learn to be in control!'*

In control of what? Ness thought about the device Bruno had used to block out noise and his use of sunglasses even on a cloudy day. What did he have to control? Could it be enhancements?

Ness gave another sigh and switched off her laptop. She'd see what else Ginny could tell her about this family.

Ginny was full of her trip to New York when they spoke the following evening.

'We'll be there in two weeks' time. Rafael and I are going to be working with the five Radicals at the soup kitchen and also on the recovery programme. If it is as good as it sounds, it will actually be a help to similar projects set up by the Compound Labs over here,' she said.

'That sounds really interesting, Ginny.' Ness asked her. 'Have you any more information about the five students here?'

'Claude is going to introduce us to them as soon as we get there,' her friend told her. 'I'm surprised you haven't come across them yet, they seem to be making themselves pretty well known.'

Ness gave a short laugh. 'I must have been working too hard! I'll have to get out more!'

'I'll make sure we both do while I'm over there, Ness! There's so much I want to see! I didn't get the chance to go to the Empire State building last week, and we *must* get to a

174

baseball game! And I want to meet your special friend!'

'I'm sure you'll get to meet him in the month you are here,' Ness said.

They chatted for another half hour before Ness said goodnight, feeling guilty as she switched off the Skype connection. She had meant to tell Ginny about Bruno being one of five, not three. And she had meant to tell her about the enhancements, too, so why hadn't she? She climbed into bed with her tablet and opened a book she needed for her MA studies but found her attention wandering. She knew why she hadn't told Ginny about Bruno – she didn't want to acknowledge that he and his family were the leaders of a ruthless political group.

CHAPTER FORTY-THREE

'They're really keen to get started, aren't they?' Ginny whispered to Rafael as the car took them from the airport straight to Claude's suite.

'That's what we're here for, remember?' he admonished.

'Of course, but it would have been nice to drop off our suitcases and I wanted to call by and say hello to Ness,' she replied.

'This first meeting is very important, Ginny,' he said seriously. 'We've been given an amazing opportunity here. We can't let the Radicals down!'

Ginny nodded and sat up straighter. 'You're right.'

An hour later she was seated in the same place as she had been a few weeks earlier. They both turned as the door opened and Claude entered, followed by a group of young people. She felt her stomach flutter again as he shook her hand and looked into her eyes.

'I don't believe you've had the pleasure to meet the rest of our New York team. Let me introduce our English friends, Ginny and Rafael, to Celeste, Jane, Bruno, Max, and Jude,' he said. They all shook hands and sat down. Ginny wondered if Bruno was the same person Ness had told her about, but remembered she hadn't mentioned he was one of five.

'We've been bringing our New York team members up to date on the research you're involved in over in the UK,' he continued. 'This is a good opportunity to give you some background information on what we are doing over here.'

Ginny pulled her eyes away from his face and glanced

around at the others. She was secretly pleased to notice that they all seemed to be under his spell. Even the men seemed to be affected by his charming manner.

'How about you start, Jane?' he suggested.

Jane blushed and pushed her hair back behind her ear. Ginny noticed a small, colourful tattoo inside her wrist, it triggered an elusive memory.

'Yes, of course,' Jane was saying. 'As we all know, the ultimate goal of the Radical party is to overthrow the Non-Lab governments and create a fair and stable way of life run by Hybrids and Labs. Radical research identified the areas where most influence can be made, that's where we come in. We five have been chosen to play an important role in those different areas. Myself and Max are role models in sports. We have several sports workshops set up around New York and a summer camp organised. We are planning on winning several gold medals at the next Olympics. The more trophies we win, the greater our influence will be on young people especially.'

'Have you decided on which sports, Jane?' Claude asked her.

She looked across at Max, who continued. 'Both of us will compete in the gymnastics team. I will also compete in the cycling and Jane is going to take part in swimming. Unfortunately, the training programmes mean we are limited to the number of events we can take part in but we can both also compete in the pentathlons.'

'And we do intend to win gold in all our competitions,' Jane added. 'We will organise celebrations at all the workshops and camps to ensure our success makes an impression on the youngsters.'

Claude nodded. 'Bruno and Jude, you have secured political internships for next year, haven't you? I will be working as an intern with Senator Jordan over the next few months. Our plan is to make ourselves known so we can have a direct influence on people's political beliefs.'

177

'Conscious Decisions is already causing quite a stir here in New York and Radical members have set up three more groups in Washington, San Francisco, and Chicago,' Jude told them.

'And we have contacts in several other cities across the US. The university groups have been speaking at High Schools, too, so we're making an impact,' Bruno said.

'And Celeste?' Claude turned to face her.

'I'm planning on beginning a film career once I have taken my degree. I've already been sent several scripts to consider,' she said. 'Today's entertainment stars have a great influence on young people and I'm the perfect role model – I do voluntary work in a soup kitchen and I give up some of my free time to tutor underprivileged youngsters. Some of the sports students who are at university gained scholarships directly through our efforts. Jane and Max have also been involved in coaching them.'

Rafael's eyes widened as he listened. 'You really have got things organised here! We've made a start in the UK but we could do with some of your ideas.'

'That's why you're here,' Claude smiled at him.

Later that day, Ginny and Rafael were taken to their rooms in a small hotel near the university campus.

'Claude said someone would pick us up from the lobby at six o'clock to take us to the Rehab Unit,' Rafael said. 'Do you want to take a look around here for a while?'

'I think I'll have a rest for an hour, Rafe,' she replied. 'We've had a lot to take in this morning, and I think jetlag is catching up on me. Aren't you tired?'

'Not a bit! I feel full of energy! They're such amazing people, aren't they?' he said.

'Yes, I can't believe how nice they are,' Ginny said softly.

'Why wouldn't they be?' he laughed as he walked away.

Ginny sighed as she sat down on the bed. She pulled out her mobile and gave Ness a call.

'Hi, Ginny! When did you arrive?' Ness asked.

She glanced at her watch, 'About four hours ago. We were taken to meet the famous five…' she heard Ness draw in her breath sharply. 'What is it?'

'What were they like?' she asked in a quiet voice.

'They were really nice, actually. They…' she began.

'You're staying at the Park Hotel, aren't you? Are you there now?' Ness interrupted. 'I'm coming over.'

Ginny raised her eyebrows as Ness came into the hotel and led her to her room, 'Hey, what's up?'

Ness sat down on a chair and looked at her friend.' So you met the five students?'

'Yes, Celeste, Jane…' she started.

'Jude, Max, and Bruno,' Ness finished.

'Yes, how do you know? When did you meet them?' she asked.

'The nice guy, remember, who I met on the first day?' she explained.

'Oh, of course! So he is your friend Bruno.' Ginny clapped her hands. 'And Jane's tattoo!' She spun to face the other girl. 'But you never told me he was part of this group!'

'I didn't know myself until two weeks ago,' Ness explained how she had discovered that Max and Jane were also part of the family.

'But that was two weeks ago and you never mentioned it.' Ginny looked hurt.

Ness looked down at her hands. 'I can't believe that they are part of a ruthless organisation. I mean, Bruno's so kind. All of them are. Celeste is a bit pushy, but they haven't done anything bad at all. I've done some research on them, and all they have done is to get involved in good works.'

Ginny sighed as she sat down next to her. 'I know what you mean, Ness. I felt so mixed up when I left this morning's meeting. They have plans for a great new life for everyone, so why are we standing against them? But then I remember that

179

the Radicals are ready to take ruthless steps to achieve their goals.'

'Not these people, though. They haven't been involved in anything like that. They're the same as you and me!' Ness insisted.

'We don't really know enough about them, do we?' Ginny shook her head. 'They're obviously programmed to persuade people.'

'Well, I think we should find out more about them before we pass judgement,' Ness suggested. 'I've checked out all I could on the internet, there's not a lot of personal details.'

Her friend looked thoughtful. 'I'll let Celia have all the details we have so far and see what she can find out about them. What do you know about their parents? I couldn't even work out if they were Hybrids or Labs, could you?'

'Funny you should say that. I said the same thing to Celeste and Bruno. I asked them about their parents, but they somehow avoided answering the question,' Ness admitted. 'I'm seeing Bruno later, I'll see what else I can find out.'

The two girls and Rafael were waiting outside the hotel for the car to take Ginny and Rafael to meet their research partners. Ness waved as they stepped into the car and turned to see Bruno and Celeste walking towards her.

Celeste was frowning. 'Was that Ginny and Rafael?'

'Yes, I was so surprised when Ginny told me that she had met you all today. They were both very impressed with the work you have in place for helping underprivileged youngsters,' Ness replied. 'What a coincidence that they'll be working with you!'

Bruno and Celeste exchanged glances.

'It does seem to be,' he said. 'Ness, I was just going to call you to say I can't make the cinema this evening, I've got an assignment to give in by Friday and I'm way behind.'

'That's OK,' Ness smiled. 'Actually, I need to get on with some of my own work so I have free time to spend with Ginny and Rafael, though they told me they'd be quite busy.'

They chatted for a few more minutes, then Celeste and Bruno turned to leave. She looked at Bruno once they were out of earshot. 'What is Ness's last name? What kind of family does she come from?'

He shrugged, 'Her Dad's a Lab, her Mom's a Non-Lab, that's all I know.'

'How does she know Ginny and Rafael?' Celeste continued.

'Maybe it *is* just a coincidence,' Bruno suggested.

'And it was *also* a coincidence that she sought you out on her first day here?' His sister didn't look convinced, despite his protests that it hadn't happened that way. 'I think we should find out a bit more about her. Let's see what Ginny and Rafael can tell us.'

CHAPTER FORTY-FOUR

The driver chatted to them on the journey to the Rehab unit later that day. Ginny hardly noticed what he was saying as her eyes were fixed on the tall, serious-faced young bodyguard sitting next to him. Robert. Her fingers felt the slip of paper with Anya's number in her pocket as she wondered if she would get the chance to pass it to him. Suddenly she felt a sharp nudge from Rafael.

'Hey, Ginny. Where are you?' he whispered. 'Wilson just asked you a question.'

'Sorry,' she said. 'I think I'm still a bit jet lagged.'

'You must feel you're on a rollercoaster ride, but we've a lot to cover in the next few weeks, so we have to get started straight away,' the driver smiled at her in the mirror. 'This evening you'll meet some of the care staff and the new youngsters we take in and assess for suitability. There's usually a fairly good selection, especially if Celeste has been involved.'

He pointed out the different parts of the building as they drew up outside the main entrance.

'Here's Nurse Gibson,' he said as he got out of the car and walked towards a young woman dressed in a clean, neat outfit. 'She'll be taking care of you now.'

Ginny clutched the paper in her hand as she opened the car door. With a quick glance at the others, she leaned in the front window and dropped it into Robert's lap. 'Robert, it's from Annette!' she whispered and noticed his eyes widen. For a moment she thought he was going to give it back, but he thrust it into his jacket pocket as Rafael beckoned her over.

'Come on, Ginny. We're waiting for you!'

Ginny turned as the driver climbed back into the car.

'We'll pick you up from here later,' he said.

'This used to be the old school house, many years ago,' Nurse Gibson explained as she led them through a tall wooden door. They were in a small hall with an office on one side.

Nurse Gibson spoke to a uniformed man in the office and gave them both a visitor's pass. Then she turned to a heavy glass door and used a fob to open it.

'This is where the youngsters are first brought,' she explained. 'It's a high-security place as some of them are still under the influence of drugs when they arrive.' As if to emphasise her point, a second security guard nodded as he walked past.

They were now in a long corridor which surrounded an open courtyard. Several French windows opened onto a pleasant garden area where teenage boys and girls sat in small groups chatting. Some looked up and smiled as Nurse Gibson walked past.

'Those ones have been here for a week now. Five of them are ready to move up to level two later this week. One or two need a bit more time.'

'Do they all recover?' Ginny asked.

She smiled. 'We don't give up on any of them. We make every attempt to find each person a worthwhile role in society, but with some it takes a lot longer than others. Once they respond, they go to level two where they are tutored in the basic subjects that enable them to follow a worthwhile career. We also have guidance and help in moving on to a suitable job or course of study.'

The nurse pushed open a large white door. 'All today's newbies have been cleaned up and assessed, so these rooms are empty at the moment.'

They looked around at a row of showers and cubicles. Two

women were unloading a trolley of white towels into an industrial-sized washing machine at one end of the corridor. At a desk in the opposite corner a young man was typing on a keyboard.

'These are results of the initial drug test which we insist all our newcomers undergo. What are today's results, JD?' the nurse asked him leaning over his shoulder. 'Not bad.'

'Yes,' he nodded. 'Only three for the secure wing. Two completely clean.'

'They'll be level two before you know it,' Nurse Gibson smiled brightly. 'And when will you be starting your new job, JD?'

'On Thursday,' he replied. 'Wish me luck!'

'I'm sure you'll do well,' she said, patting his arm. 'But we'll miss you here! JD arrived here after living on the streets for two years. Now he's turned his life around. He studied computer programming and now he's an absolute computer wizard. He set up this new database to make our lives so much easier on the newbies ward! He's been promoted to a new job in the admin office.'

'I'll miss you all, too,' JD smiled. 'But I'm really looking forward to my new post!'

Next, Ginny and Rafael were shown some of the bedrooms and the canteen area. Finally they went to a large games room where some youngsters played on virtual devices or watched a film screen. One of the girls came over to talk to the nurse for a while.

'Well, that's our department for you,' Nurse Gibson smiled. 'Let me take you to see Mac, he's in charge of the tutoring groups you'll be looking at tomorrow.'

'We cover basic written and spoken language and communication skills, maths and IT programmes. Some of our level twos go on to specialise in sports. We aim for everyone who gets through the level two to go on to a suitable post or study course,' Mac explained to them.

'And do you rely on volunteers for coaching?' Ginny asked.

'We have a qualified team, but we do rely fairly heavily on volunteers. We offer encouragement by awarding credits to the students that give up their time. They add to their own educational records and can be used for a discount at certain stores and entertainment centres around the city, so we make it worth their while!' Mac smiled. 'With Celeste and her family involved, quite a few students are interested. They're a great bunch, they really get people motivated.'

'How much does it cost to run this place?' she continued.

Mac gave a low whistle. 'I don't know much about the admin side, but I'd say it takes a few million each year.'

'Who pays for it?' Rafael asked.

'We've a small government grant, then the rest we find ourselves through our own efforts. Skyward, the construction company, are one of our biggest sponsors. They also offer job opportunities to many of the youngsters here, from building to office work. Celeste and some of the other volunteers have organised several fundraisers over the last few years,' Mac told them.

Ginny was partly relieved and partly disappointed to find there was a different driver to take them back to the campus later that evening. Even Rafael seemed tired out when they reached their rooms.

'Quite an amazing day, hmm?' Ginny murmured as they reached her door. 'Celeste and the others seem like a really nice family.'

Rafael shrugged as he turned towards his own door. 'Why would they put so much money and effort into cleaning up a bunch of useless Non-Labs? I hope we get some reasonable answers soon.'

185

CHAPTER FORTY-FIVE

Ness was seated with Bruno in a quiet corner of the college canteen. She looked up and smiled as Celeste, Jude, Jane, and Max walked towards them. Her face grew serious as she saw the expression on Celeste's face.

'Is something wrong?' she asked.

Celeste looked at Bruno. 'You haven't asked her, have you?'

'Asked me what?' Ness said, noticing Bruno did not meet her eyes.

'About your family, *Agnes Devon*, and why you don't like to talk about them to us!' Celeste had two bright red spots on her cheeks. 'Why didn't you tell us who your father was, the famous Abel, leader of the Compound Labs in the UK!'

Ness took a deep breath and looked at Bruno. 'I suppose I would've had to tell you eventually.'

The others sat down and faced her silently.

'You're right, I *have* been hiding my identity.' She looked at Celeste who had a triumphant smile on her face. 'I... I just wanted to get to know people on my own terms, I'm tired of everyone thinking I only get where I am through my famous father! I got my degree in Cambridge because I'm clever and I work hard. And it's the same story for my MA here in New York. That's why I chose a university so far away. I thought at last I could leave the famous father bit behind and just be myself!'

'I think that's really admirable, Ness.' Bruno smiled and patted her hand.

'So there's no ulterior motive, then?' Celeste looked sceptical.

'No!' Ness said emphatically. 'Why would I have?'

'Why indeed?' Celeste repeated.

'And what about your parents?' Ness countered. 'I never get any straight answers from you. I don't even know if you're Hybrid or Lab. So, now we're all being honest...'

Celeste held her hands up. 'It's funny how you changed the subject so quickly, isn't it?'

'Oh, for goodness' sake!' Ness stood up. 'I've a lecture to go to.'

Bruno looked sheepish as she walked away. 'Did you have to do that, Celeste?'

'"*I just wanted to get to know people on my own terms,*"' Celeste mimicked in a little girl voice. 'We need to keep a careful eye on her.'

'She hasn't caused us any problems so far,' Jane pointed out.

'So far...' Jude pointed out.

Celeste nodded slowly. 'She's obviously hiding something! Did you see the way her eyelids flickered? And her palms were sweating.'

'How did you know that?' Bruno asked. 'You didn't even touch her hands.'

Celeste gave a snort. 'The scent of her sweat changed! If you used your enhancements properly you wouldn't be taken in by her so easily!'

'She may well be a spy for the Compound Labs. There's too much at stake. We'll have to keep a few steps ahead of her,' Jude said.

Bruno frowned. 'So maybe it's best if I don't see her so much?'

'No,' Celeste said slowly. 'See her as much as you can. Keep us informed of what she's up to and who she spends her time with.'

Bruno nodded.

Ginny found Ness to be rather subdued that evening. She listened as her friend described the conversation that had taken place.

'It's ironic, isn't it? You're here to spy on them and I'm really here for all the reasons I gave them!' she said.

'That could help divert attention from me, I suppose,' Ginny pointed out. 'Though I know you were getting quite fond of Bruno, Ness.'

She looked away. 'Well, now we know who the famous five are, it's probably for the best that we go our separate ways.'

Ginny agreed. 'Though, like you said before, we haven't found that they are doing anything wrong - in fact we've found evidence of the opposite!' She described her visit to the Rehab Unit the previous evening and the morning tutoring groups they'd seen. 'We could use some of their ideas in the UK. Rafael isn't too happy though, he can't understand why they spend so much time and money on Non-Labs. We've a Radical meeting tomorrow morning, so he'll get his answers then.'

Ness still seemed subdued, so Ginny suggested they went to the cinema. As they were leaving, Ness's mobile rang. Her face broke into a smile as she mouthed, 'Bruno. Can he join us this evening?' Her smiled increased as her friend nodded.

CHAPTER FORTY-SIX

Early the next morning the car was waiting for Rafael and Ginny outside the hotel. Ginny had felt a nervous tremor as Robert stepped out to open the door for them, but he had scarcely looked at her, merely giving a brief nod as Rafael thanked him. They had been taken to a large office building in the heart of the business section of the city. Ginny and Rafael sat down as others joined them around the table in the centre of a conference room.

Ginny glanced around her. Claude sat at the head of the table, with Celeste, Jane and their brothers on one side. She recognised Takir, Sanjit, Shana, and Willis from the sketches Anya had made. Angus gave her a smile of recognition as he sat down. She remembered him vaguely from several years ago when he had briefly lived on the Compound. Her eyes widened as she saw Hugo, looking confident and serious. It was hard to believe he was barely into his twenties. He gave a nod as he caught sight of her.

Claude looked around the table and soon had everyone's attention. He sat back, smiling. 'Good morning. This is the first time we've all had the chance to meet up together. Let me welcome Rafael and Ginny. We're pleased to hear you're playing important roles in the Radical movement in the UK. You've already had a chance to take a look around our Rehab Unit, established by Celeste and the others here. What did you think of it?'

Rafael cleared his throat. 'Obviously a great deal of time and money has been spent on it, and it is benefitting a number of Non-Labs from difficult backgrounds.' He paused. 'But how can this help the Radical movement? Surely this money could be better spent on Hybrid and Lab investigations. Ginny is involved in research on programming mature Labs. Surely that's where the money should be going, on similar projects that benefit the Labs and Hybrids?'

Claude smiled. 'Yes, we have heard of Ginny's research and we have been very impressed. I think Willis is the best person to explain our investment in the Rehab Unit.'

Willis placed his hands flat on the table in front of him. 'Adam told me what a keen supporter of the Radicals you are and also that you don't have much time for our Non-Lab friends! But let me ask you just one question, Rafael, what percentage of the population of the UK are Labs?'

Rafael shook his head. 'I don't know exactly, about 1%?'

'0.091% in the UK, and marginally higher in the US,' Willis told him.

Rafael nodded. 'OK, but when we're talking intelligence levels, we are far ahead of Non-Labs.'

'Right again,' Willis said. 'That's why we must use that intelligence to get the Non-Labs to do what we want them to do. We have a plan for a future society superior to any that the Non-Lab rulers have ever envisioned. Plato recorded his version of the perfect society but it was never put into place. Now we are one step closer to realising his dream. But we can't do this by taking up arms against over 99% of the country, never mind the Non-Lab members of the other countries who would support them against us. No, we have to be canny. We have to use our greater intelligence levels to gain a more subtle takeover. Starting with places like the Rehab Unit. Can I hand over to you now, Celeste?'

Ginny noticed the look of pride in Hugo's eyes as he looked at the young girl. She was wearing a grey business-like suit with a crisp white shirt. Her curly, black hair was drawn back into a neat bun. She pulled at a stray curl and tucked it behind her ear. Ginny had a fleeting recollection of someone else with similar mannerisms, but couldn't put a face to the memory. It was probably because the five were so alike, she decided.

'We are immensely proud of our Rehab Unit. We have an amazing success rate with the number of young people we have taken off the streets and literally turned their lives around. Some have benefitted with light muscle enhancements to enable them to take up a career in sport. We also have a strong team who have been trained to run fairly complicated computer programmes. Another group has found employment in the retail and service areas. We are laying the basis for the producers' level,' she explained. 'And of course, the added bonus is the great publicity we receive from this work, as well as the loyal devotion of those we rescue.'

'They are a strong and growing group of supporters!' Bruno agreed. 'The efforts we put into helping this group of Non-Labs is definitely rewarded with loyalty and not just from the ones we help, but from other Non-Labs too.'

Rafael nodded. 'I can see why the Rehab Unit is so important now. I think it's really good that you are already establishing a producers' level. What concerns me is keeping these people happy in the roles they have been given. What if they decide they want a new role?'

'A very good point,' Claude said. 'That is why we have Ginny here with us.'

Ginny looked up in surprise. 'Me?'

'Yes,' he smiled. 'Perhaps you could explain your research with Carl.'

She took a deep breath. 'We've been looking at ways to programme new talents into the brains of mature, awakened Labs. Up to now all programming has been done while they were in the developing stages.'

Claude smiled. 'Now we are hoping to use this research to programme Non-Labs to fulfil a given role. This would solve

191

the problem you suggested, Rafael. They would be content to remain in their allotted position.'

'That's amazing!' Rafael beamed.

'But... I don't even know if it would be possible to use the research we've done so far,' Ginny protested. 'We were working on virtual Labs. We'd have to create virtual Non-Labs...'

'Oh, no need,' Celeste interrupted. 'Take your pick from the Non-Labs at the Rehab Unit! Everything can easily be arranged.' She turned to Claude. 'You know, I also thought it might be an idea to include a sterilisation scheme at the Unit. We can be more selective of future Non-Labs if we check their IQ levels and general health at this point.'

'That idea is worth some thought, Celeste,' he agreed.

'Why do we need to preserve the future of Non-Labs?' Rafael asked. 'Isn't the future about Hybrids and Labs?'

'Well, again, that is a good question. But we don't really know enough about our own species to decide we don't need Non-Labs anymore,' Claude replied. He glanced at Hugo who nodded and continued.

'We know that a Lab does not seek another Lab for procreation purposes, but that a Lab will seek a Non-Lab partner. Our research suggests this is because a certain raw human element is necessary for the successful production of young. We know that Hybrid and Lab can be a match and we assume a Non-Lab could also partner a Hybrid. Our latest research has taken us even further in the field of cloning.' Ginny noticed the fleeting smile that flickered across Hugo's face at this point. 'So, that's why we must ensure we have a specially selected group of Non-Labs available.'

A lavish buffet lunch was laid out by a discreet team of caterers when the meeting drew to a close. To Ginny, the gourmet food tasted like dust in her mouth as Sanjit described the research unit he had established where she would be working.

'The laboratory is just outside the city. We have all the latest equipment and if we need anything else, we can get it!' Sanjit told her. 'There's comfortable accommodation if we work late and separate accommodation for the Non-Lab subjects. There's also a farming area and small factory where we can trial the programmed Non-Labs.'

She nodded her head and forced a smile. She kept the smile fixed on her face as Hugo joined them.

'Ginny, it's so good to see you here with us!' He shook her hand warmly. 'I always knew, right back at the Compound School, that you were so much more than a Compound Lab.'

'Mmm,' she nodded. 'It's just so amazing to be here, hearing about the future the Radicals envisage. And meeting the Radical leader! He's wonderful, isn't he?'

She noticed a dark look flash across the young man's face. 'Of course, though I think his team of five are equally remarkable, myself.'

'Oh, I agree with you! They're all pretty amazing!' Ginny quickly added.

Rafael and Takir appeared beside them. 'I can hardly believe we're here in the heart of the Radical team! Ready to get right down to work, doing what we've always believed in!' the young boy said.

'The Radicals recognise smart youngsters pretty quickly, don't they, Hugo?' Takir smiled.

Ginny's head was pounding as the car drew up at their hotel later that afternoon. Rafael had been talking excitedly about the Radical future plans.

'At last, it's all becoming so real!' he said as they waited for the lift to their rooms. 'You must be so excited about the Non-Lab research! I was talking to Willis about developing a body armour for the defence level, based on Henry's fireproof material. He was really interested. You know, I think we could end up here for longer than a month, don't you?'

'Hmm?' she answered.

'Hey are you OK, Ginny?' he asked.

'Just a headache,' she replied. 'It's all been a bit too much, too quickly! I need to get used to it all. I'll feel better after a good night's sleep.'

'Yeah, it's pretty exciting stuff, OK!' Rafael said as she went into her room, 'See you in the morning, Ginny.'

194

CHAPTER FORTY-SEVEN

'What am I going to do this time, Abel?' Ginny's voice trembled as she finished a detailed account of her first two days with the Radicals. 'Yesterday at the Rehab Unit I was impressed with the good work they were doing. And now today...'

She heard him take a deep breath, 'This is a difficult situation. Hold off the actual experiments on the Non-Lab subjects for as long as you can. Tell them you need to make some adjustments to modify the programming from Lab to Non-Lab. In the meantime, I will get the team in our laboratory here to see if they can come up with an antidote that can cancel the effects of the programming. What did you say the name of the company sponsoring the unit was, Skyward? That gives us another lead.'

'Has Celia found out anything new on Bruno and his family?' she asked. 'Or about Claude?'

'Nothing new yet. Just the background that everyone knows, from when they were fostered following the death of both their parents in a car accident. Two of our Labs have visited the foster parents but were not able to unearth anything new. We're following up a few leads on Claude's father, as he is the Radicals' benefactor,' Abel said. He paused for a few seconds. 'Ginny, if this is too much for you, we can get you home, you know.'

'No... if I don't go along with their experiments, they'll just put someone else on to it,' she said slowly. 'I'll try to slow things down as much as I can.'

'Ginny, if you want to come home, let us know immediately,' Ruby's voice came on to the line. 'Don't put yourself in any danger.' She winced as she heard the slight tremor in the young woman's voice.

'I won't, don't you worry about me.'

Ruby looked up at Abel as he put his phone down on the table.

'We can't let that girl put herself in danger.'

'She's OK for the moment, but we have to move quickly. At this point it would be even more difficult to get her out of the situation without arousing suspicion,' he replied as he pulled his laptop towards him and started to tap on the keyboard. 'Let's take another look at Celeste and her siblings.' He brought up a page from the university website and flicked through several pictures of the youngsters.

'Wait,' Ruby said. 'Go back to that picture of Celeste at the charity fashion show.' She leaned over and brought up a larger image of the girl posing with her hand on the back of her head. Then she zoomed in on the image of the tattoo on her wrist. 'Ness said they all have this flower tattoo. Could it mean something? Could it give us a clue to who they are?'

Abel stared at the image. 'It looks like a flower. I can't see how that can be important.'

'Me neither,' said Ruby. 'But Anya has a keen eye for detail. Let's ask her to take a look at them. Let's get Isaac and Celia over, too. The more ideas, the better.'

An hour later Anya arrived. She stared for a long time at the tattoo pattern on Celeste's wrist, then at the same on the wrists of the others.

'They are exactly the same, all five of them,' she said.

'The same flower pattern,' Ruby nodded. 'I wonder what it represents.'

'Oh, I don't think it's a flower pattern,' Anya said. 'I think it's interwoven letters. Look, there's a C encircling an H.'

Abel and Ruby peered at the image.

'You're right!' Abel exclaimed. 'I can see it now you've pointed it out! C... H... it could be a clue to their parentage!'

'We need to list all the names of those with the initial C or H to their names,' Ruby said excitedly, pulling a notepad towards her.

'Well, there's Celeste – she could have been named after a parent or donor,' Abel said.

'And what about H?' Anya asked.

'The only H I can think of is Hugo,' Ruby said, writing down the name. 'Surely he would be too young to be considered as a parent?'

'He could've been involved on the research side,' Annette suggested. 'Or as a donor, if they are Labs.'

'So those are possible father's names; and only Celeste as a clue to the mother's identity. Unless they did something like use a male version of a female name -!' Ruby tapped the pencil on the page. 'We need more background information!'

Abel was looking thoughtful. 'I think it's time we paid another visit to Celeste's foster parents. We'll have to think of a new way of approaching them if we are to get any new leads.'

'Celia and Isaac are here,' Ruby stood up and let them in.

They sat together and discussed the latest findings.

'I could get in touch with a reporter on the *New York Times*. I'll explain what we want to find out,' Isaac said. 'I've a conference in Washington next week so I could go and see him then.'

'I'll step up the search for background information on Warner Enterprises,' Celia said. 'Ginny told me that the company Skywards is sponsoring the Rehab Unit. I'll see if there is a link between that company and Warner.'

'Ginny and Ness might be able to find out a bit more about the tattoos. In fact, I can call Ginny myself,' Anya said, glancing at her watch. 'No, she'll probably still be asleep, I'll call her when she gets up.'

'We must keep one step ahead of the Radicals!' Abel said as the others rose to leave. 'The Compound Labs need to spread a clear message on both sides of the Atlantic that each person, no matter what their background or race, has the right to achieve their own personal goals and that no one should be fenced in at a certain level.'

Later that night Anya lay in bed and looked up at the clock face on the bedside cabinet. She would wait fifteen more minutes, then call her. She looked back down at the novel she had on her tablet and stared at the same page with unseeing eyes for another ten minutes. Had Ginny given Robert her letter? How had he responded? Finally, it was time. She picked up her phone and keyed in the number.

'Hi, Anya,' she heard her voice say.

'Hi,' she replied. 'Did you get the chance to…?'

'Yes. I gave the letter to Robert two days ago. He didn't say anything to me when I saw him yesterday. So he hasn't got in touch with you yet, either?' Ginny said.

'No,' Anya let out her breath. 'They've done something to him! If only I could get to actually see him. Just for a minute!'

'I don't think you would get near him even if you were here. I'll try to speak to him again,' Ginny offered.

'Please do. Remind him that we can enjoy a free life here now. Abel helped Mum and Dad sort out things with the authorities here. I get to see them a few times every week. I told them Robert is alive and that we hope he'll be in touch soon. We all miss him so much!' Her throat ached as she spoke.

'I'll do my best, Anya,' Ginny said. 'Have you any more news on Celeste and her brothers and sisters?'

'We have some ideas about the tattoos. Maybe you and Ness can find out more about them,' Anya explained about the initials and the discussion they had had the previous evening.

'I'll speak to Ness later. Hopefully, she can get some more information from Bruno.'

198

CHAPTER FORTY-EIGHT

Ness and Ginny sat together in the canteen the next day.

'I'm starting work at the Radical laboratory in two days' time. We're going to be kept busy. They even have staff sleeping accommodation if we work late,' Ginny told her. 'Sanjit and I are going there this afternoon to make sure everything's in place.'

'You can still come and see me some evenings, can't you?' Ness said.

'I hope so, but it sounds as if this work is going to be pretty intense,' she replied. 'In the meantime, see what you can find out about the tattoos, won't you?'

Ness nodded, 'I'll try, but Bruno and his family don't really give much away about their background.'

'That's suspicious in itself!' Ginny commented as she stood up. 'I'd better get going. I'm to meet Sanjit at the hotel in ten minutes.'

Half an hour later she was being shown around a state of the art laboratory.

'This is amazing!' she said as Sanjit turned on a large screen displaying one of the 3D images of a virtual Lab brain. 'This gives so much more detail than the images we have in the UK, and I was impressed with those!'

'The Radicals strive for perfection,' Sanjit told her. 'We took your ideas and worked on them to iron out some flaws. The programming you and Carl had inputted into the virtual Labs is 99% effective, so, using that data, we should be able to calculate where we can input a programme into a live Non-

Lab brain.'

'We'll have to adapt the template to fit a Non-Lab rather than a Lab brain,' Ginny pointed out.

'There are several Non-Labs to use as guinea pigs,' Sanjit said. 'I'll send a request for a suitable male and female to be sent here tomorrow. And I'll have to run an inventory on chemical supplies.'

'Don't request the Non-Labs yet. Wait until we do a trial on a virtual Non-Lab. We can pick up any obvious differences before we start using live subjects. It will save us time in the long run.'

'Yes, I suppose you're right,' he conceded. 'I must admit, I'd prefer to run tests on virtual people rather than take unnecessary risks on healthy youngsters, even if they are Non-Labs.' He sighed. 'You know that I am a clone of Takir, don't you?'

She nodded. 'My dad told me.'

'And that I'm ageing much faster than he is.'

She nodded again. 'Dad explained why it's not a good idea to make a clone of a clone.'

'Well, as I said, the Radicals like perfection and I'm certainly not perfect, physically anyway. Some of the others have shown a distinct lack of respect for me and regard me in much the same way they see the Non-Labs we use.'

'I'm sure you have a lot to offer, Sanjit. You're still a Lab at the end of the day.' Ginny patted his arm. 'Well, I might as well take a look at the data you've stored while you're doing the inventory.'

She scrolled down the screen. 'Wow, I can see how far ahead you've gone from the work we've done in the UK.'

Soon they were deep in discussion of the work covered so far. They both looked up as there was a knock on the door. Hugo appeared.

'Hi there, Ginny, how are you settling in?'

'Just getting a bit of background information on the

Radical work so far. It's very impressive.'

'It certainly is.' He beamed. 'Sanjit, do you have a full inventory for everything you need, yet? The committee want to take a look at it.'

'I've nearly done it. It's on my tablet, I'll need to check it through before I upload it.'

'Well, if you could get that done as soon as possible...' Hugo continued.

'I'll get on to it right away while Ginny sorts out the Val.' Sanjit got up and left the room.

Hugo grimaced as he watched him leave. 'I don't know how you can bear to look at him.'

'Sanjit's fine,' Ginny said. 'This week has been unbelievable! Here I am working with the Radicals. And I've even had a chance to meet the actual leaders!'

'Claude's team of five are incredible, aren't they,' Hugo said. 'They've already prepared so much of the groundwork for him.'

'They certainly have,' she paused. 'Claude is a Lab, but do you know, I can't quite work out if his team are Hybrid or Lab, isn't that strange?'

'Actually, I know pretty much everything about them as I was very much involved with their creation and programming,' Hugo said as he glanced around then continued in a low voice. 'This isn't common knowledge, so I know you'll keep this to yourself.' Ginny nodded quickly. 'The five are actually clones from both a Lab and a Hybrid – from a spliced DNA strand.'

'What?' Ginny looked astonished. 'What do you mean?'

Hugo's eyes shone. 'That was what I was working on when I first got to know the Radicals. Dr Gil was so impressed with my ideas that he set me up in a laboratory and supplied all the help I needed to turn my investigation into reality! I spliced a DNA strand from a Hybrid and a strand from a Lab, both carefully selected over a period of two years, then I meshed the two to form a new DNA strand with the characteristics of both donors.'

'My God, that's amazing,' Ginny whispered. A frown knit her brow. 'But I thought it was… inadvisable… to clone from a clone.'

'Dr Gil perfected the procedure of producing a clone of a clone. I won't go into all the details. And he created Harlan, a clone of himself. So, with this knowledge, I was able to bring my dream of creating clones of two almost perfect beings to life,' Hugo looked smug.

Ginny's eyes opened wider. 'Oh, and who are they?'

'Well, we don't really talk about the donors, but…' he began.

'Here you are. The latest data on our programming plan.' At that moment Sanjit appeared in the room holding a small tablet. 'I've uploaded everything onto the management area. You'll be able to access them whenever you need to now.'

Hugo gave him a brief nod. 'Send an email to the committee members, would you?' He turned to Ginny. 'We'll have to continue our conversation later, Ginny. You're doing a great job here. I hope we get to work together soon.'

Ginny sat back and let out a long, drawn-out breath as the door shut behind him.

Sanjit chuckled. 'He's a bit intense, isn't he? But a clever lad, a very clever lad.'

For the next few hours, Ginny looked through the rest of the files that the Radical team had already loaded. Using data from some of the Labs at the Rehab Unit, she also designed two basic virtual Non-Labs, a male and female. She was surprised to see the time when she heard Sanjit call her name.

'Ginny, it's pretty late now. I've sent out an order for all the items we'll need. We'll have everything here before the rest of the team join us the day after tomorrow,' he said. 'How about I drop you off at the hotel?'

As they drove back, Ginny's phone rang. It was Rafael.

'I thought you'd be back by now. Do you want to meet up for something to eat?' he asked.

She agreed and they decided to meet at a restaurant near the hotel.

Sanjit slowed the car in front of the doorway.

'Why don't you join us, Sanjit?' Ginny asked him. 'We could have a chat and get to know each other a bit better as we're going to be working together for the next few weeks.'

He didn't need much persuasion and pulled into the car park. They made their way into the restaurant to find Rafael already seated at a small table. His eyes betrayed his surprise to see Sanjit with Ginny. When the older man went to fetch a chair and stopped to talk to the owner, Rafael leaned forward and whispered to Ginny, 'Why did you bring *him*? He's old, he's not even a proper Lab, for God's sake!'

'He's very intelligent, actually,' she retorted. 'Even *you* might learn something if you listen to him!'

She was pleased to notice the change in Rafael's attitude as she encouraged the older man to talk about the research he had done over the years with the Radicals.

'So Bruno and the others all have four enhancements each?' he asked. 'They can run faster than any of us and they can see, hear, and have a better sense of smell than us?'

Sanjit nodded. 'Jane and Max have greater muscle enhancements than the others as they are designed for sport.'

'Their eyes or ears don't look different to anybody else's,' Ginny said.

'No, we've perfected the design now. Our earlier ones were pretty noticeable. They were mainly used on Non-Labs. We had to achieve perfection before we were allowed to insert any enhancements into Claude,' Sanjit told them. 'His father insisted on several demonstrations as he wanted Claude to be absolutely perfect.'

'Have you used these enhancements on any of the others?' Ginny asked.

'We've trialled muscle enhancements on one of the Lab security guards. We won't be doing any further trials until you've started the programming operation. We don't want to risk a working Lab trying to use their new strengths in the wrong way!' he told them.

'I'll be involved in developing the security uniforms,' Rafael told him. 'I'll have to make a trip back to the Compound to see Henry and Cilla and their latest developments in protective materials. I'll need you to put a word in for me with your mother, Ginny, now that you and Ness are both over here.'

Rafael turned to Ginny as they watched Sanjit drive away a few hours later.

'He's OK, isn't he, even though he's pretty flawed?'

Ginny nodded. She hoped that, as he was flawed, he would be easier to persuade to leave the Radicals.

She fell into step beside Rafael as he painted a glowing picture of the Radical team he was working with. Would she ever be able to persuade *him* to stand against them?

'You won't believe the research Hugo has been involved in since he joined the Radicals,' Ginny told Abel later that evening. She went on to recount their earlier conversation.

'So Hugo was directly involved in creating the team of five,' she finished up.

'Our research staff are confident that they are close to finding a way to "clean" a cloned DNA strand so it's possible to make a clone of a clone; but no-one has even thought of splicing a DNA strand! I knew Hugo was bright, but this is amazing!' Abel said. 'If only he was on our side instead of the Radicals. They are far ahead of us in cloning research.'

'Mainly because they have few scruples about how they get their results,' Ginny pointed out.

'That's what worries me, Ginny.' Abel told her. 'Whatever you do, don't put yourself in any danger, will you?'

'Don't worry, I won't,' she reassured him.

CHAPTER FORTY-NINE

'Do you remember what simplify means?' Ness asked the girl sitting next to her.

She bit her nails nervously and shook her head as she looked down at the maths book in front of her.

'Look back at the first question we answered. It's the same working out,' Ness prompted and was rewarded with a smile.

'Now I remember!' the girl grabbed a pencil and started to jot down her workings.

Ness nodded. 'Good, I think you've got that, Helen. We've time for one more problem, then we'll have to stop for today.'

Helen's brow furrowed as she studied the next problem. She gave a loud sigh and put her pencil down. 'Who am I trying to kid? I'll never understand all this! I'll never pass the exam!'

'Come on now, don't give up,' Ness told her. 'This is your first maths lesson in years and you are doing really well! Don't you want to get on to the IT course?'

Her face lit up. 'Yes! Give me computers over maths any day!'

'Well, you need the maths to get on the course.' Ness reminded her. 'So you're just going to have to keep on trying.'

Dale slipped into the seat opposite them. 'She's right you know. It's a hard slog, but it's worth it in the end.'

Helen looked up at him and blushed. 'It's OK for you. I'm real dumb when it comes to maths.'

'You're not dumb at all, Helen,' Ness said. 'You just need to catch up on the areas you missed out on.'

'You miss out on much school?' Dale asked her and smiled as she nodded. 'Me, too, and when I was there, I wasn't all there, if you know what I mean!' He made a circular motion with his hands on either side of his head.

'You're kidding me!' Helen looked surprised.

'Without this place I'd be dead in a ditch by now. Instead I'm completing my first-year Sports Diploma!' He stood up and gave her a wink. 'We're in the building right next to the IT block!'

Ness smiled as Helen pulled the textbook towards her again. 'OK. I'm not going to let this beat me.'

'You're a natural, Ness,' Bruno said admiringly as they watched the last of the students leave the classroom shortly afterwards.

'Oh, I think it was Dale who inspired Helen tonight!' she replied.

'Do you want to go for a coffee before you head off home?' he said.

Soon they were seated in a small café close to the unit talking about the students they had been tutoring.

'I think Helen will be OK once she gets her confidence,' Ness said. 'But what happens to the ones who don't make the grade? Mac said they find them posts, what kinds of places do they end up in?'

Bruno shrugged, 'Retail and service, I suppose. We just deal with the ones who show some aptitude for sport and IT.'

'You seem to really care about people. Is that what made you go into politics?' she continued.

He nodded. 'Yes, I believe we can build an economical and peaceful society where everyone is content.'

Ness gave a wry smile. 'It sounds like a tall order to me.'

Bruno grabbed her hands and looked into her eyes. 'No, it's not! It *is* possible! All we need are the right leaders. Trust me, that day will come!'

Ness saw the passion in his face. 'I can see you really

believe this could happen.'

They sat for a few moments, hands still clasped across the table. Slowly Ness turned his hand until the tattoo showed. She ran her finger over it. 'Your tattoo fascinates me. What is it? It looks a bit like a flower. What does it represent?'

He caught her hand. 'It's a symbol of our family.'

Ness ran her fingers over the design. 'Hey, this looks like an H, and is that a C there? They're entwined. Whose initials are they?'

He frowned and looked carefully as she traced the letters again, 'H... C... that could be...' He blinked suddenly, as if remembering where he was. 'We'd better get going.' Quickly dropping her hands, he pushed back his chair.

They drove back to the campus in silence. At the door to her block, Bruno turned to Ness. 'You have a close family, don't you? You must tell me all about them next time we meet up.'

'Don't get me started, I'll never shut up!' she laughed. 'I can't wait to see them again over Christmas.'

CHAPTER FIFTY

Ginny sat with Rafael and Sanjit as they listened to the speaker detail the activities of the Radicals over the past few weeks.

'First of all, may I congratulate Claude and his support group on their campaigning on behalf of the Conscious Decision group here in New York and in Washington. We have added another fifty members over the last fortnight. I hear you're already making your mark in the political world with Senator Jordan, Claude. There have been several newspaper articles about the new kid on the scene! We'll make sure that we get as much publicity as possible for all the events you are involved in and give you a high profile.'

Claude smiled his acknowledgement.

'Following up Celeste's suggestion of a sterilisation plan, we have had our logistics and medical team draw up a plan to get that underway, maybe as early as next month. We're surprised that you don't think that your programming can begin until next month, Sanjit and Ginny. Can you explain these delays?'

Sanjit stood up and nodded. 'As you know, Ginny had been working on a similar programming plan in the UK involving Labs, using Virtual Labs as a trial. Well, we're doing the same thing here but we've created virtual Non-Labs.'

'I thought we said Non-Labs from the Rehab Unit could be used,' Celeste frowned.

'We could do that,' Ginny said, 'but we might lose a few at the outset.'

208

'Is that a problem?' Celeste shrugged. 'We have lost a few before now.'

'So far the Rehab Unit has a good name. In fact, it's one of the main reasons why you're building up such a good reputation yourselves. If some of the young men and women start to die or disappear, that would be really bad publicity. It seems a pity to risk things just for the sake of a few weeks,' Ginny said.

'I can understand your concern, Celeste, but Ginny does have a point. And if it only means a delay of a couple of weeks...' Claude looked at Ginny who nodded confidently.

'You're right. Sorry, Ginny,' Celeste gave a laugh. 'I guess I'm too impatient!' She pulled a lock of hair from behind her ear and twirled it in her fingers.

Ginny gave a sigh of relief as Claude turned to another subject.

At the end of the meeting she was collecting her belongings when she found Celeste standing in front of her.

'Ginny, what can you tell me about Agnes Devon? Why was she so secretive about her background?' she asked her. 'She gave us a story about wanting to get people to accept her for herself, but I don't believe that for a minute.'

'No, I'm sure Ness is being honest about that. She did get some unkind comments while we were at Cambridge,' Ginny told her.

Celeste shook her head. 'There are too many coincidences. She's the daughter of the Compound Lab leader; she decides to hide herself away in New York at the same university where we happen to be; she bumps into Bruno on the first day and befriends him. Does she know about your work with the Radicals?'

'How would she...' Ginny felt her face flush. 'Oh, I'd be so upset if somehow I was putting the Radicals in jeopardy! I'd better stay out of her way. I'll tell her I'm too busy, I'll make some excuses...'

Celeste patted her arm. 'Don't worry, Ginny. You and Bruno are close to her, we need you both to keep an eye on her and find out what she's up to.'

Ginny nodded silently, letting out a sigh of relief as Celeste walked away.

Sanjit suggested that he, Rafael, and Ginny went for a pizza on the way home.

'When do you think we'll get the Radical society established, Sanjit?' Rafael asked him.

The older man shrugged. 'I would say we'll be making headway in about two years.'

Rafael groaned. 'So long?'

Sanjit patted his arm. 'Rome wasn't built in a day, young man! We still have a fair bit of preparation before we are ready. How long have you been involved with the Radicals?'

'Nearly five years now,' he replied.

'Quite a while!' he smiled. 'I've been working with Takir for fifteen years now. Most of those with the Radicals.'

'And you're not getting impatient?' Rafael said.

Sanjit narrowed his eyes. 'It does seem like we are moving slowly towards our goal, but we must lay the groundwork carefully. Next year I expect Claude will have made an impact on the political scene. By then we will have built up a large group of supporters for him, led by Bruno and Jude. With the work Ginny and I are doing, many of them will be conditioned not only to be faithful supporters but also conditioned to be happy in the positions we have chosen for them. Then we can plan our political campaign, knowing we are heading for victory.'

Rafael nodded slowly. 'It makes sense when you explain it like that.'

Later as they rode in the lift up to their rooms on the campus, Rafael turned to Ginny.

'You know, I didn't have much time for Sanjit when I first met him. He looks so old and, well, ugly,' he admitted. 'But the more I talk to him, the more respect I have for him. We're lucky to have him on our side.'

'Yes, he's OK,' Ginny agreed.

Once she was in her room, she phoned Ness.

'So I have to keep an eye on you now,' she said after giving her the details of the meeting.

'Well, it does take the pressure off you, anyway,' her friend replied. 'No one suspects you, so you're safe.'

'You must take care, too, Ness.' Ginny said. 'I know Bruno seems fond of you…'

'He's not like Celeste,' Ness insisted. 'He's not so… hard…'

'But he is part of their family,' Ginny pointed out.

Ness nodded. 'I know. We talked about the tattoo today.' She told her about their conversation, 'I got the impression he doesn't really know much about his background. He didn't seem sure what the initials stood for himself, but he seemed to have his suspicions.'

'It seems strange they don't know much about their own backgrounds, doesn't it?' Ginny said. 'I wonder why not?'

CHAPTER FIFTY-ONE

'I think it's a perfect idea! The three of you play a cameo role as the three musketeers in our Christmas production!' Celeste clapped her hands with glee. 'It will get you noticed and give everyone the right message about what your political parties stand for – good versus evil! And, rumour has it that Valenzo, the film director, is sending one of his top PAs to watch me in the performance. It looks like I might have two of the big directors after me!'

Bruno shook his head. 'I don't know if it's a good idea if we appear. We're supposed to be serious about our politics.'

'It's just a bit of fun, Bruno. And, as Celeste says, great publicity,' Jude said.

'And you have to be a good actor if you want to be a successful politician!' Jane added with a laugh.

Claude nodded and gave a lazy smile. 'I wholeheartedly agree! And maybe Valenzo will talent-spot me and offer me a film contract, too! So I could be a superstar *and* a top politician!'

Celeste smiled and patted Bruno's arm. 'Don't worry, Bruno. This is just a bit of fun - but it will be good publicity for us, too.'

The performance was a resounding success. Three extra performances were put on after the first three days completely sold out. The national newspapers took up the story about the newly discovered star, Celeste, and several made favourable comments on the 'three musketeers'.

Celeste was feeling pleased with herself as she dressed for

the party after the final show. She smoothed the green silk dress over her hips, enjoying the faint rustle and the silky feel as her fingers skimmed over the delicate fabric. Looking in the mirror, she smiled with satisfaction to note how the colour perfectly matched her eyes. She had chosen well. Her head turned towards the door a minute before there was a light tap and Claude stepped inside.

'You look absolutely stunning,' he said, fingering the light material of her dress. This is exquisite.' He pulled a small leather pouch from his pocket. 'As is this.'

Celeste's smile widened as she opened the pouch and held up an emerald pendant. He took it from her hands and placed it around her neck. It sparkled, giving a soft reflection of the green of her dress.

'It's perfect.' She ran a critical glance over him. 'As usual, you also look perfect.'

He gave her one of his charming smiles. 'Of course.'

As they reached the door, she slipped her hand through his arm. 'The perfect couple. How can anyone resist us?'

'I'd like to propose a toast to everyone who made this show a success,' Celeste said later that evening.

'With real champagne, too!' one of the drama students commented loudly.

'My treat, I think we all deserve it,' Claude said. 'From what I have read in the papers, this has been the most successful production the university has put on.'

'That success is due to Celeste!' another student said, raising his glass. 'To our starring lady!'

'She was awesome!' Dale gazed at her and shook his head. 'She's definitely a star!'

'Are you trying to make your girlfriend jealous?' Ginny asked him.

Dale turned towards Helen with a dismayed expression. 'Oh, no! You're the only one for me, babe!'

'You're lucky I'm not the jealous type!' she laughed,

slapping his arm playfully. 'It's OK, I know you've always had a soft spot for Celeste. I can't blame you. Her family have done so much for us. Neither of us would have got this far without the Rehab Unit.'

Rafael nodded. 'We were very impressed with it. We're going to take some of their ideas back to England with us, aren't we, Ginny?'

'It is a great place,' Dale agreed. 'They helped us get back on our feet and they have continued to make sure we're on track. We're due another check-up next week, aren't we Helen.'

'Yeah. I hope it's all good news again,' Helen nodded. 'I want us to be in tip-top condition when we're thinking of starting a family later.'

'Hey, you and me with kids!' Dale chuckled.

Shortly afterwards Ginny and Rafael left them talking to some other students.

Rafael grinned as they walked away. 'I'm relieved that they won't be allowed to have any kids of their own!'

Ginny stopped and faced him. 'Are they down for the sterilisation programme?'

'Yes. That's what the "check-up" is that they're going for next week. They're starting with those two and six others who have been through the Unit,' he replied. His face grew serious as he caught her expression. 'What's up? Surely you don't think Non-Labs like *them* should be allowed to have young?'

Ginny shook her head slowly. 'They seem so happy together. Now they're talking about their future and planning a family and they're going to discover it's just not going to happen. Someone else has made that decision for them.'

'Don't get soft, Ginny! They're Non-Labs and not very clever ones. Someone has to make the important decisions for them,' Rafael said.

'You're right!' Ginny laughed and looked away. 'It would be stupid to let them go ahead and have children! Hey, Ness is over there talking to Jane and Celeste. Let's join them.'

His brow furrowed as he watched her walk towards her friend.

'Celeste! You were brilliant!' she said as she reached them. 'The three musketeers were so funny!'

Jane agreed with her. 'It was definitely a great idea to include them!'

Ness smiled and looked up as Bruno and Claude joined them. 'Talking of musketeers; here are two of them!'

Celeste raised her eyebrows. 'You two were talking to Valenzo's man for quite a while. I thought maybe he wanted to offer you a contract, too.'

'Actually, he did say if we changed our minds about following a career in politics to let him know,' Claude said.

'As if I could be an actor!' Bruno laughed.

'Well, he seems to think you've got what it takes!' Jane smiled.

CHAPTER FIFTY-TWO

'We've got to do something quickly,' Ginny said to Ness the next day. 'Rafael told me they are starting the sterilisation programme next week with Dale, Helen, and six others!'

She paced around the room. 'What can we do that won't blow my cover?'

Ness bit her lip and was silent for a while. Then she said, 'You could send them an anonymous letter.'

Ginny stood still. 'Yes, it's worth a try. We could type it up so no-one recognises the handwriting.'

Ness opened her laptop as they sat down together.

To Dale and Helen,

'No, make that "Dear Friend",' Ginny suggested.

Dear Friend,

I want to warn you about the medical check-up arranged for you at the Rehab Unit.

I have been informed by a reliable source that you may be offered treatment which has serious side effects that may have an impact on your future fertility.'

Ness slipped the letter into an envelope and sealed it. 'If we walk down to the mall we can post it from there so it will be harder to trace. Dale should have it by tomorrow.'

Dale sat with a worried expression on his face as Helen joined him the following afternoon outside the university.

'What is it, hun?' she asked.

He handed her the letter and waited silently as she read it.

'I don't understand. Who sent this?' she frowned. 'Surely

216

the Rehab Unit wouldn't put us at risk?'

Dale shook his head. 'It's probably some prank. Or maybe someone who's just jealous.'

'Yeah, maybe, but...' Helen paused. 'What if there's something in it? I don't want to take any risks. What are we going to do?'

'I think we should talk to Celeste about it,' Dale said. 'She'll know what to do.'

Celeste's green eyes were cold as she read the letter. She held it near her face and gave a slight sniff. 'When did you get this?'

'This morning,' he replied.

'I'm glad you brought it to me,' she nodded. 'Some scaremonger who hasn't even the guts to sign their name.'

'Is there any truth in it?' Helen's brow furrowed.

Celeste laughed. 'Not at all! Any medical tests the Rehab Unit carry out are always fully trialled until they are guaranteed to be safe!' Helen still looked unconvinced. 'You can listen to this anonymous person who has not given a shred of evidence to back their fears; or you can trust me.'

Dale gave a sigh of relief. 'Well, we know who we can trust, don't we, Helen? I told you, Celeste would know what to do!'

'So everything will go ahead as planned.' Celeste smiled and tapped the letter. 'If you get any more of these, let me know immediately. I'm going to get someone to take a closer look at this.'

As she walked away Helen turned to Dale. 'Dale, I'm sorry, but if there is any chance of risking a future baby...'

'Hey, you heard Celeste; it's just some nutter! We don't have to worry about anything. The Rehab people would never put us in any danger,' he said.

'All the same, I think we should wait for the moment. There's no rush for us to have any check-ups yet, is there?' she insisted. 'We'll ask Celeste if we can think things over for

217

a while.'

'I don't want her to think we don't trust her, after all she's done for us.' Dale looked at his girlfriend's strained expression. 'But I don't want to see you all upset, either. We'll tell her we'll leave it for the moment.'

That evening, Celeste paced the living room as she waited for Jane and her brothers to arrive.

Jane and Max were laughing as they walked in but their faces grew serious as they saw her expression. Bruno and Jude arrived shortly after them.

'Just take a look at this.' Celeste tossed the letter on to the table.

Jude picked it up and gave a low whistle as he glanced at it. He read it aloud and watched the others' reactions.

'How could anyone know about this?' Jane began.

'Dale and Helen have told a few people about their check-up next week. They don't know any details about it, so they couldn't have given anyone any ideas,' Max said.

'Well, they're not going ahead with the check-ups for the moment; Dale said Helen is feeling a bit nervous about things.' Celeste picked up the letter and handed it to Bruno. 'It's quite obvious who sent the letter, isn't it?'

He held it to his nose and nodded. 'It's Ness alright. But how would she get to know anything about it?'

'She seems to be picking up quite a bit of information about us,' Celeste snapped. 'If you used your enhancements properly you would have a better idea of what she's been up to. I think you are becoming too fond of the girl to think clearly. Next term it would be better if you cool things down with her.'

Bruno looked away and said nothing.

CHAPTER FIFTY-THREE

Ness could hardly contain her excitement as Abel drove her and Ginny from the airport on Christmas Eve.

'I can't wait to see everyone!' she said for the tenth time in half an hour.

'They are just as excited to see you again, Ness,' her father told her. 'Your mother is waiting for you at the office, Ginny.'

Ruby met them at the door of the house and ushered them inside. She hugged Ness to her. 'It's so good to see you again!'

There was a loud shout and two boys ran into the hall.

'Ness!' the younger one cried as he rushed into her arms. She spun him around then put him on the floor.

'Finn! Look at you! You've grown so much these last few months!' she said, then turned to the older brother. 'Zac! You're as tall as me now! And where's Tilda?'

Brit appeared, carrying Ness's younger sister who jumped down and ran to Ness.

'Come and see the Christmas tree!' Tilda cried, pulling her into the lounge.

'We decorated it ourselves,' Finn added.

'I put the lights on it,' Zac said.

'Oh, it's beautiful. The best yet!' Ness smiled. 'The whole house looks so Christmassy!'

'Wash your hands ready for lunch now,' Ruby told them. Soon they were all seated and dishes were passed around the table.

'This looks delicious,' said Ness, spooning potatoes and

vegetables on to her plate. 'And tastes even better because I didn't have to cook it myself!'

'I helped Shiva make the chocolate dessert!' Tilda told her.

They continued to chat during the meal, Ness listening attentively to all the news her brothers and sister had to tell her. After the meal, Zac offered to show her around the Compound to see the changes of the past few months. They stopped by the garden area where Zig was working in one of the greenhouses. Jethro, her two-year-old son, was pouring compost from one plant pot to another beside her. 'I'm helping Mummy,' he told her.

'I'm sure you're a great help now you're getting bigger!' Ness grinned as Zig raised her eyebrows. 'Mum told me you've moved into one of the houses on the new estate, Zig!'

'Yes,' she replied. 'It's lovely being back on the Compound!'

'This place has changed so much over the last few months,' Ness said, looking around her. 'The boundary wall is completely gone now, isn't it? What are they building down where the old gateway used to be?'

'That's going to be the new primary school. It will take in children from the old village school and the ones from the new houses,' Zig told her.

'What about the Compound School?' Ness asked. 'Ginny told me it was going to be extended.'

'Yes, that's what the plans are,' Zig said. 'There are some objections to the Compound school being virtually only for Hybrid children.'

'But it has always been open to Non-Lab children if they pass the entrance exam, hasn't it?' Ness pointed out. 'If they can't pass then why would they want to go there?'

'We had two Non-Lab children in my class last year, but only one of them stayed more than a month. And he went on to a private high school this year,' Zac shook his head. 'He was such a swot! Always studying and worrying about his grades!'

'IQ level isn't everything,' Zig grinned. 'I should know that!'

'You're right, Zig,' Ness said. 'There's a lot more to life than being clever!'

'So are you saying I shouldn't work hard at school?' Zac tilted his head.

'Not at all!' Zig nudged his shoulder, playfully. 'You find your own talents and you work on them!'

As they reached the play area, Zac spotted some of his friends.

'Go and join them, Zac,' Ness smiled. 'You don't want to waste your football skills!'

They watched them play for a while then continued on their walk.

'Do you miss your touring days, Zig?' Ness asked her friend.

'It was great to see so many countries, but it was time to settle down,' she replied. 'I was so pleased when Keith suggested starting a family. Neither of us can imagine life without Jethro, now! Keith is doing really well with his special effects business with Pellier. The cat contact lenses are still in demand and now they're thinking of some new ideas they can sell to the public and to other bands. Now we've moved back here Jethro loves going to the Compound nursery and I'm happy to be working here in the garden again. Bailey and his team are trying out some new plants suitable for growing all the year round. They're working on accelerating the growth of a crop so you can have several crops in one year.'

'There must be plenty of governments interested in that,' Ness commented.

'Mmm, and a lot of sceptics, too,' Zig said. 'There are still a lot of people who don't trust new things, especially if they are invented by Labs! Anyway, what about you? How is life in

New York?'

Ness smiled. 'Really good. There are great resources and I've several advisors, Lab and Non-Lab, to help me.'

'What about the other students?' Zig asked. 'I hear you've been hanging out with Radicals.'

'Yes. I didn't realise who they were for a while. And they didn't know who I was, either,' she said.

'What are they like? Are they preparing to exterminate us Non-Labs and take over the world?' Zig asked half-jokingly.

Ness sighed. 'Not exactly. Their ideal world would be one controlled by Labs and Hybrids with Non-Labs doing the jobs they are allocated.'

'What if we don't like the job we are allocated?' her friend asked.

'Ginny told me that the Radicals have a plan for those who are not in the ruling level to be programmed to accept their given role,' Ness looked uneasy. 'They are beginning the programming next month.'

Zig raised her eyebrows. 'Phew! Do Abel and the other Compound Labs know of this?'

Ness nodded.

'I don't know if you should be mixing too much with this crowd, Ness,' her friend said. 'They sound like a bunch of control freaks to me.'

The younger girl looked unhappy. 'They're not all bad, really. I think it's just the way they have been conditioned themselves. I think if we could somehow persuade them to look at things from a different point of view…'

'What's his name?' Zig interrupted.

'Who?' she said.

'The guy you fancy. The one you want to rescue!' she said. 'No, don't deny it! I was there with Angus, remember? Look where that got me!' She pointed to her eyes.

'Bruno,' Ness murmured. 'Zig, I know this sounds silly, but I really believe there's more to him than the others. He can't even cope with his enhancements.'

'Abel said they had some pretty amazing enhancements,' Zig nodded. 'What do you mean he can't cope with them?'

Ness explained her first meeting with Bruno and Celeste's angry reaction. She described the ear plugs he usually wore. 'And he usually wears sunglasses. Lights and noise seem to bother him.'

'So the others don't have the same problems,' Zig looked thoughtful. 'That could give us some leverage with him.'

What do you mean? You're not planning on hurting him, are you?'

'No, quite the opposite! Have you told your father about this? No? Well, I think we should have a chat with him and the others as soon as we get the chance,' Zig looked pleased. 'I'm going to get in touch with Dr Shultz. He's the one who helped me with the contact lenses after my Radical op! I wonder if he can help Bruno. If he accepts our help, we might be able to win him over to our side!'

It was late the next day, Christmas Day, before Ness got the chance to find out more about Zig's plan. The day had been filled with excitement and laughter. For a while, Ness forgot about New York as she helped Finn and Tilda unwrap and try out their new presents.

Zig, Keith, and Pellier arrived, with Jethro, for lunch, followed closely by Isaac and Celia and their son. After lunch, the older children disappeared outside to play with their friends and their new toys when Ginny and Amanda arrived.

'Henry's mother is making a brief appearance for a few days to spend time with him before her next trip to some far-flung place in pursuit of a rare plant,' Ginny explained. 'So we thought we'd come over here and see how you're getting on. The kids outside seemed pleased with their presents! Zac has promised I can have a go on his mountain bike later. I wonder if I can still do a few tricks – without falling off!'

The younger children were excited to see the bags they

were carrying, containing even more presents. Amanda left shortly afterwards but Ginny stayed. She and Ness entertained the young ones until, eventually, they were tired enough to settle down to watch a film. Then Ginny and Ness joined the adults in the dining room.

'I know it's a holiday, but I think we need to catch up on anything you have to report, Ginny,' Abel said.

She sighed. 'The programming is due to start the day after we get back to New York.'

Abel nodded. 'Out team are working on a corrective programme. Thanks to the details you forwarded us from New York, we should have something prepared before you leave.'

Ginny looked relieved. She went on to explain how they had prevented Dale and Helen from attending the sterilisation programme the Radicals had planned.

'But it now means that Ness is suspected of being a spy for the Compound Labs,' she added.

Ruby looked worried. 'Ness, you never said anything.'

'It's OK, Mum, no need to worry,' she told her.

'And, we do have the good news that Bruno isn't handling his enhancements very well, don't we, Ness?' Zig explained her ideas. 'So it could work in our favour. I made a phone call last night to Dr Shultz. He's very keen on meeting Bruno and the others.'

Abel agreed. 'We've heard so much about these youngsters from Ginny and Ness, I would like to actually meet them.'

'Perhaps you could arrange a trip with Dr Shultz to New York?' Ruby suggested.

'I think they might be suspicious,' Ginny frowned. 'But we could give it a try, I suppose.'

Their discussion ended shortly afterwards when the older children came in with Amanda, Dylan, and Henry. Ruby sighed as she watched the two older girls laughing as they pulled Christmas crackers with the younger ones.

'They're just kids themselves, Abel. We can't let them put

themselves in danger,' she whispered.

'We'll keep a careful eye on them both. Nothing will happen to them,' he answered in a firm voice, only his eyes betraying the anxiety he felt.

Celia moved up beside him as Ruby was called away by Tilda.

'Are you sure they will be OK?' she asked. 'The Radicals can be ruthless.'

'Reuben has several people watching over them here and in New York,' he said. 'They can't just walk away now, they are in too deep.'

Celia pulled a stand of hair from behind her ear and twisted it around her finger, 'They'd better keep a close eye on them.'

Ginny glanced up at her and felt a memory stirring, but it was soon lost as Anya arrived with her parents.

'Happy Christmas!' she beamed and hugged Ginny to her, pulling her to one side as Ruby and Abel led the older people into the lounge.

'Robert phoned us today! He's fine and he'll be in touch again as soon as he can. Thank you so much for giving him my number, Ginny,' she said.

'So is he happy working with the Radicals?' Ginny asked.

'No! I'm sure he's not!' Anya answered too quickly.

'What did he say?' Ginny continued.

'He didn't really have time to say much,' Anya said. 'He just told us he loved us all very much and he'd be in touch again as soon as he could.'

Ginny frowned but was not able to say any more as Tilda appeared with a crying Finn. 'He's tired and he can't find his teddy.'

Anya swung the boy up into her arms. 'Come on, let's take a look around the playroom, shall we? That's where he usually hides out!'

CHAPTER FIFTY-FOUR

In New York on Christmas Eve, the Radicals had called a meeting of their senior members.

'Leela will work with you while Ginny is in England, Sanjit,' Willis told him. 'Then we'll be ready to start the programming straight away.'

Sanjit nodded and sat down with Leela, a young Hybrid. He opened his laptop and was beginning to explain what they had been doing over the past few weeks.

'It's OK, I have already been brought up to date on your progress, Sanjit,' she said sharply, a look of distaste flashing across her face as his arm brushed hers. 'It's just a matter of readying the Non-Labs once the holiday period is over.'

'Rafael,' Willis called him over. 'Have you updated the results of the materials to be used for body armour?'

'The last trials we did were the day before yesterday. We need some new supplies, but the chemical company is not open until the end of the week,' he told him.

Shana smiled. 'We're not going to be able to get much done until after the holiday period. Why don't we pack up early today, Claude?'

'Yes, I think you're right, Shana,' he answered. 'We'll meet up again on Friday morning.'

As Willis walked past him, Claude called him over. 'Once Ginny is back, will she and Leela be able to organise the programming themselves without...' He tilted his head towards Sanjit.

Willis nodded. 'Yes, and Denton can do the backup checks,

so there will be no room for error.'

Claude nodded. 'Good. I think Leela feels the same as I do about him. He really makes my skin crawl. It's time he was moved out, Willis.'

Willis held his gaze. 'Consider it done.'

Rafael looked up to see who the two men were talking about. They both had their eyes on Sanjit.

'Are you ready?' Adam asked him. 'Takir and I are going to Sancho's. Do you want to join us for lunch?'

'Yes, that would be great,' he replied. 'Sanjit, are you up for Mexican?'

It was beginning to snow as they made their way across the road to Sancho's.

'It looks pretty quiet here today,' Takir commented as they neared the door.

'I imagine most people will be eating at home today,' Adam said.

'I hope that means we'll get served quicker,' Rafael grinned. 'I'm starving!'

A moment later there was a screech of brakes as a car swerved around the corner and mounted the pavement. Rafael grabbed Sanjit's arm and pushed him into the restaurant, landing heavily on top of him. A couple about to leave stepped back in alarm.

Rafael stood up and rushed outside just in time to see the car disappear around the corner. He stood looking at the deep impression of the car tyres in the snow. They reached almost to the steps of the restaurant.

'Drunken driver!' Adam spat out. 'He could have killed someone!'

'Thank goodness you reacted so quickly, Rafael,' Takir said in an unsteady voice. 'Sanjit could have…'

They walked inside to find Sanjit sitting on a chair rubbing his shoulder.

'That was quite a good rugby tackle, Rafael!' he joked. He

insisted he wasn't hurt as they were led to a table.

The conversation Rafael had overheard ran through his head during the meal. Surely they wouldn't stoop to murdering a Lab? It must have been a drunken driver.

CHAPTER FIFTY-FIVE

The time hung heavily on Rafael's hands over the next week. He felt really happy as he made his way to the airport to meet Ginny and Ness. In the arrivals lounge he met Bruno who seemed as excited as he was, his broad smile reflecting Rafael's own as the two girls emerged, dragging large suitcases behind them.

'Hey, Rafael!' Ginny smiled and nudged his shoulder as they sat in the back of Bruno's car a short while later. 'Had a good holiday? Did you miss us?'

'I was glad to have a rest from your incessant chattering!' He gave a mock sigh.

Ness's roommates welcomed them all into the apartment. Each girl had a tasty selection of foods from their own homes and soon there was a party atmosphere as they sat around enjoying an impromptu feast.

'What is England like at Christmas?' one girl asked. 'Can we see your photos?'

Ness needed no encouragement. 'Here's Zac on his new mountain bike.'

'Is that your sister in the background?' another of the girls asked, leaning towards the laptop image. 'She looks so much like you!'

'Yes, we all look pretty similar, I suppose. That's me and Ginny at the shopping centre by the Christmas tree,' Ness said as she clicked to the next picture. 'It's not half as big as the malls you have over here! And the tree isn't quite as big as the one set up in the campus! Hambleton is only a small town.'

'Oh, that's the video of Tilda and Finn at the end of term school production. They were so funny!' Ginny laughed. As the rest of the group clicked through the pictures she looked up to see Bruno watching Ness with a gentle look in his eyes. Rafael was looking down at his hands, a troubled look on his face. She wondered what sort of holiday they had enjoyed. Rafael gave her a smile as he looked up and caught her eye. She smiled in return, happy to see him again.

It was quite late as they walked back to their rooms.

'What's bothering you, Rafe?' Ginny asked as they neared the building.

Without looking at her, he related the conversation he had overheard and the near miss Sanjit had had shortly afterwards.

He stopped and faced her. 'It's probably just a coincidence. I don't think Willis would kill Sanjit! Sanjit's a Lab, for God's sake!'

Ginny was silent for a few moments. Rafael looked at her expectantly.

'A flawed Lab,' she said quietly. 'I think we need to keep a careful eye on him, Rafael.'

As they reached her room Rafael leaned forward and patted her shoulder, 'It's good to have you back, Ginny. I have missed you.'

'I missed you, too,' she replied.

CHAPTER FIFTY-SIX

After a restless night Ginny was eager to get to the laboratory the next morning to see Sanjit. He greeted her warmly when she walked in.

'I'm just getting things set up for Leela. She's quite a stickler, but I'm sure you two will get on. She's nearer your age,' he told her. 'We've made a start on programming two Non-Labs so far. We selected the ones with the lowest scores on the IQs tests. They're quite happily repairing the fence on the bottom field at the moment. Do you want me to take you down to meet them?'

'It's cold out here, isn't it,' Ginny commented as they made their way across the yard from the laboratory building.

Sanjit nodded in agreement, pulling his coat collar up about his ears. 'I must admit, I'm glad it isn't me working out here! Ah, there they are, Neil and Charlie.' He waved his hand and beckoned them over. The two young men put down their tools and walked towards them.

'Can I introduce you to Ginny who is working in the laboratory? This is Neil and Charlie,' Sanjit said.

'Hello, Ginny. Pleased to meet you,' Neil said, pulling off a work glove and shaking her hand.

'Nice to meet you, Ginny,' said Charlie, holding out his own hand.

'You're making good progress there, aren't you?' Sanjit nodded towards the wire fencing at the edge of the field.

'Yes,' Charlie smiled. 'We'll have the longer side finished by lunchtime and get the two shorter ones done this afternoon.'

Sanjit nodded. 'Then you could take a look at the stream along by the roadside. It's quite blocked up.'

'We could make a start on that tomorrow,' Neil said.

'Have you done much of this kind of work before?' Ginny asked them.

'No, not at all,' Charlie answered. 'I'd done one or two driving jobs before I went to the Unit.'

'In fact when Sanjit told us what he had planned for us, I was all ready to pack up and leave!' Neil smiled. 'But he said sleep on it and the next day it didn't seem such a bad idea after all.'

'Well, we'll leave you to your work, boys,' Sanjit said, leading Ginny away. 'Before they came to the Rehab Unit, those two young men had been in and out of prison a few times and now, thanks to our intervention, they're entirely happy with their roles! Let's see what else we have to work on.'

'So it's just the lowest scorers we are programming, is it?' Ginny asked.

'That's what I have recommended,' Sanjit nodded. 'I know they are only Non-Labs and I never thought I would say this, but I must admit I've become quite fond of some of them from the Unit. Some have overcome quite formidable obstacles in their lives and are determined to do well. There are a few who could achieve quite high positions at the producer level. It would be a pity not to acknowledge their abilities.'

Inside the laboratory they found Leela at her desk. She gave a brief nod as Sanjit introduced them.

'Ginny and I are going to continue with this now, Sanjit,' she said. 'I think Willis has something else lined up for you.'

Sanjit knit his brow. 'No-one has said anything to me about this, Leela. Are you sure?'

'He left a message for you to call him.' She shrugged and turned to Ginny. 'I've selected the next two Non-Labs, females, Carol and Gill. They're to work as chambermaids at a Warner hotel in the city. We'll carry out the procedure this afternoon.'

'Carol's IQ suggested she could be eligible for IT training,' Sanjit said. 'If you look at the list I prepared you'll see I recommended -'

'I've made some amendments to your suggestions, Sanjit,' she said curtly. 'Carol's too much of a rebel. She could be a threat later.'

'Maybe we could use her rebellious streak to help us?' Ginny suggested.

'Too risky,' Leela said, leading Ginny from the room. 'Well, let's make a start.'

Ginny glanced back at Sanjit who stood with a bemused look on his face. 'See you later,' she said.

The two Non-Lab girls were seated in a small lounge. Both were in their mid-teens, one tall and thin, the other shorter with a more rounded figure. They both looked up as they entered.

'The guys at the Unit said you had some work for us,' the taller girl said.

'Yes, Gill, we do,' Leela said sitting down opposite them. 'There are a couple of jobs as chambermaids we thought you might be interested in.'

'Chambermaids? That's just another word for cleaners, isn't it?' Carol looked disappointed. 'I don't think I'm really interested in that.'

'It might be OK for a while,' Gill said. 'While we look around for something else.'

'Exactly,' said Leela.

'No,' Carol stood up. 'Thanks, but I'll go back to the Unit. They said they might be able to get me on to a training scheme or something.'

'It's your choice,' Leela smiled at the two girls. 'Either way, the Unit wants us to give you both a medical test so you

233

can go to your new job, or training, with a clean bill of health. Don't forget, with your history of drug abuse, it is necessary. We know that you're clean now, but you'll need a certificate to convince your next employers.'

Carol gave a loud sigh and sat back. 'OK. Let's get it over with!'

A young Hybrid nurse joined them and led Carol to an adjacent cubicle.

'You'll have more of my blood than I have soon!' Carol was heard to say.

Gill was led to a second cubicle. Soon it was quiet.

Ginny felt her hands shaking as Leela pulled a machine into the first cubicle where Carol lay sleeping. She quickly attached leads to Carol's head and looked at the image on a tablet screen.

'Are you ready?' she said sharply to Ginny.

'Of course, sorry,' she sat in front of the screen and typed in the programming details.

After an hour Leela and Ginny returned to the office, leaving the nurse to tend to the two girls.

'Well, they won't be giving us any trouble from now on!' Leela laughed as she sat at her desk. 'I'll send a record of the procedure to head office. That's four now. If the next week goes well, we could increase the number of procedures by the end of the month.'

Ginny's heart was still racing and her mouth felt dry. She opened a bottle of water and took a sip.

'Is Sanjit around?' she asked the nurse when she came in.

'He left about an hour ago,' she told her. 'He seemed a bit upset, actually.'

Leela suggested they pay a visit to the Unit while the two girls recuperated.

'We'll see them tomorrow morning,' she explained as she drove there. 'I can't see any problems arising, so we might as well take a look at the rest of the week's intake. There are two more girls and three boys suggested, so far. Take a look at that list.'

Ginny scanned the list. 'Some of these have pretty high IQs. Sanjit recommended several of them for training for higher positions. Why are they being programmed for unskilled work?' she asked.

Leela shrugged. 'We don't want rebellious Non-Labs with high IQs in positions where they could be a danger.'

'But if they're happily settled into a suitably demanding job, surely they won't be rebellious. From the ones I spoke to at the Unit -'Ginny began.

'Your role is to programme, Ginny. I'll sort out suitable candidates,' her partner said sharply. 'Personally, I think *all* Non-Labs should be programmed to carry out the roles we decide on. It makes things far simpler and safer for us.'

After an hour at the Unit talking to the young people there, Leela arranged for six more youngsters to visit the Laboratory over the next few days. Ginny was relieved when she was dropped off at her lodgings. Pulling out her mobile, she called Sanjit.

'Hi, what's happening? Are you being moved?' she asked.

'I'm now to work at home collecting and indexing data,' he sounded dejected.

'Well, someone has to do the job!' Ginny tried to cheer him up.

'Yes, it's the perfect job for a Non-Lab or a flawed Lab. No, I'm being tucked out of sight, away from the beautiful new creatures,' he said.

'Oh, Sanjit, I'm sure it's not like that…' she began.

'I've been expecting something like this for a while now, Ginny,' he told her. 'Call around and keep me sane when you get the chance. Bring young Rafael with you, won't you?'

'For sure. How about we call round tomorrow evening? We could try out that Thai restaurant?' she agreed.

She gave a sigh as she put her phone on the table. She

would miss his company at the laboratory. He seemed to be developing a more tolerant attitude towards Non-Labs, unlike the other Radicals she had met.

The next morning, as Leela had predicted, both Carol and Gill were compliant with the new posts suggested to them.

'It sounds OK, doesn't it?' Gill asked her companion as she read their job descriptions.

Carol nodded happily. 'Sounds fine to me. And you say we've new accommodation, too, Leela?'

Leela smiled. 'Yes, a hostel quite near where you'll be working. It'll make it easy when you have split shifts.'

Shortly afterwards the two girls cheerfully set off for their new lives in a taxi.

Leela watched them leave then picked up a list. 'What next? Mmm two youths, nineteen and eighteen. I remember the older one, he has quite a mouth on him. It'll be a pleasure to put him in his place.'

Ginny gave a quiet sigh and was following Leela towards the back office when her phone rang. Looking at the screen she noticed it was from Rafael.

'Hi, Ginny,' he said in a faltering voice. 'I've some bad news, I'm afraid.'

Her pulse raced, 'What is it, Rafael?'

'It's Sanjit… they think it must have been a heart attack…' he began. 'They said it must have happened in his sleep… he… he's dead.'

She put her hand to her mouth, 'No!'

Leela gave her a questioning look.

'It's Sanjit. He's had a heart attack. He's dead,' she whispered, sinking into a chair.

'Oh, dear. How sad,' Leela shook her head.

Rafael went on to explain how Willis had called to see Sanjit about his new job early that morning, but had not been able to get a reply when he rang the bell or when he phoned. He'd alerted the caretaker of the building who'd let him in with a master key. Sanjit was still in bed and had probably been dead for a few hours.

'Takir wants someone to arrange to collect his belongings from the laboratory,' he added.

'Oh, poor Takir,' Ginny said. 'What a terrible shock for him. Tell him I'll sort Sanjit's things out and make sure he gets them.'

After a few more minutes, Ginny put her phone down on the table. She sat for a while, staring into space. She tried to remember how Sanjit had sounded when they had spoken the previous evening. The sound of a slight cough brought her back to the present.

'I'm really sorry about poor old Sanjit, but we do have quite a lot to get through today, Ginny,' Leela said.

Two days later, Ginny attended a private ceremony for Sanjit. They all rose as the leader of the service stood at the front of the tiny room. Ginny recognised her as a speaker at some of the Radical meetings they had attended in New York. She gave a short speech on Sanjit's good qualities and loyal devotion to the Radicals. As she talked, Ginny looked around the room at the assembled mourners. Claude sat in the front row, his shoulders still, his eyes fixed on the ground. Next to him, Takir sat upright, his face etched with grief. Willis sat beside him, occasionally giving a surreptitious glance at his watch. Leela and Shana were talking together as they waited for the service to begin. Leela smiled at a comment her companion made until she caught Ginny's eye and quickly composed herself. There were several other faces that Ginny knew by sight only, some with concerned and others with indifferent expressions on their faces. As the speaker sat down, music was played and the coffin was wheeled from the room. She felt herself trembling and was thankful when she felt Rafael's hand in hers. He was still holding it tightly as they all filed outside a short while later.

'Takir, Jackie, and Liz are going to his cremation

237

ceremony,' Rafael told her as they watched the three climb into a car behind the hearse.

'So sad,' Claude was saying to the leader of the service, as he shook her hand.

'Yes, though he was aging quite rapidly lately, so maybe it is not so surprising,' she replied.

Willis gave a slight smile as he caught Claude's eye. Ginny noticed that for a moment the look of grief on Claude's face was replaced by a glint of amusement as their eyes met. She turned to Rafael, fighting back a feeling of nausea. 'Let's go!'

'I don't think half of those people were bothered about Sanjit!' she said bitterly as they walked back to their lodgings. 'He said himself he was flawed! And the Radicals have no room for imperfection.'

Rafael stopped and faced her. 'You know, Ginny, a few weeks ago I would have felt nothing at Sanjit's death. He looked old and physically ugly. But these last few weeks I got to know him as a person. I'm going to miss him.'

'Yes, that's just you, me, and Takir!' She wiped a tear from her eye.

CHAPTER FIFTY-SEVEN

Two days later, Ginny sat listening as Leela scrolled through a list of the people they had programmed over the past month.

'So we've six men working on the farm next door and ten men and women working at Gillings Distribution Warehouse. This week three more girls started as chambermaids at the Central Hotel, with another three cleaning at the hospital. They all seem satisfied in their roles. We've had great reports of their efficiency and positive attitudes. Once we have enough evidence that all is going to plan, we will be extending these premises. We'll need more staff so two Hybrids will be joining us next week,' she said. 'They want to get the sterilisation programme up and running as soon as possible. The Non-Labs we select will be programmed in the morning and sterilised in the afternoon. It makes sense really.'

'Won't that be a bit much for the... patients?' Ginny asked.

Leela shook her head. 'No. They don't actually operate with the new method. It's just two different types of injections, one for male and one for female. There are no scars, no evidence of what has happened at all. We just keep them here for a bit longer to check for any side effects, then they can get off to whatever work they've been assigned to do.'

'If this programme is extended, where will we get future workers at producer levels if we sterilise so many?' Ginny asked.

'Eventually, we'll work out a selection procedure and keep enough fertile ones above a given IQ level to provide for the

239

future. We won't need too many for the really basic tasks, we can use automatons,' Leela tossed her head towards the window where some of the programmed Non-Labs were working in the field outside. 'That lot aren't much more than automatons anyway!'

'It's so awful, transforming Non-Lab kids of my own age into mindless workers. Leela actually said they were not much more than automatons!' Ginny told Abel that evening. 'And they are planning on starting the sterilisation programme shortly, too.'

'Don't worry,' he reassured her. 'Reuben has a team picking up ten of them tonight from the different workplace addresses you have given me. We are confident that we can override the programming and restore them to their original characters. Let me know what the outcome is as soon as you can.'

'You've actually started?' Ginny felt her spirits lift for the first time in over a week. 'I'll be in touch as soon as I get any news.'

The next morning, Ginny looked up and smiled at Rafael as he joined her for breakfast.

'I'm glad to see you looking happier,' he said.

'Yeah, I've been a bit down lately,' she replied. 'Do you fancy doing something this evening? I could see if Ness is free and maybe Bruno, too.'

'Yeah. That would be good.'

They chatted for a few minutes until Ginny rose to leave. Rafael smiled as he watched her wave goodbye.

Ginny had not been at the laboratory for long when Leela answered the phone. She could see from the expression on her face that something had happened.

'No! I'm absolutely sure nothing was tampered with here!' she said. 'Please do! I would have insisted on a security check anyway. We'll get all the equipment ready for you. We'll cancel programmes for the rest of the week until we find out what has happened.'

She slammed the phone down and turned to Ginny. 'Something's gone seriously wrong! Get all the data up from the beginning of the programming. The security force will be here any minute.'

'What's happened?' Ginny asked. She kept a look of disbelief on her face as Leela told her how ten of the programmed Non-Labs had reverted to their previous characters overnight.

'And they think someone has tampered with our work here!' she said. 'Call the Unit and tell them we've a technical hitch and can't arrange any more interviews this week. We'll be in touch. Then come and help me check out the equipment in the cubicles.'

Ginny sat back and watched as Leela sat stony-faced during an interview with the security team.

'So you can see there is absolutely nothing wrong with our equipment!' she said.

'Yes, we can see that, but the fact remains that the programming hasn't been effective on ten of your patients. They have caused us a great deal of trouble. Two of them have agreed to go back to the Unit but the other eight had left their places of work before we could get there and so far we haven't been able to trace five of those,' an equally stern faced security officer commented. His badge read *Chief Officer Reed*. 'The programming obviously hasn't been sufficiently tested before being implemented. Someone will be held responsible for this!'

'The programming was fully tested on virtual and real Non-Labs!' Leela insisted.

'We will be running our own tests in future,' Reed told her. 'All procedures will be suspended until further notice.'

Ginny phoned Ness as she headed back to her lodgings an hour later.

'This evening's plans will have to be cancelled,' she told her. 'They've called an emergency meeting at six o'clock.'

'They won't suspect you of having anything to do with it, will they?' Ness sounded anxious.

'No, they've checked out all the equipment and data, everything is as it should be,' Ginny reassured her.

She felt rather less confident three hours later as she sat down at the hastily called Radical meeting.

Reed, the security officer she had met that morning was the first to stand up.

'Well, we have the results of the scans done on the two of the failed programmed Non-Labs that we managed to hold on to.' His lips and eyes narrowed into slits as he looked around the room. 'It appears that secondary programming was carried out to override the initial treatment!'

Murmurs of surprise went around the room.

'How could that be possible?' Jude shook his head. 'That would mean that…'

'Someone has been passing on information to an outside source!' Leela completed his sentence.

'Yes, indeed! We have a spy!' Reed said.

'Or maybe we *did* have a spy,' Willis suggested. 'It could have been Sanjit. He was pretty upset about being moved out of the laboratory.'

'No, I think if he had passed on any information this would have taken place before now,' Jane said.

Ginny noticed a look of relief cross Takir's face. She looked around the room as some people exchanged suspicious glances. Claude was looking intently at each individual. Bruno was looking down at his hands. Celeste had pulled a strand of hair from behind her ear and was twirling it between her fingers thoughtfully.

She was woken from her reverie when she heard her name spoken.

Celeste was staring at her, her green eyes cold. 'Do you

have anything to tell us, Ginny?'

Ginny felt her face flush and her hands grow clammy.

'Go on, Ginny, don't hold back; just speak the truth!' Celeste's voice sounded hard.

Ginny shook her head, 'I don't know what you mean…'

'I know she's your friend, but you can't keep on protecting her!' Celeste continued. 'It must be Ness! She must have got hold of the information from your laptop and passed it on to her father!'

'No, she couldn't have!' Ginny protested. 'No staff are allowed to take any sensitive data away from the laboratory.'

She was glad to see Bruno shake his head at Celeste, too.

'Celeste! You have no proof that Ness…' he began.

'What more proof do we need?' she gave a short laugh. 'She's here anonymously, she's wheedled her way into our lives, via yourself, and now she's using Ginny, her close friend, to get information! Why can't you see it?'

Ginny saw a look of hurt cross Bruno's face. Jude stared at Ginny.

'Ness is certainly high on the list of suspects,' Jane said.

'We should get her in here and make her come clean!' Celeste continued.

'No!' Everyone looked around in surprise as Rafael stood up shaking his head. 'No,' he repeated. 'We need *proof* that Ness is the spy. And at the same time we can turn this to our advantage. We could set things up so that she passes on incorrect information to her father.'

Claude looked at him for a few moments. 'I agree, Rafael. That does sound a better idea than rushing to conclusions. And we need to look carefully at *all* the people we come in contact with and tighten our security measures if the Radicals are to succeed. Maybe we have become too complacent.'

A sombre mood hung over everyone as they left the meeting room that evening. Ginny and Rafael walked silently back to their hotel. As they parted ways at Ginny's door she looked up at him.

'Do you really think Ness has been passing on information?' she asked.

'I hope it isn't her, but she is the most likely suspect,' he said. 'I'm afraid for her, Ginny. What will they do if they find out it *is* her?'

Ginny looked alarmed.

'Politically, she may not have the right ideas, but she's… a friend,' he said softly.

'That's how I feel, too, Rafe,' she agreed. 'We'll have to keep an eye on her.'

She gave him a brief smile and went into her room.

At midnight when the rest of the building was quiet, Ginny rang Abel and told him of the meeting that evening and of Rafael's fears for Ness.

'I'd already heard about this from Reuben. He's going to step up the security around her,' he replied. 'Ness was planning on coming over for a few days just before the Hambleton election; now we'll change the plans and get her over here as soon as possible with the excuse that I need her here to help with the campaign. Reuben is going to increase security around you, too, Ginny. You mustn't do anything that can put you in danger.'

'I won't,' she promised.

It was a long time before she fell asleep that night.

244

'Guess what!' Ness told Bruno two days later. 'Mum phoned last night. They've arranged for me to fly back to England for ten days so I can help Dad in the election campaign. We're all so excited! My dad could be the first ever Lab MP!'

'That really will be something,' Bruno laughed. 'England will beat us to it, if he is elected!'

Later that evening, Celeste looked thoughtful as he told them the news, 'So Ness is going on a trip to England, is she, Bruno? Is the timing a coincidence, do you think?'

'Why don't you join her, Bruno? Someone needs to keep an eye on her,' Jane suggested.

Jude looked up. 'That's a good idea, Jane. And you could also find out more about the Compound Labs at first hand and see if the UK is ready for a Lab MP yet.'

'Why don't I go, too?' Celeste suggested. 'Two pairs of eyes and ears, especially ones like ours, are better than one! Let's see what Ness and her family think of our proposal.'

Ness was pleased when they suggested they join her. 'My parents would love to meet you! The only thing is, I'm going to be pretty busy helping Dad out - but if you don't mind looking after yourselves for some of the time, it's a great idea!'

On the Friday the three of them boarded the plane for London.

'Are you OK?' Ness whispered to Bruno as they settled themselves into the aeroplane seats.

He nodded, adjusting his earphones and shading his eyes.

'It's just the take-off and landing; the pressure I suppose.'

She squeezed his hand. 'I'm so glad you are coming with me, Bruno. I can't wait to show you both a bit of England!'

She glanced across the aisle at Celeste who gave a brief smile and then grimaced slightly as the engines revved.

Once the aeroplane was airborne, they both seemed more relaxed and listened as Ness listed the sights she wanted to show them in the next week.

'I'll be pretty busy with my dad at first but once the election is over, we'll have time for some sightseeing before we come back,' she said.

'We can keep ourselves busy,' Celeste said. 'I am really interested in seeing the Compound and the Labs there.'

'And taking a look around the Compound School, too' Bruno added.

'The school is thriving, but there's not much left of the old Compound now,' Ness told her. 'The boundary wall has gone and there is a mixture of Lab and Non-Lab families living in the new estate that has been built there.'

'The Compound Labs get on well with the Non-Labs, don't they?' Bruno said.

'Most of the time,' Ness nodded. 'There are still a few Non-Labs who find it hard to accept Labs and Hybrids. But things are steadily improving.'

'Your father even has Non-Labs working with him in politics, doesn't he?' said Celeste. 'It always amazes me that Labs can accept advice from people intellectually inferior to them.'

'Sometimes you need more than a high IQ to make the right decisions,' Ness said. Celeste gave her a sceptical look.

At the airport, Abel hugged his daughter and welcomed the two visitors.

'We have been following your campaign in the news with interest, Abel,' Bruno told him.

Abel smiled. 'You are heading for a political career

yourself, aren't you?'

'Yes,' Bruno said. 'We believe that Labs and Hybrids hold the key to a future peaceful society.'

'I would include Non-Labs in that, too,' Abel replied.

'We noticed that you have support from both Non-Labs and Labs around Hambleton,' Celeste said.

'Yes, I've been very pleased with the support I have been shown from everybody,' Abel said.

'I can't wait to join you on your campaign, Dad,' Ness said. 'Celeste and Bruno are interested in finding out more about life for the Labs over here in the UK while I'm busy with you.'

'You'll be staying in one of the school staff quarters, so you could start with a tour of the school tomorrow,' Abel told the visitors. 'Amanda is looking forward to showing you around.'

They chatted on about Abel's campaign while Celeste and Bruno listened with interest.

The house was bustling with people when they arrived. Shortly afterwards, Abel excused himself and left for a meeting.

'It's been like this for weeks now,' Ruby apologised as the phone interrupted them several time during their evening meal.

Bruno seemed uneasy with so much noise and as soon as he could, escaped to the comparative quiet of the garden. Noticing him slip outside, Celeste said they were both ready for an early night after the long flight.

'Amanda, Ginny's mother, will be here at about half past nine tomorrow to show you around the school. I'm going to be out all day but I'll see you at some point in the evening,' Ness told them as she left them at their rooms.

Bruno smiled and squeezed her arm, 'Don't worry about us. We knew you would be busy and we'll have plenty of things to keep ourselves occupied. There's so much we want

247

to find out about life for Labs over here.'

Ness's brothers and sister were in bed and her mum was stacking the dishwasher when she got home.

'Isaac phoned. He'll be here at eight tomorrow morning,' Ruby told Ness.

'I can't wait to join Dad's campaign,' she replied. 'Do you think he'll be elected?'

'I hope so,' she replied. 'He has worked so hard to improve things between the Labs and Non-Labs.'

'Well, I'm going to help as much as I can!' Ness said. 'I'm so glad I was able to get time off uni to help out!'

'What about your Radical friends?' Ruby asked. 'Your father told me they have come to keep an eye on you as they think you are the Compound spy. He said he has people watching them carefully.'

'Don't worry, Mum,' Ness hugged her. 'Celeste and Bruno are OK. I know they are Radicals, but Bruno and I are also good friends.' She wiped the table and looked up. 'You know what I really hope, mum? That on this trip, Bruno and Celeste could see things from our point of view. And leave the Radicals.'

Ruby looked at her daughter. 'That's a pretty tall order, love. They have been conditioned by the Radicals for all their lives.'

'But people do change, Mum. If they meet someone really influential, someone who could make them see things from another perspective, it could happen,' Ness said firmly. 'Someone like Dad.'

Ruby hugged her daughter. 'I think it would take more than your father's influence to persuade them, love.'

Amanda was delighted to be able to show off the school to Celeste and Bruno the next morning.

'This is the new science block. The first laboratory is where Henry and Cilla work,' she said. 'But there are six other laboratories too now we have expanded.'

Celeste exchanged looks with Bruno. They had heard so much about Henry from Rafael. 'Can we go in?' she asked.

Amanda nodded and pushed open the door. 'Henry, Cilla, you have some American visitors today.'

'Hey, great to meet you. Do you mind if we ask you about what you're doing here?' Celeste asked, holding out her hand.

Henry shook it solemnly. 'You're most welcome. At the moment we are working on ways to improve a wetsuit material. We've analysed a sample of the original material used and so far we are considering two different chemicals in the liquid state...' He continued to talk in great detail about their investigation, with occasional remarks offered by Cilla.

After a while, Bruno shook his head. 'I know quite a bit about basic physics, but you have left me far behind, now!'

Amanda led them out while Henry and Cilla were still discussing the next step of the investigation.

'They certainly are dedicated!' Celeste commented.

Amanda nodded. 'We found that with most of our Hybrid students. Once they find their subject, they can become quite engrossed in it, so we give them every opportunity to develop their skills as far as they can go.'

'And do you accept Non-Lab students here, too?' Bruno asked.

Amanda smiled, 'Non-Lab students can sit the entrance exam the same as any Hybrid or Lab student. But it is rare that they pass. We have had three students over the past two years. Two lasted a term, one lasted a year, then transferred to a private secondary school. He had to work so hard to keep up with the rest of his class.'

Celeste and Bruno listened with interest as Amanda showed them the rest of the school and told them of the positions many of the students went on to.

'Do many of them go into politics?' Bruno asked.

'Yes, but we haven't any MPs yet. I hope Abel will be

elected. There is still a fear of the Labs and Hybrids having too much power,' she said.

'As a Non-Lab yourself you don't share this attitude, do you?' Celeste said.

She shook her head. 'The Labs and Hybrids have exceptionally high IQs. They hold the key to our future! What is there to fear?'

'Well, we have a Non-Lab who appreciates the higher IQ levels of Labs and Hybrids,' Celeste commented as they made their way back to their rooms later that day.

'Yes, and there must be others judging by Abel's popularity,' Bruno agreed.

'I've arranged to meet up with some UK Radical members tomorrow,' Celeste said. 'We must find out what their plans are if Abel is elected as MP.'

They saw Ness briefly at her house that evening.

'I'm so sorry I can't spend much time with you tonight, I'm helping Isaac out as Celia is away at the moment,' she apologised.

'Don't worry,' Celeste told her. 'We'll be fine. It's fascinating talking to everyone!' She drifted away to join a small group. Ness frowned as she saw Bruno wince as he stood in the noisy room. Zig glanced over and made her way to them.

'Don't worry, Ness, Isaac is waiting for you. I'll make sure Bruno is OK,' she said.

She followed Bruno as he slipped out of the room into the garden. He was leaning against the fence with his eyes closed when she touched his arm. She felt him jump.

'Are you OK?' she said.

He quickly regained his composure. 'Yes, yes. I'm fine. I just needed some air.'

As he started to walk away, Zig grabbed his arm. 'It's the enhancements, isn't it?'

He spun around. 'I don't know what you mean.'

Zig cupped her head in her hands and slipped the contacts from her eyes, then faced him. He drew back as her pupils narrowed into slits.

'I was one of the earlier ones!' She gave a wry grin. 'More noticeable than yours!'

He drew back. 'I don't know what you mean!'

'They're obviously not working as they should be. You need some help,' she continued.

'I just needed a breath of air.' He gave a polite smile and started to walk away.

'Have they made any comment? About you being flawed?' she asked. 'I don't think they tolerate…'

'I am not flawed! I just need to adjust…' He faltered.

'You can't adjust them yourself, but I know someone who can help you,' Zig said.

'I don't need any help,' Bruno turned away again.

'OK,' Zig said. 'It's going to be a noisy few days. Ness was worried you'd have trouble.'

'Ness doesn't know about this,' he said with an uncertain note in his voice.

Zig shrugged.

Bruno stood looking at the house, the sound of loud voices carrying across the air. He turned back to her, 'What do you mean, you know someone who can help me?'

Zig smiled. 'The guys at the medical centre. They worked wonders for me. Dr Shultz always works late. I'll give him a call. We could go over there now. Celeste won't even notice you're gone.'

CHAPTER FIFTY-NINE

Leonard smiled as he opened the door to Celeste and Bruno the following morning, 'We are so pleased to meet you! We have arranged for several Radical members to join us this morning to hear your progress in America.'

Celeste held out her hand. 'It's a pleasure to be here and get the chance to learn about the UK Radicals!'

'You have come at a particularly exciting time – hopefully we'll see the election of the first Lab MP in two days' time!' Leonard continued as he led them into a conference room.

Bruno nodded. 'And what will that mean for the Radicals here in the UK? Abel is very close to Non-Labs, too.'

Leonard nodded. 'Yes. But that's what is going to get him elected. A lot of Non-Labs are still wary of us. Let's think of this as a foot in the door, so to speak.'

'It will make it easier for us over in America when we are ready to start our own election campaigns,' Bruno agreed.

Denzil joined them, shaking their hands as he introduced himself. Over the next half hour, twelve more people arrived and sat around the table.

'Well, we're all here,' Leonard said. 'Unfortunately, not all the Radicals who wanted to attend were able to, but there is quite a good representation from around the UK.'

Further introductions were made, then Leonard turned to the two American guests.

'Perhaps you could start by telling us more about your future plans. Adam said we would be hearing more about Claude on this side of the Atlantic soon. What's he like?'

'At first we had our doubts about him,' Celeste admitted. 'We had been led to believe that Bruno was to lead the party with our support.'

Bruno smiled. 'But once we met him we realised that Claude is the perfect leader for the Radicals.'

'With his physical presence, his charm, and his programming, he knows how to capture an audience,' Celeste said.

'Yes, Adam told us Claude has been well designed and trained for his role,' Leonard said. 'I'm sure we'll be hearing more about him. Then it won't be long before the US Radicals start to introduce the new way of life. It's an exciting time! Adam told us that preparations are underway over there.'

Bruno nodded enthusiastically. 'Jude and I set up Conscious Decisions at the university, which has attracted a good deal of interest. We've not linked it to any political party yet, but once Claude is established we will do. We have Non-Labs as well as Labs and Hybrids as strong supporters.'

'You had a similar organisation, Green Shoots, at High School, didn't you?' Denzil looked thoughtful. 'We need to establish more Non-Lab friendly organisations here in the UK. Adam told us about your Non-Lab programming – and the unfortunate setback. When you get that back on track, it will play such a big part in overcoming any opposition in the future!'

Celeste's lips narrowed. 'It's probably the Compound Labs who have tampered with the programming.'

'We're taking a close look at all the Labs and Hybrids from here who have been working with you,' Leonard said.

'If it is one of them, we'll find out who and eliminate them!' Denzil added.

'Through Ginny and Rafael we have heard quite a bit about your work over there,' one of the other Radicals said. 'We're starting up similar schemes here. Perhaps you could give us some advice.'

Celeste and Bruno talked for some time about the ground work they were laying in New York and the plans they had for rolling it out in other states in America.

'It will take a few years but eventually we'll be moving here to the UK and on to the rest of Europe,' Bruno ended.

'Mmm, we're already considering the young Hybrids who are possible candidates for future politicians,' Denzil told them. 'We need to consider the best way to guide and condition them for their future roles.'

Celeste and Bruno were questioned about their preparation for the roles they were to play. Celeste described their upbringing and education.

'We were destined to fulfil our roles from the beginning. We have never known any other life,' she told them. 'We are completely dedicated to the cause.'

'Have you ever doubted the role you have been given?' one of the UK Radical members asked.

Celeste and Bruno looked at each other and shrugged. 'Never.'

'Is there anything that could make you change course?' another said.

Again they shook their heads.

'No,' said Celeste.

CHAPTER SIXTY

'There's nothing wrong with me, Celeste,' Bruno insisted the following morning. 'You know I need a bit of quiet time so I can keep on top of things. You go with Ness and Isaac. You can find out more about the campaign. It won't be long before we'll be experiencing something similar!'

'OK, if you're sure,' she sighed. 'I wish you could get a grip with your enhancements, Bruno.'

'I'm making progress, it's just the jetlag and noise and... well, I just need a break. You better go. Ness and Isaac have just pulled up outside.'

He breathed a sigh of relief as she turned and walked to the front door. Pulling his mobile from his pocket, he dialled a number. 'Zig? OK. I can be there in five minutes.'

Half an hour later he was lying on a hospital bed.

'Once we have completed this scan we will have a clearer picture of what's inside your head,' Dr Shultz said as he pressed a button.

They sat side by side in front of a screen a short while later.

'Everything is perfect,' the doctor said, pointing to different areas of the brain image. 'The only problem is that your receptor cells are magnifying your sight and sound responses before transmitting them to your brain. This is causing your distress.'

'Can you do anything about it? Will it involve an operation to remove the enhancements?' Bruno looked worried. 'Why is it only me out of the five of us?'

'I'll answer your last question first. For some reason you

seem to have naturally heightened sensitivity and this has caused the distress you are experiencing with your enhancements,' Dr Shultz explained. 'It will not be possible to remove the enhancements as they replaced your eyes, ears and olfactory glands. But I have already given this matter some thought since seeing you last night. For your hearing I have used these tiny devices modelled on a Non-Lab hearing aid. They can be slipped into your ears, where they expand; but instead of magnifying sounds, I have modified them so they act as a simple sound shield. They are disposable and must be removed and discarded every day. These similar devices, but obviously of a different shape and material, can be used in your nose. For your eyes, you will need specially designed contact lenses, much like the ones Zig wears, but more opaque. You will need to be measured for the contacts but the other devices you can use straight away.'

Bruno sat motionless for a few moments after Dr Shultz had inserted the devices. 'This feels so much better! I'm not being assaulted by such powerful sounds and scents!'

'Wonderful! If you step into the next room Nurse Jones will measure you up for the contacts. We can have them ready for tomorrow. She'll give you enough supplies to last for a month. We'll need to produce more as you need them.'

'You don't know what a relief this is!' Bruno beamed at Zig. 'Thank you so much, both of you!'

'And as we agreed last night, my team will be analysing your enhancements and using data from them for our own research in improving the sight and hearing of others, Lab and Non-Lab,' the doctor reminded him.

'It's a deal. As long as none of the other Radicals know about our agreement.'

'You have my word,' the doctor shook his hand.

'Where is Bruno?' Ness asked Ruby when they returned that evening.

'He's in the kitchen with Zig. We've prepared enough food

256

to feed an army!' she laughed. 'We're expecting quite a crowd here tonight to watch the final speeches of all the candidates, so we've booked the community hall and set up a screen there.'

There was the sound of loud laughter as Zig and Bruno appeared in the doorway.

'Hi,' he said. 'You're just in time to help carry some of these dishes down to the hall.'

'Are you OK?' Ness asked. 'I've got to go to the airport with Isaac to pick up Vince.'

'Fine,' he smiled disappearing out of the front door. 'I'll see you later.'

For the next half hour, there was a procession of both children and adults carrying a variety of containers which they set up on the tables in the hall. Celeste put a plate of garlic bread on the table and looked around for her brother.

'Have you seen Bruno?' she asked Ruby.

'He was here a minute ago with Zig,' she replied, looking around. 'He's probably gone back to the house to get more supplies.'

Another twenty minutes passed before she found him walking towards the hall with Zig.

'Hey, are you OK?' Celeste whispered to him. 'Do you think you'll be OK with all this noise and fuss?'

'I'm getting on top of it all now. I'll be fine,' he smiled. 'How did today go?'

'Good,' Celeste said. 'Abel has a lot of supporters in most of the small towns and villages around here.'

'I'll join you all tomorrow,' he promised. 'Where's Ness?'

'She went with Isaac to pick Celia and Vince up from the airport.' She sniffed her sleeve and held her arm out towards him. 'Smell this.'

Bruno sniffed and shrugged.

'You can't smell it? It's still quite strong. Isaac had this strange smell about him. It was on the kid's blanket in the car, too. It's… I don't know… just so familiar. Surely you can smell it?'

Ruby joined them. 'What's up?'

'Oh, I spilt some coffee on my jacket, I think I'll go back and change it,' Celeste laughed. 'I won't be long.'

As she neared the school block, a car drove past, Isaac and an attractive black woman sitting in the front. Ness, who was sitting in the back seat with an older man, gave her a wave.

Isaac glanced at Celeste through the rear view mirror.

'She's a bit of a strange character, isn't she?' he said to Ness. 'Today she kept, well, sort of sniffing me.'

'Well, she does have an enhanced sense of smell,' Ness pointed out.

'Yes, but she wasn't sniffing anyone else!' Isaac said. 'Just me - oh, and that blanket that's on the back seat.'

'Perhaps Seth was sick on it or something?' Ness held it to her nose. 'Smells OK to me.'

Celia took it from her. 'Smells OK to me, too. But then we don't have enhanced senses, do we? I'll put it in the wash, anyway.'

'Do you and Vince want to go down to join the others while I get Seth to bed?' Isaac asked Celia as they drew up at their house.

'I'm ready for a rest after the flight,' Vince told him. 'I'll stay home tonight and watch Abel on TV. I'll need my energy for the big day tomorrow.'

'OK, I'll just get changed and go down with Ness for an hour or so,' Celia said.

Meanwhile, Celeste shook out her jacket, frowning as she gave the sleeve a last deep sniff before hanging it on the back of the door. Then she pulled on a warm woollen sweater and headed back to the hall.

All eyes were on the screen as she re-entered the building. A Non-Lab MP, Gerard Darling, was smiling as he spoke to a reporter, answering her questions on the developments around the Compound and their effects on the town of Hambleton.

'We have seen a growth in businesses here, run by Labs and Non-Labs,' he said. 'There is a strong community spirit. On the surface it appears that we are all working together to ensure a bright future for everyone on an equal level but there are many residents who feel that the Labs are, well, taking over our community. That's why I am standing again as MP for Hambleton. I want to continue to make sure that the balance doesn't swing too much in favour of our new, clever neighbours.'

Celeste glanced around the room. Bruno and Ness were talking together, heads close. Bruno seemed unaware of the noise and distractions around him, though he still wore the dark glasses he'd hardly been without these past few months. At last he was getting to grips with some of his enhancements, she thought. The woman from the car had joined them as Celeste made her way over to them. She looked up and smiled as Celeste reached them.

'Celeste, meet Celia, Isaac's partner,' Ness said. 'She's just back from America with Vince, her father.'

Celeste looked up and felt her whole body freeze. The scent she'd noticed on Isaac was even stronger on this woman. As she studied her face the feeling of familiarity grew. She took the outstretched hand and shook it.

'So glad to meet you, after hearing so much about you and Bruno,' Celia said.

Even her voice compounded the feeling that she knew her very well. Celeste sent a questioning glance to her brother, but he seemed unaffected by this woman. A sharp realisation of the truth struck her almost physically.

'We need to talk,' she whispered, still holding Celia's hand tightly. Understanding slowly dawned on Celia's face as Celeste held her gaze. She nodded and they headed out of the hall, followed by a bewildered Ness who looked at Bruno. He shook his head and slipped away from them. Once they were far enough away from the building, Celia and Celeste stopped to face each other.

'What's up?' Ness asked as she drew near. The two women seemed unaware of her presence.

'Your scent, your voice, your feel, your appearance. Everything is so familiar because…' Celeste breathed.

'You must be one of our donors,' Bruno reappeared, his nostrils flaring. He pushed up his sleeve and traced the 'C' on his tattoo.

Celia stood silently, her eyes bright with tears. She swallowed and blinked hard. 'You are my… Labs?'

Bruno and Celeste exchanged glances.

'Can we go somewhere and talk?' Celeste asked.

Celia nodded and led the way to her house.

Isaac and Vince were seated in front of the television when they arrived. Isaac was holding a sleeping Seth on his knees. He gave Celia a questioning look.

'Is anything wrong, love?'

Bruno stepped forward, his eyes riveted on the child. 'Your son?'

She nodded and whispered, 'Seth.'

He looked at his sister. 'Sort of like another brother, Celeste!'

'Brother?' Isaac looked from face to face. 'You mean… the five in America?'

Celia took a deep breath and nodded.

'Can you be certain, Celia? Don't you think you need to make sure… DNA tests…?' Vince suggested.

Celia, Celeste, and Bruno exchanged glances.

'We *know*,' Celeste said simply. She took Celia's hand again. 'The feel of your skin, your scent, your face, everything… it is so familiar because it is *us*!'

Vince cleared his throat, 'Ness, how about we go to the hall and join the others? These people have a bit of catching up to do.'

The others hardly noticed as Ness and Vince left the house.

'We won't say anything about this to anyone else at the moment,' Vince said as they reached the hall. 'There's enough happening here already and they need a bit of time to get their heads around the whole situation.'

Ness nodded.

Isaac carried the sleeping toddler upstairs.

'How long have you known I was one of your donors?' Celia asked the two visitors.

Celeste shook her head. 'We didn't know. Not until I saw you just now. But the scent of you, and of the kid's blanket in your car. It was so familiar!'

'And the male donor, do you know who he is?' Celia continued.

Bruno started to speak but Celeste put her hand on his arm shaking her head.

Isaac had rejoined them. 'Surely you have some idea?'

Celia moved towards him and put a hand on his shoulder. 'Hey, we have to deal with this calmly.' She took a deep breath. 'You're almost… my children. We need to get to know more about each other.'

Isaac looked at Celia and then at the other two. 'We certainly do.'

'So, tell us about yourself, Celia,' Celeste said. 'How did you come to be one of our donors and not know about it? You said something happened.'

Celia gripped the arms of the chair and took a deep breath. 'Yes. When I was mugged.'

'Mugged?' Bruno echoed.

'You didn't know about that?' Celia asked. Both shook their heads. 'Then I think I'd better start from the beginning.'

They listened in silence as she described the night she and Hugo had been mugged and her car stolen. They had thought it was a straight forward theft until someone noticed a syringe puncture in Celia's arm, disguised as a cut.

'So, we are the product of a Compound Lab female and -' Bruno began.

'Most probably a Radical male!' Celia finished his sentence. 'Yes, we do know of your Radical backgrounds.'

'Through Ness!' Celeste's eyes narrowed. 'She's the spy in our camp!'

Celia shook her head. 'Ness has nothing to do with it.' She noticed a look of relief cross Bruno's face, but Celeste remained unconvinced. 'The Compound Labs have been keeping an eye on the Radical movement for quite a long time.'

'We *knew* the Radicals were involved with Celia's mugging and we have never given up searching for an answer to the question why!' Isaac clenched his fists.

'So you were selected as the perfect female donor for our creation,' Celeste whispered.

'Can I ask you about yourselves, about your lives up to now?' Celia ventured.

Bruno smiled. 'And we'd like to know more about you, too.'

Celeste looked confused as if she was been pulled in two directions at once. 'But we cannot tell you anything that will put our future plans in danger.'

'Of course not,' Celia agreed. 'But I do want to know about you. Tell us about your early years.'

Celeste frowned in concentration. 'I remember my awakening. I was in a long, white room in a narrow bed, covered by a thin sheet. A woman was smiling at me. She said something to me and helped me to stand up. There were three boys and one girl sleeping in four other similar beds in the same room. She woke those up, too. She told us that we were siblings and that we were special Labs with a special purpose in life. Later we learned that we were equivalent to fourteen Non-Lab years old as we had undergone an accelerated growth programme while we had been kept in a sleep-like state.

'Over the next six months we learnt that we had been created to lead a future society. One that would replace the present dismal, war-torn world that we were to find out about soon enough. We studied and trained hard for our future roles for a year then we were taken to a suburb of New York to our Lab foster parents and were enrolled at the local high school like all the other young people equivalent to our age,' Bruno said.

'What were your foster parents like?' Celia asked. 'Did they feel like *real* parents?'

'We had nothing to compare them to, but they seemed to behave pretty much the same as the parents of our school friends,' Celeste said. 'They looked after our physical needs. The Radicals took care of any other aspects of our training. We spent some weekends and most of the school holidays with them.'

'Once we finished high school we began our studies at New York University on the courses selected to fit our future roles. And that takes us up to the present time,' Bruno said.

'And they never told you who your donors were?' Isaac asked.

'We were told it was not in our interest to be personally acquainted with them. They did not want the possibility that we could be swayed by their opinions and emotions, our job was too important. We were told that our donors had been specially selected to ensure that we were of the highest standards in all areas,' Celeste said.

'We now know that I am the "C" on your tattoos,' Celia said as Bruno absentmindedly rubbed at the flowery pattern on his wrist. 'What about the letter "H"? That must be the initial of your male donor's name. Surely you have some idea who that might be?'

Bruno looked at Celeste who gave a brief shake of her head. 'We have no idea,' she said curtly.

'Tell us about your background, Celia,' Bruno continued.

'I'm sure you know the story behind the Centre and the Compound, don't you?' she said.

Bruno nodded. 'Yes, but we'd like to hear what it was like for you in your own words.'

The next hour passed quickly as Celia recounted the early life to the Labs, frequently stopping to answer questions asked by the two youngsters. They stopped talking when they heard Vince arriving back at the house.

'Well, Gerard Darling met his match in Abel tonight!' he said. 'We didn't mention anything to anyone as we thought you'd want to do that in your own time.'

'Thank you, Vince. I think it might be an idea to keep this to ourselves for a while. What do you think?' Celia said looking at the others.

Bruno and Celeste nodded. 'We need to get used to the idea ourselves.'

Vince stretched his arms. 'I'm off to bed now. I can hardly keep my eyes open!'

The others rose, too.

Celia walked with Bruno and Celeste to their rooms.

'Whatever happens, I feel you are my children. And I am so glad to meet you. I do hope we can be friends.'

CHAPTER SIXTY-ONE

Bruno walked into the lounge to find Celeste seated looking out of the window into the darkness.

She looked up and smiled. 'Couldn't you sleep either?'

He shook his head and sat down opposite her. 'Why didn't you want to tell Celia about Hugo?'

She looked at him. 'It didn't seem right to tell her. It isn't even openly acknowledged that he *is* our male donor by the Radicals, although he has always felt more like us than the others, especially since we've had our enhancements.'

Bruno raised his eyebrows. 'And how many times has Hugo hinted that he had been closely involved in our creation? He never actually said it, but we were left in no doubt that he is one of our donors. It was Hugo himself who had the tattoos put on our wrists.'

'Yes. I remember how furious Takir was when he saw them and the terrible argument they had. Hugo said we needed to be reminded of how important we were. Takir said all he was thinking about was his own importance and that he could jeopardise our future,' his sister nodded.

'So, we are the products of a Radical male and a Compound female,' Bruno sighed. 'Where do we go from here?'

Celeste frowned. 'I don't know. I felt the bond with Celia so strongly. But she's also a Compound Lab! Our greatest enemy.'

'But does she need to be? Can't we persuade her to see things from our point of view and to join us?' he suggested.

265

'I don't know if we can, Bruno.' She looked solemn.

'Well, we're going to have to try. We just need to get her to listen to us!' A determined look crossed his face. 'We have one more week to convince her. To make her see the flaws in the Compound Labs' way of thinking.'

'Without giving away too much about the Radicals,' Celeste reminded her brother.

Meanwhile, Celia sat looking out of her bedroom window.

'Can't you sleep, love?' Isaac joined her.

She shook her head.

'Even though we've been searching for answers for so long, this is all a bit of a shock,' he said.

'Perhaps we can persuade them to see things from our point of view,' she said. 'Get them away for the Radical way of thinking.'

'I can't see that being easy,' he said.

'And there's another thing, Isaac.'

She felt his body tense. 'I know what you're going to say, Celia. They're… related to you, not to me.' He rubbed a hand over his face and let out a long, slow breath, closing his eyes. 'I won't say this is easy for me. And I know it's a difficult situation for you, too. I can see the bond between you three already.'

Celia waited as he slowly opened his eyes. 'As you already said, they're like your children. Sort of Seth's half-siblings and, well, we've been through too much already to let something that was not your fault at all and not the fault of the five youngsters, come between us. I would welcome them as part of our family.'

Celia realised she had been holding her breath as she let out a long sigh and leaned against him. 'Oh, Isaac.' She looked up at him. 'We only have a week to somehow persuade them to stand against the Radicals and to join us.'

'Well, we can give it our best effort, love.' He pulled her closer to him so she couldn't see the look of doubt on his face.

CHAPTER SIXTY-TWO

'Bruno and Celeste said you'd invited them over for breakfast to watch Abel on catch-up,' Ness said, arriving at Celia and Isaac's house the next morning.

'Yes,' Celia replied. 'I'd like to know their opinions on Abel's views. Are you joining us?'

'No, I'm off to see Dad and support him on his final tour of Hambleton. This time tomorrow we'll have the election results!' she said.

'We've decided - Isaac, myself, Bruno and Celeste – that we'd keep our news to ourselves for the moment. At least until after the election.' Celia told her.

'I think that is a good idea,' Ness turned to go and then paused.

'What is it, Ness?' Celia asked.

'Well, we now know who the "C" is on their tattoo. Have you thought about who the "H" represents? Hugo, maybe?'

Celia looked at her. 'From what they said, the donors were considered the best in all areas - physically, intellectually, and so on. I don't think they'd use a teenager as a donor as the person would need time to have proven himself.'

Ness creased her brow. 'But according to Hugo's research, a Hybrid reaches maturity much earlier than a Non-Lab. So any Hybrid over, say, fourteen or fifteen could have proven his worth.'

'Hugo was around that age when he disappeared,' Celia said thoughtfully. 'So if he continued his research after that, he could very well be the male donor…'

'And taking into consideration his reaction to meeting me in Romania, it does add up.' Isaac's face grew hard.

'Well, we must remember the youngsters can't be held responsible for what happened,' Celia pointed out. 'We are going to use this week to try to convince them that the Compound Labs are right and to join us.'

Ness's eyes shone. 'What a great idea! I've been thinking of that myself. I'm sure between us we could influence them!'

She left shortly afterwards as the two visitors joined them. After breakfast they sat down to watch the recording.

Abel looked confident as he sat down with his interviewer.

'Oh, oh! It's Hugh Johnson!' Isaac made a face. 'He can be a tough interviewer. And he's not exactly the Labs' greatest supporter!'

'Well, Abel,' Johnson began. 'We've already listened to your opponent's point of view. I expect you've heard most of what he had to say, haven't you? He doesn't feel that you are really the person to make a fair representation for the majority of people living in this area.'

'Yes, I have listened to the points he had to make,' Abel said. 'If he or anyone else takes a look around Hambleton today, especially around the renewed Compound area, they will see how both Labs and Non-Labs are working hard together to build up our town on an equal footing.'

'That's how it is at the moment, isn't it?' Johnson leaned to one side and tapped the arm of his chair, 'but it's early days yet. What about the future? Will the more intelligent Hybrids and Labs really be happy to allow their Non-Lab neighbours to make important decisions? Especially if they have a Lab MP to support their own ideas?'

'I am standing for the rights of everyone here,' Abel insisted. 'The very planning and development of the new area was carried out according to the wishes of all members of the community. The proposed plans for the new housing estate were laid out for comments and criticism of all town members. We decided to display these plans anonymously so that there was no bias in the choices made. The final plans that won the approval of 70% of the public were a merger of several different proposals put forward by both Labs and Non-Labs.'

'Yes it does seem that you are giving equal weight to the interests of the Non-Labs at the moment.' Johnson nodded. 'But if we look back through the history of your people we know that you are capable of extreme measures to protect your own interests. How do we know we can rely on your unbiased judgement now? Is this just a pre-election stunt? We've all seen how would-be politicians, on any side, can present their point of view to fit in with the views of the public just before an election. And how quickly things can change after taking up office! For example, you said that you are working hard to ensure that there are employment opportunities in the area, especially for the young people. But we all know which ones are going to have the higher qualifications, don't we, and who will have the pick of the jobs!'

'We have several young people, Hybrids and Non-Labs, on the local committee involved in developing the area,' Abel told him. 'They have taken a look at what they want to see in here and the skills they have to offer. Some of the youngsters have also suggested new courses that they would like to see at the local colleges.'

'Mmm,' Johnson looked sceptical. 'I can't help but wonder if the ordinary kids around here will be left with the jobs your people don't want!'

Abel shook his head. 'The committee was formed to ensure there is a balance of Lab or Hybrid and, as you call them, ordinary people, in all areas of employment. And to maintain that balance for the good of everyone.'

'And what about the schools here? There's the Compound school churning out university candidates every year and Hambleton High with a much smaller percentage of their students going on to university. The figures speak for themselves. You can't deny that,' Johnson shook his head.

'You are right. Many of the Compound students do go on to university,' Abel answered. 'Following discussions with parents and students of the high school we have set up a scholarship scheme, funded by the Compound, whereby students who do not wish to pursue an academic career can apply for the training of their choice. There is a small percentage of our own Compound students who don't choose a university education. We believe the choice of job or training is very much up to the individual, we don't want to push anyone into a role they do not feel is right for them.'

'It does seem like an ideal society - at the moment!' Johnson said sceptically.

'We all enjoy living here in Hambleton. It is not only one of the oldest towns, steeped in hundreds of years of history, but it is the creation centre of my people, the Labs. So it is an important place for all of us. We want to show everyone that it *is* possible for Labs and ordinary people to live and work happily side by side as equals.'

Bruno and Celeste exchanged glances as Isaac switched off the screen.

'He spoke well,' Bruno admitted.

'Yes,' Celeste agreed. 'Though I can't understand why he is reluctant to acknowledge that the Labs and Hybrids would be much better at making decisions for the whole area. Why does he downplay the advanced intelligence of his own kind?'

Isaac bristled. 'You seem to think that only IQ levels have a part to play in the running of a community! Non-Labs do have a lot to offer, including a vast amount of experience to draw on!'

'And plenty of mistakes,' Celeste replied tersely. 'Which they don't seem to have learnt much from!'

'It's not just this community, it's the bigger picture we need to think about,' Bruno added.

'That's what the Radicals are all about, isn't it?' Celia said. She placed a hand on Isaac's arm as he was about to speak. 'Let's listen to what the youngsters have to say about the Radicals' vision, Isaac.'

Celeste gave her brother a knowing smile before she turned back to them. 'Claude told us all about our benefactor. He wasn't a Lab, he was an average young ordinary American. In fact, in his early life no-one, not even he himself, had any idea that he would later become involved in such an important political movement.'

She described in detail the story of Arnold Warner's life as Claude had described it to them. And how he had devoted the last decade of his life to enabling his dream of the future, of a peaceful and happy world, to become a reality. 'He knew he would not be able to lead the newly formed Radical movement himself so he created and perfected a clone of himself, Claude.'

'What's Claude like?' Celia asked. 'I've seen him on the news lately. He certainly is handsome.'

'Oh, he's more than just handsome,' Celeste's eyes glowed. 'His voice, his movements, everything about him is perfect! He is certainly the one to persuade people to see things from the Radical point of view.'

'So how do the Radicals hope to achieve the perfect society?' Isaac asked with a note of sarcasm in his voice.

Bruno gave Celeste a sharp glance. 'As we have said, we want a peaceful and happy society, where everyone fits into their own role and each level of society works towards the good of all.'

Isaac gave a short laugh, 'Ha! Just look back at the thousands of years where people have tried to establish the perfect society! What makes the Radicals think they can change things?'

'Hmm. Non-Labs are such cynics! That's why they have never achieved a peaceful world!' Celeste said. 'The Radicals are going to create a world where everyone feels valued and motivated to work for the society they live in.'

'How can you ensure that everyone will be happy?' Celia asked.

'Each person will be trained and given a suitable role to meet their own individual needs at their own particular level,' Bruno said carefully.

'How many levels will there be?' Celia asked.

'Three basic ones,' he said. 'The producer level, the security level, and the governing level. With a certain variety of roles within each level.'

'But if someone has chosen their level and their role and then later changes their mind about it...' Isaac began.

'They won't change their minds, their first choice will be the correct choice,' Celeste stated.

'How can you guarantee that?' Celia asked.

'Because the rul -' Celeste began, but Bruno interrupted her.

'They will be carefully guided in their decision making. It will not be taken lightly.'

'It sounds as if they are not going to be given much free choice in the matter,' Isaac commented drily. 'In fact, I don't think you yourselves have been given many free choices.'

Celeste's head shot up indignantly. 'You don't know what you are talking about!'

'We are going to be future leaders!' Bruno exclaimed.

'When did you make that decision?' Isaac continued.

Celia looked concerned. 'Isaac, maybe this is a bit...'

He shook his head. 'Tell me, Bruno, when did you *decide* you were going to be a great leader?'

Bruno looked confused. Celeste shot an angry glance at Isaac. 'We were all offered the chance to play a major role in establishing a society free from war and the petty squabbles of the Non-Lab led world we belong to now! Would you turn down such an opportunity?'

Isaac's gaze flicked from face to face. 'I suppose you're right there. Given the choice to be a slave or a ruler, who wouldn't choose ruler?'

Celeste bristled again, but Isaac raised a hand before she could speak. 'Just let me ask you one more thing. *If* this brave new world does come into existence - and I say *if* – what happens when one of the rulers decides that he or she wants to grab a bit more power? That person isn't happy with the way their part of the world is run? If we look through the history books, this does seem to have a habit of happening!'

Celeste shook her head vehemently. 'It won't happen! There will be no need for power struggles!'

'So all the Radical individuals who are at this moment planning the new society - they are all perfectly happy with their roles? There is not even a murmur of discontent from any one of them?'

Celeste shook her head sympathetically. 'We were warned that there would be many negative arguments from those who would not understand, especially from the Non-Lab ranks!'

CHAPTER SIXTY-THREE

Celeste walked into the lounge where Bruno sat watching the screen.

'It looks like Abel is going to be representing Hambleton, doesn't it?' she said. 'What is the count so far?'

'What?' he looked up.

'I thought you were catching up on the latest results,' she said. 'You've been miles away since our conversation with Isaac this morning. You're not letting the ideas of a Non-Lab bother you, are you?'

He frowned. 'No, not really...'

'I think coming here might not have been the best decision for you, Bruno.' Celeste sat opposite him and muted the television. 'I know it can look like the Compound Labs have discovered a wonderful life living happily along with their Non-Lab neighbours, but we are aiming for so much more than that! Don't forget that.' She stood up. 'I think once we get back to New York it would be better if you don't see Ness any more. We'll get someone else to keep an eye on her. Someone less involved.'

Shortly afterwards they joined the others in the hall. There was a great feeling of excitement as the number of votes in favour of Abel mounted, leaving no doubt that he had been chosen to stand for Hambleton.

Zig stood with Celeste and Bruno in the crowded room in front of the large screen. 'This is so exciting! Abel and Ness have just arrived back at the house and are coming over for the final count!'

As she spoke a cheer went up as Abel, Ruby, and Ness entered the hall. They all looked exhausted but elated. There was a flash of cameras and several reporters pushed microphones in front of them shouting out questions. Suddenly a voice called for quiet. All eyes were on the screen as the final results were read out, giving a clear majority to Abel. An even louder cheer went up and cameras flashed again as Ruby and Abel hugged each other then turned to shake hands with some of the Lab and Non-Lab supporters standing nearby.

Ness pushed her way through the crowds to Bruno and Celeste, her eyes shining. 'He's done it! The first Lab MP! My Dad!'

'Yes. Congratulations to Abel. It's good news for Labs all over the world,' Celeste smiled.

It was well after midnight when the people in the hall started to show signs of leaving. They had listened to speeches from winners and losers, words from the Prime Minister as well as comments from politically minded people, both Lab and Non-Lab from around the world.

Celia and Vince stopped to speak to Bruno and Celeste as they were leaving.

'I'm so glad you two were here to witness this!' Celia said to them.

'Yes, history in the making!' Isaac nodded. 'And it's actually a big story about the Labs that I am allowed to print!' He waved at a photographer across the hall and went to join him.

'There's going to be a big celebration along the South Bank tomorrow - I mean, later today!' Ness laughed, looking at her watch. 'Shall we go? You can see a bit more of London.'

'An excellent idea, Ness!' Celia agreed. 'Let's relax and enjoy ourselves without thinking of politics all the time!'

Ness chattered away as Bruno walked her home.

'Oh, God, just listen to me jabbering on! I'm on such a high, I don't know how I can sleep!' she burbled.

'Ness...' Bruno took her hand as they reached the door.

'Yes, Bruno?' she smiled.

He shrugged. 'You'll need some sleep if you're going to show us London tomorrow.'

'You're right! I'm really looking forward to spending the next few days with you. And Celeste.' She leaned forward and kissed his cheek before slipping in the front door.

'Oh, this is so spicy!' Ness panted, fanning her mouth.

'It certainly is authentic Indian street food!' Celia laughed turning to Bruno and Celeste. 'Are you two OK?'

'We're fine.' Celeste grinned. 'Bruno and Jude quite often cook up a spicy curry for us all!'

Bruno nodded and said, 'You'll have to come around for one of our special evenings, back in New York, Ness. And you, too, Celia, when you come over.'

'Yes, I want to come over soon to meet your sister and brothers.' Celia's expression grew serious. 'And we have to decide when we're going to tell the others here, too.'

'How do you think they will react? We are sort of rivals, aren't we?' Bruno looked worried.

The tension of the moment was suddenly shattered by the sound of a steel band.

'Come on! We can worry that later! Let's go and see what's happening!' Ness grabbed Bruno's hand and pulled him towards the music as the others followed them.

They pushed their way into a crowd that had gathered before a group of seven young people dressed in brightly coloured outfits. Three of them beat out a lively tune on steel drums while the other four performed a spectacular street dance routine of flips and turns. The crowd gasped as several times the smallest of the group was flung high into the air.

'My God,' Celia cried. 'That must be dangerous!'

'Well they haven't dropped her yet!' Ness laughed, unperturbed.

The group ended up scrambling on top of each other with the smallest member in the highest position. Suddenly she somersaulted even higher and flew through the air, landing at Bruno's feet. He was speechless as she rose up smiling at the crowd and bowed gracefully. The drummers played on as the rest of the group circulated amongst the crowd, holding out embroidered bags to collect their donations.

Celeste moved away, a look of annoyance on her face. 'They aren't much more than beggars, are they?'

Celia laughed. 'They're not beggars; they're entertainers! Look at how happy they have made the crowd!'

Celeste shrugged as they started to walk away. 'Where are Bruno and Ness?'

Looking around she frowned again to see them both in deep conversation with two of the group and strode towards them.

'So, you're planning on travelling across Europe to Turkey? That sounds exciting!' Ness was saying.

'And can you really make enough to live on with your show?' Bruno sounded amazed.

'Well, we have done in the last five years,' the girl told them. 'Although two winters ago we did have a bit of a slow time. Still, we got through and we're still here!'

'Why don't you get a steady job and settle down?' Celeste looked incredulous. 'I can't imagine anything worse than living on the road, not knowing whether you'll make enough money to live on!'

A young man joined them. He put his arm around the girl and smiled. 'I can't imagine being stuck in a nine-to-five job every day for the rest of my life!'

His girlfriend beamed at him. 'Me too. But it's a free country! Everyone has to follow their own dream!'

She waved as they turned and walked away.

Bruno seemed lost in thought as they continued along the crowded pathway. The crowd stopped suddenly as loud music blared out from either side of them and twenty or more people ran forward, pulling off their everyday clothes to reveal identical silver spacesuits. They all began to dance in time with each other, much to the delight of the crowds.

'What…?' Celeste began.

'It's a flash mob! How amazing! I've always wanted to see one of these!' Ness laughed pulling out her phone to record it. 'Just wait till I show Ginny this!'

As suddenly as it had begun, the dancing and music stopped and the dancers disappeared into the crowds.

Celeste shook her head with a bemused look on her face. 'I just don't understand the point of all that!'

'There is no point, it's just for fun!' Ness smiled.

Celeste looked at Bruno who shrugged.

A short while later, Celia stepped up closer to Celeste as they wandered past a group of pavement artists who were creating chalk pictures on the ground. Bruno and Ness had struck up a conversation with a young man over one of his pictures depicting a strange dream-like scene.

'Some of these pictures are quite good, aren't they?' she said. The younger woman shrugged.

'OK, I suppose. I didn't realise that there were so many people without suitable employment on the streets of London.'

'Not everyone can be slotted neatly into levels in society,' Celia suggested gently.

'You're right, Celia,' Ness remarked as they joined them. 'These people add so much colour and interest to our lives but they don't fit in to what most people see as normal society. Everyone should be free to choose their own way of life if it is not harmful to others.'

Celia noticed a wistful look cross Bruno's face.

Both the young visitors were quiet on the way back to the Compound later that evening.

'Well, that was quite a day!' Celeste stifled a yawn as they reached Ness's family home. 'I think we'll have an early night tonight. What do you think, Bruno?'

He nodded silently and gave a smile to the other two as he turned to follow his sister.

'Bruno?' Celeste said as they sat in the lounge. 'I saw how you looked at Ness today. You know it's not going to work out. Our plans are the Radicals' plans...'

'But they're not *our* plans, are they, Celeste?' He waved his hand towards the window. 'Out there, there are so many people who don't fit into what the Radicals' vision of the future is. But they are free. They make free choices every day! When have we *ever* made a free choice?'

'We were created with a special role to play in the future of the planet, which is much more important than having the freedom to scrape a living as a travelling entertainer!' she retorted. 'Is that what you see yourself doing, Bruno?'

'Of course not!' he replied. 'But I want the freedom to make a choice about my own lifestyle. Doesn't that idea appeal to you? Making your own decisions?'

Celeste looked flustered. 'This trip wasn't a good idea. We need to get back to New York, back to the plans we have worked so hard for all our lives!'

'Maybe we were wrong,' her brother said quietly.

Celeste's voice rose. 'No, we were not wrong. It's just the excitement of the elections... meeting Celia... it's all just knocked you off course for a while. Once we get back to the others everything will be fine. We'll be back on track!'

'And what about Celia?' he asked. 'Is she going to be a part of our life now? And Isaac and Seth?'

She closed her eyes and rubbed her forehead. 'I don't know! I just don't know!'

Ness sat at the kitchen table as Ruby brewed a pot of tea and put a plate of biscuits in front of her.

'You know, Mum, I think that Bruno is having second thoughts about the Radicals. He really enjoyed himself today. He had so much to say to the street entertainers. It was like he was waking up to reality!'

'Don't get your hopes up too high, Ness. All of his life he has been conditioned and prepared for a future role with the Radicals. I think it will take more than a few days to convince him,' her mother replied. 'And it doesn't sound as if Celeste was really impressed.'

Zig walked in at that moment. 'I think Ness does have a point, Ruby. I also got the impression that Bruno is not as dedicated to the Radical way of thinking as his sister is. He agreed to let Dr Shultz do some research on his enhancements quite willingly.'

'That was because Dr Shultz helped him manage the enhancements. Ness told us how he had struggled up to now,' Ruby pointed out.

'And there's Ce…' Ness stopped herself at the last minute. The two older women looked at her and waited. 'I'm not supposed to tell anyone else this news. It has to come from them.' she faltered.

Ruby sat down opposite her and stroked her hand. 'It's Celia; she's their donor, isn't she?' Ness's eyes grew wide. 'It's OK, love. Abel guessed when he saw them together yesterday.'

'Wow! Celia's their donor? That makes Seth sort of their little brother!' Zig broke into a huge smile. 'Surely they can't see the Compound Labs as the enemy now!'

'If only it were that simple, Zig.' Ruby gave a wistful smile.

'Well, I'm not giving up on them!' Ness said determinedly. 'We've five days left! Let's see what we can do!'

'I'm with you!' Zig said. 'I think we should work on making them appreciate family life, make them feel part of our community, so they'll choose us!'

'Maybe Dad could speak to them,' Ness began.

'Yes. Abel will be with us tomorrow evening. Let's ask them to join us for dinner!' Ruby said. 'They'll get to meet Beth and Frank, too. The first Lab and Non-Lab couple to have children!'

'More people to convince them about how good life is here!' Ness added.

CHAPTER SIXTY-FOUR

'"From society's prisoner to society's leader!"' Isaac read from the paper the following evening. 'Your whole life in print, Abel, complete with pictures! Our team did a good job.'

'Not all the dailies were so supportive,' Abel replied. 'According to the *Star*, I am the thin edge of the wedge. An interview with Bob Furnace, head of Stand for England, really digs into my past! They've a picture of me with my hand bandaged after hitting John Baxman but they don't mention it was straight after he suggested turning off the power supply of the sleeping Labs in the Centre. They've reprinted part of my speech saying I hated Non-Labs, without pointing out in the next sentence I said that was in the past and I'd moved on since then.'

'Well, we weren't expecting everything to be plain sailing, were we?' Ruby patted his shoulder. 'But you do have the majority of the people in Hambleton behind you and it won't be long before you have followers in other areas once you make a start on your next plan.'

'What is your next move?' Bruno asked him.

'We're going to start by implementing one of your ideas from New York,' Abel said. 'We're setting up a centre run on the lines of your Rehab Unit to get some of the youngsters off the streets, cleaned up and into education or training before they get in trouble with the law. Our first one will be here in Hambleton in the old town hall building. It'll be run by Labs and Non-Labs and with Hybrid volunteers as mentors and tutors. And if it is a success, we'll be liaising with government officials in London to set up similar ones in the city.'

'That's a great idea, isn't it, Celeste?' Bruno smiled.

She nodded. 'It certainly is.'

'Perhaps you could take a look through our plans so far. We'd appreciate your input.' Abel smiled. 'I'm sure Celia would be happy to take you up to the office to see them.'

'Did I hear my name?' Celia asked as she arrived with Seth running behind her. She listened and nodded as Abel repeated his ideas. 'We could go tomorrow morning,' she said.

Seth smiled as he caught Bruno's eye.

'Hey there, little guy!' he said.

'You're from America, aren't you?' Seth said. 'My mum told me. But I would have known from the way you speak, anyway.'

'So you recognise the American accent?' Celeste asked. 'Have you ever been there?'

'No, but there are lots of films with American actors, even the kids' ones.' He nodded. 'They have big cars in America, don't they? I like cars, look, these are my favourite ones.' He pulled out two toy cars from his pockets and demonstrated how well they ran.

Celia caught Abel's eye as he looked across at the three of them and gave a brief smile. Ruby had told her and Isaac that he had guessed at their relationship.

'So what are your plans for your children's future careers, Abel?' Celeste turned to him.

'Well, we'll wait and see what they choose to do and support them in every way we can,' he replied.

'And how will you guide them in their choices?'

'All the children here in Hambleton have the chance of a good education either at the Compound School or Hambleton Hillside. After that it's up to them to make their own decisions.'

'Surely you can't expect a young person to make such an important decision without guidance?' She looked shocked.

'What if they make the wrong choice?'

Abel nodded. 'You are right. Often a young person sets out on one career path and later decides that it's not for them and changes to another.'

'That's exactly what I did,' Isaac said. 'I started out studying engineering in Cardiff, then got involved with producing the uni newspaper and after a few months decided that journalism was the career for me!'

Ruby smiled. 'And your second choice was obviously the right one, as you have proved to us again and again, Isaac!'

'But if you had been given the right guidance at first it would have saved such a waste of time,' Celeste said.

Isaac smiled. 'If someone had told me what to do as a youngster, I would have stubbornly decided to do the opposite! I had to be free to find the right choice for myself!'

Celeste looked unconvinced. 'Everyone needs to be prepared for their role in the future if they are to be worthwhile members of society. This needs to start at a young age.'

'I think most people are capable of making their own decisions and their own mistakes!' Beth said.

'I can see what Celeste means,' Frank said. 'I wish I had more guidance when I was at school. I wasted quite a few years of my life.'

'Yes, you made mistakes and wrong choices earlier, but you learnt from them and turned your life around by yourself,' Beth said. 'Like Isaac, I don't think you would have welcomed interference when you were younger.'

Frank grinned. 'Well, maybe not.'

'Sometimes pushing young people to do one thing does have the opposite effect,' Abel turned to the two youngsters. 'Haven't you ever felt you wanted to rebel?'

Celeste looked amazed. 'Of course not! We have an important role to play!'

'And you, Bruno?' Abel asked.

Bruno frowned and looked down at his hands. 'I know the kind of society we are aiming for and I know what part I am to play in it.'

'But what are your opinions on the role you have been allocated? Your *own* opinions.' Abel continued.

'We know our place in the society we are aiming to build. We know what we have to do to achieve our ultimate dream.' Two red spots appeared on Celeste's face. 'Look around at the world you are happy to live in, badly run by generation after generation of Non-Labs! We are not going to settle for anything less than a society where everyone is happy and content to play their part in maintaining a happy, peaceful life.'

'We are not going to sit back and accept the shortcomings of this way of life,' Abel said. 'But we are not going to change things by taking away the freedom of the individual. We can all, Labs and Non-Labs, work together to bring this about. But it won't happen overnight.'

Celeste shook back her hair. 'It won't happen at all your way! Bruno and I know what we are doing!'

Ness looked at Bruno who seemed increasingly unhappy. She smiled and squeezed his arm. 'Well, enough of these serious discussions. This afternoon, you're in for a treat! Today one of the children from the Compound, Marlene, is five and she's having a party in the hall.'

Ruby looked concerned. 'Henry and Cilla have arranged a firework display, haven't they?'

'Yes, but don't worry. Amanda has arranged for a group of the older students to supervise this time!' Ness smiled.

'Fireworks! Much more fun than a cake with candles!' Henry told them outside the hall later that afternoon.

'And fireworks are such great fun to make!' Cilla giggled.

'Adam let them prepare them at his house,' Amanda confided. 'They do most of their experimenting over there these days.'

285

'Really?' Ness said.

'Mmm. Well, as Adam pointed out, if we let them continue with their investigations at the school, we would probably fail a government inspection, so he offered to supervise the more *volatile* ones at his place.'

Celeste sank down on her bed later that evening. 'I didn't know little children could be so exhausting!'

'Or that they could be so much fun!' Bruno smiled. He looked at her. 'I don't remember having fun when we were growing up.'

'We were awakened at fourteen, remember,' she pointed out.

'Some of those kids were in their teens at least. They were enjoying themselves.' He raised his eyebrows. 'And the things those kids are allowed to get up to! Making fireworks? I certainly don't remember anything like that!'

'Who knows how they'll turn out! Probably arsonists!' Celeste said.

'No, the fireworks were just for fun. Henry and Cilla are the inventors of a fireproof material. Rafael brought a sample to New York,' her brother told her.

'Oh, *that's* Henry? I thought he'd be much older,' she replied. She stretched again. 'We'd better get some sleep. I want to talk to Leonard tomorrow about plans for a new estate similar to Hambleton set up by a group of Compound Labs in France, just outside Paris. The Radicals have infiltrated the team and I'm to be given details to take back to New York. It'll be good to get to talk sense with some Radical supporters after these last few days.'

'But we've arranged to go and watch Leon and Johnny play their friendly soccer match tomorrow,' Bruno said. 'Zac and the other kids are really excited about it!'

'I know. I'll say I have a headache at the last minute and you can go without me. I'm meeting Leonard shortly after you leave,' Celeste told him.

'You don't need me with you?' A look of relief passed over his face as she shook her head.

'No, it'll be easier for me to slip away by myself.'

Celeste was seated by the window when Bruno returned late the next day.

'You missed such a great day, Celeste!' he said. 'Those boys sure know how to play soccer, I mean, football! If you'd have seen...'

She looked at him, her face hard. 'Bruno, I don't want to talk about some trivial sport! I've had a very interesting day with Leonard and some UK Radicals who are working on the French project. They're hoping they can really make an impact there, in fact, we may start the European campaign in France rather than the UK as there's less Compound Lab support there. I can't wait to tell them this news back in New York!'

He watched her as she walked to her bedroom. As she closed the door behind her, he pulled his coat on and slipped out quietly.

A few minutes later he stood in front of Isaac's and Celia's home. He waited a moment, then raised his hand and rang the bell.

'Bruno, come in!' she smiled.

'I hope I'm not disturbing you?'

'Not at all. It's lovely to see you. How is Celeste? I hope her headache is better?' she said, leading him into the lounge. 'Isaac is just putting Seth to bed. He'll be down in a minute. Tea?'

He nodded and sat down. She noticed his hands were shaking as she passed him the cup.

'Are you OK?'

He sighed and put the cup down on the table beside him. 'I don't know. This is all so strange. I don't even know if I'm doing the right thing.'

Celia waited as he clasped and unclasped his hands.

'Being here, seeing how you all live, finding out about you... I always thought the Radical way of life was the only way... but now I don't know anymore.' He paused for a moment. 'I'm finding this hard because, like Isaac said, I've never really made a decision of my own before.'

'So you're having doubts about the Radical way of life?' Celia asked softly.

'Yes. I look at you all, even the children, you are free to decide what you want to do with your lives. I know it's not a perfect society, but you are free.' Bruno ran a hand over his hair. 'The more I think about it, the Radicals' vision of the future does mean taking away freedom. I've seen what is happening to the Non-Lab kids they pick up. They say it's all for the best. I can't go along with it anymore, but I can't leave my brothers and sisters, either. And I can't see a future without you in it. Or Ness.'

Celia sat down beside him and put her arm around his shoulders. 'This is a hard decision for you to make, Bruno.'

Isaac had come into the lounge. 'It *is* a hard choice. I expect both you and Celeste were hoping to convince Celia that the Radicals' way was the right one?'

Bruno smiled and nodded. 'Celeste still is.'

'And we've spent the last few days trying to convert you both to our way of thinking!' Isaac admitted.

'I don't know if you can persuade the others to leave the Radicals,' Bruno said. 'And I don't know if I can leave my brothers and sisters.'

'You know,' Celia said slowly. 'I think there is a possibility we could solve the problem.'

Both men looked at her expectantly.

'I can't say anything else at the moment,' she said. 'I need some time to think my idea through.' She sat down at the desk and opened her laptop.

'Celia will tell us what she has in mind as soon as she is

ready, Bruno,' Isaac said as he led him to the door. 'You'd better go and get some sleep now. Just let me tell you, when Celia has an idea, it's usually a pretty good one!'

Bruno headed back to his rooms with a lighter step.

'I've got it, Isaac!' Celia stood up, her eyes shining as he walked back into the lounge. 'We don't need to persuade them to *leave* the Radicals. We'll bring the whole Radical movement *down*!'

Isaac gave a low whistle. 'Quite an ambitious idea, Celia!'

'Ginny said that the Warner Company is the sole financial backer of the Radical group. So if we could bring it down, we've brought down the Radicals, too!'

Her partner frowned. 'But Warner has stakes in, I don't know, hundreds of companies.'

'Yes,' Celia nodded. 'We have the names of some of them, but we need to know the names of many more, especially the larger ones. And then we have to find a way to access their bank details.'

'That's quite a job!'

'It will be. I'll need help from Vince and Dette. And I can think of a few others who can work with me on this. And I'm going to need some good spies over in New York. It could be dangerous.'

'Are you going to let Bruno in on this?' Isaac asked.

She shook her head. 'Not just yet. It's not that I don't trust him, but he is very close to the others and I wouldn't like him to give anything away or put himself in danger.'

CHAPTER SIXTY-FIVE

Bruno shook Isaac's hand as they reached the departure gate at the airport at the end of their stay. 'Goodbye, Isaac. It's been a pleasure meeting you and all your family and friends.'

'We've enjoyed getting to know you!' he replied.

'I'm so much looking forward to meeting your brothers and sister!' Celia said as she pulled Bruno to her.

He hugged her back. 'Yeah, in just over a week! They'll have time to get used to the idea by then. It won't be such a shock as when we first met you!'

Celeste hugged Celia briefly, then quickly turned away. She remained silent as they boarded their flight and she settled down in her seat.

Ness peered out at the dwindling image of houses, rivers and roads below her as the plane took off.

'I can see why you miss your hometown,' Bruno said to her. 'Are you planning on returning once you've finished your MA?'

'Yes. I can't wait - only a few months to go,' she said. 'But living in New York is a great experience. I'm glad I came.'

Bruno looked at her and squeezed her hand. 'I'm glad you did, too.'

A few hours later, as Ness dozed off in her seat, he turned to his sister. 'Don't you think that somehow the Compounds and Radicals could reach a kind of compromise?'

'I don't see how that could happen. We're so different.'

'But we have a lot in common, too,' Bruno insisted.

A fleeting look of sadness passed over her face as she

shook her head.

The taxi dropped Ness off at her rooms then continued to the siblings' apartment, where Max and Jane had joined Jude.

'Hey, great to see you back!' Jane hugged and kissed her brother and sister.

'Sounds like you had a good time,' Jude said.

'Did you find out anything interesting about the Compound Labs?' Max asked.

Bruno and Celeste exchanged glances. 'You'd all better sit down.'

Half an hour later the room was silent.

'You mean, one of the leading Compound Labs is our female donor?' Jude looked shocked.

'What is she like? Do you think she could really care about us?' Jane asked.

'When you get to meet her, you'll know she does. And you'll just love her! Hey and here's Seth, he's sort of our brother.' Bruno pulled out his phone and flicked through the pictures of the toddler.

'It's like having a real family,' Jane whispered.

Max balled his fists. 'We should confront Hugo! He always knew we were aware that he's our male donor! How could he keep this from us?'

'No! That could put Celia in danger. It's better if we keep this to ourselves for the moment,' Celeste said. 'We have to persuade her to join us! To join the Radicals.'

'Yes. She's obviously an intelligent person, Hugo always said she was carefully selected, so it shouldn't be too hard to do,' Jane agreed. 'And once we've convinced her and we're all working together then we can deal with Hugo.'

'She's a Compound Lab, one of the leaders, as you've already pointed out, Jane. I don't think she will be easily persuaded!' Bruno said softly. 'And if we can't, then what?'

'Well, we'll have to!' Jane insisted.

'When are we going to meet her?' Jude said.

'She's already booked a flight for herself and Isaac in ten days' time. They're going to stay in a hotel near the airport. We thought it best not to let anyone else from here know about it just yet. They weren't too keen on us finding out about our donors before now, were they?'

Meanwhile, in another part of the city, Ginny was listening in amazement as Ness recounted how Celeste and Celia had recognised each other. She also told her about Abel's theory on the spliced DNA used as donors for the five.

'So they met their female donor, discovered they had another brother, and witnessed the election of the first Lab MP in the UK. What a trip!' she exclaimed.

'And discovered their female donor is a leading figure in the Compound Labs, the Radicals' number one enemy!' Ness added.

'But now they all know about her and know they are family, maybe they can be persuaded to leave the Radicals,' Ginny said thoughtfully.

'That's what we were all hoping for, too, Ginny,' her friend said. 'We did our best to convince them in England.'

'We'll have to work on it here, too!' Ginny said.

CHAPTER SIXTY-SIX

The following morning Bruno followed Celeste into the meeting room where the others were already waiting.

'Bruno, Celeste! It's good to have you back!' Claude said smiling as they sat down. We've been hearing all about Abel's election. He has certainly caused a stir!' Claude read out the lead article of the *New York Times*: '"*New Lab MP not resting on his laurels: already Abel has made a big impact on his hometown Hambleton, promoting harmony between Labs and Non-Labs, and has ambitious plans to roll out some of the successful schemes in other towns and cities across the UK.*" He seems to be building up his Non-Lab supporters. What did you make of him?'

'He is certainly a character to be reckoned with,' Celeste said. 'He presents his views well and obviously has a sincere belief that Labs and Non-Labs can live as equals.'

Bruno nodded in agreement. 'And he is also a strong believer in freedom for the individual.'

'Did he give you a chance to explain how we see the world?' Shana asked.

'Yes, he listened to us; they all did, Celia and Isaac, too,' Celeste said, noticing how Hugo looked up at the mention of Celia's name. 'But they weren't convinced. As Bruno said, they are great believers in free choice!'

'So you met Celia and Isaac?' Hugo said, watching their faces.

'Yes. And Ruby, Dette, the two footballers and their families!' Bruno said quickly. 'And quite a few others. And they are all firm supporters of Abel.'

'Luckily, not all Labs are firm supporters of the Compound Labs' way of thinking. We have a good number of Radical followers over there,' Adam said.

'Yes, we met with some of them. Leonard introduced me to some French Radicals who have managed to infiltrate a Compound Lab team setting up a community just outside Paris. Like Abel, they are working with the local Non-Labs to build closer relationships. I have the details here on my tablet. If we could get our members in at the planning stage of a community, we could really make an impact!'

For the next hour they discussed the influence of the Compound Labs in Europe and how they could use this to their advantage. Bruno found his mind wandering. Could Celia really have found a way to stop the Radicals spreading their ideas?

CHAPTER SIXTY-SEVEN

Bruno felt his heart beat quicker as he watched the arrivals board indicate that the plane had landed. Glancing around at the others, he could see the same excitement and apprehension written on their faces, too. Jane gripped his hand tightly as the first few people started to come through the doorway.

'Is that her?' she whispered as a woman in her thirties appeared. The woman smiled and stepped forward as an older woman waved to her.

'You'll know her straight away, believe me,' Celeste said, moving closer to her sister.

Finally, Celia and Isaac appeared behind a group of Japanese tourists who were heading for a young woman holding a placard aloft. Bruno watched as Celia scanned the crowd until her eyes fell on them. She stood gazing at them silently until Isaac took her elbow and guided her towards them.

'Well,' she said as she reached them. 'You must be Jane.' She took both of the girl's hands in her own.

Jane whispered, breathing in the scent of the older woman. 'Celeste said we would know you straight away! It's true, everything about you is so familiar!'

'I feel it, too,' Celia agreed. She turned to the young men standing beside her holding out her hand. 'And you're Max and you must be Jude!' They both nodded silently.

Bruno turned to Isaac. 'Let's help you with your cases. Our car is over here.'

A short while later they were shown into a suite in a nearby hotel. As the bellboy closed the door behind him, Celia looked around at the youngsters and sighed. 'So, we're all family, really, aren't we?'

Over the next few hours there were many questions and answers and stories recounted. Celia watched the videos of the youngsters at school and university and peered closely at images of themselves at an earlier age and at those of their foster parents. Isaac proudly showed them pictures of Seth, their brother over in the UK. Celia told them of her life with the Compound Labs and how she had become unwittingly involved in their creation.

'So, you didn't even know about us,' Jane said in a small voice. 'And we didn't know about you.'

'Well, we can change all that now, can't we?' Bruno said.

'There is the small problem of you being a Compound Lab, and we... well, we're on the other side!' Jude pointed out.

'Bruno and Celeste saw what life is like for the Compound Labs. This is a chance for us to show you the Radicals' vision of the future!' Jane said eagerly. 'Who knows, perhaps we can persuade you to join us!'

'Now, wait a -' Isaac began, but Celia put a hand on his arm.

'No, let's give them a chance to see if they can convince us, Isaac!'

'It might end up the other way round,' Isaac countered. 'We get *you* to see things from *our* point of view!'

As it grew dark Bruno looked at his watch and said they must leave. 'We don't want to raise any suspicions, do we?'

Celia stood up and hugged each one of them. 'Could we meet for lunch tomorrow?'

Celeste frowned. 'We have lectures in the morning and then a meeting with Claude tomorrow. Max and Jane have training all evening.'

'But we could get away for a half an hour at about five o'clock,' Jane said. 'We must make the most of the time you are here.'

'We're here until Wednesday,' Isaac said. 'So we have a few days to get to see you all, even if not all of you at the same time.'

'You are right, Bruno. She is wonderful. Even Isaac, he's OK for a Non-Lab,' Jude said as they drove back to their apartments.

'We're going to have to really work hard to convince Celia to join us!' Max said.

'She's sort of our mother. She has to join us,' Jane said quietly. 'Oh, what if we can't persuade her? We've only just found her, we can't lose her again!'

Bruno squeezed her hand. 'We won't lose her.'

Mixed emotions ran through Celeste's head.

CHAPTER SIXTY-EIGHT

Ness and Ginny stepped out of the taxi in front of the hotel the following morning.

'Celia Craig, please,' Ginny said at the reception. 'She's expecting us.'

The receptionist spoke into the phone and nodded. 'Go right up, Room 612.'

Isaac was waiting for them as the lift door opened. 'Come in. Room service has just delivered breakfast.'

They chatted about the surprising events of the past few weeks.

'So you finally found out why you were attacked all those years ago,' Ginny said. 'How do you feel about Bruno and the others?'

'They feel like my family,' Celia said simply.

'If only they weren't a big part of the Radical group,' Ness sighed.

Isaac raised an eyebrow. 'This is to go no further, but Celia has plans for the Radicals...'

Both girls looked at her. She nodded.

'The simplified version is to bring them down, ruin them financially.'

'Phew! That's certainly an ambitious plan!' Ness said.

'And what can *we* do?' Ginny leaned forward.

'*You* don't need to do anything, Ginny.' Celia told her firmly. 'Reuben is going to get one of his team to implant a password on one of the computers in their admin offices to give me remote access. He has someone there as a maintenance worker. Then our team will do the rest!'

Ness's eyes shone. 'If there wasn't a Radical movement, maybe Bruno and his brothers and sisters could be persuaded to join us!'

'I have been talking to some of the psychologists at the Compound about re-educating the five of them,' Celia said.

'It won't be easy. They have been created and programmed to oppose the Compound Labs' way of thinking,' Isaac pointed out.

'But there's hope!' Ness smiled.

The talk continued to their plans for the week. Ginny half-listened, her mind going over Celia's plan. The sooner it went ahead, the sooner she could get out of the soul-destroying atmosphere in the Radical laboratory. She put her coffee cup down on the table, knocking Celia's handbag off as she did so. Leaning forward, she picked the items that had fallen out. One of them was Reuben's business card. On the back was a code. Her breath quickened. She slipped the card into her pocket and headed for the bathroom.

This must be the code for the computers! Perhaps she could find a way to input it herself she thought. Scribbling it down onto a piece of paper she pushed it down into her pocket.

Rejoining the others, she was glad to see Ness ready to leave. As she picked up her jacket, she slipped Reuben's card under Celia's bag.

'Hey, what are you doing over here?' Rafael asked as Ginny stepped into the hallway of the Radical building the next morning. He fell in step beside her as she made her way to the lift.

'I'm picking up an order on my way to the laboratory,' she told him. 'Just tea and coffee supplies. They don't let any outsiders into the laboratory these days.'

'Are you meeting up with Ness this evening?' he asked. 'Perhaps I could join you?'

Ginny wasn't listening to him. She was fingering the piece of paper in her pocket. She reminded herself she would only use it in an emergency. She wanted to see if she could spot Reuben's handyman and find out if he'd succeeded in his mission yet.

'Ginny?' Rafael repeated.

'Oh, sorry, Rafael,' she said. 'I was miles away.'

'So I'll see you this evening?'

'Yes, sure!' she fixed a smile on her face. 'See you back at the hotel.'

Rafael smiled as she followed him out at the fifth floor. 'I thought you were heading for supplies? That's the sixth floor.'

'Oh, I need the exercise!' she joked. 'I'll take the stairs the rest of the way.'

She gave him a brief wave as she continued up the stairs. Her friendship with Rafael would be coming to an end soon, and it upset her more than she would have imagined a few months ago.

Rafael listened as Ginny's footsteps rang out on the concrete stairwell, then frowned as she continued on to the seventh floor. Keeping near the wall, he quietly followed her. She had stopped by the doorway and was peering through the glass. A moment later she stepped out of sight as a maintenance man appeared with a young woman.

'The lower stairwell is dangerous with only one working bulb. The cleaning crew have refused to go down there now,' she was saying as she led the man down the stairs. 'You have to fix that before you see to the window in Accounts. They don't really need to open it with the air conditioning so that can be done any time. We've plenty of more urgent jobs!'

Ginny saw the look of frustration on his face as they went past. It looked as if Reuben's man had been foiled in his attempts to key in the code. Rafael watched as she spoke into her mobile. The call ended and once again she peered through the glass pane, ducking back out of sight for a moment then finally slipping into the corridor. He sprinted up the stairs and caught a glimpse of her disappearing into the first office. Hoping that no-one would stop him he strode confidently towards the door. Ginny was leaning over a computer, tapping her fingers impatiently as she looked through different icons.

'Come on! Come on!' she whispered.

'Ginny?' he said in surprise. 'What are you doing?'

She jumped up screwing up the piece of paper in her hand. 'Rafael, I...'

'What are you *doing*?' he repeated.

Ginny's eyes grew wider as a tall figure appeared in the doorway.

'I think it's quite obvious what the young lady is up to,' Robert said. 'I think you'd better come with me, miss.'

'Wait a minute!' Rafael stepped forward as the guard grabbed Ginny's arm. 'I'm sure there's a reasonable explanation. Ginny?'

A second figure appeared in the doorway. 'Someone called to say I was wanted in reception straight away but reception didn't know anything about it.' He glared at Ginny. 'It was a female voice!'

'I think the young lady can explain herself to the proper authorities,' Robert said. He pushed Rafael aside and led the trembling girl behind him. She looked back at him with tears in her eyes as she left. 'I'm so sorry, Rafael.'

CHAPTER SIXTY-NINE

All eyes looked up as Claude entered the room and seated himself at the top of the table.

He cleared his throat. 'You all know why we're here. Robert caught Ginny attempting to steal or sabotage data from one of the computers in the Accounts department.'

'So it wasn't Ness at all,' Bruno said. 'Ginny was the spy in the camp.'

Claude looked at Robert. 'Where is she now?'

'Isolated in a secure position, sir,' came the quiet response.

'Where exactly?' Claude continued.

'I'd prefer to inform you privately,' he continued. 'With all respect, we did not suspect Ginny and who knows who else...'

'Of course,' he replied. 'Our IT security team is checking out all computers in all departments and so far have assured us that nothing has been removed or altered. They have now set up a safety scheme to guard against any further attacks in any department. I'm glad you were so vigilant, Robert.'

Robert gave a slight nod.

'What will happen to her now?' Adam asked in a low voice. Rafael trembled as he looked down at the pencil he held tightly in his hands.

'I can continue to have her held in isolation. Or she can be eliminated,' Robert continued in an even tone.

There was a sharp sound as the pencil in Rafael's hands snapped. 'No!' he cried.

'There must be some other way of dealing with her,' Jane said. 'I mean, anything she did know she has already passed on to the Compound Labs anyway. And now she is no threat to us.'

'And how would the Compound Labs react if anything happened to her? The last thing we want is the place swarming with police!' Rafael ventured.

Several others nodded in agreement. Adam remained still and pale with his eyes fixed on Claude's face.

'We need to know just how much information she has passed on and if there are any other Compound spies amongst us,' Willis said. 'I suggest we question her as soon as possible!'

Robert spoke again, 'If we keep her isolated and under close observation for a few days, it will unnerve her and she should be more willing to talk.'

Claude agreed. 'Continue to hold her in isolation for the weekend.'

Robert nodded. 'I've used her phone to text her Compound contact to say that she'll be away for the weekend. That gives us time to decide on our next move.'

'Good.' Claude stood up, looking at his watch. 'I'd like the main committee to stay here but all research and admin offices will be closed to everyone else for the moment. Set up a security system, please, Robert.'

'It's been attended to, sir,' he replied.

An hour later Robert entered the Warner Enterprise building. 'All OK here?' he asked a security guard who nodded. 'Quiet as a grave!'

Robert walked along the corridor until he reached the room where Ginny had been discovered. He unlocked the door and stepped inside. 'She came up here via the stairs, didn't she? Have you checked them out?'

'Yes. All stair doors are locked now and the outside emergency exit.'

'When were they last checked?' Robert asked.

'Well, we just checked them the once, and locked

everything up securely. I didn't think we'd need to...' the guard stammered.

'It's because people didn't *think* that she got in here in the first place,' Robert said in an even tone, his face a cold mask. 'I suggest you check everything again now and put it on your nightly schedule.'

'Yes, sir. Right away! I'll do that right away, sir!' The young man almost ran from the room.

Robert waited until he heard the stairwell door being unlocked before he walked up to the computer furthest from the door, turned it on and waited for the screen to spring to life. He opened an app and tapped in a short code. Pulling out a mobile phone, he keyed in a message and pressed send. A second later he received a reply. Smiling, he switched the screen light and the overhead lights off, leaving the machine humming quietly in the darkness. He heard the voice of the young guard talking to a colleague as they both appeared through the doorway.

'Everything is in order, sir. And we'll be checking on all exits and entrances all night, don't you worry. Everything is under control.'

Robert smiled and nodded. 'Yes, everything is under control.'

He had left the building and was heading for the metro when he heard a shout. He turned to see Rafael running towards him.

'Robert! Wait!' Rafael stopped beside him. His eyes looked wild. 'Where is she? What have you done with her?'

'She's safe.' Robert carried on walking.

Rafael grabbed his arm. 'I must see her!' He winced as Robert peeled his fingers off his arm and pushed him away. Nursing his hand he hurried after him again. 'Please! I must see her!'

Robert shook his head. 'It's impossible!'

Rafael stepped in front of him putting his hand against his

chest. 'Let me talk to her for one minute; that's all I ask.'

The young man looked at him for several seconds. 'You don't know what you're letting yourself in for.'

Rafael shook his head. 'I don't care; I've got to see her.'

'Come with me.'

They walked in silence for twenty minutes until they reached a block of apartments. Robert pressed a card against the outer door and they took the lift up to the seventh floor. He called out as he opened the door of one of the apartments.

'You have a visitor.'

Ginny stepped from the lounge into the hallway and stopped suddenly on seeing Rafael in front of her. He rushed forward and pulled her into his arms. 'You're all right, Ginny! Oh, you're all right! I've been out of my mind with worry!'

She hugged him tightly. 'I thought you'd never want to talk to me again, Rafael!'

He held her away from him. 'They all thought it was Ness, you know, the Compound spy; but I knew you were up to something. I didn't want to think it could be you! Then when Robert took you away, I wished I'd done something! I knew I couldn't stay with the Radicals if they had done anything to you.' He paused. 'So have you just been using me all this time, Ginny?'

She shook her head. 'No, Rafael. I was beginning to think of you as more than just a friend, but if we're on different sides, is there any hope for us?'

'Perhaps you won't have to worry about different sides soon,' Robert suggested.

Rafael looked at him. 'How long have you been working with the Compound Labs?'

'Since I had news of my sister. But we decided to keep it quiet; the fewer people who knew, the better.' The intercom rang. Robert picked up the handset and listened. 'Come up,' he said.

A few minutes later he opened the door and Isaac stepped

inside. He raised his eyebrows as he caught sight of Rafael and gave Robert a questioning look.

'He wanted to see her. I'll keep him here now until it's out in the open,' he answered.

Isaac strode into the lounge. 'What were you thinking of, Ginny?'

Robert stepped forward and signalled for Rafael to follow him.

'What were you thinking of, Ginny?' Isaac repeated again after they had left. 'What if it hadn't been Robert who found you?'

'Well, Reuben's man was finding it difficult to get into the accounts department and the opportunity just presented itself... so I took it!' she pleaded.

'Abel is furious – I don't know if he's angrier with us for being careless with the code so you could find it, or with you for trying to use it!' he said.

'And Mum?' Ginny said in a small voice.

'Well, luckily for you, she's away at an archaeological conference with Dylan in Egypt at the moment, so we haven't been able to speak to her yet.'

'Phew! That's a relief!' Ginny let out a breath. 'Robert said that now he's set up remote access for Celia over here, she's able to go ahead with the plan tonight. What exactly is she going to do?'

'I can tell you the details now. By Monday morning it will have hit the headlines anyway.' He sat down on a low sofa and signalled for her to sit down, too. 'As you know, the Radicals are entirely financed by Warner Enterprises.'

'Yes,' Ginny nodded. 'Warner Enterprises is in the sole hands of Claude, Arnold Warner's Lab. Warner left strict instructions about this in his will.'

Isaac smiled. 'Exactly! Arnold Warner made the Radicals rely on Claude financially to make sure he would be the undisputed leader of the new society he envisaged. However, that has been his undoing. That's what is going to lead to the imminent fall of the Radicals!'

'How will Celia do that?' Ginny asked.

'Warner Enterprises has controlling shares in many other companies. Celia, with help from Vince and Dette and a sizeable team, has managed to trace a large number of these companies and now she has remote access to enough of their major accounts. Tonight she is going to hack into their accounts, divert their funds and bankrupt them.' He glanced at his watch. 'It's a synchronised operation. Celia, Vince, Dette and several others will be keying in the same data in each of these companies at exactly the same time so all companies will go under at exactly twenty-three hundred hours GMT tonight.'

'So tomorrow, all hell will be let loose!' Ginny's eyes widened.

'The worst will come to light on Monday morning when the stock exchanges around the world start their business week,' Isaac said.

'Won't the police be able to trace the money?' Ginny asked.

Isaac shook his head. 'Celia has experience covering her tracks from the early days when she obtained funds from the Centre to establish the Labs in society. She has arranged an even more complicated scheme to ensure the money diverted from Warner Enterprises and associated companies will not be traceable.'

'That gives Reuben and his team the next two days to organise a swoop on Monday morning. The Warner Enterprise building, the Rehab Unit, the laboratory and any other building used by the Radicals are already under surveillance,' Robert said as he rejoined them. 'I am involved in the security manoeuvres.'

Isaac stood up and pulled a small black mobile from his pocket. 'You'd better ring Ness on this. I told her you were safe, but she made me promise I'd let you speak to her. It's best if we keep the details to ourselves at the moment. We can't risk jeopardising anything.'

Ginny nodded and eagerly took the phone from his hand.

Much later Robert locked the door after Isaac had left for his hotel. He walked with Ginny towards the bedrooms.

'If he gets any ideas about breaking out of here, he'll have me to deal with!' he whispered as he pushed a door open. Rafael was lying spread out on the bed, still fully clothed, breathing deeply.

Ginny smiled. 'It doesn't look as if he's thinking of going anywhere.'

CHAPTER SEVENTY

Fall of a Giant!

Stock exchanges around the world reeling with sudden fall of one of the USA's most prominent businesses.

Warner Enterprises has been declared bankrupt this morning. Along with the main company, hundreds of other smaller companies have also been adversely affected by this news.

A Wake up Call for Warner!

The collapse of a World Giant – was it due to mismanagement or corruption?

We all need to see this as the writing on the wall. When a company becomes too big to manage how can everyone be accounted for?

Takir sat ashen-faced as he looked around the table at the other equally stunned expressions.

'How could this have happened?' he murmured again. 'How is it possible?'

Angus entered the room with a frown on his face. 'What's happening?' he asked.

Takir gestured towards the newspapers spread across the table.

'We heard something on the news. What's going on?' Shana said as she arrived with Willis a few minutes later.

Leela entered the room followed by two young nurses. 'We went to the laboratory this morning to find it locked up.

What's this all about?'

During the next half an hour more and more of the staff appeared, bewildered and looking for answers.

Finally Claude entered the room. 'Good morning – or maybe I should say, it's not actually a *good* morning,' he said with an ironic smile. Only the slight shake of his hands as he held up a sheaf of papers betrayed any nervousness he was feeling. He flicked through the papers he held. 'This is a list of the companies that have been declared bankrupt. That covers all of Warner Enterprises businesses and anything we've been involved in sponsoring. Warner's is completely, utterly broke. I only own the clothes I stand up in.' He gave a short laugh. 'In fact, I think I still owe money to my tailor!'

Murmurs spread around the room and then a young woman asked, 'What's going to happen to us?'

Adam looked around the room and headed for Jude as the others drew closer to Claude. He caught his arm and pulled him to one side.

'Memorise this number,' he said showing him a slip of paper then slipped it back into his pocket as Jude nodded. 'It's my number, make sure you don't use a phone they can trace to you.'

Jude looked bewildered. 'What's all this about?'

'You'll know soon enough! Call me in a day or two,' Adam said turning away and once more scanning the room. Catching sight of Hugo he beckoned him to follow him out of the room. 'We need to get out of here as quickly as possible. We don't have much time,' he said. He flipped open a tablet and started to type in data. 'They're going to search this place over the next few hours. Where do you keep your back-ups?' Hugo hesitated for a few seconds. 'Don't pretend you didn't make copies!'

'Data-Space,' Hugo replied.

Adam shook his head. 'It's not secure enough. You'll have to move it straight away.' He typed for a few more seconds

310

then passed the tablet to him 'Set up an account at this site, Chameleon, and transfer everything now. You can access it through my recommendation.' He frowned at Hugo's reluctance. 'If we're to save anything from this shambles, we've got to act quickly!'

Hugo took the tablet from his hands and began to type. After a few minutes he passed the tablet back to him. 'What are we going to do?'

'Can you arrange for the south door to be released for a short time, without it being flagged up on security?'

Hugo raised his eyebrows. 'I could probably manage it for twenty, possibly thirty seconds.'

'That should do it. I'll see you down by the door in five minutes. Take it easy, we don't want to raise any alarm.' He was once more tapping on his tablet before Hugo had left the room. A small voice made him look up and he stared impassively at his daughter.

'Dad?' Ginny's eyes were red and swollen. 'I'm so sorry! But I couldn't let…'

'Don't say anything!' He sighed and closed his eyes. 'I should have realised that you are too much like the Compound Labs to ever believe you would join us. But I so *wanted* to believe it!'

Ginny moved forward slowly and gave a sob as he hugged her to him. 'I'm sure that many of the Radicals will be joining the Compounds now, Dad. You can still…'

She faltered as he shook his head and kissed her forehead. 'Take care, my love.'

They both froze as Abel and Reuben entered the room and called for attention.

Adam frowned. 'Earlier than I thought.' He pushed his tablet into his pocket as a young man in uniform headed their way. 'Can I just have a moment to talk to my daughter, please?' he asked curtly. He waited until he was out of earshot then whispered, 'This is goodbye.'

'Where are you going?' she asked.

'It's better if you don't know, Ginny. Keep them occupied for a few minutes?' He squeezed her hand and then headed for the door.

'Where is your father, miss?' the young man had reappeared. Silently, with tears rolling down her face, Ginny gestured towards the crowded room in the opposite direction to where Adam had exited.

Hugo was nearing the south door when he heard a familiar voice. He turned to see Celia and Isaac.

'It was *me* who brought Warner Enterprises down. I just wanted you to know that, Hugo,' Celia said, an edge of steel in her voice. 'Finally *my* Labs are going to see reason. They're going to lead happy, fulfilling lives free of your influence.'

'Those five were created to be the most important leaders in the future and you destroyed everything! Can't you see what you have done?' Hugo spat out. 'If I had realised what limited vision you have, I would never have selected you!'

'You used me to create them to be your puppets! To run the world as you saw fit. They were as much Radical prisoners as the original Compound Labs in the Centre were! I hope there is enough of my blood in them to make them realise how warped the ideas of the Radicals are. I'm glad we have been able to rescue them and the others that you were ready to trample over – Lab and Non-Lab!' Celia glared at him. 'There's nothing in *you* to rescue!'

Hugo's eyes narrowed. 'I would rather be *dead* than shackled to your short-sighted *Compound* boundaries.'

Isaac stepped forward. 'I would love to oblige you there!' He swung his arm back and landed a punch squarely on Hugo's face. Hugo gave a cry of pain and clutched his bleeding nose.

'You'll pay for that, you Non-Lab lowlife!' he shouted, rushing towards Isaac and head-butting him to the floor. Adam arrived as Celia was trying to separate the two men and pulled

Hugo around to face him.

'Stop, Hugo!' He turned to Celia. 'I think you'd better leave, and take *him* with you!'

Isaac was breathing heavily. 'You haven't heard the last from us!'

Hugo sank back on to the floor wiping his nose as they listened to their footsteps receding along the corridor. Adam pulled him to his feet. 'Come on, we've no time to lose! I've a hire car waiting for us by the square.'

Back in the main hall, Willis was speaking. 'So we're all broke? Well, are we free to go now to collect our meagre belongings from the apartments that were once owned by Warner Enterprises?'

'I'm afraid not,' Reuben told him. 'We have several concerns about the work being done here by the Radicals and will be interviewing each of you before anyone is allowed to leave. You will be escorted to separate rooms until we can speak to each of you.'

There were several protests as they left the room. Finally, only Claude, Reuben, and Abel remained.

'We'd like to start with the work you have done at the Rehab Unit,' Reuben began as he gestured for Claude to take a seat.

'We're well-known for the help we have given many youngsters to turn their lives around. In fact, Abel has asked for help in setting up a similar scheme in the UK, haven't you?' Claude said.

'Yes, without the compulsory brainwashing and sterilisations,' Abel said dryly.

'Can any of this be proven?' Claude asked. 'You can interview as many of the youngsters as you want and I'm sure they won't have any complaints against us.'

'Ginny has let us have proof of the work done here,' Reuben said.

'Well, maybe *she* should be questioned if she was actively

involved in any underhand procedure that we were unaware of.' Claude held Reuben's gaze.

'I'm certain there will be others to support the information Ginny was passing on to us over the past year,' Abel said.

Claude gave a short laugh. 'I'm sure you have all the information you need about us. So what will the next step be?'

'The end of the Radicals,' Reuben said calmly.

The young man shook his head. 'No! You can't stop the Radicals. There are too many of us. We have accomplished so much!'

'Without financial backing, the Radicals can't continue,' Reuben pointed out.

'It's what I was created and designed for. To lead the Radicals. To be the one to bring about a new society, free from war, where everyone can be happy. To fulfil my father's wish.'

'Your own conditioning will be a point in your defence,' Reuben said sadly. 'And for the other youngsters brainwashed to fulfil a role they had no real choice in.'

'I think you will all need some kind of rehab yourselves, Claude,' Abel said gently.

314

CHAPTER SEVENTY-ONE

'What's going to happen to us?' Celeste asked.

Reuben looked around at the six people in front of him. 'All members of the Radical group are to be microtagged so we can monitor your movements and behaviour. You six people will all attend an initial two-month rehabilitation course, with the hope that you will begin to understand a more moderate view of society and how we can all live together as equals.'

'What if we don't all "see the light", as it were?' Claude asked.

Reuben shrugged. 'You people didn't choose to become Radicals, you were created and designed to think as you do, and until you have the opportunity to see a balanced argument you can't really form your own opinions. I am optimistic that you all will respond to the rehabilitation course. However you will have to liaise with your mentors over the next few months until we deem you fit to live independently in society.'

'Who are our mentors?' Jane asked.

Celia and Isaac came in and sat down opposite them. 'We are.'

'I don't think I can accept you as my mentor when you are responsible for the fall of the movement we have dedicated our lives to,' Claude said in a strangely level tone.

'Yes, it *was* me who brought Warner Enterprises down,' Celia said. 'Not to destroy you, but to free you from this evil organisation.'

'The Radical movement is not evil! Our vision is of a

society where everyone has a role at their suited level and everyone is happy in their role. This is the only way to bring about peace and to end war,' Claude insisted. Celeste, Max and Jude nodded their heads vigorously in agreement, while Bruno and Jane looked less enthusiastic.

Isaac shook his head slowly. 'No, Claude. It won't work. You've already seen how people had to be brainwashed or worse than that to make them fit their given roles!'

'Yes, sometimes the rulers must be harsh, but it is for the best of society as a whole,' Claude argued. 'Once they adapt to their roles, society can function smoothly.'

'He's right! Can't you see how the Non-Labs have spoiled and destroyed this world in all the generations they have been rulers?' Max added. 'It is not a coincidence we are here at this point. We have been designed to lead everyone to a new and better life!'

Celia shook her head. 'Things have changed now, Max. You must rethink your own role in a world where everyone is free to make their own decisions, including you. You can't force people to fit the role you want them to play!'

'You'll have to forget the ideals you have been indoctrinated with!' Isaac said. He turned to Jane. 'Given a free choice, Jane, what would you do with your life?'

Jane was taken aback. 'Well, that's not a question I can answer. I've never thought about it, my role was decided long ago.'

'And what about you, Jude? And you, Max?' Isaac continued. 'Celeste, Bruno, Claude?' He looked around the room. 'You all need time to come to terms with what has happened and to make your own decisions on your own futures.'

'There's a lot to think about. You will probably need weeks or even months to make your decisions,' Celia said. 'You will be supported financially for the next few months until you are able to earn a living for yourselves.' She stood up. 'Isaac and I are going to stay in New York for a while and we'll meet up with you each morning. If you wish to contact us at any other time, just pick up the phone. And remember, we're here as your friends, not your enemies.'

As they left the room, the others sat in silence.

At the end of the day some of the staff were allowed to leave while the more prominent members of the Radicals were given rooms to stay in overnight.

Abel, Reuben and two of his officers, Celia, and Isaac sat around a table. Ginny placed a tray of tea and sandwiches on the table and sat down with them.

'Well, we interviewed most of the staff, except for Adam and Hugo. We know they were here earlier, but there doesn't seem to be any sign of them now,' one of Reuben's officers said. 'I don't know how they slipped through our fingers. I've organised a widespread search for them.'

Abel glanced at Ginny but she kept her eyes on the cup in her hand.

At the same time, the two men were speeding along the Western Highway. Hugo looked back as New York disappeared behind them.

'How did you manage to arrange all this so quickly?' he asked his companion.

'Oh, my escape plan has been in place for years. After my first setback, I learnt to be prepared for the unexpected. I've a house in Washington no one knows about where we can lie low and decide on our next move. What are your ideas on the subject?' Adam glanced at Hugo.

'I don't know. I'm still so angry that we've lost so much! We had got so far, too!' the young man replied.

They travelled on in silence, reaching a sprawling house in a leafy Washington suburb late that night.

'You've a nice place here,' Hugo commented as he sat down on the sofa which, apart from a coffee table, was the only piece of furniture in the room. 'A bit sparse on furnishings, though!'

Adam sat down beside him. 'It's just a bolthole. We need to relocate as soon as possible.'

'Your daughter messed things up for us completely, didn't she?' Hugo's face was grim.

'She didn't do it all on her own! Anyway, maybe this is an opportunity for us to start afresh,' Adam said. 'And maybe we won't have to start completely from scratch. I didn't want to leave the youngsters behind. Not after all the work we have put into them.' He told him that he had told Jude to get in touch. 'Of course, we'll need to tread very carefully if they do want to join us. They could be setting us up for the Compound Labs.'

Hugo agreed eagerly. 'Certainly. But we don't want to turn them away if they are genuine, either, do we? They are valuable assets.'

318

CHAPTER SEVENTY-TWO

Two months later, Claude sat opposite Bruno and Celeste. Jude rose from a nearby chair as the doorbell sounded. He returned to the lounge followed by Jane and Max.

'So, what about the future?' Claude asked as he looked around at the solemn faces.

'The rehabilitation talks are pathetic! Those soft-talking Compound Labs aren't convincing me that they have it all sussed out!' Jude scoffed.

Jane creased her forehead. 'I don't think they are pretending to have it all sussed out, Jude. Sometimes their way of looking at things makes a lot more sense than the Radical way.'

'Just what they want you to think!' Jude retaliated.

Claude held out a placatory hand. 'What are your plans now, Jane?'

'Long-term, I don't really know. I keep expecting Willis or someone to tell me what I should be doing,' she gave a nervous giggle. 'For the moment, I'm going to carry on training for the Olympics as we had planned. After that…'

'Are you continuing with your Olympic training, Max?' Claude asked him.

'No! What's the point now?' he said angrily. 'I'm taking some time out to think about everything. After we graduate, Jude and I are planning to travel for about a year and see a bit more of the world.'

Jude nodded. 'Yes, it'll give us a chance to clear our heads, find a new goal.'

'That sounds like a good plan,' Claude agreed. 'Bruno?'

'I suppose this may make me sound like a traitor,' Bruno shuffled uneasily. 'But I think a lot of what the Compound Labs have to say makes sense. I'd like to work in a place similar to the Rehab Unit but without the conditioning that was carried out here. I've spoken to Abel about working in the unit they have set up in Hambleton over in the UK.'

Jude raised his eyebrows. 'But without the conditioning you wouldn't be guaranteed success, would you? So what would be the point in working to change people's lives when you would *fail* with some of those people?'

Bruno shrugged. 'I'll do my utmost to help them get on their feet, but I'll have to accept that, as they have free will, they could choose to accept or reject my offers of help.'

Jude rolled his eyes at the ceiling. 'Sounds pretty pointless to me!'

Celeste looked thoughtful. 'No, Jude, maybe Bruno is right. If you are dedicated you could enjoy persuading someone to freely choose the right path. And let's face it, we are especially equipped to be more sensitive to the feelings and reactions of others than any Non-Lab and many other Hybrids and Labs! With that and all our training, our persuasive powers are superior to just about everyone else's.'

'And what are you going to do now, Celeste?' Jane asked her.

Celeste leaned back, pulling her thick, curly hair to one side. She gave a wide smile. 'I am completely happy with the role chosen for me. I would have chosen it anyway. I'm going to go ahead and be a famous actor and perfect role model with everyone, Labs and Non-Labs, worshipping me!'

'Yes, you have been living your ideal life anyway, Celeste, adding to your fan club wherever you go,' Bruno smiled.

'And what about you, Claude?' Celeste looked at him. 'Are you ready to share your plans with everybody?'

For a moment Claude seemed to lose his usual air of self-assurance. 'I was invented to fulfil my father's role; now I've had to reinvent myself; a daunting prospect. So if I'm not going to fulfil my father's dreams, what are my own dreams of the future? The truth is, I don't know yet. In the meantime, I need to make a living, so I've signed a contract with Valenzo to star in his latest film with Celeste as the leading lady.'

Celeste smiled at them all. 'So we're both going to be film stars! We'll be the perfect couple, won't we, Claude? There'll be no stopping us!'

Claude sat up straighter, his usual air of confidence returning. Smoothing his hair back, he winked. 'Yes, we'll be the perfect couple, Celeste.'

'So we all have something positive to report to Celia and Isaac when we meet up with them tomorrow,' Bruno smiled. 'I'm feeling more optimistic about the future these days!'

Isaac smiled as the six entered the office at Reuben's headquarters the next morning.

'Come in and sit down. Celia will be joining us in a minute.'

In a room nearby, Celia watched the young people through a two-way mirror.

'I know it's necessary, but it feels dishonest, Anya,' she said to the girl sitting next to her.

Anya patted her hand. 'I understand how you feel. It is difficult. I felt I was betraying his confidence when I watched Robert here a few days ago; but Reuben and Abel are right, we must be absolutely sure that they are not still under the influence of the Radicals.' She smoothed out the pad on the table in front of her and gave her an encouraging smile. 'The results of last week's discussion were very positive, for most of them, anyway.'

Celia's brow creased. 'Yes, I wonder if Max and Jude are going to be less hostile today.' She took a deep breath and joined the others.

Anya peered closely at each of the youngsters as Celia

321

appeared and sat down with them. She watched each face very carefully for the next two hours as they talked about their plans for the future. She noticed their body language as she jotted down notes on her pad and sketched particular expressions.

Bruno sat forward in his chair, his expression open, a smile ready on his face. Jane seemed somewhat anxious and at times confused as if torn between two worlds. Celeste alone seemed completely relaxed and sure of herself when talking of her future plans, often patting Claude's hand and encouraging him as he spoke. Max and Jude still seemed very aggressive, although Jude did grudgingly agree with a few favourable comments that Celia made about the Compound Labs' beliefs. Anya added a few scribbled notes as the youngsters prepared to leave. Shortly after that she sat with Isaac and Celia to discuss the progress they felt they were making with them.

'Bruno is definitely a convert to the Compound Lab way of life,' she smiled as Celia nodded.

'Yes, he's already spoken to Abel about working in the Hambleton Rehab Unit. I think the fact that Ness also wants to work there as psychologist might have influenced his decision!'

'Jane is really undecided at the moment, isn't she?' Isaac said, looking at the sketch Anya had made of her. 'Once the Olympics are over I think she will need to be given a choice of roles to try out rather than being left to decide for herself.'

'Yes, I think you are right there, Isaac,' Celia agreed. 'She shows a very caring side to her nature. We could make a list of possible places where she could fit in, such as nursing or some kind of therapy…'

'And if it was linked to her love of sport, it could very well work,' Anya said.

Isaac rubbed his chin as he looked at the sketches and notes Anya had made of Jude and Max. 'These two are still pretty hostile to any criticism of the Radical movement, aren't they?

322

Abel has suggested that they may actually be reclassified, along with Takir, Willis and some of the others as still posing a serious threat. That would mean an upgrade to their tags and a much longer period of monitoring.'

Celia looked alarmed. 'I thought that Jude seemed a lot more open to discussion today. Anyway, it's early days yet! We've still a few weeks to work with them before we need to make any recommendations!'

'Yes, the final test will be the polygraph test they take in just over six weeks,' Anya said. 'Between then and now they'll be learning about the Compound Lab way of life in a much more practical setting.'

'And seeing why freedom of choice is so important,' Isaac added.

CHAPTER SEVENTY-THREE

'Did anyone think it strange that this is your second visit to Washington in a month?' Hugo asked the two young men as they sat in a restaurant in Washington.

'No, this time we're here to see an old friend of Isaac who has just returned from Paris after living there for most of his life. He's going to give us some tips on travelling in Europe and some contact numbers when we head off on our travels,' Jude told him.

'And no one has any suspicions?' Adam asked.

Max shook his head. 'No-one is really surprised that Jude and I have decided to have a gap year.'

'We do have one problem though,' Jude frowned. 'We'll be getting the microtags off next month – if we pass a polygraph test!'

Hugo looked thoughtful. 'So you'll need something to override your tags…'

There was silence for a few moments then Adam snapped his fingers. 'Not a block on the microtag! You need something to make your mind work in the way they want it to work!'

'Just as we conditioned those Non-Labs at the Radical rehab centre!' Understanding dawned on Hugo's face. 'We can condition your mind to give the sort of responses that Celia and Abel would approve of!'

'Don't worry,' Adam reassured them as Jude looked sceptical. 'We can counteract the effect afterwards, so it will only be a temporary state of mind! We could apply the conditioning the day before the polygraph test and counteract

324

it the day after. I assume you are having vaccinations to protect you from different illnesses before you set off, aren't you?'

Max nodded. 'Yes, we have quite a few!'

'Good,' he continued. 'We can set this up as an extra vaccination at Washington Medical Centre. That will make it even easier!'

'We'll have to make sure that you are conditioned to return for the second "vaccination" or we could lose you to the Compounds!' Hugo added.

CHAPTER SEVENTY-FOUR

'All of the thirty most prominent leaders of the Radicals are listed there, except for Hugo and Adam. We have no news of their whereabouts up to now,' Abel told the rest of the company seated around the table. 'As you can see, they are each to be placed in a different location with no communication between them. They will be treated much as we have suggested Non-Lab offenders could be treated. In the mornings, they will all work in a job suited to their skills that allows them to help rather than control the lives of others. In the afternoons, they will take part in a community-based activity.'

'How long will they be held?' Celia asked.

'As long as it takes for us to judge that they are no longer a threat to society,' he replied.

'What if they don't agree to these terms?' Keith said.

'They can choose the alternative – serve a sentence in a Lab institute structured along the lines of the usual type of Non-Lab prison until they are deemed no longer a threat to society,' Abel said.

'How will you be sure they are no longer a risk?' Zig shuddered. 'I'm sure they'll go along with all this to get their freedom. I don't trust any of them!'

'This group have been given a high-security microtag which will also act as an advanced form of polygraph testing so we can take readings on their true feelings at any time. Hence the indeterminate sentencing.'

'And are the UK and US police force aware of all this?'

Isaac raised an eyebrow.

Reuben and Abel exchanged glances. 'No. We don't feel it will be beneficial to share this knowledge, as it could cause widespread alarm,' Abel said.

'And although my organisation feels this is the best way to handle the situation, we don't think a similar Non-Lab organisation would take the same view,' Reuben added.

'What about the five youngsters? Six, counting Claude.' Celia frowned.

'We're looking at the feedback on their progress at the rehabilitation course,' Reuben said. 'If they can pass the polygraph test after they graduate, and we're hopeful that at least some of them will, we'll remove their microtags and let them get on with their own plans for the future. There are some concerns about Max and Jude, though. They may need further monitoring.'

Celia looked more anxious. 'But they have shown a much more positive attitude over the last few weeks, Reuben. They haven't responded as quickly as the others but I feel we are beginning to build up a closer relationship with them. They admit that they have found it difficult to reject the ideals of the Radicals, but they both feel they would benefit from a few months travelling and readjusting to this new way of life. Just like any other kids, sometimes a gap year could be the making of them! They just need to be given a chance!'

Isaac squeezed her hand as Reuben continued. 'I understand how you must be feeling, Celia, but it all depends on how they do in the polygraph test before we can make any decisions on their future.'

327

CHAPTER SEVENTY-FIVE

Celia smiled as she and Anya placed plates of food on an already laden table.

'I've never seen so much food!' Anya cried as her mother joined them with two more platters.

'Well, there's quite a gathering today. Robert and the other youngsters have hearty appetites!' Denise said. 'I'm so pleased that Robert turned down an offer of a job in New York and decided on working for Reuben in England instead.'

'Me, too,' Anya agreed. 'We'll be able to get together as a family again and this time without all the worries we had before, Mum! We have to thank Celia for sorting out the legalities for us.'

Denise smiled at Celia. 'We can never thank you enough!'

'I'm glad everything worked out OK,' she said.

Cam walked up and helped himself to a large slice of cake. 'This is really good,' he said as Brit joined them. 'Celia said you did most of the cooking.'

She rolled her eyes upwards. 'Don't speak with your mouth full! Your table manners still haven't improved, have they?'

He took a drink of water before he winked at her. 'No. I need a good woman to help me out! Know anyone? She'd have to be a good cook!'

She blushed and gave his arm a playful slap. 'Can't think of anyone willing to take you on!'

Celia walked outside. Ruby and Abel were seated with Ness on the veranda. Opposite them sat Zig and Keith. Zig watched their young son, Jethro, complete a chunky jigsaw on the floor with the help of Seth and some guidance from Celeste. Claude and Celeste were quickly becoming one of the most talked-about celebrity couples since they had signed contracts to star in the latest Valenzo film, due to be released in a few months' time.

Other changes had happened in the six months since the Radicals' rehabilitation. Bruno had moved to the UK and now both he and Ness were working at Hambleton Spring, the Rehab Unit established by Abel and a committee of Non-Labs shortly after his election.

Ginny had been surprised to receive a letter from her father through his solicitor in England. He had put the deeds of his house near Hambleton in her name. She now lived there with Rafael, who also worked there with several of the Compound School students during the day, mainly those involved in the more volatile science investigations. He had become firm friends with Henry and Cilla. Ginny herself had decided to return to Cambridge to study medicine with the aim of becoming a brain surgeon.

As well as training for the Olympics, Jane was studying to be a physiotherapist and now worked at a clinic for injured military personnel in Washington. She sat talking to Rafael and Henry with her Non-Lab partner, Connor, whom she'd met as a patient at the clinic. They were discussing the merits of his prosthetic limb.

'I think the design could be improved,' Henry said. 'You can't swim with it, can you?'

Connor shook his head. 'No, and that's one thing I do miss. I'm too lopsided with just one leg.'

'We could redesign the frame using a lighter metal,' Rafael suggested. 'And then we could cover it with the material from the wetsuit you designed, Henry. What do you think?'

Henry nodded. 'That could work, Rafael.'

'Oh, at the military hospital they've had me trial several different types "that could work" but I've never found anything I've been comfortable with,' Connor told them.

'Well, yes, but they were just Non-L...' Rafael began. Standing nearby, Ginny cleared her throat and gave him a warning look. 'Just not looking at things from the same angle as we do.' He gave her a sheepish grin as he finished his sentence.

'Come and take a look at the latest video from Max and Jude,' Celia told them as she opened a tablet on the coffee table in front of Celeste. 'Jane, Bruno, come and see what your brothers are up to!'

Her smile widened as the video started.

'Greetings from Oahu!' said a tanned Max into the camera. 'They say it's the birthplace of surfing! And it's absolutely incredible! So good, in fact, we're extending our stay here for a month or two. We're seeing some guys later about taking on some casual work.'

'Yeah!' an equally tanned Jude joined in. 'Max has persuaded me we could do worse than spend a few months here while he learns to rule the waves. It didn't take much to persuade me, I must admit! There are so many great places to explore around here.'

The camera scanned around the white sandy beach. There was a beach bar where several people were seated. Then it homed in on the sea view. Several surfers were riding huge waves.

'Hey, get me in on the next shot!' Max cried, grabbing a surfboard and heading into the sea.

There were whoops and cries of delight as the next scene showed Max hurtling through a tunnel of water.

'There he goes!' Jude's voice was heard to say. 'I don't know how I'll ever get him away from Hawaii!'

His face reappeared. 'Speak again soon. Take care!'

Behind them Anya leaned forward as Jane replayed the video of the two boys. Looking at them and listening carefully to their voices, she felt a twinge of misgiving.

330

'They look so happy, don't they?' Jane said.

'Yes they do. I'm so glad they are sorting themselves out,' Celia smiled at Anya. 'We were worried for a while, weren't we?'

Anya looked up and was about to comment when Isaac walked up and slipped his arms around Celia's waist. 'Life doesn't get any better than this, does it, love?' he whispered. She looked down, hiding her expression as Celia nestled against him. 'No, it doesn't! This is perfect!'

CHAPTER SEVENTY-SIX

'This certainly is a bit of paradise!' Max looked out at the stunning sea view from the balcony of the sprawling house.

'Hugo suggested this remote island as we needed somewhere where it will be very difficult to find us!' Adam smiled.

'There are many smaller, uninhabited islands around Hawaii,' Hugo explained. 'I did quite a bit of research as a kid. I used to fantasize about setting up my own laboratory out here. Now that fantasy has become reality!'

Adam nodded. 'We've enough funds to cover us for the next year, but we are going to have to find ways to generate capital to finance our research in the long term. We're hoping you boys can come up with some ideas.'

'With the data we have, couldn't we set up a "semi-legal" Lab centre?' Max suggested. 'They're pretty lucrative.'

'And using the enhancement techniques we could even create people suited to security posts or something the military might be interested in. Maybe not in the western world, but I'm sure there are other countries who would be potential customers,' Jude added.

'We don't want to end up with security guards like Robert. His judgement was impaired by emotional influence. But if we could modify the human brain, maybe using AI, we should be able to create the ideal protector,' Hugo said. 'We need people with unfailing loyalty and who are devoid of emotional weaknesses. An AI brain would be easier to control.'

'But we would have to be wary of AI creations making

independent decisions that override those of their creators,' Max said.

'Yes, we'd have to consider that,' Adam agreed.

'And I think we'd need to redefine our aim,' Hugo added. 'I'm not sure I totally agree with Warner's vision of an ideal society.'

'Yes, I'd like to give some serious thought to what constitutes an ideal world,' Jude nodded.

'Well, we have the time to do that now,' his brother said.

Adam rubbed his hands together. 'The future is in our hands!'

'The possibilities are endless!' Hugo smiled broadly.

Á

Proudly published by Accent Press

www.accentpress.co.uk